C 2

THE CHARM BRACELET

Many years ago she was sent one mysteriously, just a single charm attached. Some
time later another charm appeared, and the
same thing happened a number of times over
the years until the bracelet was almost full.
Each charm proved significant too, as if her
anonymous benefactor knew she needed a
little bit of magic in her life. So when Holly
stumbles across another bracelet — one that
somebody else has lost — she recognises a
lifetime spelled out through the charms, and
knows she must try to reunite it with its
owner. Using each charm to help discover
more about the bracelet's owner, Holly gradually begins to piece together details of this
other charmed life. But her quest leads her
somewhere she never expected . . .

Books by Melissa Hill
Published by The House of Ulverscroft:

BEFORE I FORGET
SOMETHING FROM TIFFANY'S

MELISSA HILL

THE CHARM BRACELET

Complete and Unabridged

CHARNWOOD
Leicester

First published in Great Britain in 2012 by
Hodder & Stoughton
London

First Charnwood Edition
published 2013
by arrangement with
Hodder & Stoughton
An Hachette UK company
London

A catalogue record for this book is available
from the British Library.

ISBN 978–1–4448–1515–3

Published by
F. A. Thorpe (Publishing)
Anstey, Leicestershire

Set by Words & Graphics Ltd.
Anstey, Leicestershire
Printed and bound in Great Britain by
T. J. International Ltd., Padstow, Cornwall

This book is printed on acid-free paper

Especially for Mam
With lots of love

Acknowledgements

Lots of love and thanks to my wonderful agent Sheila Crowley and everyone at Hodder UK and Hachette Ireland for looking after me so well, and to the lovely booksellers all over the world who continuously give my books such amazing support.

To Kevin and Carrie for always putting a smile on my face.

This book is dedicated to my mother, Nell, who many years ago introduced me to the delights of the charm bracelet. Thanks also to my dad, Noel, and two lovely sisters, Amanda and Sharon, who are all wonderful supporters.

To Alexandra Konecki and Inga Laurila, who each make a special appearance in this book because of their wonderful support of charities Autism Speaks (thank you Rosemary Konecki) and Authors for Japan.

As always, special thanks to readers everywhere who buy and read my books. I'm so very grateful and I love hearing from you via my website www.melissahill.info or chatting on Facebook and Twitter.

I very much hope you enjoy *The Charm Bracelet*.

1

Holly O'Neill always figured that life was just like a snow globe. From the outside things looked peaceful, until you shook it and everything inside got jumbled up.

She pressed her nose closer to the window-pane as a delicate snowflake landed on the glass in front of her before quickly dissolving into nothingness.

Holly loved the first winter snowfall of the year. It meant that Christmas would be here soon — time for curling up next to warm log fires in her cosy walk-up apartment. It meant twinkling lights, mulled wine and pink cheeks, while immersed in a bustling city made all the more romantic under a blanket of snow.

Closing her eyes, she imagined the goodwill that seemed to automatically blossom in Manhattan when the temperatures outside dropped, and general feelings of cheer permeated. She smiled in anticipation of the holiday season and wondered what fantastic things the snow would bring with it.

'Mom! I can't find my iPod!'

Holly opened her eyes and quickly brought herself back to reality. Smiling, she turned from the window at the same moment the door to the living room flew open to reveal a ten-year-old in the midst of a technological-related meltdown.

'I don't know where I put it, and I need it

1

now. I just downloaded a new Kanye song and I want Chris to listen to it at school.' Her son Danny stood before her, his bright blue eyes wide with worry, and the dark brown hair that Holly had already so diligently smoothed down with water once again in the throes of bed-head.

'Danny, calm down — I borrowed it, it's right there.' She pointed to the antique rosewood side table that she had rescued from certain doom at a thrift store on Canal Street.

He raised his eyebrows sceptically. 'You . . . borrowed my iPod?' He went to retrieve the little device and quickly turned it on, as if to make sure his technologically challenged mother hadn't done anything to time-warp it back to a long-forgotten era. 'I didn't think you even knew how to use it.'

Holly puffed out her chest. 'Now, I'll have you know, I have truly mastered the BlackBerry Carole bought me for my birthday.' She thought back to her boss's attempt at bringing Holly into the twenty-first century, thinking it would be valuable for her to have a way to easily manage the client list, deliveries and other goings-on at the Secret Closet, the Greenwich vintage store in which she worked.

'Only 'cause I taught you, Mom,' smiled Danny sheepishly as he scrolled through his playlist. 'Uh, who is Dean Martin?' he asked, as if he had just smelled something bad.

Holly threw up her hands in mock disbelief. 'A son of mine who doesn't know who Dean Martin is? 'When the moon hits your eye like a big ole pizza pie that's . . . amore!'' she sang

2

while Danny rolled his eyes.

'A song about pizza? Weird.'

Holly giggled. 'It's not about pizza; it's about love. Listen to it, I downloaded it. I think my record must be somewhere in storage because I can't find it.'

'I'll listen to it, if you listen to Kanye.'

Holly laughed. 'Ha, quite the negotiator as usual. Maybe later, sweetheart, but we need to go soon. I'm running late, and the store has a shipment coming in this morning.'

Her son sat down on Holly's expertly made bed, which was hidden behind a pretty silk curtain in the living room. She had given Danny the apartment's only bedroom so he could have space for his things and privacy.

'I don't get it.'

'Don't get what, honey?' Holly asked as she perused her closet, looking for the vintage Dior jacket she had salvaged from the bottom of a heap at work. Her employee discount was the only way she could afford beautiful clothes from another era, or more importantly, keep Danny in shoes and pay rent.

'Why do people want to buy other people's old stuff?'

Holly sighed. This was a conversation they had had many times before and, as always, she tried to explain about the appeal of vintage clothes, things that had a real history and had been worn when their previous owners fell in love, when they cried, and all throughout life's great adventures. She truly believed the clothes that passed through the store were each unique in their own way: they had a personality; they had lived.

Danny, however, being a young boy, only truly loved the new Nikes on his feet.

'Someday you will understand — or, more likely, you will meet a girl who understands.'

Danny rolled his eyes, a typical response. He was still at the age when girls were considered 'gross'. Holly figured that in a couple of years or so, he would be singing a different tune.

'Whatever, Mom.'

'*Whatever*, you'll see. Many a man comes into our store desperately searching for a handbag, or a scarf, or a dress that his girlfriend, fiancée or wife saw and just simply *can't* live without. Someday that will be you. Rummaging through a store like ours in search of a particular handbag.'

'Not a chance. I'm *never* going to like a girl who is into handbags.'

Holly found the jacket that she had been searching for and turned round to face her son, a grin on her face. 'Ha, that's sort of like saying you only like fish that don't swim. It's simply not possible.'

Danny shrugged and conceded a tiny smile. 'Well, I guess as long as she doesn't make me listen to pizza music it might be OK.'

'Ha-ha.' Holly smiled, glancing around the room. 'OK, I think I'm ready.' As organised as she tried to be most days, there was no denying that she usually struggled to get out the door in the morning. 'How do I look?'

She had on a brown pencil skirt that skimmed her figure and a white blouse with a ruffled

4

cravat that complemented her orange brushed velvet jacket. Slouched brown leather knee-high boots finished off the ensemble.

She wasn't very tall, and only stood about five foot five in her stockinged feet, so she felt compelled to wear heels almost all the time. The boots, though lovely, would have been impractical for some, as they sported four-inch heels. Fortunately Holly had been wearing heels for so long that she was adept at walking in them, and wore them as if they were a pair of running shoes. She was reasonably slender, though in her mind she was never slender enough. She never really dieted, but tried to stay away from junk food, and of course all the walking helped. What didn't help was living so close to some of the Manhattan modelling agencies.

Her auburn hair was piled loosely on her head, and her emerald-green eyes sparkled, setting off the creaminess of her skin. With a surname like O'Neill, and looking the way she did, people naturally assumed she was of Irish background. But while Holly had been brought up by Irish parents, she wasn't altogether sure if she was Irish by blood, as she'd been adopted by Seamus and Eileen O'Neill when she was just eight months old.

They were practically New Yorkers by then, having emigrated from different parts of Ireland in their youth, and met and fallen in love in Queens, where Holly's mother still lived. Sadly her dad had died years ago.

Danny was sizing her up. 'Actually,' he said pensively, 'I think you're missing something.' He smiled at her, wiggling his hand back and forth to see if she would catch on.

Holly looked down at herself, a frown on her face. 'Well, I don't see what . . . Oh!' She pulled her sleeve back, displaying a right wrist that was usually adorned with a very important piece of jewellery.

Danny got up and walked to Holly's dresser, and looked through a small crystal bowl that contained several pieces of jewellery. He found what he was looking for and turned round to face his mother.

'Here you go.' He placed a silver charm bracelet in her palm. 'You almost forgot.'

Holly smiled warmly at the boy who knew her so well. True, she rarely ever took her bracelet off, but she'd removed it the night before when she was cleaning the kitchen, afraid to tarnish it or snag it on something. But even if Danny hadn't reminded her about it just then, she knew she wouldn't have gone far without realising it was absent from her wrist. She felt naked when she didn't have it on.

'Can I see my charm again?' her son asked.

'Of course,' she said, fastening the bracelet round her wrist. 'There it is, right here.' She wiggled the bracelet and displayed a charm in the shape of a stork carrying a small bundle, a baby. 'I got this one not long after I found out I was going to have you.'

Danny studied the tiny trinket. 'From Dad, right?'

Holly smiled tightly, her heart speeding up a little. 'Erm, yes, I think so. Anyway, it's time to

6

go. You don't want to be late for school, do you?' She hoped to distract Danny from asking any other questions about his father. Holly really didn't feel like going down that road again, at least not now.

Danny caressed the charm one more time. 'OK, let me grab my backpack. Are you picking me up from school today?'

She shook her head, regretfully. 'No, not today, but I should be home a little earlier than usual. Kate has a date,' she said, referring to her good friend who usually did the honours with the school run.

'Oh, OK,' he said, slightly melancholy all of a sudden.

She leaned down to his level, worried. 'Hey,' she said, tilting his chin up. 'What's wrong? You like Kate, don't you? You guys always have fun.'

He shrugged and avoided Holly's eyes. 'I know, she's cool. It's not that. It's just . . . ' He stalled for a moment, looking ashamed and uncomfortable.

Holly furrowed her brow. 'What is it, Danny? What's going on?'

'It's nothing, it's just I know you work so hard, and Kate is a lot of fun. But sometimes, the other kids, their dads pick them up at school.'

She smiled sadly. The subject of 'Dad' was always such a sensitive topic, and one Holly usually worked to avoid at all costs, but inevitably it came up. Usually during the worst times, like now when she was running late.

Danny looked up at her guiltily. 'It's just the other moms, they have help from the dads, you know? I wish you had a bit of help sometimes.'

She smiled at her son's gallantry. 'Hey, buddy, I have everything I need. Don't you worry about me. I think we make a good team, don't you?' She pinched his cheeks and kissed his forehead.

'I just want you to be happy. The other dads buy their wives flowers and jewellery and stuff. Someone should do that for you.'

Finally, she laughed. 'What do I need flowers and jewellery for when I have you to educate me on the finer workings of the iPod? Trust me, Danny. I'm fine. I have you and that means I have everything I want. Now let's get you to school. And maybe later on this week, you and I can head down to the Apple Store — see what you want from Santa this year. Christmas is right around the corner, you know.'

Danny rolled his eyes. 'Mom, you know I don't believe in Santa any more. That's for little kids.'

Holly gathered up her handbag and looked again to the window, where the snow was coming down, harder than before. She smiled in anticipation of getting outside and smelling winter in the air, of feeling the wind on her face. During this time of year, New York truly was like a fairy tale.

She hustled Danny out through the door as she switched off the light. 'Well, humour me for now, OK? I happen to believe in him. Anyway, take it from me, you're never too old to believe in a little magic.'

2

As she made her way to Greenwich Village after seeing Danny safely to the school gates, Holly marvelled once again at the fairy lights that seemed to dominate the city streets in this part of town. Bleecker Street was often covered in lights anyway, but at this time of year they were festive rather than just funky.

She checked her watch and stopped by her usual deli, a Korean place on the corner of Tenth and Waverly, for a cup of coffee. Warming her hands round the hot cardboard cup, she held it to her face, letting the steam rise. Even though she had been working at the vintage store for almost four years, she still could not get the journey to work down pat. She was always late, despite the short walk from her place via Danny's school only a few blocks away.

As she quickened her pace, she stole a look at some of the other store windows and paused for a moment in front of Encore, the Secret Closet's main competition. Encore had some hot-pepper lights around the window frame and a display of handbags in muted leathers and plaids. A mannequin wearing a full-on fifties evening dress stood in one corner of the window, and a second wearing a motorcycle jacket and jeans *à la* James Dean crouched in another. Holly shook her head fondly. An out-and-out thrift-store display. Pity, as she could tell the bags were authentic, and it was even possible that the evening dress on the mannequin might well have been worn by someone like Greta Garbo at some point.

Frank, the owner, just did not know how to dress a window. Suddenly the man himself appeared from behind the James Dean mannequin and waved at her happily, pointing to the display and giving her a thumbs-up suggesting, 'Not bad, huh?' Holly laughed and returned the gesture.

Her boss, Carole, was already at work when she arrived at the store, as the shutters were up but no lights were on yet. Holly pushed the door open, letting in cold air, and the bells that hung from the knob jingled.

'Morning, Carole!' she called cheerily, as she worked to brush some stray hair out of her face and wipe melting snow from her pink cheeks.

'I'm in the back. Be out in a sec,' a thin voice called from the rear of the store.

Holly unwound her scarf and folded it up along with her bag behind the counter.

She began switching on the lights that accented the various clothing racks around the store. Her boots clacked on the polished hardwood floor, and she could glimpse flashes of herself in the floor-to-ceiling mirrors that graced each wall.

There were only about ten racks out at a time; Carole liked to rotate clothing by season, keeping an eye on the trends that her many stylist clients (as well as the latest issue of *Vogue*) clued her into.

Each rack was stainless steel and uncrowded,

and each beautifully restored and pressed vintage piece hung carefully on its own wooden hanger. Carole was strict about every garment being hung four inches apart from the next; she hated customers having to dig through piles of clothes to find something.

There were simple ladder-style shelves in one corner of the store, upon which hats and scarves were meticulously displayed, and in front of the windows, facing inwards, were two long benches with glass cases full of smaller accessories — brooches, hairclips and fascinators.

Holly leaned into the store window to make sure there was no dirt on the glass. Their window display could not have been more different than Encore's. Carole found regular store manne-quins tacky, so ages back she had got hold of two dress dummies from a Metropolitan Museum of Art costume exhibit.

How she had managed it, Holly never knew, but they looked great. Beautifully sculpted in wood and covered with a sheer layer of creamy velvet, one dummy wore a black Ralph Lauren pinstripe suit from the sixties, and the other an Oscar de la Renta early seventies ivory lace floor-length dress.

There was nothing else in the display but good lighting and a view to the inside.

Most days Carole was out on the prowl for that perfect vintage piece, even attending Sotheby's auctions when she knew a big estate was being sold off, but most of her mornings were spent going through new stock and donations. A percentage of all their profits automatically went to the Red Cross, and as the store had a distinguished and wealthy client base, the prices were not for the faint of heart.

Holly looked up, suddenly noticing the UPS delivery person standing in front of the counter. 'Oh gosh, Harold, I'm sorry, I was daydreaming . . . Can I help you?' She recognised their usual delivery person, who visited their store at least once a week. 'I hope you haven't been waiting long.'

'Not long. A real winter wonderland out there today, isn't it?' he commented in a thick Brooklyn accent.

'I know, isn't it beautiful? The perfect start to the season,' Holly said dreamily, completely missing the sardonic undertone.

'Yeah. Ho-ho-ho,' Harold replied dully. 'You might change your tune if you had to drive that monster around the streets of Manhattan all day.' He motioned to the brown UPS truck that idled by the kerb, turning the snow under its wheels to a dull grey sludge.

'Oh, Harold, stop. Surely you can still appreciate the holiday spirit,' Holly smiled. 'New York is especially magical around this time of year.'

'Yeah, well, I'd appreciate some holiday magic in the form of a signature. Park an extra minute longer than necessary in the Village and I'm cited for blocking traffic. Corporate just *loves* when that happens, and I need my bonus this year, so if you don't mind . . . '

'Of course. We wouldn't want you to get in trouble.' Holly took the electronic signature pad from him and scribbled her name with loops and swirls. 'Here you go.'

Carole emerged from the backroom of the store, looking completely on task and focused, and well put-together in an Yves St Laurent suit. She held a variety of clothes on hangers, all ready to be displayed out front. Holly's boss was in her sixties and had been living and working downtown since the 1970s. She had held on to the Secret Closet all that time, transforming it from a dowdy thrift store that once sold mismatched tea cups and old toasters next to used pea coats into what it was today, a streamlined and chic designer vintage clothing store.

Plump with a short pixie cut, Carole dyed her hair a deep red and always wore dramatic eye makeup. 'It's my signature,' she had told Holly once, and Holly could see why. Her eyes were huge and almond-shaped, stunning. Her boss was typically brusque by nature, but Holly knew she appreciated her work. The two women had become close over the years, each knowing they could depend on the other to do whatever needed to get done.

'Oh, I'm sorry, Harold. I thought I heard the front door open. I was up to my elbows trying to get this stuff out before we opened,' she said.

'Don't worry about it, Carole. Holly was here to help me,' Harold said. 'She was just telling me all about the magic of the season,' he added mischievously.

'Ah yes, I should have figured,' Carole said drolly. 'As if you couldn't already tell from her name, our Holly just loves Christmas.' She turned to her employee. 'I'm sure you were skipping through the streets singing 'Jingle Bells'?'

Holly shrugged off the teasing; they knew her well. 'Well, if I thought I was going to be facing the Ghost of Christmas Past and Ebenezer Scrooge, I would have taken my time getting here.'

Carole chuckled. 'So what do we have, Harold? How many boxes?' No aspect of operations slipped through without Carole noticing. Her organisational skills and attention to detail were two of the reasons the store was so successful.

'Looks like there are about three or four,' he told her. 'You want me to carry them out to the backroom?'

'If you wouldn't mind,' Carole agreed.

Holly relieved her boss of the clothes that she had been carrying and quickly went to work getting the store set up for the day's business. There was no denying it, she was in an energetic mood, and she knew that the weather outside would only help custom today. While it might be normal human inclination to stay bundled up inside when the weather got messy, conversely New Yorkers tended to be driven out, filling the streets with holiday shopping treks and other festive wanderings. She knew that they would have a busy day.

'Ready to do some psychic sorting?' Carole reappeared from the backroom and plopped a big box on the counter between her and Holly.

She grinned. 'Yep!'

Carole detached the packing slip and ripped open the box. She pulled out the first piece, a big beautiful beige leather bag. Holly could immediately tell it was a Kelly original, still in almost mint condition. Most of their stock came from upscale clients who thoroughly inspected and cleaned what they wanted sold.

'Well?' Carole enquired, eyeing her.

'Kelly original for sure, immaculate as far as I can see.'

'Well, I know *that* much . . . '

Holly closed her eyes and dramatically held the bag out in front of her. 'Tall, beautiful, in her twenties, no children, adored Grace Kelly, in a secretary pool at — ' she peered through one eye to see Carole smiling — 'the *New Yorker* maybe? Wound up marrying her boss, who was much shorter, but that didn't matter. He was wealthy beyond her wildest dreams.'

'So that made her happy?' Carole asked, trying to hide a grin.

Holly stroked the leather bag, kept in such perfect condition by its owner, probably on a high shelf in a protective pouch, with other bags lined up military style next to it.

'The bag definitely did.'

'And would money make you happy?'

Holly laughed. 'No way: love only for me. I need to feel it like a ton of bricks.'

Carole shook her head. 'Such a softie . . . Good luck with that.'

Holly delved further into the box. She loved new deliveries — the thrill of finding something

15

unique always gave her a rush, and there was truly something bittersweet about going through the discarded remains of someone's life, of bygone times.

She marvelled as she pulled out one designer piece of clothing after another, hanging each on an empty rack as she worked. There were some fun party tops, two sequinned dresses — good pieces, but a little flashy.

Holly smiled as she admired each piece in her arms. Her breath caught as she noticed a particularly gorgeous fifties Givenchy party dress. She hung it on the rack for a better look, certain that this dress would not be around for long. She stroked the rich, black silken material and gazed longingly at the tiny delicate crystals that graced the full tulle skirt. It really was a special dress.

She closed her eyes, wondering where it had come from and the kind of person who had worn it . . . what parties it had actually experienced in its past life, the fun and romance it had inevitably inspired when it was worn by some young, beautiful woman of another era. A dress like this had surely seen some good times, and she was positive the fun to be had wasn't over yet. Holly smiled, realising that destiny would soon deem someone else suitable to meet this dress . . . that the next chapter of this beautiful garment's life was about to begin, right here.

'It's just so beautiful, don't you think?' she said to Carole. 'Can you imagine the life it's had?'

'I'm sure it's had a very interesting existence,' Carole noted dryly, reading the delivery record.

'Seems this lot came directly from Anna Bowery's collection.'

Holly's eyes widened at the mention of the well-known, elderly New York socialite. Anna Bowery had been famous during the 1950s and 1960s for rubbing shoulders with people like Frank Sinatra, the Kennedys, Clark Gable even. Truly this dress must have seen some incredible times.

'Wow . . . can you imagine? She might have danced with Marlon Brando in this dress, or talked about books with J.D. Salinger while wearing it . . . ' Holly felt goose bumps. 'Such an amazing life already. Whoever buys this is genuinely getting a piece of history,' she said reverently. 'It's a dress that is made for magic. What girl wouldn't want to be kissed in this? It's simply meant for falling in love.'

'Sounds like someone else has actually fallen in *lust*,' Carole smiled. 'I bet it would fit you,' she ventured.

Holly laughed and shook her head ruefully.

'Nope, not even *with* my store discount could I afford that. Besides, where would I wear it? This dress needs to be danced in — on a big occasion, like New Year's Eve or something. My New Year's Eve consists of popcorn on the couch with Danny, watching the ball drop on TV.'

Carole raised her eyebrows. 'Spoken like a true spinster. Go on, Holly, try it on. Just to see. It will be fun.'

Holly smiled, and for a moment the urge to try on the dress was so strong that she was sure she would cave. But there was no point. Even if

17

it did look good on her, the reality was that she had nowhere to wear something this lovely. It didn't deserve to live out its days going unworn in her closet.

Of course, she wished she had somewhere to wear it, and, more to the point, she wished it were that easy just to hand over her Visa and think only of her own desires. But it wasn't how things were in her life — she had Danny to think about, and every year she was more and more determined to make his Christmas magical, even if it meant forgoing the parties or events to which she was occasionally invited. While sometimes she felt it might be nice to go out on the town, she didn't resent Danny for preventing her. She was happy with how things were.

Which meant playing Santa instead of splurging on Givenchy.

Her sudden melancholy mood didn't escape Carole.

'Is everything OK, honey? I'm sorry, I didn't mean to go on about the dress.'

Holly shrugged and waved her hand airily. 'Oh no, it's nothing. Sorry, just have some stuff on my mind. Danny started talking about dads again this morning. Apparently, he has taken note that some of his friends' fathers pick up their kids at school.'

'I'm sure he just thinks that you could use someone else around,' Carole offered. Holly looked up to protest, but Carole cut her off. 'I know, I know. You are Superwoman and you can do it all. But I'm sure that Danny's just thinking about your happiness, not his.'

'But I am happy,' Holly insisted.

'I know you are,' Carole continued. 'That's plain to see. You are one of the most optimistic people I know. You see romance and joy around every corner and infect everyone you meet with all that positivity. Do you think Danny doesn't see that? All I am saying is that you, too, deserve a little magic. You're too young to take yourself out of the game completely. You don't want to end up like me, all by myself,' Carole said with a self-deprecating smile.

'Oh, Carole, I'm sure I could do much worse than end up like you,' Holly teased, referring to her boss's whirlwind social life.

'Well then, you need to get your diary filled. No way are you going to add more charms to that bracelet if all you do is sit at home in your pyjamas.' Carole patted Holly's arm knowingly, aware that she had a tradition of adding charms that signified important life events and experiences to her charm bracelet. She also knew that Holly hadn't added a charm in several years.

'Thank you, you're right. I'll make a start on filling up my social calendar.'

'Good.'

'Just as soon as I unpack all those boxes out back,' she added with a wink, skilfully evading the topic.

Carole shook her head as Holly headed towards the back of the store. 'Well, it's your life, but do you think Anna Bowery waited for Sinatra to ask her to dance? Absolutely not. I bet she took the bull by the horns. Especially in that dress!'

19

Holly pushed open the stockroom door with her hip. 'I believe it,' she called back. 'In that dress, a girl could do anything.' She quickly brushed through the doorframe, hoping to avoid any further discussion of her social life, the dress or her lack of either. That simply was not reality. She knew where her responsibilities lay: firmly with Danny and what was best for him.

She shook her head as if to rid herself of the cobwebs of gloom that had now descended upon her. Determined to recapture the optimism with which she had begun the day, she picked up a box cutter that lay on a folding table and turned to the boxes that Harold had delivered. Who knew what treasures were waiting to be discovered within?

She applied the box cutter to the top of the first one, slicing it open quickly and expertly, realising that it was a true garment box. Some of their stock came in anything: garbage bags, cardboard boxes, milk crates even. This box was beautifully packed, as if the owner understood well the worth of the clothes. There were a few gorgeous leather handbags on top and then some suits, all carefully wrapped in tissue paper. Three suits, to be exact. Holly pulled them out and lined them up on a rack in front of her. Three perfectly kept Gucci suits: one pink, one brown plaid and one in black. She gave a low whistle.

'Wow, this is good stuff,' she whispered under her breath. Why would anyone want to part with it? Then she smiled as she answered her own question. Someone with lots of money, of course. It was typical for the time of year, actually, especially among New York's wealthy, who routinely purged their closets, readying themselves for the onslaught of holiday shopping. Nice . . .

She went about the business of inspecting them for tears and blemishes and going through the pockets. People rarely used the pockets in designer pieces and most times they were sewn up to keep the lines of the garment smooth.

Then, going back to the box, she pulled the flaps wider to reveal a red velvet jacket . . . a very expensive, classic red velvet jacket. Chanel, no less.

'Oh my, this is beautiful . . . just beautiful,' Holly gasped, pulling the jacket from its packaging and shaking it out gently. She smiled as she examined the workmanship; the quality the Chanel brand put into their individual pieces was truly exquisite.

As she admired it, she couldn't resist wondering what it would look like on. 'Oh what the hell.' Holly peeled off her own jacket and placed it aside. Unlike the dress, she just might be able to afford this — plus it was practical and she could wear it anywhere, no special occasion required. Slipping into the jacket, and buttoning it up, she ran her hands over the delicate fabric, checking the way it fitted.

But as Holly turned to a mirror to admire the effect while smoothing the jacket along her torso, she felt something. Something hard inside the jacket, beneath the material.

'What in the world . . . ?' Holly unbuttoned the jacket and pulled open the lapels, wondering if something from the box had got snagged on it. But there was nothing immediately apparent against the interior lining.

Her hand returned to the spot where she had first felt the hard bulge. It was still there.

She turned the Chanel jacket inside out and was examining the lining when Carole came into the stockroom. 'Holly, have you seen that beaded purse we had on display last week? Has it sold? Someone is asking about it . . . Oh wow, that's beautiful.'

Holly shook her head. 'There's something wrong with it, though. I tried it on and there's something . . . hard inside.'

Carole stepped closer. 'Something hard?'

'Yes . . . right here . . . Oh, there's a pocket!' Holly ran her hands along the seam and pointed out a small, barely concealed zipper that was secreted away in the lining.

'Let me see.' Carole peered over her shoulder. 'Well, Chanel certainly never put inner pockets in these. This must have been altered by the original owner — or for her, at least.'

Holly gently tugged at the zipper and it opened easily. 'There's definitely something in here.' She put her hand in the secret pocket, and her fingers sought out an object cool to the touch.

Taking it out, she revealed a silver chain. Actually no, she realised quickly, it was a silver *bracelet* — full of dangling trinkets and pretty objects.

The room seemed eerily quiet as Holly held the bracelet in her open palm and the morning light, leaking through the windows, illuminated the dust particles around the charms, giving them a slight luminescence.

'Oh my goodness,' she exclaimed to Carole, 'a charm bracelet.'

'It's just like yours.'

Holly inspected the piece of jewellery, running her gaze over the individual charms. She noted a horseshoe, a baby carriage, a heart-shaped key, a building of some kind, a carousel . . . there were so many. Yes, it was indeed just like her own bracelet, but with many more charms.

'So many of them,' she whispered almost to herself. Then she looked at Carole. 'Obviously it was left in the jacket by accident. Someone is missing it.'

Carole turned back to the boxes. 'Well, I'm sure we can send it back. Where's the docket?' She duly picked up the UPS delivery documentation and read through it. 'No name or address that I can see, just the UPS branch it was shipped from. I'm sure they'll have some record of it.' She frowned. 'And according to this it's a straight donation — no commission required.'

Which meant that the sender of these clothes intended that their percentage of the proceeds earned on any sales should go directly to charity. While this wasn't unusual in the business, it was becoming rarer and rarer due to the downturn in the economy.

Holly nodded absently, her eyes not leaving the bracelet. 'But why on earth would you put a bracelet in that little pocket in the first place? You'd think the owner would have missed it and

23

remembered that they'd put it there. I know I rarely leave the house without mine.'

As she took in the variety of charms, she knew that this bracelet had to be of great value and importance — to the owner, or indeed to anyone who had chosen the charms and perhaps given them as a gift, helping the owner build up so many significant memories. It was so full that Holly could tell that whoever owned this bracelet had really *lived*. Her spine tingled with anticipation as she started imagining the stories that accompanied each trinket.

She instinctively glanced at her own bracelet, sitting prettily on her wrist, and ran her fingers over the individual charms. It was her talisman and each charm was a special reminder of the most important times in her life. She'd had it for what . . . ? Goodness, it was going on eighteen years now. Where did the time go?

Holly gazed down at the charms. There might be many now, yet once upon a time there had been only one . . .

★   ★   ★

Queens, New York, 1994

Holly looked down at the frumpy black dress her mom had bought her for the funeral.

She felt tears well up and she pulled the skirt of the dress to her face, hastily wiping it. She was broken-hearted, miserable, and she didn't care if her appearance justified it. Besides, the service was over, they'd returned from the cemetery

24

ages ago and no one had to see her. She just had to try and get through the endless stream of people that flowed in and out of her house, commiserating with her and her mother over her father.

Dad . . . She would never see her beloved dad's face again. It was like a nightmare, a terrible dream Holly wished she could wake up from. She curled up in the foetal position on her bed, and lay there for a very long time, feeling terribly alone. Why did it have to be him who'd died? Why couldn't it have been . . . ? The thought came unbidden, and Holly immediately felt guilty. They might be fighting a lot lately, but of course she wouldn't wish her mother, Eileen, dead. She just wished this horrible day, this horrible *time*, could be over.

Wiping her tear-stained face on the pillow, she focused her gaze on the window in front of her. Sunlight streamed into her bedroom, and she watched beams of light dance across the ceiling above her bed. She felt angry that the sun chose to show its face on such a day. It should be overcast, rainy, gloomy. It would be more appropriate if the weather matched her mood, appreciated what was happening in her life.

Holly sat up at last and swung her feet over the side of her bed, finding her footing and walking to the window. She cast her eyes across the rear lawn of her family's home. The tiny patch of grass was packed with mourners, and in the midst of all of it, she spotted her mother. Her heart softened a little as she saw the misery that was etched in every line of her mother's face.

There was no denying that this was hard on Eileen too. Even when they had realised it might be a possibility for some time. With the cancer and all.

She knew that she should probably go down there and support her mom. If anything, she should go and give a hand to Sarah, a neighbour who had volunteered to help out in the kitchen today, and organise the crazy amount of food that people had brought. Casseroles and vegetable plates and baked goods . . . Holly had never understood why people thought that funerals or memorials were a time to eat; she had never been less hungry in her whole life.

She was about to step away from the window and retreat back to her bed when her mother looked up towards her bedroom. Their eyes locked and a weak smile touched the corners of Eileen's lips and she raised her hand slightly, as if encouraging Holly to come down and join the living. Holly didn't understand how that one simple gesture allowed for so much pressure to build in her chest. She felt as if a vice had tightened around her heart. She knew she would have to face all those people, but she really didn't want to. This sadness, this funeral, was bad enough, not to mention having to wonder about the private thoughts of the people around her.

Eventually, Holly left her room and walked down the hallway that led to the stairs descending into the entry hall of their tiny house. She was well aware that her footsteps echoed on the bare wooden floors, and that it would be easy for anyone to tell that she was up and about. There would probably be people down there waiting for her, all wanting to talk and hug her and tell her how much Seamus had loved her.

Seamus her dad. A man too young, too lively and too full of energy and ability to be lying in a coffin under six feet of earth. But it was true. She reached up and pinched the bridge of her nose as if this effort would push the tears to the back of her eyes, but it didn't. Two large drops of water spilled forth. She wiped them on her sleeve just as Sarah walked into the room.

'Oh, Holly, I thought I heard you coming down.'

Sarah spotted the teardrops on Holly's face and her heart melted at the sight of such suffering.

'Honey, come here, come here,' she cooed as she encircled Holly in her arms. 'There, there, don't cry. I know it hurts, I know it hurts terribly. We are all going to miss him.'

Holly nodded sorrowfully as she rested her head on Sarah's shoulder. 'Come on now. Let's go and get something to eat. You must be hungry.' Food. Sarah's answer to everything. Holly smiled in spite of herself and shook her head. 'I'm not really hungry.'

'Of course you are,' Sarah insisted. 'I haven't seen you eat all day. Oh, and I almost forgot, there is a package for you on the counter.'

Holly looked up. 'A package?'

She had been getting the mail ahead of her mother, so as to weed through the condolence cards. It was fascinating to Holly the types of cards that came in. *Wishing You Well, Sending Prayers* . . . they were so stupid, and she could see why they upset her mother, but they just made Holly angry. She wanted to get a card that told the truth: *Life Sucks, It's Not Fair,* or *I Have No Idea What You Are Going Through But I Am Glad I'm Not You.*

Sarah shrugged and led the way through the hallway to the kitchen that ran parallel to the backyard. 'Yes. It was delivered just a little while ago.'

'Are you sure it's not for my mom? Everything else has been for her.'

'No, it's definitely for you. Has your name on it. It doesn't say Eileen O'Neill. It says Holly O'Neill.'

Holly followed her into the kitchen and sat down at the polished Formica table in the breakfast nook. 'Right there.' Sarah pointed to a small package next to a bowl of fruit. 'Came about an hour ago.'

Holly reached forward and took the small package in her hands, turning it over and over.

'Well? Aren't you going to open it?'

Holly shrugged a non-verbal answer like any sullen teenager, even though on the inside she was burning with curiosity, as well as some relief at being offered a temporary distraction from her otherwise terrible day.

What could it be? Who was it from? she wondered, hoping that her anticipation wouldn't show on her face. It felt wrong somehow.

As the plain brown packaging paper was peeled away, a beautiful velvet lilac-coloured box

28

adorned with a white satin ribbon revealed itself.

'Oh, looks nice. What is it?' asked Sarah, moving closer to the table with a plate of sandwiches she had prepared for Holly. She placed the plate on the table and pushed it towards her, but Holly ignored it.

With trembling fingers, she untied the ribbon and lifted off the top of the box, wondering what it contained. And what's more, who was it from?

Then she sucked in her breath and gasped. 'Oh my goodness. How pretty.'

Inside the box was a silver bracelet made of delicate loops that sparkled beneath the kitchen lights. Holly lifted up the chain and examined it more closely. A single item dangled from the centre of the bracelet. A charm. It was a charm bracelet.

'Well, isn't that lovely?' Sarah said, moving closer. 'What's that?' she asked, pointing to the charm.

'It looks like . . . an hourglass,' Holly replied finally. The tiny hourglass charm was made of silver and glass, with sand particles inside the glass.

She turned her attention from the bracelet back to the box that had been discarded on the table. Looking inside the lid, she felt around under the cushion that the bracelet had rested upon but found no note, no receipt or explanation. Just . . . nothing.

Right then her mother appeared in the kitchen doorway. 'I think we need more iced tea outside,' she said. 'Patsy Collins said that the jug is empty . . . What are you two doing?' She turned her attention to Holly and Sarah, who were both still studying the bracelet. 'What's that?'

Holly looked up at her mother, her eyes wide with fascination.

'It's a bracelet. A charm bracelet. It's just arrived out of nowhere addressed to me,' she said, holding up the piece of jewellery for Eileen to see.

Forgetting about the iced tea, Eileen crossed the room to get a better look. 'Isn't that gorgeous! An hourglass . . . beautiful. Who is it from?'

Holly shook her head. 'I have no idea.'

Her mother let out a chuckle. 'Looks like someone has a secret admirer . . . '

Colour flooded Holly's cheeks as she considered the thought. Everyone knew that her father had passed away recently, and her classmates were well aware that she hadn't been in school for the past week or so. However, when she thought about who might possibly have sent her the bracelet, it seemed unlikely that it could be anyone from there. Most of the boys she knew were as subtle as a battering ram, and what's more she couldn't imagine any of them picking out such a pretty piece of jewellery, let alone taking the time to select a charm like an hourglass.

Even Corey Mason, who had been following her around lately (and who *definitely* liked her), was the type of guy who was more interested in showing off his biceps than taking the time to figure out a thoughtful gift.

Holly shrugged, awkward about the idea of

discussing boys on the day of her father's funeral. 'Don't be stupid,' she said defensively, while inside her head her thoughts were racing.

'You know, the hourglass . . . that's a symbol of passing time,' said Sarah after a beat. Her voice was gentle. 'Maybe . . . maybe somebody wanted to help you realise that today is also about celebrating your father's life, about realising that things are always moving forward, and life is for living.'

'Sarah's right,' Eileen agreed, her voice cracking a little. 'Your dad would have wanted you to be happy, to be whole. He loved you so much and cherished every second he spent with you. You know that, don't you?'

A lump in her throat, Holly stared at the hourglass, beginning to understand the significance. Days of sadness and uncombed hair, of her and her mom bumping into each other in the night because neither of them could sleep. Of mumbling in the morning as they avoided Dad's favourite chair in the kitchen, eating separately in their own rooms. She and her mother would pass each other in the living room, again avoiding his chair, but mostly avoiding each other.

A surge of optimism pulsed through her veins . . . Holly would miss her dad desperately. For ever. And Seamus would have known this, known how lonely and adrift she'd feel without him.

Which was why she knew in her heart that the bracelet must have been arranged by her father, arranged before . . . everything, so that it would arrive at a time just when she needed it.

She slipped the bracelet on; the weight felt good and solid, as if someone was firmly touching — holding even — her hand.

Thank you, Dad, she told her father silently, knowing that she would treasure his final gift to her for the rest of her life.

3

Greg Matthews tapped his fingers on his desk, nervous about what was about to happen, what he was about to do. He had been in the office since seven thirty that morning, and had been working through this onslaught of frantic energy, debating with himself, making sure he wasn't going to regret it. It was now ten, time to get this done.

It *was* the right decision, wasn't it?

He looked around his tiny cubicle. Even after eight years at Foster, Cummings and Tyler — a top Wall Street brokerage firm in Lower Manhattan — he still had barely enough room to get comfortable. His desk chair needed replacing; this he knew because of the pain that had lodged itself in his lower lumbar region about two years ago, a pain that he paid a masseuse dearly to get rid of, but still felt return after a few days of being back in the chair.

The office was a grim building on Vesey Street, with grim lighting and this grim cubicle. Greg had always hated it, but enjoyed the money. He liked his clients, but usually got sidetracked into talking to them about a gallery opening or how their kids were doing, rather than trying to sell them the next hot commodity.

He'd started out on the floor of the New York Stock Exchange and had worked his way up to the cubicle he was in now. There was no denying that it brought him little joy, just a big bank account balance.

'It's now or never, Matthews,' he said under his breath. 'Time to make the call.'

He poked his head up over his cubicle walls hesitantly, like a prairie dog hoping to go unnoticed by its prey. Looking straight ahead, he scanned across the sea of cubes, ignoring the noisy activity of his co-workers, into his boss's office. He could see the stately figure of Dave Foster at his polished mahogany desk, like a king on his throne.

Greg had known this day was coming for a long time. Recent events had brought it home that life was short and there was little time to waste. Now it was nearing Christmas. The end of one year, the beginning of another. He couldn't face the thought of entering the New Year still sitting in this cube. He cringed at the idea of another ignored holiday season and regretted, for his family's sake, that he hadn't done it sooner.

That's not to say that he didn't have a good life. He had been happy, blissfully happy, when he wasn't inside these walls. The problem was that the time he spent outside the walls was limited. And with everything that was going on in his personal life at the moment, that just couldn't continue.

It wasn't as if he was bad at his job. Over his eight years as a broker he had amassed plenty of money: money that had bought trips, a nice townhouse, expensive dinners, the whole she-bang.

But, frankly, he was burned out. His eyes were

red at the end of the day from staring at the computer screen, his heartbeat accelerated from tracking all of his investments, for himself and his clients, and his free time was . . . non-existent. Depending on his trades he could be up and out at three to five a.m., and not be home till late at night. He knew it would have to be this way for at least another ten years if he were to have a career like his father's; he had built his own stockbrokerage from scratch. But Greg had already made a tidy sum (and was on every fancy gala list and main event in the city as a result) and he found the job a fruitless, endless effort in the pursuit of money for clients who already had enough.

Greg bit his lip. He just hoped people would understand, his dad especially. Unlike Jeff Matthews, Greg had grown to loathe standing in the pit, and most of his clients hated to hear from him anyway, the way the economy was going. No joy on his customers' faces. More like panic, or disgust.

Smiling gently, he thought of his mother; she would definitely be supportive about it, was always urging him to follow his dreams, and do something he was passionate about.

What's more, after nearly three years together, he and Karen could finally begin concentrating on what was important. The rest of their lives.

Yes, Greg knew it was time for him to make a choice that he was sure would make him happy when he looked back and recounted his life.

He shuffled some papers around, finally creating a neat pile. His stomach felt as if it was tied in a knot. Maybe he should have spoken to someone about it before today, just to make sure that he was doing the right thing.

He shook his head. 'No, it's my life.' And he thought of his mother once again.

Cristina had been such an inspiration to him for as long as he could remember. And it wasn't that he was a mama's boy. Far from it. His mother always said that thirty-six years ago when she found out that she was having a baby she'd been hoping for a boy, because she could raise him to be a man. She had always been intent on teaching him to be strong, honourable and brave. 'No matter what, never compromise on your morals or ideals,' she would say. 'Those things make you who you are.'

He knew that she hadn't wanted him to return to the firm after 9/11 and it wasn't just that she was scared of the 'what if?' that had been on many people's minds since that day. Rather, she had believed — correctly — that life was too short to spend it working in a cube. Nevertheless she had respected his choice to play the role of the young corporate maverick. Even when she knew about the hobby he had had since childhood that had turned into a full-blown passion of his.

Photography.

Greg loved New York as much as he loved anything, and had spent countless hours and days exploring this city, photographing everything — from day-to-day life in the boroughs to the magnificence of the Manhattan buildings that seemed to become one with the sky. He loved it all. Earlier this year he'd even sold an arty shot of the Flatiron Building to a downtown art gallery, something his mother had been intensely proud of, and a piece of his past that he considered a fierce accomplishment. It had given him a renewed sense of faith.

Then the week before, the Ninth Precinct had let him ride with them as they made their rounds in Queens. Greg had put in the request months ago in the hope of capturing drama in the city at night through a lens.

He was thrilled when they finally got back to him, and he had spent the entire night tagging along with the cops as they not only saved lives, but in some cases just put lives back on track.

He had got some great shots of a relieved mother staring gratefully into the eyes of her three-year-old, who had just recovered from an asthma attack. Of a drunk teenager being pulled out of an elevator shaft he had tumbled into, and of an elderly man being pushed in a wheelchair to the local church because there was no heat in his apartment. It was part of a 'People of the City' portfolio he was working on. He had just finished a series on the construction downtown, focusing on St Paul's Church and the work on the Freedom Tower and the other newer buildings at Ground Zero. While he always loved to photograph the cityscape, he felt he had overdosed a bit on the buildings recently, and had been looking forward to getting some faces in front of his lens again.

That morning, walking by Zuccotti Park had made up his mind for good. He'd been wearing his suit and carrying his briefcase, and slowed down as he passed. There were people of all kinds just milling around talking with each other. It looked like a modern-day Rome. The businessman exchanging ideas with the woman with dreadlocks and a baby strapped to her chest. The student with bare feet in an intense debate with the concrete worker on his lunch break. Greg felt frustrated he didn't have his camera. His fingers itched to adjust the lens and he felt like a junkie without a fix. The suit he was wearing suddenly felt heavy and the briefcase like a shackle, even though his camera equipment was ten times heavier. It was at that moment that he had felt complete clarification. He wanted to run back to his house, get into a pair of jeans, grab his photography gear and get back there, quickly, before it all went away.

Sure, this was New York and there were plenty of photographers everywhere, but Greg knew he had talent, and what's more he had passion. Passion that had led to his decision today. And while his new career might not be anything like as lucrative as being a broker, he was certain that it would pay tenfold in happiness.

Steeling himself, he ran his fingers through his closely cropped dark brown hair.

It was a Monday morning. The markets were long open, and trading was in full swing. He glanced at his co-worker Mark, who sat in the cube across from him. His face was flushed and his eyes bulged as he studied figures on three computer monitors and yelled into the phone, placing an order to the trading floor of the stock exchange.

Mark suddenly became aware of Greg's presence and turned to face him in a full-blown panic.

'Matthews, what are you doing? Don't you *see* what's happening? There's another goddamn issue with the euro and oil prices are going nuts because some new shit-storm is brewing in the Middle East! You'd better get on the phone with Carmichael. He's going to be pissed if you aren't on this right *now!*' Mark picked up a bottle of Tums and flicked it open with one hand before putting it to his mouth and pouring several tablets down his throat.

Greg stared at Mark, feeling a sense of disconnect. Sure, he should probably get on the phone with his biggest client, Leonard Carmichael, and tell him what they needed to do to protect his investments, but he found he didn't want to, that it didn't matter. There was always some new crisis, something that caused fortunes to collapse or developments that created windfalls and landed vast amounts of wealth into the laps of people who did nothing but push buttons and issue orders.

He shook his head; he was tired of the constant state of panic that everyone here operated in, including himself. He was sick of the stress and the stale air of the office. There was more to life than this.

He left his cubicle as Mark shouted behind him, 'It's your ass, Matthews! It's your ass Carmichael will have for breakfast if you don't tell him about this shit NOW!'

Greg ignored Mark's message of impending

doom and walked straight forward, with conviction, towards Dave Foster's office. He saw the man sitting calmly at his desk, seemingly oblivious to the meltdown that was occurring just outside his door.

It was the way it always was, though. The rest of them suffered heart attacks, panic disorders and acid reflux, while Foster sat at his desk thinking about the next yacht he was going to buy.

As he closed the distance between him and the door to his boss's office, he caught the eye of Foster's bulldog executive assistant, Claudia. Fiercely protective of guarding the inner sanctum, she could melt the skin off your face just by looking at you. Usually Greg worked to stay off her radar — there was no denying she was a cow; he had the attitude that if he didn't get in her way, she wouldn't get in his.

Today, though, was a different story.

Greg continued to march forward, even after Claudia stood up and took her usual vicious canine pose.

'I have to see Dave,' Greg stated in a voice that meant business.

Claudia placed her hand up. 'Mr Foster is busy. You can't go in there.' Greg kept walking. 'Hey, stop,' she ordered.

He pushed past her, reached for the doorknob to his boss's office and turned it. It was open.

'You do not have an appointment. You cannot see him!'

He ignored Claudia completely and went into Dave's office uninvited. Sure enough, he could see what Dave was looking at on the Internet. OK, so he wasn't shopping for a yacht, but a villa in Tuscany. Same difference.

'Ah-hem,' Greg cleared his throat and the noise startled his boss. The man quickly turned round and met his employee's eyes.

'Matthews. What are you doing? I'm up to my eyes here.' He quickly minimised his screen.

'Mr Foster,' Claudia huffed as she pushed past Greg, 'I'm sorry, I told him he couldn't come in, that you were busy. I apologise. Do you want me to call security?'

Greg rolled his eyes and put up his hand. 'No need for that. This will only take a minute.'

Dave puffed up his chest in an attempt to gain control of the situation. 'I don't have a minute. And what the hell are you doing in here anyway? Look at that out there, it's chaos! Get to work!' He pointed to the office as if he had been monitoring the situation this entire time, instead of only just noticing it.

Greg shook his head. 'No, Dave.'

His boss's eyes bugged out. 'No? No? I'm going to tell you what you are going to do right now and that's — '

'No,' said Greg calmly. 'I'm going to tell you what I'm going to do right now. I quit.' He smiled pleasantly at Claudia's shocked expression.

'Can't take it no more, huh?' Dave said calmly, in one of his infamous mood changes. He nodded briefly at Claudia, who got the message and left.

Greg shook his head. 'Nope.'

His boss calmly took out a cigar, lit it and blew the smoke up at the ceiling. Greg knew he had dismantled the smoke alarm ages ago. Dave wasn't much of a rules guy, which is probably why he had got so far. 'Must admit, I envy you.'

'Why?' Greg asked, surprised. 'You want out too?'

Dave slapped his hands down on his desk. 'Nah, I love the job. It's dangerous, always unpredictable . . . addictive. I'd just like to know that if I did walk away, I wouldn't be ruining so many lives.'

Greg nodded. 'Right, wife, kids . . . '

Dave chewed madly on the end of his cigar and waved his hand. 'Mistress, and her kids, and my sister who can't hold down a damn job, and my mother-in-law who always needs surgery on something or other, and . . . ' He stopped short and grinned at Greg's surprised face. 'What got you? Mistress, or the fact that I'm keeping my mother-in-law maintained?'

Greg stumbled. 'Both?'

Dave nodded satisfactorily. 'You're too nice for this job anyway. Go and be a shutterbug, or an *artist*, or whatever you want to call it these days.' He stood up and slapped Greg hard on the back. 'But whatever you do, don't get married — take it from me, they're all leeches.'

'Erm, thank you,' Greg said, his head spinning a little at the unexpected ease of it all. 'I really appreciate that. Of course, goes without saying that I'll work out any notice if you — '

'Nah, doesn't work like that in this business, you know that.'

Greg did but he wanted to make the offer anyway. 'I'll clear out my desk right away.'

'No worries, kid. Have a great life.'

Exactly, Greg thought, turning on his heels, his heart soaring. He *would* have a great life, and it was about time he got on with it. After all, like his mother always said, life was too short to spend in a cube.

Half an hour later, he stood in the elevator, holding a brown box that contained the few meagre personal possessions from his cubicle. Still feeling slightly dizzy after what he'd just done, Greg thought about the first time he'd ever used a camera. He was ten at the time, and his parents had bought him a Kodak for his birthday. He had turned it over and over in his hands, wondering what on earth he was supposed to take pictures of.

'Just take it with you when we go out,' his mother had said. She loved to walk around her old neighbourhood, the East Side, spotting all the changes that had taken place since she was a girl. She would excitedly point out different buildings to Greg. 'There, that's where I went to grammar school. Do you know who else went there? James Cagney, can you believe it?' and she would sound so amazed that Greg would pull out the camera and take a picture of the building.

Later he was glad he did, because many of the buildings from back then had since been torn down and replaced by cheap high-rises. His mother too adored looking at the old photo-graphs, her face lighting up as she recognised various familiar landmarks that no longer existed.

His mother had been raised by Italian immigrants in Alphabet City — just near the East Village in Manhattan; they had worked in an Italian deli 'every day of every hour of my life, until they both dropped dead', she would tell Greg. She had only two photos of her childhood. One was a black-and-white shot of her in a bassinet on top of a freezer in the deli, her face a pink smudge, her mother in the photo too, her arm resting on the meat slicer. The other photo was of her in high school, taken by a professional photographer. She was striking a Grace Kelly-like pose, her head titled slightly, looking past the camera wistfully.

His grandparents' deli had changed hands many times since and had finally closed in 1990, a victim of poor management by the then owners. The modest three-storey building had been torn down and a twenty-three-floor high-rise built in its place.

Driving around in Queens last week had energised Greg, given him purpose, made him realise he had made the right decision. He hadn't truly noticed until after 9/11 how much and how fast the city changed. The bulk of his photography work so far had been on the buildings protected by the Landmarks Preservation Commission, those that were deemed historical and would never be torn down.

But who was to say that his grandparents' deli, owned and operated from 1936 to 1990, wasn't a historical building as well? And since those types of buildings weren't protected, maybe those were the landmarks he should be concentrating on.

Greg felt a jolt of energy like an electric shock shoot through his body and right out of the top of his head. That could be his next project, photographing local, architecturally nondescript buildings that were in fact the lifeblood of the city, but were disappearing all too quickly.

Greg smiled.

If this was what loving what you did for a living felt like, then bring it on.

★ ★ ★

Later that afternoon, Greg pushed open the door of his Upper Seventies East Side brownstone feeling like a brand-new man. After leaving the office, he had picked up a coffee and walked almost the entire way from the Financial District back home, stopping to hail a cab only when the wind and the snow started whipping his face violently. He wasn't usually averse to winter weather, but there was only so much a cab-loving New Yorker could take.

But now, as he got home, he was eager to get out of his suit, shed his corporate work uniform and get on with the next part of his life. He figured there was no time like the present. So, first things first, he was going to organise all of his camera equipment and start documenting the work that was already on film. If he was going to start a new career, then he was going to have to make sure he stayed on task.

He smiled to himself, feeling giddy with excitement. And just a little bit nervous. He hadn't told Karen yet about his decision to quit and he felt slightly guilty that he had left her out of the loop. But, then again, she had always stood behind him. He couldn't imagine it would be any different now. He loved her and she loved him. After all, they had been committed to each other for almost three years and it was time to start thinking about what came next. He was sure she would be fine with his decision.

He also had the rest of the day to think about how he was going to tell her — it was just past lunchtime and she wouldn't be home for hours yet. Karen worked at Macy's, in the marketing department, and Christmas was one of their busiest times.

Greg still couldn't believe that he'd bitten the bullet and that for him there would be no more working late hours in a cramped office, no more slaving away on Christmas Eve or skipping parties because his boss wanted him at his desk for no good reason. Nope, no more of that. From now on, *he* was the boss.

Greg walked inside the foyer of the townhouse and suddenly had a funny feeling in the bottom of his stomach. He slipped off his shoes, trying to be extra-vigilant about not tracking snow across the wooden floors. Karen hated when puddles accumulated on the polished oak; she was convinced that if the wood became warped, it would affect the resale value of the house, which, for all intents and purposes, was prime real estate.

No arguing with her there, thought Greg, realising where the sudden feeling of worry came from. Admittedly, the place was almost paid off. He had written a cheque for a considerable chunk of the mortgage with his last bonus. But it had been his job that had funded the creation of this beautiful home, from its initial purchase to the remodelling that Karen had helped him with, right down to the littlest details provided by the (very expensive) interior designer. Greg also knew that he was sitting on a nice savings account. And, of course, he had always made sure he funded his retirement account, so he felt perfectly stable. But . . .

Just might have to be a little more conscious of what we are spending, at least until business takes off, he thought. He put his briefcase down and slid it under a side table in the entryway. It was only then that he noticed that Karen's handbag was there. Was she home?

'Karen? Honey?' he called out.

He heard the click-clack of her stilettos from deep inside the townhouse making their way to the front. When Karen emerged into view, he found her resplendent in an Armani suit of deep red that showed off her trim figure. Her light blonde hair was pulled back in an expertly coiffed knot at the nape of her neck that showed off her Swedish cheekbones and flawless complexion. As usual there wasn't a hair out of place. Her makeup was always perfect and Greg suspected that she had help from the counter girls in the actual store, although Karen never admitted to it. 'I barely wear any: that's all you need to know,' she would playfully chide him.

Greg's heart sped up as he looked at her. Brains as well as beauty, and she was all his — the whole package. However, the only thing that was missing from that whole package at the moment was a smile.

'Hey, babe, what are you doing home? I didn't expect you until later,' he said, smiling. He moved forward to kiss her on the cheek.

'I was uptown for a meeting this morning, so I decided to just come home for lunch. And I could say the same for you,' she replied, arching an eyebrow. 'What's going on? Why are *you* home? Let me guess, did the office lose power because of this weather? I swear to God, I don't know why more backup generators aren't used. The threat of data loss alone — '

Greg smiled and cut her off. 'No, babe, nothing like that. Actually — '

'Then why . . . ? What happened?' Karen's face changed suddenly. 'Oh my God, did you get fired? Did they fire you? Jesus Christ on a cracker. Is this about that one account of yours? Carmichael, that son-of-a-bitch . . . '

Greg had to admit, he loved her intensity and the way her mind worked, but sometimes she could be really dramatic. With event marketing he guessed it came with the territory. 'Karen, honey, no. I didn't get fired. Everything is OK.'

'Oh thank goodness. Don't do that to me ever again.'

She took a deep breath and raised a hand to the back of her hair, as if making sure she was still well put together in light of her recent scare.

'It's not that. Like I said, I didn't get fired,' he continued, unable to resist a smile. 'Actually, I quit!' He laughed as if the admission out loud had allowed his soul to take flight right there in the middle of their hall.

The smile dropped from Karen's face. 'You what?'

Greg grinned even more brightly. 'I quit. I told them all to shove it this morning. I'm not going to go through another holiday season working eighteen-hour days and missing out on life. I have bigger and better things to do, we both do. Like my folks always say, we should work to live, not live to work. And now you and I have the opportunity to spend more time together, and I can help Dad out more too, try and make things easier for everyone. So what do you think?'

He reached forward and pulled Karen towards him, encircling her with his arms, but she didn't melt into his embrace like she usually did. Greg looked at her, suddenly nervous.

'Well, I . . . don't know what to think.'

He frowned. 'But I thought you'd be happy. You're always talking about how we can never go anywhere as a couple because I'm forever stuck at the office. That's all changed now.'

'Greg, I'm happy for *you*, but not happy for *us*,' she said shortly. 'You didn't tell me you were going to do any of this; I thought we'd be making decisions together by now. This . . . you quitting your job is a big deal, one that really affects our future. A one-income household . . . ' She shook her head.

Money . . . was that all she was worried about? Greg felt relieved.

'Oh, honey — ' he grabbed her hands and held them — 'things will change a little, that's all, just for a short while. Maybe not so much eating out, or as many cab rides . . . no big deal.'

'Not as many cab rides . . . you are planning on working somehow?'

Greg barked a laugh. 'Of course I am. I was just getting round to that bit.' He smiled. 'I can't believe you thought I was just going to turn into some unemployed bum . . . '

Karen exhaled. 'Phew. So have you been interviewing? Why didn't you tell me? Is this about that executive position at Wells Fargo? I remember you mentioning it to your dad ages ago, but then didn't hear anything about it. It is, isn't it?' She smiled broadly. 'Oh my God, Greg, this is fantastic — we should go to St Barts for Christmas to celebrate!'

Not meeting her gaze, Greg grimaced.

Indeed, he had spoken briefly to his dad and Karen about an open position at Wells Fargo a while back. He had even interviewed for it, and had been offered the job, but ended up passing on it. In essence, while the move would have been vertical, it would have meant even longer hours, the last thing he wanted. He didn't think that taking it would have improved anything other than his bank account. Because of this, he had never mentioned his decision on the offer to Karen. He knew he should have, and realised now it was a sort of sin of omission — but really, what was the point in bringing it up in the first place? Especially if he had already decided it wasn't for him.

And as for going to St Barts for Christmas this year with everything else that was happening? Not a chance.

He pulled away gingerly and looked down at her glowing face, now realising that maybe he should have told her about the Wells Fargo decision, or even in advance of the choice he had made today. Did he mess this up?

'Actually, this isn't about the Wells Fargo position,' he replied. 'Come on, let's go into the living room. I'll tell you all about it.'

He led the way down the hallway that opened up into the entertainment-friendly kitchen-cum-living room. Karen followed him hesitantly, as if she was Superman and he had just offered her a surprise that might well be laced with Kryptonite.

'Come on, babe, sit down.' Greg smiled encouragingly as he took her hand and led her to the Pottery Barn couch that she'd insisted they get a month ago. Karen had moved into the townhouse over a year before, and since then he had accumulated considerably more than twice as many possessions. He thought back quickly, trying to remember if he had put that piece of furniture on a credit card or had paid cash for it.

It was cash, he recalled eventually, feeling slightly better that it wasn't accruing interest right that minute.

Karen sat down and crossed her legs. 'OK, so if it's not Wells Fargo, where is it?' She was still talking interviews. 'Where's the new position, and when do you start?'

'Well, actually I start today,' he said simply. He

51

had felt so confident this morning that she would be excited by his decision, by his choice to be his own boss. Now he hoped he hadn't been wrong and overplayed his hand.

Her eyebrows went up. 'Today? You quit your job today and you are going to start somewhere new?' She pulled up the sleeve of her suit jacket and looked at the Movado watch he had bought her last Christmas. 'But it's almost two o'clock. How are you starting a new job today?'

'Well, here's the kicker . . . ' He smiled. 'I am going to be my own boss. I'm starting my own business.'

Silence permeated the room and Greg shifted uncomfortably in his seat. Eventually he cleared his throat. 'I have been playing around with this idea of starting my own company, a photography business. You know, ever since I sold the Flatiron shot. It's what I love doing and . . . ' He shrugged. 'I figured that there was real potential there.'

He studied her face, hoping for encouragement, or any hint in her expression that she approved of his decision.

'Photography?' Karen said quietly. She cast her eyes down, as if she was having a problem meeting his gaze.

'Yes,' he said with resolution.

'A photography business?' she clarified, still not looking at him. 'Freelance, you mean?' She finally turned her eyes towards him, and even though she was questioning him to clarify his intentions, he noticed that her expression was full of worry, and her voice lacked confidence.

'Well, I suppose you could describe it like that. But really, I have a lot of ideas about growing my client base — '

'You mean beginning,' she said, interrupting him.

'What?'

'Beginning your client base . . . starting it,' she said bluntly. 'You don't have a client base to grow.'

He shifted in his seat as he considered the reality of her statement. 'Well, yes, but all entrepreneurs have to start somewhere and, like I said, I have a lot of ideas. The only way to go is up. And I think I can really do something with this, Karen, be successful, but also enjoy it too. You know . . . Mom always thought that I had a knack for this sort of thing; she thought that — '

'Greg, come on,' Karen interjected sharply. 'Of course your mother said she loved your photos. All mothers love their kids' work. Have you ever seen a mother who didn't put up a finger painting on their refrigerator? They're supposed to do that.' She sat back and sighed. 'I really wish you would have talked to me before you did something this rash. Do you think that you can go back to Dave and apologise? Say you changed your mind?'

Greg recoiled at her words. He had to admit they stung. She was more or less calling him a delusional mommy's boy; she had taken everything completely out of context.

'That's not what I was trying to say, Karen. No, I can't go back. And yes, I'm sorry. Maybe I should have said something about this, but I thought you'd be happy I was out of the rat race. I believe in it and I know I can make this work. Come on, you've always had faith in me. And I'm sorry, I'm sorry that I didn't tell you, but I wanted it to be a surprise. Now we will all have more time together. And time is important, Karen, now more than ever.' He wished that he didn't sound so pleading, as if he was asking for permission.

'I understand what you're saying and that's all fine and good but, Greg, New York is an expensive city. I don't think I have to tell you that.'

'Come on now. Of course I know that. And I have thought about this. We will be fine. You still have your salary, and I have a nice nest egg — it will keep us in a good position until the business grows. OK, of course it means we'll have to cut back in a couple of areas, a few austerity measures, as they say, but nothing serious. And it will all be worth it in the end.'

'Oh, I know what it means,' she said drolly. 'I'm well aware we are certainly *not* talking St Barts for the holiday.'

'Karen . . . '

'Anyway,' she continued quickly, 'I have to get back to the office. One of us has to work.'

'Now come on . . . '

She breathed heavily, as if she suddenly felt the weight of the world rest upon her shoulders. She looked around at their well-appointed living room, as if trying to figure out what they'd need to sell first.

'Baby, come on. Think positive. We are going

to be fine.' Greg stood up and reached for her. 'I have faith in myself. I believe in what I can do. I thought you did too?' He hated how pleading he sounded. This is not how he pictured this conversation.

Karen locked her eyes on his face and she said, blankly, 'I do have faith in you, but I also thought that you considered me an equal partner in this relationship.'

'I do!' he said defensively.

'I'm not so sure, Greg. You just put a lot of responsibility on my shoulders and you didn't even care about my opinion enough to consult me before you did it. You just *assumed*.'

She had just turned the tables on him, making him out to be some sort of loser, some guy who sits back and does nothing and expects to be supported. She knew him better than that!

'I did no such thing,' he said. Or did he? He took a deep breath, preparing what he was going to say next, but she held up a hand. He had seen her use that move on the people she was in charge of at work; it was an icy gesture that immediately silenced the other person. It worked.

'I don't have time for this now. I have to get back. We can talk about it later, OK?' she said, turning her back to him and walking towards the door. She looked over her shoulder quickly. 'Oh, your dad called — there's a message on the machine. You probably should call him back.'

Moments later, Greg heard the door close behind her, leaving him in frigid silence.

His formerly good mood had been crushed

and now he was left with a worrying sinking feeling. He stared at the phone, hoping that his father's call wasn't the harbinger of more bad news. He didn't think he would be able to deal with that right now.

4

Holly didn't have a whole lot of time to think about her surprise discovery of the charm bracelet because, immediately afterwards, one of the Secret Closet's regular (and most demanding) customers arrived at the store with 'an emergency, and money to spend'.

Burn was more like it, Holly thought. A stylist by profession, Mona Sachs had been coming to the Secret Closet long before Holly worked there, and relied on them for many of the clothes she used for her clients, who ranged from movie stars to Hampton housewives.

Today she looked gracefully unkempt as usual. Her bright blonde hair was wound up in some sort of white cotton scarf and a huge pair of sunglasses slipped down her tiny pointed nose. A magnificent suede and fur poncho fell as far as her denim-encased knees, and on her feet were towering spike-heeled brown leather boots. Mona was not only short, but skinny with it, and reminded Holly of a little girl dressing up in her mother's clothes. She carried a Louis Vuitton bag in the crook of one arm that was so big Holly was sure she could fit a small child inside, and in her other hand was a BlackBerry. Holly had never seen Mona without the device, and often wondered if she showered with one hand sticking out of the shower curtain.

'What do you need?' Holly asked helpfully.

'I need a wrap for the Met Gala, and it can be real fur but, if it is, it has to be really old . . . and preferably pale, you know, like white or grey or bluish . . . no tails or heads flopping down or anything, a clean line.'

'Oh, I see, a starlet who will only wear fur if it's been 'grandfathered' in?' Holly teased.

'Ha. I also need a Halston, eighties party style. Have you anything new in?' Mona leaned towards the back, as though she wanted to run in there and rip through whatever boxes Carole was most likely going through.

'Let's start with the fur . . . ' Holly walked over to a nearby rack and pulled a stole off a hanger. It was silver fox and in great condition. 'Look at this one. Pure Elizabeth Taylor — if she were tall and blonde.'

'Oh my Lord, that's perfect!' Mona grabbed the stole and ran her hands across it. 'I'll take it.'

'Well,' Holly said wryly, 'that was easy.'

Mona's BlackBerry started to beep and she pulled it out of her bag and started texting. 'Gotta go . . . ' she mumbled, without looking up. 'Can you courier the Halston over direct if you find something?' Mona's office was based uptown on Seventh Avenue and she usually trusted Holly and Carole's judgement.

'No problem.' Holly wrapped the fur in tissue and slipped it into a Secret Closet monogrammed bag.

'Thanks, sweetheart.' Mona never even looked up from her phone as she jangled out through the door and hailed a cab.

After that, Carole went out on an errand and

58

Holly was kept busy until well past lunchtime, helping customers and occasionally going into the back to unpack a box and sneak another look at the mysterious bracelet. She planned to give UPS a call just as soon as she had a free moment, but by lunchtime there was still lots of work to get through and three more boxes waiting to be opened.

Well, they'll just have to wait, Holly thought, switching the sign to 'Back in 30 minutes' and dashing out with the latest round of arrivals for the dry cleaner. The service they used was just round the corner on Sixth Street, and when Holly walked in, Thuma, the girl manning the counter, was on her usual perch, slurping soup from a cardboard container.

'Don't you ever take a lunch break?' Holly greeted her, carefully laying the clothes on the counter.

'How can I? You and Carole are in here every damn minute.' This was typical Thuma, ornery to the last. From what little Holly could gather, she had come to the United States ten years before and had the kind of Slavic beauty that usually graced the covers of magazines. She wore too much jewellery, too much makeup and kept her hair cut short and slicked back. While Holly never smelled smoke from Thuma, looking at her hands she could see the nicotine stains.

Because they knew so little about Thuma's past, Holly made wild stories up about her for Carole. Stories like she'd once been a burlesque dancer in Las Vegas, and was fleeing the Mob for knowing too much, or that she had held up banks, Bonnie and Clyde style, with the man who brought her to the United States, and that's why she was always looking over her shoulder.

Of course it was more likely that Thuma was always looking over her shoulder merely to make sure that the dry-cleaning steamer wasn't overheating.

But Holly couldn't help it: she had a vivid imagination and adored mystery and romance, especially when combined. Which was why the job at the Secret Closet was so perfect for her.

She pitied Thuma's customers, though. She knew everything about them: who was cheating, drinking too much, who overate, who was changing jobs, who was going broke and who was doing drugs — and was able to derive all this from the smell and spills found on their jackets and dresses, by the labels they wore and the forgotten notes and bank receipts they left crumpled in pockets.

Thuma huffily got off her stool and smoothed her hands over the clothes Holly had brought in. 'Mmm, nice. Did Mata Hari die?'

Holly laughed. 'I suppose they are a little gaudy.'

'You think?' Thuma pulled out one of the gold blouses. 'This will be no small feat. See how thin it's got?' She put her hand under the vintage blouse, and studied it through the worn lamé.

'Maybe it's so worn because the owner was a high-priced hooker?' Holly ventured.

Thuma leaned towards the blouse and gave it a hearty sniff. She was the only person Holly knew who was obsessed with the history of

60

clothing as much as she herself was.

'Smell it,' Thuma demanded, shaking it under Holly's nose. She complied, unsure about what Thuma wanted her to see, or rather smell.

She inhaled. 'OK . . . perfume, roses and . . . bergamot maybe?'

'Yes, that's no hooker perfume: that is prim lady with money and arthritis.' Thuma held the blouse up and eyed it sadly. 'Poor lady, maybe she thought it would make her feel young.'

She grabbed her receipt book and started scribbling out a short description of each garment before handing it to Holly. 'OK, this time tomorrow, good?'

Holly nodded; she knew she was being dismissed. She gave a little wave as she left the store.

Next, she made her way to the Korean deli next door, ordering butternut-squash soup and crispy bread to go. She impatiently checked her watch as she waited at the counter; she only had ten minutes left to eat, and the knucklehead in front of her couldn't find his wallet. *Typical*. Holly eyed the impeccably tailored midnight-black suit and the scuff-free Bruno Magli shoes. Wall Street for sure.

Back at the shop, Holly set out her lunch on the counter over a cloth napkin. Carole was very strict about keeping the place clean, and bug and rodent free (not an easy task downtown). She checked the time. Great, five minutes to eat. She drank the soup like coffee instead of enjoying it, and only took one bite of the bread before throwing the whole lot away.

The store got even busier as the day went on, and by the time she had a free moment, it was almost five.

Darn. She had promised Kate that she would be home by five today, yet there was still a customer in the store, painfully making a decision over a Dior riding jacket.

She watched the young woman turn in front of the mirror for the umpteenth time, anxiously biting her lip.

'I think it looks great!' Holly said, sliding off her stool and walking over to her.

'You're supposed to say that.' The woman eyed her dourly.

'Maybe, but I wouldn't want you to come back for a refund either.'

'I just think I can't . . . I'm not sure if I can pull it off. It's too . . . much for me.'

Holly knew from experience that 'too much for me' usually meant 'too good for me'.

'Not if you wear it the right way,' she said pleasantly. 'By the way, do you know who wore that jacket?' she added. 'Well, maybe not that particular jacket, but something almost identical.'

The woman shook her head.

'Faye Dunaway. She used to have a house upstate, with horses and everything.' She smoothed the back of the jacket across the woman's shoulders, and began pulling the sleeves down for a better fit. 'She used to throw riding parties there, with people like Al Pacino and Clint Eastwood.'

The young woman's eyebrows shot up. 'Seriously?'

'Yeah,' Holly continued, 'right before Al broke

62

her heart, but it didn't matter, she rebounded with . . . what's his name? You know the one.' She continued to shape the jacket and could see the woman physically become more relaxed and comfortable in it, finally looking at her reflection with a smile rather than a frown. 'You have hair just like her, you know. Maybe blow it out, add some tight jeans and heels with the jacket and you're good to go.'

The woman nodded receptively. 'You really think so?'

'Absolutely.'

Then she smiled and shook her head. 'OK, you've got me. I'll take it.'

Holly grinned. 'I promise you won't regret it.'

She was just starting to cash out and run receipts when Carole breezed in. 'Sorry I was gone so long . . . ' She paused and looked at Holly. 'In a hurry?'

'Sort of. Kate has a date tonight and I promised I'd be home by five.'

A good friend as well as helping her out with Danny, Holly wanted to give Kate moral support before her date, not just thank her for collecting Danny from school and giving him mac 'n' cheese. Kate had had terrible luck with men lately — not that Holly's luck was any better. But at least she was choosy, whereas Kate seemed to date anyone . . . the guy she met at a hot-dog stand, the bass player from a club last month, not to mention the guy who did her taxes and got her audited by the IRS.

'Well then, shoo, it's almost five after,' Carole chided. 'I'll take care of that.'

63

'Are you sure? I hate leaving you in the lurch . . . '

'Don't be silly; usually I can't get rid of you!' she joked. 'Seriously, go.'

Holly duly handed the cash and receipts over and gathered her things.

'Thanks, Carole, see you tomorrow.' Heading out the door, she flipped the sign to 'Closed' so that no one would bother her boss after hours.

She made it back home in record time, and pounded up the stairs to her apartment. Before she could slip her key in the lock, Danny opened the door.

Holly kissed him on the head as she walked in. 'Hey, honey, what's up?'

He motioned to the couch, rolling his eyes and shaking his head. 'Dump City,' he muttered, before going back to his big comfy armchair and his Nintendo DS.

Kate, brown hair newly styled and dressed to the nines, was on the couch, weeping over a cup of tea and a box of Kleenex. Holly sat down next to her and handed her another tissue.

'I'm sorry,' she sniffed. 'Danny's fine. He made me tea.'

Good boy, Holly thought proudly. With his father in and out of his life so much, and Holly never going on dates, she always worried that he had no good male role models, but it seemed like he knew what to do in a crisis.

'What happened?' She turned her attention back to Kate.

'Tim called just a few minutes ago. He said he couldn't make it, and had to stay home with

64

his . . . ' She started to sob again.

'Stay home with what — his dog?' Holly ventured.

Kate shook her head.

'Mother?'

She shook her head again and finally took a deep breath. 'Wife!' she exclaimed, before collapsing into tears again. 'Why can't I ever meet anyone?'

Danny duly turned up the volume on his DS.

'Danny, please — the headphones?' Holly chided. 'Maybe,' she said gently to Kate, 'it's because you meet *everyone*, and that's why you are not meeting *the* one.'

Kate stopped crying and sat up to blow her nose. 'You think so?'

'Yeah, I think so. I mean, where did you pick up this one?'

Kate giggled ashamedly. 'The crosstown bus.'

Holly nodded. 'The crosstown bus. At least next time try and aim for a guy who's hailing a cab?'

Kate laughed this time and Holly felt relieved.

'Look, why don't you stay on here for a while and let's order pizza or something.'

As if on cue, Danny jumped out of his chair. 'Pizza? Yes!'

Holly smiled indulgently. Of course he could hear that through the headphones.

Kate gave a weak smile. 'Thanks, that sounds great. I'm sorry for dumping on you again.' She sniffed. 'I'm going to get cleaned up.' She stood up and headed for the bathroom.

Holly walked over to Danny and gave him a

hug. 'That was so nice of you to make Kate tea — someday you are going to make a girl very happy.'

'Girls? Gross, Mom!' Danny pulled away from her and flopped back on the chair.

Holly gave him a look that told him she knew better, and went into the kitchen to search for the pizza menu. She rummaged through the drawers, pawing through used candles from Danny's birthday and old wine corks. She couldn't remember why she'd kept them. (Perhaps she'd liked the bottle?) She pulled one out and gave it a sniff. It smelled like nothing more than the inside of her kitchen drawer now. She sighed as she tossed it back in; maybe Danny might need it for a school project sometime. Then she stumbled across some bits of random bakery string, and one of Danny's baby soothers. Her heart melted as she picked it up and she shook her head. Why she was keeping a ten-year-old soother was beyond her. But her father had been the very same way, sentimental to the last. Probably the Irish blood — or the upbringing, at least.

It was her mother whose favourite motto was 'When in doubt, throw it out.'

Eileen and Seamus used to argue over the value of oddly shaped cardboard boxes that her father claimed were hard to find, the guitar with no strings, and a number of various mismatched blue willow plates that had belonged to his mother back in Dublin.

'But where am I supposed to put all this stuff?' her mother would demand.

'In the attic,' he would answer. 'You never know, Holly might need them someday, right, Holly?'

And as a girl Holly would nod, excited at the prospect of setting up her own house with a random set of blue willow from Ireland, not understanding that as she became older, she wouldn't want them, would never learn guitar and she would have her own taste and her own money to spend, not to mention her own plates to buy and break.

A couple of years after her father's death, Eileen had phoned one day out of the blue. She was going through the stuff in the attic, and was there anything that Holly wanted her to keep? Twenty years old and living away in her college dorm at the time, Holly had thoughtlessly replied that no, there was nothing.

Now she leaned against the counter, the search for the pizza menu suddenly forgotten. Right then there was nothing more she wanted than that odd set of stupid blue willow plates.

Why hadn't she asked her mother to keep them? Or, more to the point, why hadn't she taken them? Was that why she was keeping all this random stuff in the drawers? Was she afraid to forget?

Danny had turned ten a couple of weeks ago and Holly remembered the look on his face when he tore into the gift she got him, a Nintendo DS system. The apartment was too small for a Wii, and their TV was tiny. And getting him a Wii system would have been like asking the downstairs neighbours to complain even more about the noise. It was difficult enough as it was, trying to keep the energy level of a ten-year-old at bay in a one-bedroom apartment with wooden floors.

Danny's father, Nick, couldn't even show up for his birthday, so Holly *had* to keep the ten-shaped candles, and the string from the bakery cake box, and a little piece of shiny star wrapping paper, otherwise who would remind her?

'Mom, did you find the menu?' Danny called out from the living room.

Shaking her head, she dug back into the drawers. There, folded under a bunch of Danny's homemade cards to her, was the pizza menu. 'Yup, got it!'

She ordered a pizza and the three of them sat in the tiny kitchen nook when it arrived. As they ate and chatted about the day, Holly wondered if it would always be like this, such a small circle of friends but no real family for Danny. The thought saddened her a little.

After Kate left, Holly and Danny did their usual evening ritual of reading next to each other in the living room on Holly's bed. He was curled up next to her, with a Harry Potter book, while she was trying to concentrate on a Margaret Atwood novel that Carole said she 'just *had* to read', but instead she was absently scanning the pages.

'Mom?' Danny shifted next to her, looking up from his own book.

'Hmm?' She ruffled his hair.

'I want to change my name.'

'What?' Holly put the book down and held her breath. She had not been expecting this.

'Yeah, I want to change my last name from Mestas to O'Neill.'

Holly felt her heart freeze and a rush of dread flooded through her. This is exactly what she was always worried about. With her dad gone and his own father usually missing in action, Danny had never had any consistent male role model and it was beginning to show. While Nick had always supported them well financially, his parenting skills were decidedly more 'miss' than 'hit'. That was, whenever he actually remembered that he was a parent.

'Mom?' He looked at her anxiously.

'Hey, go make me a cup of tea since I know you can do that now, and we'll talk about it.' She pushed him playfully off the bed and he hurried to the kitchen, perhaps pleased to be treated as an adult, to be in charge of his own fate or, indeed, name.

Holly clasped her hands together and thought about what to say. Way back when Danny was born, Nick had sworn he would be involved, that he would care for them and be 'the best dad ever'. Of course, this was short-lived enthusiasm once the tough reality of caring for a child became apparent, and instead, Holly had wound up trying to be both a mother and a father.

Danny returned with two mugs of tea and handed one to her.

She took a sip, taking her time. 'Mmm, good!' and he beamed. 'Come here, sit by me.' She patted the space next to her and he climbed up,

69

careful not to spill his own mug.

'So . . . ' Holly held her mug between her hands, taking care not to cuddle him — she wanted this to be an adult conversation. 'I appreciate that you want to change your name to mine, but I need to ask why?'

'Because Dad is never here,' Danny said angrily. 'How is it fair that he gets to have me walking around with his name when he's done nothing to deserve it?' He started to get flushed and stopped abruptly.

Holly nodded. 'That's a good point.' He was obviously still sore that his dad hadn't shown up at his birthday. Double digits were important in the grammar-school set. 'But he is your father, and nothing you can do will change that. You can try changing your name, your looks — ' Danny looked just like his dad — 'whatever you like, but he is your father. He may not have given you much — '

Her son rolled his eyes. 'You think?'

Holly smiled. 'He may not have given you much besides his name or that iPod last Christmas,' she added jokingly, 'but it is something. It's a part of who you are, and you can't dismiss it. And your dad is part of you, whether he is around all the time or not.'

Danny was looking sourly into his mug.

Holly touched his arm. 'Look, I know he's not the best dad in the world, but it's up to you to take what he gives you and make it into something better. If you feel all he has given you is his name, then embrace it. Take the name and make it the best name in the world.'

He looked up at her, his eyes full of thought.

'You and I, we have something special — we are together all the time; we know what it's like to be a family, yes?'

He nodded appreciatively.

'So take the name and spin it into gold, OK?' She hugged him. 'You think I need you to have the same last name as me? You are too silly . . . What next, matching outfits?'

Danny shoved her away playfully. 'Oh, Mom!'

She laughed and pulled him tighter. 'You were born Daniel Joseph Mestas, *my* son. So don't ever change it.'

He hugged her back. 'OK.'

'Now go to bed!'

He groaned and shuffled off to his room, but seemed happier.

Holly listened as he creaked into bed and shut off his light. That was certainly a conversation she didn't want to have again anytime soon. Putting her head on the pillow, she lay there for a long time, wondering where she went wrong and where she went right.

The discussion had thrown her for a loop. She knew it would only be a matter of time before Danny started to feel bitter towards Nick — as it was, she'd needed ten years to calm down herself. She looked at the picture on her bedside table, of Danny the night he was born.

She blinked back tears. She had vowed not to obsess about Nick and had told herself that the father and son relationship was *their* relationship, autonomous from hers.

But it was hard; hard when Danny was hurting

71

because of Nick, because it brought back memories of when she was hurting because of him too. She ached for Danny; she wanted him to be happy and well adjusted, but who was she kidding? She was a single mom and Nick, for the most part, an absentee dad.

She toyed with her charm bracelet. 'Iron sharpens iron, so one man sharpens another,' Seamus always used to say, and her father was right.

Holly switched out the light and prayed for sleep, which did not come easily. She tucked her arm under her head and gazed out through the window across from her bed.

Her flimsy curtains only barely concealed the goings-on in the rest of the building. She could glimpse people's shadows as they turned lights off and on; she knew who watched too much TV and who was single. Much as they probably knew about her, she thought.

Holly watched through the curtains as a blurry couple across the way entered their apartment. She watched them turning on the lights, settling in, tossing coats and looking in the fridge, then shutting lights out on their way to the bedroom, where, Holly imagined, wonderful unseen things would probably take place. She sighed and turned to the wall instead. She wished she could shut her brain off and go to sleep, instead of finding new things to worry about. Finally she watched the shadows on the wall and ceiling as all the lights in the courtyard started to expire, and once the building and her apartment were completely dark, she managed to drift off.

5

The next morning, she felt nervous and jumpy. She walked Danny to school, trying not to let him see how last night's conversation had caused her so much worry. But he seemed OK. She stood for a while across the street from the school building, watching him and the rest of the kids make their way in. The sky was grey and heavy with snow today; it felt as if it was five o'clock, the way the clouds blocked out the sun. The children were made to line up in an orderly fashion before being let inside. A teacher blew a whistle and they all started marching in, quietly. Holly watched her child shuffle in with the rest, his back stooped a little with the load of books that seemed too much for a fourth grader. She wanted to run across the street and pull him out of the line, take the day off and go to the zoo and watch the penguins, and eat hot dogs off a cart, which she never allowed him to do.

She clenched her fists in her black wool pea coat — at least she had had the sense to dress warmly today. She snuggled her chin firmly into her scarf and started walking back up Sixth Avenue. Hot dogs, she thought. I'll stop at the grocery store and pick up some hot dogs later. That would cheer them both up. Summer food on a cloudy day. Maybe next summer she could take him camping. She shuddered a bit at the thought — no, maybe three days at the beach was enough.

Having been born and raised in the city, Holly felt a little short on some of the experiences that other people had had. She hadn't even learned to drive: it was embarrassing actually. But she had never been able to afford a car, and her mother didn't drive, so Holly hadn't bothered to take a course or test. When she took Danny to the shore, there was always a train out of Penn Station, and New York City was loaded with public transportation and cabs. And of course there was no parking, or at least that's what it looked like to her. Every street in Manhattan seemed to be crammed with cars parked so tight she wouldn't even know how to manoeuvre one out of the space. And wasn't that the excuse for almost every New Yorker running late? 'Sorry, couldn't find parking,' or, 'Sorry, I hit traffic'?

Having to get up early to move a car that she might only use on weekends seemed ridiculous.

Anyway, Kate drove, so on those rare occasions that Holly had needed a car, she simply called on her friend. Like when she found, on the street, the amazing big armchair that now sat in her living room. It had been too large to carry home. Danny had been eight at the time and appalled when his mother had come to a screeching halt on Tenth Street to inspect the chair. She had then eagerly pulled out her cell phone to call Kate and have her meet them.

'We're picking up someone else's *garbage*?' he had asked, mystified.

Holly laughed. 'Remember, one man's trash is another man's treasure.'

'But it's in the *street* — who knows who

74

owned it?' he had said, eyes wide.

'Exactly!' Holly had said, pinching his cheek. 'Who knows? Maybe it belonged to that guy who played Wolverine.'

'Really?' Danny asked, looking around. 'He lives here?'

'Oh yeah,' Holly told him. 'All those celebrities get apartments downtown after they make it big. They think no one cares down here, that we won't notice them.' She had leaned in close to Danny and pointed to a tall passer-by with a black baseball cap pulled tightly down over his eyes. 'So keep your eyes peeled.'

Kate had appeared in less than five minutes, and the two women hauled the chair into the trunk of her Volkswagen, tying it down with twine. Kate never complained. She was always there for her. Thinking about it, Kate had been raised in Minnesota, so she probably knew about things like camping — Holly would ask her about it later.

She had been so deep in thought while walking that before she knew it she was standing inside the Secret Closet.

'Thank God you're here,' Carole exclaimed when Holly went out back to her boss. 'We are *swamped* — look how many boxes there are to go through. This is insane.'

Holly looked around; the three boxes she had left unpacked yesterday had now turned into twelve, as if cloned overnight.

'Oh my,' she murmured. It wasn't that they couldn't go through them easily enough; it was that Carole was due to go out to Long Island that week to visit her daughter for Hanukkah, which was early this year. And Carole *hated* leaving unfinished business behind, and Carole *hated* not going through the boxes, or at least seeing every piece that came out, and deciding whether she was going to sell it or not.

She was always afraid that even her trusted Holly would let a vintage piece slip by. Usually when they went through boxes, what wasn't kept went to the shelter at Sacred Heart a few blocks away. The last thing Carole wanted to see, she always said, 'was a homeless person in a Dolce and Gabbana overcoat'. As a percentage of all the store's profits went to charity, it wasn't that Carole wasn't charitable; she was just obsessive.

Holly put her hand on her boss's shoulder. 'Oh, you are such a control freak. I can handle it. I'll go through one box at a time at the desk, OK?'

Carole stood with her lips pursed.

'And if I'm not sure about a piece, I'll call you, but I am usually pretty good at spotting the tags from Walmart.' Holly grinned and gave her shoulder a little shake. 'It'll be fine, I promise.'

Carole laughed nervously. 'I know, you'll be fine and that's great, you can call me. I'm sorry, sweetie, I just get wound up at the holidays.'

Holly smiled. 'We all do — that's why there's eggnog. I'll take a box out with me now, all right? You go do what you have to do.'

She loved having Carole as a boss, but she also loved having the shop to herself now and then.

'You're right, I will.' Carole pecked Holly on the cheek. 'Oh, did you call UPS about the bracelet?'

'Not yet, but it's on my list.'

'Great. I want to make a decision on whether or not we can sell that jacket. If it happened to get there by mistake . . . ' She rolled her eyes. 'You and I both know there'll be hell to pay.'

But as it turned out the UPS service lines were jammed all morning, and try as she might, Holly couldn't get anyone to answer her call.

So, during lunch, she decided to take a walk over to the nearest UPS store and see if she could get her query dealt with in person.

As she walked, a blast of icy wind hit her in the face. The weather had certainly turned colder today.

Reaching the address, Holly pulled open the door to the brightly lit store and was immediately comforted by the rush of warm air. Somewhat less comforting was the long line of customers who were waiting, albeit begrudgingly, for their turn with the sole — and seemingly harried — store clerk.

She sighed. So much for being quicker in person . . .

Still, it was all a necessary evil. Holly prayed that if — heaven forbid — she ever lost her charm bracelet, it would fall into the hands of someone who would try to return it to her.

'It's all good karma — especially at this time of year,' she muttered to herself, taking her place at the end of the line. 'Season of goodwill . . . pay it forward and all that.'

Hearing her words, the man who was standing in front of her turned round quickly. He looked her up and down and she smiled politely at his frowning face.

'Pay it forward?' he barked. 'I wish this line would *move* it forward. Bunch of holiday bullshit, can't get anything done quickly.' He turned back round and Holly took a deep breath.

She plucked the charm bracelet out of her purse and studied it for what seemed to be the hundredth time since stumbling across it yesterday. She turned each of the individual charms over in her fingers and wondered if the owner of the bracelet had collected her charms with the same intention that Holly had done over the years, by associating a special moment or memory with each new addition.

Interesting that this was the second time in her life that a mysterious bracelet had appeared out of the blue.

She thought again about the initial appearance of her own bracelet and how she'd tried to work out the significance of that first charm, and indeed who had sent it to her.

Lost in thought, Holly eventually looked up and was happy to see that she was next in line. However, she was not so happy to see that the angry man in front of her was now making the UPS clerk's life hell.

'What do you *mean* you can't have it delivered by then? You are friggin' UPS!' Angry Man bellowed.

The clerk held out her hands, looking exhausted. 'I'm sorry, sir, we have our drivers working overtime this time of year and — '

'But that's not good enough!' the man yelled. Holly couldn't help but feel embarrassed for him. Someone should tell him that you always catch more flies with honey than you do with vinegar. She looked past the man's shoulder as he continued his verbal abuse and tried to make eye contact with the clerk. The young woman looked dangerously close to tears.

'You people are a bunch of morons! This is the last time I come here for anything. From now on it's the other guys or nothing!' The man threw up his arms and looked around, centring his gaze on Holly. 'Good luck, lady. Pay it forward, my ass!' He hurtled through the store, slamming the glass door behind him. Holly grimaced as she watched the clerk try to recompose herself. She stepped forward gingerly. While she adored this time of year, she also hated the fact that the holiday season seemed to bring out the worst in some people.

'Are you OK?' she asked kindly. 'Maybe this weather will help cool him off.'

'Thanks. It's been a long day,' the woman said with a shaky voice.

'I'm sure it has,' Holly soothed. 'It's this time of year. It brings out the beauty in some and the ugliness in others. I've always said that everyone should, at some point in their lives, be required to work in retail or at a restaurant. It teaches a good lesson in how you should treat others.' She smiled warmly at the young woman, whose name tag read 'Lila.'

'Oh, how right you are,' Lila laughed, a smile finding its way onto her face. 'Anyway, holiday-related stress goes with the territory, and I'm fine really. Where do you work?' she asked.

'The Secret Closet, off Bleecker. It's why I'm here, actually. I'm hoping you might be able to help me.'

Lila nodded. 'Sure, I know that store. I can't afford to shop there most days, though. What can I do for you?'

'Most days I can't afford to shop there either,' laughed Holly. She pulled out the shipping document from the box in which she had discovered the charm bracelet. 'Well, yesterday morning we received a shipment at the store, three boxes in total. This is the reference.' She handed the document across the counter. 'The problem is, when we opened up one of the boxes, we found a bracelet inside a jacket that had been sent to us for resale. But there's nothing on there about the sender.' She pulled the charm bracelet out to show her. 'And I know this is valuable. I'm sure someone is missing it.'

Lila leaned in closer to take a look at the bracelet. 'That's really pretty, look at all those charms. Let me see what I can do. Usually we do have sender information, but it's weird nothing was on the label.'

She started typing on her computer, entering the UPS tracking reference to pull up the file. She pressed 'Enter' on her keyboard, and a moment later a crease appeared on her forehead. 'Huh,' she said. 'That's odd.'

Holly cocked her head. 'Is there a problem?'

'I'm not sure really,' Lila said, frowning. Then she shook her head. 'See, there is a tracking number associated with the shipment that came to us, but here's the problem. We reuse tracking numbers, especially this time of year. So there is no information about origination for the other tracking number associated with the boxes, because Corporate already put the tracking number back into the system. When I run that number, the one that is associated with it being delivered here, it shows that there is a package currently using it, and it's in transit . . . to Boise, Idaho.'

Holly made a face. 'So you can't tell me where our delivery came from?'

Lila shook her head. 'I'm sorry. It's our policy to reuse these tracking numbers . . . the older tracking information might be saved, but I have to call Corporate. Problem is, I'm on my own today so it might be a while.' She looked at the long line behind Holly.

'Of course, I understand.' Holly reached back into her handbag. 'Here's my card. If you do find anything out, I can be reached at those numbers.'

'Thanks. I'll do that. It's not a problem at all.' Lila smiled. 'It's nice that you are trying to find out who that bracelet belongs to. Many people might not bother. Good to know there are still nice people out there.'

'Thank you, but it's the least I can do.' Holly picked up the charm bracelet and looked at it again. 'I know it has lived a good life. I just need to help it find its way home.' Smiling at Lila, she placed it solemnly in an inner pocket of her handbag. 'Thanks again.'

'You're welcome. And I'll be in touch as soon as I can.'

'Great,' Holly said as she turned to leave. She'd taken a couple of steps towards the door when Lila called out to her. The customer who had been behind her in line had already moved to where she had stood just seconds before.

'Oh . . . miss?'

'Yes?'

'Well, it's just that, this might sound silly, but my mom always told me that if you lose something, you should retrace your steps . . . try and remember what you had been doing before you realised you were missing it. Maybe that's what you should do.'

'But I'm not lost,' Holly replied, puzzled. 'The bracelet is.'

Lila smiled. 'I know, but maybe if you worked out where it's been, you might learn where it's supposed to be. Just a thought.'

Holly felt the hair on the back of her neck stand up.

The girl was right.

She thought about the individual charms on her own bracelet. Each one had a story behind it, and held special significance. Maybe if she learned more about the charms on the other bracelet and what they signified, it would help lead her to the person who had lost it.

After all, Holly thought, looking again at her beloved bracelet, the charms on this illustrated a direct path through her life, didn't they?

★　★　★

City University of New York, Manhattan, 1997

'I honestly don't know how I am ever going to get all of this done. Seriously, Warner is such a

82

creep, it's like he gets a kick out of punishing his students,' whined Holly as she ran her hands through her frizzy auburn hair. 'And this hair, I need to do something about it.'

She looked at the books spread out around her on the library table, a veritable Mount Everest of college textbooks, and sighed. 'Above all, I need to get a life.'

Her roommate, Laura, looked up from her own stack of work and smiled. 'I concur.'

They both laughed. 'Maybe that will happen after this semester. This psych class is killing me.'

Laura pushed her books away. 'I don't see why you are taking it, anyway. Isn't it unrelated to your major?'

'You mean, how does psychology relate to fashion merchandising?' Holly replied. She shrugged. 'My adviser says it should be valuable, especially when determining customer purchasing habits. Still, maybe I should have gone into an easier major . . . like physics or microbiology.'

Laura groaned. 'Look at us, in the college library on a Friday night in one of the coolest cities in the world. Our life is passing us by. I mean, when did anything exciting ever happen in a library?'

Holly raised an amused eyebrow. 'I'm sure that some of the world's great thinkers would argue with you on that.'

'Yeah, yeah, yeah. What I mean is, when was the last time you met a cool guy at a library?'

Holly looked at a guy sitting several seats down from them, poring over a chemistry textbook. He met her gaze, then shushed them and scowled.

Laura flipped her hair, rolled her eyes and gave him the finger. 'See my point?'

Holly shook her head. 'OK, what do you have in mind?'

'Ah,' Laura replied, jumping up and down in her seat. 'I thought you would never ask. There's actually this party tonight, at the Kappa house. I know a guy in my feminist theory class, he asked me to come along.'

Holly rolled her eyes. 'A frat party? I thought you said something about meeting *cool* guys? And you met him in a *feminist theory* class? What — does he think that it's a good place to pick up chicks?'

Laura swatted the air. 'Whatever, it's just for fun. Plus he is kind of cute. Come with me. *Pleeaaassseee* . . . ?'

Holly considered her friend for a moment and looked at the alternative, her books and the shusher, who had just stood up from his seat — probably to report them to the head librarian. He was wasting his time — Holly knew Inga, the librarian, wouldn't entertain his complaints. A kind, friendly woman who knew Holly and Laura well, Inga Laurila was well used to student shenanigans.

It was true, though; Holly kind of did need a night out. And she supposed a frat party was better than nothing.

'What the hell . . . ?' she conceded. 'But I have to go change and put some makeup on. I can't go anywhere looking like this.'

'Oh? I didn't think you cared about what some frat boys thought of you.'

'I don't, but it's Manhattan. And here, standards are necessary.'

As they left the library, Inga smiled and called out in her native Boston accent, 'Leaving so soon?'

'A different kind of research!' Laura called back, winking at Holly. 'See you tomorrow.'

A little later, the two girls rushed through the doorway of their dorm building, eager to get changed and ready for their impulsive night out.

Just as they were pushing through the heavy metal door that led to the stairway, their resident adviser called out to Holly from the lobby.

She turned round. 'Hi, Kirsten. What's up?'

Kirsten rummaged around underneath the front desk. 'Glad I caught you. There was a delivery for you earlier.'

'A delivery?' Holly repeated, eyebrows raised. She took the package from Kirsten, eyeing it suspiciously. Then, noticing that there was no return address on the packaging, she felt her fingers tremble.

This was the second time a package with no return address had been delivered to her. The first time was the day she'd been sent her bracelet and the hourglass charm from her dad. But that had been over two years ago.

And, more to the point, her dad was long since cold in the ground.

'Holly, come on, hurry up,' Laura said, tapping her elbow.

Holly snapped out of her reverie. 'Sure, sorry.' She began to follow her roommate up the stairs, her feet on autopilot. She continued to stare at the package in her hand, wondering what it was and who it had come from.

When they reached their room, Laura immediately hustled about, shuffling through drawers and plunging into her closet.

Holly, however, sat down at a small table and turned the box-shaped parcel over and over in her hands.

Her fingers shook as she found scissors to cut through the packaging tape and reveal the contents.

When she did, her stomach did an almighty flip-flop.

Inside was a lilac box adorned with white satin ribbon. While it was a little smaller, it was exactly the same type of box as the one before that had contained her charm bracelet.

Laura finally took note of Holly's mood. 'Hey, is everything OK? What is that? You're staring at it like it holds a bomb. Who's it from?'

Holly's voice trembled. 'That's just it, I don't know.'

'What do you mean, you don't know?'

Taking a deep breath, Holly launched into the story of the charm bracelet that had mysteriously arrived on the day of her father's funeral, and her conclusion that it had come from him.

'But you never knew for sure that your dad was the one who sent it?' Laura asked when Holly finished her story.

She shook her head, feeling very uncertain now. 'I just assumed it was something he'd arranged before his death.'

'Like a message from beyond the grave? Shit,

sorry, I didn't mean to sound insensitive.'

But Laura was right. That was exactly what Holly had assumed at the time. 'But this one couldn't possibly be from Dad.'

'Well then, what about your mum?'

Holly shook her head determinedly. 'Not a chance. Me and my mother . . . well, you know we're not exactly best buddies.'

'Are you absolutely sure it was from your dad, though? You said that your parents were pretty well known in Queens. Maybe it was someone who read the obituary and wanted to connect?'

Wanted to connect . . . Holly looked at her, wondering if she might be right. Her thoughts galloped. 'But then . . . why would they be sending me another box, and why now?'

Laura moved closer to peer over her shoulder. 'Maybe what's inside might give you the answer to that?' she suggested.

Opening the box, Holly revealed a small silver charm displayed on a piece of purple satin. She gently lifted it out, taking in every detail.

'It is another charm,' Laura stated. 'But what . . . ?'

'It's a book, an open book,' Holly confirmed. 'And look, there's an engraving on it.'

The wise man reads both books and life itself.
Lin Yutang

'What do you think it means?' she asked quietly, more to herself than to Laura.

'I have no idea.' She glanced surreptitiously at her watch, as if suddenly recalling they had things to do. Then she grinned. 'Maybe it means that you should get dressed so that we can go to this party to experience some college *life*?'

Holly rolled her eyes, amused by her friend's short attention span.

It was true, her academic life as of late could use some balance, but there was something else too, an expression that was coming back to her, as she tried to recall something that her father had told her when she was young and just learning to read.

That books should provide for learning, but that they should also provide for enjoyment.

When was the last time that she had actually picked up a book to read just for the sake of reading? When was the last time that she had cracked open *Gone with the Wind*, or *Pride and Prejudice*, or any one of her other favourite books? There had been a time when all of those novels had been her best friends, when they had been a part of her soul and much more than just a hobby.

She smiled at the memory, suddenly feeling comforted by it. She wasn't sure how he'd done it, but clearly her dad had somehow arranged to have this one sent too. But yet, how could he have known she'd end up going to college here, or where her dorm was, or —

'How would the person who sent you that know that you have been spending all your time in the library?' Laura, who had already gone on to change into a mini-skirt and a halterneck top, returned to where Holly was sitting.

Holly's mind was reeling as she thought the very same thing.

'I'm not sure. Clearly someone has been

keeping an eye on me.'

Laura's eyes widened. 'You mean like a stalker? Eww, that's creepy.'

But for some reason, Holly knew it wasn't quite like that.

'No, not like a *stalker*. More like . . . a fairy godmother.' She smiled at the idea of someone watching over her, sending her encouraging messages and providing guidance on how to live her life.

A new thought was playing at the edges of her mind, but one that she couldn't quite yet process.

She looked back down at the new charm. The idea made sense, and it certainly fed Holly's imagination. She liked the idea of someone on the periphery thinking about her, giving her a small push in the right direction.

'You know I'm adopted, don't you?' she said to Laura, almost reluctant to share her thoughts out loud.

Her friend's eyes widened. 'Oh, so you're thinking . . . ?'

In all honesty, Holly wasn't sure what to think. But there was no denying it was nice to think that somebody was looking out for her.

So maybe she should do justice to her mysterious benefactor, whomever it might be. After all, without her love of reading, Holly might not have the ability to dream and imagine and wonder about the charm that she now held in her hands.

Mind made up, she decided that, tomorrow, she would pick up a book, one of her old friends, just to read for fun.

But tonight, *tonight*, she would go to this party with Laura, and keep an open mind. A recognition of sorts, of what the charm might be trying to tell her.

After all, her future could be likened to an open book and, Holly thought, surely the best part of life was enjoying writing your own story?

6

Greg rummaged around in the bread drawer and came up with a heel from a loaf of white and an end from a loaf of rye. He slapped together a makeshift sandwich of tomato and mayo, and leaned up against the counter to eat.

His grandfather, Nonno, from the deli, would be spinning in his grave about that sandwich. Despite his heritage, they were the only Italian words Greg really knew: *Nonno* meaning Grandpa and *Nonna*, Grandma. And only because his mother would say, 'Oh, your nonna would have loved that,' or, 'Your nonno could make a mean grilled cheese sandwich.'

Both had died long before he was born, and he often wondered what impact they would have made on his life. His father's parents had also died young, a product of the hard work and sacrifice necessary to make it in America.

He made his way to his darkroom, filled the trays with chemicals and switched off the lights to begin exposing the film. As he worked, he felt a sense of calm that only happened in the darkroom.

'Or just all those chemicals making you stoned,' Karen would tease.

She'd come round a little since the other day, once she'd had a chance to get used to the idea of his leaving the firm and going out on his own. In truth, it was Greg's own fault for landing such a huge change on her completely out of the blue. Who could blame her for being concerned? But she needn't worry for long: Greg wasn't one for sitting around, and today he was going to get out there and start work. It might not be paying work just yet, but everyone needed to start somewhere.

He let the chemicals do their thing and, once he had everything pinned up to dry, he slipped out through the door to wait.

He noticed the answer-machine light was blinking. He'd been so absorbed in his work that he hadn't even heard the phone ring. He pressed 'Play' on the machine — it was Karen.

'Hey, babe, just wrapping things up here on Further — back in town later.'

She was at a staff team-building exercise in the Hamptons. The event management crew had just finished with the Macy's parade, and were now knee-deep in planning the January promotions.

Her boss Bradley's house was on Further Road in East Hampton, and Karen always joked, 'You never know, if we push a little 'further', we could wind up there.'

She was in love with the idea of a summer place, like so many other New Yorkers, but Greg couldn't really understand it. His parents never had a summer place: if they wanted to go out of town, they usually rented.

And they were right, Greg thought, the simpler the better. Owning multiple properties would surely turn into a full-time job and, besides, with his reduction in pay, that wasn't going to happen anytime soon. He grabbed his phone and texted Karen. *Got your message. See you later. Let me know when you're back.*

He returned to the darkroom to check on his photos; they were developing nicely. He studied the one he'd taken the week before in Queens of the girl who had suffered the asthma attack. She and her mother were sitting on the front steps of their brownstone with paramedics in various states of work around them. They were oblivious to anyone, and looking with joy into each other's eyes, as if to say, 'We got through it.'

The mother's grey knit cap stood out like ash against the dark stone behind her. Apparently she had run out of the building holding her near-unconscious daughter in her arms. There was no phone in the building and she had no cell — hard to believe in this day and age, Greg thought. So she'd run out into the street, screaming for help, and a cabbie had radioed it in to his call centre, from where they had called 911. After the incident, Greg had asked one of the police officers if there was any way to arrange a cell phone for her. The officer, older and seasoned, had wagged his finger over the steering wheel as they had driven away. 'You're just an observer, man. You take your pictures and that's it. Don't even think about getting involved.' Greg later learned that most of the officers carried cards from city social workers that they would hand out, and it was a shot in the dark as to who would call wanting the help and who didn't.

Was there a huge stretch between want and need? Greg wondered.

Then, satisfied that the other shots were also

93

coming up well, he stretched and looked around.

He felt restless and was itching to get out and about in the city again — now that he was master of his own destiny. All those years cooped up in that cubbyhole . . . he was anxious to make up for lost time. Greg eyed his bike standing guard near the front door. Maybe he should take it out and about today, and see where he ended up.

He might pay a visit to his mate Rob, who worked at the *New York Times*. He hadn't even told him yet that he had quit. Digging around in his pocket for his phone again, he sent Rob a text saying he'd be in the area later, then slipped into sneakers and a sweatshirt, before grabbing his camera and a new roll of film.

As he rode, his calves burned; he had to get used to biking again — no more cabs. In any case, it was also the best way to see the city. As the cold air filled his lungs, he was again struck by how free he felt, how in sync with everything.

He manoeuvred his way through the busy streets, avoiding collisions with cabs and other bikers, and as he passed the Metropolitan Museum of Art, he felt a pang of guilt. Usually he gave a big donation every year; now, with this new career change, he wouldn't be able to.

He took out his camera and took a few quick shots of the steps. It was cold so there were relatively few people hanging out on them. In the summer, Greg loved to walk on the other side of the street and watch the tourist and art students piling in and out of the doors. He glanced up at the banner — advertising the highlight of a forthcoming gala evening in February. Greg stopped in his tracks. The gala . . .

As a patron of the museum he was always given two tickets, and Karen adored such events. Well, she was bound to be a little disappointed about missing it this time, but what was a fancy dinner compared to a lifelong dream?

Greg continued whistling a little under his breath.

He reached the *NYT* building about half an hour later, chained his bike and went inside. Rob was a writer for the travel section of the paper, and he and Greg had met when they were both attending Columbia. Rob was the nearest thing Greg had to a brother and, no matter what was happening, they had always managed to stay in touch all these years. He gave his name at the reception desk and was motioned through metal detectors to the elevator bank.

Getting out of the elevator, he admired the office. It was a totally open space with no walls or cubicles. People worked side by side on long, deep desks while perched on rolling chairs. There were coffee and snack areas with fresh fruit in each of the four corners of the room. Multiple flat-screen TVs were scattered about, some on, some not. When Greg had first seen Rob's office, he'd queried how he could work among such commotion, and his friend had taken him to a corner of the office and sat him down at one of the long desks. It was calm and quiet; the huge ceiling and expanse of the room basically sucked the noise up and out.

'Pretty cool,' Greg had said, thinking of his

own depressing cubicle on Vesey Street. He'd always felt faintly jealous of Rob, who'd pursued his dream of writing, while Greg had followed in his father's footsteps and gone into trading because he wasn't sure what he wanted to do, wasn't confident enough of making a living as a photographer. But now things had changed. He scanned the room looking for his friend and saw Rob waving at him from one of the rolling chairs.

When Greg reached his friend's desk, he saw the naked surprise on Rob's face. 'How come you're out and about in the land of the living?'

Greg shrugged modestly. 'I did it,' he said.

'Did what?'

'Quit. My J-O-B,' Greg spelled out slowly.

'So you're finally gonna give the photography a proper shot?' Rob chuckled. 'Excuse the pun.'

'That's the plan.'

'That's amazing, man, and about time too.' Then Greg noticed his friend was looking distractedly past him to someone who had just come off the elevator.

'Hey,' Rob called out, waving. 'Hey, Billy, over here!'

Greg stood up. 'Look, man, if you're busy we can always hook up later . . . ' He felt confused and somewhat hurt by his friend's reaction.

'Just hold on a second.'

A short man with a square head and body lumbered over to them, a huge folder balanced on his hands.

'Billy,' Rob began, 'I want you to meet Greg Matthews — remember I told you about him? He's a good friend of mine, a photographer

. . . been documenting the city since . . . ' He glanced questioningly at Greg, who felt oddly proud of being introduced as a photographer.

'Since I was about ten,' Greg replied, sticking out his hand.

'This is Billy Harrington. He's one of our photo editors here at the paper.' Rob grinned at Greg's look of surprise.

Billy tried to manoeuvre the folder he was holding so he could shake Greg's hand but gave up. Both men laughed. 'Yeah, Rob talked about you before, said you were really good,' Billy said. 'Have him give you my number and I'll take a look at your portfolio.'

Greg was stunned. 'That would be . . . great, thanks . . . '

Billy scurried away and Greg looked gratefully at Rob. 'Wow, thanks, man. I really, really appreciate that.'

'Hey.' Rob held his hands up. 'It's just an introduction. You gotta bring the gold, OK? Get some of that stuff together you did with the Flatiron, and maybe some of those neighbourhood pieces you were talking about, and I reckon he might offer you at least a trial contract position.' He shrugged. 'Pay's not great, but . . . '

'That would be incredible,' Greg said, hardly able to believe his luck. Never mind the pay, the experience would be invaluable. The *New York Times*!

'Well, let's meet up for a beer or two soon and we can talk some more about it — it's already been too long.' He glanced at his computer screen. 'Wish I could talk more now but I'm

97

kind of on a deadline.'

'No problem. I'll get out of your hair — or at least what's left of it,' he joked to his friend.

As Greg made his way back to the elevator, he turned round to take a look at the office one more time. He couldn't believe this opportunity. Granted, as a contractor, and a trial one at that, he'd be making very little money, but it would still be worth it. Being in charge of his own schedule, being creative. He felt like jumping in the air and doing a fist pump.

He couldn't wait to get home and start gathering together what he wanted to show to the photo editor.

Outside on the street, as he unlocked his bike, a text came in from Karen. *I'm back. A few of us just popped to the Oyster Bar — can you meet me there?*

He paused, surprised by his automatic, unenthusiastic reaction.

As much as he wanted to see Karen, he didn't fancy socialising just then; he wanted to go home and work. It was a new feeling. But, seeing as she was being so understanding about the changes in their life, Greg replied telling her that he would meet her there, but to start without him. Then he hopped back on his bike and peddled as fast as he could through the Times Square traffic towards midtown.

★   ★   ★

The Oyster Bar was located in Grand Central Terminal and was reasonably fancy, but not so much that anyone would raise an eyebrow at Greg's casual attire of jeans and fleece pullover. The knit cap had to go, though. Greg slipped it over the seat of the bike he had anchored on the street outside and, going inside the cavernous building, he headed for the subterranean restaurant area.

Inside the restaurant, he hastily combed his hair with his fingers as he spotted Karen at a table with a few of her co-workers. She was wearing a black suit with a short skirt and a red cashmere scarf peeking out of the neckline. Her long legs were elegantly crossed at the ankle and her black alpaca coat was slung neatly on the chair next to her. She had on a pair of black Louboutin shoes and the red soles coordinated perfectly with the rest of her outfit. Seeing Greg approach, she waved and stood up to greet him.

'Hello, sweetie, glad you could make it,' she enthused before making introductions to people he was sure he'd never met before. 'This is Blake — ' she gestured to a short, balding man in an Armani suit, who stood and pumped Greg's arm up and down — 'and this is Stacy.' Stacy did not get up, but looked at Greg with interest as he sat down. Stacy was also in Armani.

'They work in the advertising department,' Karen added brightly.

The Armani couple looked vaguely interested as Greg tried to work out why Karen had invited him to what seemed like a work confab. The four of them regarded each other silently for a moment, and then Stacy took a swig of her almost empty wineglass and gestured at the waiter for another.

'So you are a photographer,' she said to Greg, her voice the tiniest bit slurred.

'Well, yeah . . . ' he replied hesitantly, still trying to get used to this new job description.

'Karen's been chatting you up a storm. Says you're the greatest thing since Mapplethorpe.'

Karen squeezed Greg's knee and looked at him proudly.

'I was an art major, did you know that?' Stacy said.

Greg shook his head. How could he know? They had just met. He glanced quickly at Blake, who was looking bored into his own wineglass. The waiter came back with Stacy's wine and a glass of iced water for Greg.

'Yep. Really good too. I even showed downtown once. Oils.' She took another gigantic gulp of wine. 'But of course, I needed to eat . . . ' She chuckled. 'I needed money. So here I am, artistic director for Macy's Department Store.'

'Sounds . . . impressive,' Greg said, stiffening a little.

'Yeah, well, it's not.'

Karen tried to rope Blake into the conversation. 'Blake is in charge of layouts for the store circulars. They are always looking for new talent, aren't you, Blake?'

He nodded. 'Absolutely, and Karen says you're good — really, really good. We could always use a fresh eye, you know, and the pay is pretty OK too.'

Greg simply nodded, his lips pressed into a firm, thin line.

'So, if you have a — ' Blake stumbled, a bit

100

thrown by Greg's lack of enthusiasm — 'portfo-lio, or something you can show us . . . '

Greg shook his head. 'No, I don't, but thanks for the offer. Maybe I can get your card,' he added politely as he felt Karen's hand slip off his knee.

'Yep, good call there, Greg.' Stacy was busy ordering another glass of wine. 'Stick to the arts. Don't fall into the corporate trap.'

Karen stared down at the table, refusing to meet Greg's eyes. Soon after, they asked for the bill, and Blake carefully navigated Stacy out of her chair as they said their goodbyes.

When they were gone, Karen turned to him. 'Well, you can't blame a girl for trying,' she said, her dark gaze penetrating his.

'No, I suppose you can't,' he said dully. 'But, Karen, I take pictures of buildings, architecture, people in the city . . . '

'Well, I'm sorry for trying to help,' she replied, her tone defensive. 'I know what you take pictures of. I am so very sorry that my line of work is not . . . ' she paused, searching for the right word, ' . . . artistic enough for you.'

Greg put a hand on her arm. 'That's not what I meant at all. It's just that I've only just quit my corporate job and am starting to get my feet wet, and today I found out that I might be able to get something at the *NYT*. I'm only just finding my feet, sweetheart, and already I'm loving it. You know I hated the corporate life. So why would you want me to sell out again so soon?'

Karen looked down at his sneakers beneath the table. 'Because I can't help but worry about the future — especially in this economy . . . '

Greg sighed. 'I know, I'm sorry. I'll admit that life is probably not going to be as . . . comfortable as it was for a while, but we have to give it a little time. And I'll be happy — I am happy. Surely that counts for something too?' He waited for her to look up at him again, but she didn't. 'Karen . . . '

He understood that she enjoyed and worked hard to afford the finer things in life. Born and bred on Long Island, she came from a big family, completely different to Greg's privileged, only-child upbringing.

Her parents were great, and were always asking the two of them to come over for dinner, see a show or spend weekends. Karen had three sisters and one brother, all only a year or two apart in age.

It was just the kind of big, close-knit family that Greg had been envious of his whole life, and he marvelled at how they finished each other's sentences, how they picked on each other and yet never seemed to get really mad at each other. They had welcomed him into the fold happily, pleased that Karen had met someone so successful, so nice, who treated her so well. Karen herself was the eldest daughter and the most successful out of the whole clan. She had worked her way through college waitressing, and had held off on getting into a serious relationship long after all her siblings had got married. Her mother, after meeting Greg for the first time, had said, 'I see why you waited, Karen. I see it perfectly.'

Because of her working-class roots, Greg had thought that she would understand better than most that people can be happy no matter what they had, and even without a regular job, he and Karen were still better off than most. He knew for a plain cold fact after meeting Stacy that he did not want to end up like that. Married to a job he had no passion for, the realisation that you could have made it if you'd just tried harder.

No, he'd done the corporate thing and he was not going back, especially now that he felt that — given a chance — he could be successful at something he truly loved.

Karen finally looked up, a slight smile on her face. 'I still can't believe they let you in here with those sneakers.'

Relieved, Greg laughed, and they made their way outside.

'Do I really have to get used to you never being in a suit again?' She linked her arm through his. 'At least at the Met Gala you'll be in one — and on the right side of the ropes that night, I hope?' she teased.

Greg swallowed uncomfortably — now was definitely not the moment to tell her the bad news about the Met Gala. She could only take one disappointment at a time.

Thinking about it, though, maybe he had been too wrapped up in himself and his own needs lately; maybe he needed to bring the romance back to their relationship.

He thought of his mother and father, of the way his dad brought Cristina sunflowers every Friday, no matter what and for no reason. Of how his mother loved to recount how he had come downtown to find her so many years ago.

She'd been sitting outside her parents' deli and, according to her, had been wearing her best blue dress the day that she and Greg's father first met. She didn't know why, but something told her to put it on that morning, as if something special was going to happen. She had taken her post on the chair next to the pickle barrel outside the deli and waited.

'There he was, striding down the street,' she would say, her eyes lighting up. 'Can you imagine, in our little neighbourhood of small-boned people comes this tall, fair-haired giant. He walked right up to me, as if it were the only reason he had come downtown, and asked what was in the barrel.' At this point, Greg's mother would crack up laughing, wiping tears from her eyes. 'Can you believe it? He had never seen a pickle barrel before!' She would laugh and laugh, and his father would squeeze her arm, the two of them caught up in that moment, the moment they had met and changed each other's lives for ever. Greg never tired of hearing the story even as an adult. But his mother hadn't laughed at his father that day, but had daintily pulled a pickle out of the barrel and handed it to the 'tall, fair-haired giant' who would eventually become her husband.

Every year his parents would celebrate their anniversary, not by going to Le Cirque, buying each other jewellery or going on a cruise, but by going downtown to Alphabet City to look for pickles. Since the city was always changing, they never knew if a deli was still going to be there or if it would close by the following year. So 17 May was their pickle-hunt day.

They only seemed to get closer as the years progressed, especially after his father retired. Most men Jeff's age — and who had been in the business he was in — suffered a heart attack after retirement, their bodies unused to the lack of excitement and stress, but not Jeff. Cristina had plans for him. Every month it was something new. 'I signed us up for tango lessons!' she would announce suddenly over the dining-room table.

'What? What the hell are you thinking?' he would bark at her, smiling the whole time.

'Oh come on — we should try it.'

And they would and they would love it. Two people who had worked hard their whole lives finally enjoying themselves and each other. After tango came watercolours, then organic cooking, and then a small, lively theatre class at the YMCA.

For one year they were volunteer guides at the New York Historical Society, giving tours in tandem with each other, finishing each other's sentences as they described a Hudson River Valley painting or gave a tour of the library.

That's what Greg wanted, he decided as he wheeled his bike along the streets beside Karen: he wanted Karen and him to finish each other's sentences; he wanted a life full of love and laughter like his parents had.

Forget careers and fancy galas. Love, laughter and great memories — wasn't that what life was truly about?

7

'This bracelet really is a pretty thing; it's incredible just how much it's like yours,' commented Kate. She twirled the bracelet gently in her hands, inspecting the individual charms.

'It's kind of uncanny, isn't it?' Holly agreed.

On her lunch break from the Secret Closet, she'd hustled across the street to Best Bagels to meet with Kate. Her friend was already sitting at a table when she arrived, flirting with the guy behind the counter.

Leopards and their spots . . . Holly walked up to her, smiling. 'Hey, I thought we talked about this!'

Kate grinned sheepishly.

'Well, as long as he's quick on the job. I have to be back in — '

Kate interrupted her: 'Thirty minutes or less, I know. Maybe we should have gone to McDonald's, then. But yep, I ordered for you already. Plain bagel with butter and black tea.' She gave one last playful wave to the bagel guy and Holly rolled her eyes.

'Thanks, sounds great.' She peeled off her gloves and shrugged herself out of her coat.

'So what do you want for Christmas?' she asked her friend.

Kate ogled the guy behind the counter again.

'*Besides* a healthy relationship with a man,' Holly added, groaning.

'Oh, I don't know, nothing? A trip to Queens to see Eileen and her famous mince pies?' Kate retorted.

Holly's mother believed God had made pre-cooked food for a reason and it certainly wasn't her place to argue over it.

Although, Holly recalled sadly, when Seamus was alive Eileen used to make Christmas pudding — an old Irish recipe that had apparently been handed down through generations. Holly still remembered how delicious it tasted, but after her father died, these family traditions had been abandoned over the years.

Holly and Danny usually went to Eileen's for Christmas dinner, and Kate had tagged along once or twice if she wasn't going home to her family in Minnesota.

'You do know she buys the mince pies at ShopRite and then plates them up?'

'No!' Kate pretended to be shocked. 'And the turkey? You're saying she doesn't raise one herself on the fire escape and butcher it in the bathtub?'

'Well, as long as it was raised in Queens . . . ' Holly laughed; she always joked that her mother never left Queens.

'That's not true,' Eileen would protest. 'I go to the opera, don't I?' Holly had to concede that yes, her mother managed to make it in on public transportation to see her beloved Wagner Circle every year. Holly and Danny would pick her up after the performance and take her to their apartment in a taxi, where she would spend the night and then travel home the next day by subway. Danny and Holly had a running joke. He would ask, 'When is Nana coming over?' And she would reply, 'I don't know; who's playing at Lincoln Center?'

It was then that Holly remembered the bracelet and yesterday's failed attempt at tracking it down. With Carole's permission, she'd taken it upon herself to locate the owner via any means she could, and now she pulled it out to show Kate, who was in the throes of admiration.

'This looks a bit like Tiffany,' her friend said, studying the bracelet.

'Really?' Although Holly was as familiar as any New Yorker with the famous jewellery store, she wasn't familiar (or lucky) enough to be able to recognise one of its creations.

'Well, maybe not the bracelet, but this charm is anyway,' Kate indicated the heart-shaped key. 'See the maker's mark just there?'

Holly followed her gaze. 'Good spot.'

'A little worn, but it definitely looks like a Tiffany mark.' Kate continued examining the various charms. 'Oh, and look at this — a Date to Remember charm! Thirty-first of December.'

Holly reached out and pulled the bracelet back towards her. 'I didn't notice that either. Not the date anyway.' But Kate was right: on the other side of the disc-shaped charm was inscribed: *December 31 — Same Time, Same Place.*

She looked away into the distance, her thoughts racing.

'Oh no,' Kate chuckled. 'I know that look. It's the same look you had when you found that old couple's photo. You dragged me all over the city to find them, remember? It took us weeks!'

Holly smiled; she did indeed remember that photo. She had found it tucked inside a book she'd borrowed from the library. It was of a middle-aged man and woman sitting at a café in what looked like an exotic part of the world, beaming at each other. It had taken a while to find the owner, but with the library's help, Holly had managed. Turned out he had lost his wife in 9/11 in the meantime and had moved out to Brooklyn. When Holly and Kate managed to track him down and showed up at his door with the photo, he had broken down in tears. No one said a word; he just hugged her, and she hugged him back. The look on his face had been worth all the hours of searching.

'I remember too,' Kate sniffed, her voice filled with sudden emotion.

'What?' Holly looked up, startled, and then felt stupid, Of course, she thought. Justin.

Kate had been in a serious relationship with a man who had worked at Cantor Fitzgerald who had also died on 9/11. 'I'm sorry, Kate, I forgot for a second. I'm so sorry.'

She had tried her best back then to comfort Kate, but it was hard. Watching her friend suffer was something Holly never wanted to experience again.

Justin and Kate had seemed like the perfect couple: engaged and blissfully happy. Holly had first met them both in Washington Square Park, not far from her apartment. She had been around six months pregnant with Danny at the time, and Kate's dog, Lily, had jumped up on her as they passed. Kate was appalled, and while Holly had insisted she was fine, Kate had in turn insisted on making her rest on a park bench and they had all got talking. Kate and Holly's friendship grew quickly, and the first time Justin visited Holly at home, he had surveyed her tiny apartment and immediately walked over to her window facing the courtyard.

'Wow, you are so lucky,' he'd said. 'If I had this place, I would park myself in front of this window with a telescope all the time, *Rear Window* style.'

Holly adored him from that moment on.

After 9/11 she had gone to the site with Kate, posting his photo everywhere they could. Kate could not believe it.

'He's a rock climber, Holly,' she would say tearfully, as they roamed the streets. 'A jogger. He's strong and fit: he could survive *anything*.'

Holly would nod, hoping against hope that she was right, but after seeing the wreckage, she knew in her heart it was impossible.

After that, the two women became inseparable. In the months that followed, Holly gave birth to Danny and very quickly realised that she and Nick had no future, and Kate finally accepted that it was impossible for someone to face down such destruction and survive.

Then, a few years back, after the city officials had sifted through much of the rubble that used to be the towers, they had sent Justin's mother his ID badge from the office. It was all that was ever found of him.

His mother had sent it to Kate with a note. *I can't bear to keep it but I can't throw it away.* Kate wasn't sure what to do with it either, but Holly knew exactly what. She tucked it in the space between the frame and windowpane in her apartment, facing out to the courtyard. Justin would have his wish after all: a front-row seat to life that would continue on without him.

'Anyway,' Kate said, determinedly turning her attention back to the bracelet, 'if you're taking the UPS girl's idea seriously — that is, to try and find the owner by way of the charms — where do you plan to start?'

Holly picked up the bracelet from where Kate had placed it on the table and looked through the charms again.

'I'm not exactly sure; there are so many, aren't there? Is there anything that looks familiar to you? Other than the Tiffany key.'

The two women huddled over the bracelet, both studying the charms.

'Well,' Kate said, looking up, 'the Eiffel Tower one would suggest she's been to Paris.'

Holly laughed. 'Well, thanks, *Captain Obvious*, I appreciate that. Doesn't tell us anything other than that, though, does it?'

'She's lucky. I'd love to go to Paris . . . be whisked away by someone special.' She eyed the guy behind the counter again.

Holly smiled and shook her head. 'Erm, I think Paris, Texas is about as far as you'd get with that guy.'

'Don't I know it,' Kate laughed, and put her head back down, considering the charms.

She looked at Holly. 'Of course, the pink ribbon could suggest — '

'I know.' The pink ribbon, a now universally recognisable symbol for breast cancer, had been one of the first charms that had stood out for Holly. 'But she could be a big supporter of the charity — or have a friend or family member who — '

'Actually . . . ' Kate picked the bracelet up again to look more closely at the heart-shaped key charm. 'This one from Tiffany . . . ' She held up the key for Holly to see. You know the way they stamp 'Return to Tiffany' on their key rings and stuff?'

Holly nodded. 'Yes, I know there's a reason behind that, but I can't remember what.'

'Well, when someone buys something from Tiffany with one of those 'Return to Tiffany' stamps on it, supposedly they're given the key ring's registration number on a separate card. If the key ring is lost and returned to the store, Tiffany contacts the customer and arranges to get it back to the owner. Isn't it romantic?' She shook her head dreamily. 'So maybe it's as simple as that.'

'Yes, but there's nothing like that on the bracelet,' Holly pointed out.

'But there is a Tiffany charm. Maybe they keep records of this kind of stuff anyway?'

'You could be on to something there,' she agreed, the wheels in her brain turning.

Maybe Tiffany did keep records of some sort. At the Secret Closet, even though they weren't anywhere near the size or scale of Tiffany & Co., they kept records of all their best and returning customers, so as to contact them when something they thought might interest them came in.

When she explained this to Kate, her friend nodded excitedly. 'Well then, there's your starting point. Off to Tiffany you go.'

★   ★   ★

'Sweetheart, hold on a second . . . I know you're excited, but really, you've also got me lugging all the bags!'

I turned round and, seeing the love of my life struggling with some of the shopping bags, gave him a guilty look. I suppose I went a little overboard in the Oltrarno district, but then again, how often does a girl get to shop in Florence? However, I also supposed I could only use that line so many times . . .

'You know, if I thought you were going to have problems keeping up with me, I would have brought a younger man.'

'Watch it. Besides, the ink is surely dry on our marriage certificate. Too late — you are stuck with me for life.'

I pulled him close and kissed him, truly amazed that such a wonderful man was now my husband.

He put both arms around my waist and we looked out over the precipice in Piazzale Michelangelo, overlooking Florence's famed Duomo. The setting sun highlighted and gave added mystique to the red dome of the structure, and I couldn't help but sigh at the beauty spread out before me.

'Isn't that just the most gorgeous view? Florence really was a great idea for a honeymoon.'

'It's not nearly as gorgeous as you. And, sweetheart, this is just the beginning of our adventures.'

Feeling happy, content and whole, we wandered on for a bit, while I kept snapping pictures with my Kodak Instamatic 30 of the places I had only ever read about or seen pictures of. I hoped all the pictures turned out well, as I definitely wanted to frame some for what would be our new home. It still tickled me that we were actually walking through the ancient streets of Florence. It all seemed too good to be true!

'What do you think about stopping and getting a carafe of the homemade vino?'

'Sounds magnifico,' I said in my best Italian accent, the one that had been making my husband laugh since we stepped off the plane three days ago. 'What about there?' I pointed to a tiny little restaurant that had a few small tables on the street outside. 'We can watch the world go by and I can consult the map.'

Moments later, we sat at a small wicker table, a glass jug of the house red before us. I opened the guidebook that I had purchased weeks before at a used bookstore back home and looked over an illustration of the city.

I looked up as he gave a snort of laughter.

'Put that thing away. I think we have already determined that the map in that book is wrong or out of date.'

Indeed, we had. We'd got miserably lost the day before because of this map, but even so, I felt that there had to be some truth in what had been printed.

'Stop it, I trust in maps. It's how I will learn my way around Florence.'

'You learn your way only if the map is right, though.'

I peered across the table, marvelling again at those bright blue eyes, and the fair hair that flopped over the back of his shirt collar. I thought about running my hands through it right then and there, but decided it might be better to save that for the hotel room.

'You know, if you behave right now, I might feel the urge to misbehave later, when we are alone.' I said this as seductively as possible, and ran my tongue over my lips, until I couldn't take it any longer and burst out laughing.

'You minx,' he laughed with a twinkle in his eye. 'I'm going to hold you to that.'

'I hope you do, but in the meantime, what street are we on?' I peered up at the corner of the building in which we sat. I had learned quickly that there were no street signs the way there were in New York, but rather that the street names were actually marked on the buildings. 'Can you see what that says?' I asked, pointing to where the name was inscribed in the marble of the building façade.

'I think it says Viale Donato Giannotti.'

I looked back down at the map. 'OK, so if that's right, that means we are on this street right here. And our hotel is there.' I pointed to each place.

'I trust you, you're the navigator,' he

shrugged. 'I'll follow you anywhere.'

I put the book down and reached across the table to take my new husband's hand, the charm bracelet round my wrist jingling happily. 'Likewise,' I cooed. 'Oh, this is all just so exciting, don't you think? Doesn't it feel magical, like all of our adventures are only just beginning? I feel like it's a fairy tale, and that you are my knight in shining armour. I know it's corny, but I can't help but get caught up in the romance of this place. I feel as though our lives are just getting started.'

He squeezed my hand and toyed with my bracelet. 'It's just beginning. Everything is. Our whole life, together. There is no other person I want to experience everything with. And I know we will. I have never loved anyone the way I love you. You are my everything,' he said softly.

I felt my eyes tear up, and I leaned across the table to kiss him again. 'Such memories we are making.' I tapped the top of my camera. 'There's no way this thing can ever do what's in my mind justice. I love you, and I just know I am going to love where our lives take us, the family and the home we will make. Like I said, I'm a lucky girl.'

He kissed me again. 'Well then, lucky girl, how about we finish this wine and head back to the hotel? I see some room service in our future.'

I smiled again. 'Perfect.'

As we started walking back to our hotel, navigating the cobblestones of the street and holding hands, an interesting storefront came into view. A red awning bedecked the outside, and polished brass and other metals shone like a treasure chest from inside the small leaded windows. Italian corna in all shapes and sizes were displayed. An Italian talisman of ancient origin, a corno was a long, gently twisted horn-shaped object, believed to protect against the evil eye. I'd noticed that they were quite prevalent in Florence.

'Oh, look at that!' I let go of his hand and crossed to the store. 'How pretty! Let's go in.'

He held up the shopping bags that we had been accumulating throughout the day and made a look of surrender. 'Sure, I mean, what's one more shop in the scheme of things?'

'Get used to it, mister!'

We entered the store and were immediately hit by sensory overload. The entire store was covered in corna. It appeared to be all that this store sold.

I crossed the room quickly and came upon a display case like you would find in a jewellery store. Inside it was a selection of smaller horns — cornicelli — pieces in silver and gold to be worn round the neck or on a bracelet.

'Look, how great is this? Look at these!'

He came up behind me and peered over my shoulder. 'They're very pretty.'

At that moment, a man emerged from somewhere out back. He had a jeweller's loupe on a string round his neck and, seeing he had customers, wiped his hands off with a handkerchief he had stowed in his back pocket.

'Buonasera. Come posso aiutarla?' *Good evening. Can I help you?*

117

I thought quickly to the rusty Italian I had been struggling with for days. I loved trying new languages, even though it definitely wasn't my strong suit.

'Um . . . Mi piacciono i ciondoli, molto carini, quanto costa?' Sure, it was a broken translation of 'I like charms, very pretty, how much?' But the shopkeeper caught my drift. As well as the fact that Italian was not my native language.

'Grazie, lei è americana?'

I smiled, feeling as if I had just been rescued. I didn't know if I could conduct an entire conversation in Italian.

'Yes, we are,' I giggled nervously.

'No problem, I speak English,' the man said smoothly. 'I am Giovanni. Welcome to my store.' He raised his hands as if he was summoning the heavens to attention.

'Thank you. You have such beautiful things.'

'Ah, yes,' Giovanni smiled. 'This I know, all crafted by hand. I do all of this. And someday, when I can no longer, my son will. Do you have children?' He pointed to us both.

'No, not yet, but maybe someday, maybe lots of bambinos!' I laughed. 'We just got married. We are on our honeymoon.'

'Ah, beautiful, congratulations to you. Maybe Florence will bless you with a baby while you are here.'

I blushed and tried to change the subject. A honeymoon baby wasn't necessarily in the plans. A baby someday, just not right now. We had a lot to do together before baby made three.

My lovely husband sensed my discomfort and

interjected to redirect the conversation. 'Signore, this charm, we like it very much.' He pointed to a tiny Italian horn made of silver within the display case. 'How much is it?'

'Ah, for you, venti, ah, twenty lira.' He opened the display case and removed the tiny charm. 'For your wife, yes?'

He nodded.

'See, I have a bracelet.' I held up my wrist and showed him.

'Can you add this right now to her bracelet? So she can wear it today?'

Giovanni nodded in agreement and I removed the bracelet from my wrist. Taking the money, Giovanni retreated to what had to be his workroom. My husband wrapped his arms around my waist and placed a kiss on my neck.

'I'd say that'll be a pretty good souvenir of this trip,' he whispered.

It was perfect. Exactly right to commemorate our time here together.

Minutes later, Giovanni returned with my bracelet. Behind him scampered a little boy who couldn't be more than four or five years old.

'Here you go now — enjoy,' Giovanni said. 'You see, this here is my son, Lupo. He is only little today, but this someday will all be his.' He once again raised his hands to the store. 'Lupo, say ciao.'

'Ciao,' the small boy replied.

'Ciao, Lupo,' I said, leaning down to look at him. 'You are a very lucky boy to have such a talented father.'

Giovanni threw up his hands. 'Ah, he no

speak any English, not yet. He learn, though. Giusto?' Right? The little boy nodded his head. 'And now, you have fun in our city. And much luck in your new matrimonio. May you be blessed. May you remember here always because of this.'

He pointed to the charm and I smiled.

'Thank you so much, Giovanni. Thank you. I'll never forget this place. We'll always remember because of this beautiful charm.' I took my new husband's hand and we began our retreat from the store, my new charm getting settled into its new home on my wrist. 'Arrivederci.'

Indeed, I would remember this place for the rest of my life. I looked again at my bracelet and smiled. That much was guaranteed.

8

It was Sunday morning and, as Danny was fast asleep, Holly had the peace and quiet of the morning in bed with her coffee and paper.

Thank God for delivery, she thought, as she cracked open the *New York Times*. She scanned the front page — too depressing, just the picture was enough to make her turn the page. She immediately flipped through to the book reviews and scanned the fiction list to see if there was anything good. After that she turned her attention to the crossword.

Holly could do the *NYT* crossword practically in her sleep. She smiled to herself. Today, the theme was old movies.

Let's see . . . She bit her lip as she read the clues.

1941 Frank Capra film: MEET JOHN (– –)E

Too easy. She pencilled the letters D and O in to read 'Doe' and then, just as she was ready to move on to the next clue, she heard Danny start to rustle in his bed.

Holly got out from beneath her own warm covers. Having briefly freshened up in the bathroom, she moved to the small kitchenette and got out a pan and some pancake mix. She had pre-made it and stored it in a jar for just this purpose. As the pan began to sizzle, she heard Danny call out, 'What's for breakfast?'

'Pancakes,' Holly grinned, predicting the response.

'Yes!' Danny's feet hit the floor.

They ate in the little breakfast nook off the kitchen and Holly studied Danny, who was looking more and more like his father every day.

He had the same straight nose and dark hair, so different from her own colouring, and a nose with a bump on the end. His cheekbones were high and his hair curled around his small ears as if it had been styled that way. He was practically tanned all through the dead of winter, a tribute to his father's Mediterranean roots. Holly burned or got red if she was out in the sun for more than ten minutes, winter or summer. Danny seemed to be made for the sun: he never burned, nor complained of the heat.

Having practically inhaled his pancakes, Danny stood up and put his dish in the sink without being told.

Then, for the first time, he looked out of the window.

'Snow again, yay!' he exclaimed, excitedly hopping from one foot to the other.

She smiled indulgently at him. 'You mean you only just noticed?'

'Let's go out. Can we, Mom, please?' He pushed his face against the cold glass of the window. 'Maybe there won't be any school tomorrow?'

'Not with that light dusting.' Holly gulped down the rest of her coffee and got dressed — no use torturing him.

Besides, she wanted to try and see if she could make it over to Tiffany today. It was near enough to Columbus Circle, so they could take a quick walk through the park while they were there.

When she got out of the bathroom he was waiting by the door, dressed and ready to go. He took her coat off the hook and pointed to her boots on the floor. 'Here you go.'

'Are you a golden retriever now?' she joked, shaking her head indulgently as she slipped on her coat and got into her warmest walking boots.

When they got out onto the street, it was wonderfully calm and quiet — a world away from the usual weekday hustle and bustle. She looked at the snow softly falling on cars and lying undisturbed on the ground. Soon the paths would be a slushy mess and most of the young people in the neighbourhood would have missed it. But the snow definitely wasn't wasted on Danny.

He was trying to catch flakes on his tongue as they walked. Holly threw her arm around him. How could she not be the happiest woman in the world? Danny's shoulder felt bony and muscular at the same time, the shoulder of a boy on the verge of becoming a teen. Not long now, she thought sadly, until he tries to pull away from me. Would it be harder or easier than it was for her and her mother?

Holly recalled the day her mother, during one of their infamous arguments, had blurted out the news that had shattered her heart. She'd just turned sixteen. Overcome by teenage hormones, Holly had been complaining resentfully that her mother was continuously on her case.

'It's like you wish I'd never been born!'

'More like I'm glad you're not actually my daughter!' Eileen shot back, before putting her hands to her mouth, horrified.

The words had washed over Holly like a tsunami of betrayal, fear and anger. Adopted? Impossible!

Everyone was always commenting that she was petite like her mother, and looked like her dad. Was it all lies? Everything? Maybe she wasn't smart and pretty either, or creative, or interesting, or fun . . .

Her world had ended on that day. It was like the Holly she knew had died, or was erased, non-existent . . .

The memory made her squeeze Danny's shoulder tighter, who in turn wriggled away from her grasp. He jogged ahead of her, sweeping snow off cars as he went to make snowballs and throwing one at a passing crosstown bus. As she watched him, Holly tried to remember herself at that age: carefree, with two parents at home who loved her.

How that had all changed when Eileen had gone on to admit the awful truth.

Holly had stared at the woman across from her, the woman she had called Mom all those years. It was as if she'd suddenly been given a pair of glasses that completely altered her vision. Instead she saw Eileen as separate from her: small and dowdy, with a bad haircut and poorly outlined lipstick.

'I'm . . . not your child?' Holly screamed, hysterical.

Eileen grabbed her hands and Holly snatched them away. The blood drained from her mother's face. 'I'm so, so sorry. I never meant you to find out like this. Your dad and I had planned to sit down together one day and . . . ' She trailed off.

'When? When were you going to tell me that I'm not your daughter?' Holly started to cry and was angry with herself for it. She swatted a tear away as if it were a fly.

'Oh, Holly, you *are* my daughter. You were sent to us — me and your dad . . . ' Eileen reached for her again and Holly stood up from the table, knocking the chair back.

'Maybe someday you might want to find her — maybe when you have children of your own . . . ' her mother continued pleadingly.

'Children of my own?' Holly spat at her. 'I'm sixteen. What — you think I am going to follow in her footsteps and get knocked up?' she hissed, assuming that was what had happened with her real mother. Her real mother . . . it was all so horribly surreal.

'Holly . . . ' Eileen pleaded.

But Holly did not hear her; she was gone, leaving the house in a whirl, running down the stairs and out into the street. She had started walking and found herself in front of the hardware store. Her beloved dad was behind the counter, ringing up a can of paint for a young man in tight pants. When she entered, the young man grimaced at her lewdly.

'Hi, sweetheart,' her father said calmly, leaning his full weight on his hands on the counter. Looking the young man square in the eye, he said, 'Couldn't be luckier, having a daughter who likes to stop by to help her poor old father.'

But poor and old were the last words Holly

would have used to describe her father that day. He stood about six feet two and was built like a large square, with broad shoulders and a long jaw. He pushed the can of paint across the counter to the now nervous-looking young man. 'Enjoy!' he said cheerily as the guy scampered out through the door.

When the door shut, Holly burst into tears. The next thing she felt were her father's large, solid arms around her and him saying, 'Shh, it can't be that bad, you haven't got a worry in the world.'

When she finally calmed herself enough to tell him what had happened, he switched the door sign to 'Closed' and gave her a cup of coffee with a dash of whisky in it, his Irish coffee special for bad days, he called it.

'Do you know where I came from?' he had asked her, very seriously. 'Do you, Holly?'

She had shrugged in her impartial teenage way and waited for him to tell her, but he had just kept asking her questions.

'Where was I born?'

'In Ireland, Dad,' she had sighed.

'Yeah, but where?' he insisted.

Holly paid attention now. 'Your mother's bed, in the Liberties.' She had no idea where that was or what kind of a place it was, but it sounded like a good place for a childhood, carefree.

'Yeah,' he nodded sadly. 'I was born to a woman who wanted another baby like she wanted a hole in the head. My older sister had sat out on the front step with her ears covered as my mother screamed her agony to the whole world.'

126

Holly looked at him. She knew the story about him being born at home, but he had never said he wasn't wanted. He had come from a large Irish Catholic family, where lots of children were inevitable — no one complained about it.

He pulled her closer. 'Holly, my mother had me and barely looked at me, hardly said two words to me my whole life with her, which was only up to the age of fifteen.' Holly had heard this story too, but in her mind she assumed he had left for New York at such a young age because he had just been wild and rebellious.

'You know, when I left for the boat to America, all my mum said was, 'Good luck.' She didn't even say my name. I think the whole time I was in the Liberties with my family, I never heard my mother say my name once.'

'Oh, Dad.' Holly hugged him back, suddenly tired of knowing more than her years.

'All I'm trying to say,' he added, squeezing her tightly, 'is that we are all born — that's the easy part. It's being loved and wanted that's tricky.'

Now, walking the snowy streets of New York, Holly watched her son, who ran ahead of her, then waited, then broke away from her again, like a colt experimenting with leaving its mother. She kept a steady pace, letting him be free and return as much as he wanted. There was no question that Danny was wanted and very much loved, at least by her.

They reached Twenty-Third Street, where the crowds were beginning to come out on the hunt for coffee, papers and fresh-baked goods. Danny's pace had slowed from a boisterous

127

snowball pitcher to a shivering ten-year-old. She linked his arm through hers. 'Let's take the crosstown bus to Madison and then catch the uptown?'

He nodded and took her arm. 'Where are we going?'

'Well,' she said with an enigmatic smile, knowing this would appeal to his imagination, 'we are going to solve a mystery.'

When the bus got near enough to walk to Fifth Avenue, the two of them hopped out and started to walk to Tiffany.

When they got there, Holly paused to look in the windows and admire the wonderfully elaborate displays.

'So we're going to a jewellery store,' Danny said flatly.

She punched him in the shoulder. 'Yep, but I know a great movie theatre near by that might be playing . . . the Marx brothers.'

'Really? YES!' Danny did a goofy happy dance on the sidewalk.

Holly pushed him towards the entrance. 'But here first, OK?'

They passed the swarms of tourists posing for pictures in front of the iconic store sign, and found refuge inside the revolving doors that led to the main ground-floor jewellery hall.

They walked past the opening display cases that showcased a variety of glittering jewels, and Holly quickly sought out a quiet area towards the rear, leaving Danny to wander around at his leisure. She caught the eye of a pleasant-looking salesman and smiled brightly.

'Hello, I was wondering if you could help me?'

'Of course, madam. What can I do for you?' he smiled, and she saw him surreptitiously take in her vintage Chanel handbag and chic, expensive-looking waffle-weave jacket — somewhat different to the majority of the 'I ♥ New York'-type tourists in the store just then.

Holly took a deep breath and pulled the charm bracelet from her pocket. 'Actually, I was hoping to show you something. I found this bracelet . . . '

She quickly recounted the story. 'It's just so important that I get this back to the rightful owner. I know I would be missing it terribly, if it were mine. See this heart-shaped key charm here — it has a Tiffany mark on it. Do you think you could tell me a little bit more about it? Something that might perhaps help me trace the owner?'

The man, whose name badge read, 'Samuel,' looked closer, inspecting the charm. 'Well, you are right, it is one of ours — a Tiffany key — possibly one of our most popular lines,' he added, with a smile. 'But,' he continued, 'this charm is produced en masse, so I doubt you could trace it back to the owner.' He turned to his computer and quickly started pressing buttons. 'There are hundreds of thousands of these sold worldwide — over a hundred thousand here in New York alone.'

'One hundred thousand . . . ' she said, crestfallen. 'So there's just no way records would be kept on . . . ' She trailed off, and gave Samuel a bleak smile. 'Oh well, I thought that this would

129

be the place to start, but maybe I was wrong. I guess it's back to square one. Thanks for the information.'

'Actually, could I see the bracelet again?'

'Sure,' said Holly, putting it back down on the display case.

Samuel took the piece with his long fingers and flipped through the charms, before stopping on one. He turned it over in his hands several times, before going behind the counter to take out a jeweller's loupe. Inspecting it through the monocle-like piece, he nodded, as if confirming something to himself.

'This one here — ' he held up a gem-encrusted egg wrapped in a gold-coloured ribbon — 'is rather distinctive in its craftsmanship.'

'OK . . . ' Holly's face brightened.

'It's an expensive piece, made from gold and diamonds. The workmanship is quite exquisite actually.'

Holly tried to stop her jaw from falling to the floor. Gold and diamonds? She looked at the egg, which to her untrained eye looked no different to the ones on her own bracelet — little trinkets really. To think that she'd been carrying around a bracelet with a teeny tiny charm on it that could be so valuable . . .

'Oh my goodness! Are you sure?'

He nodded. 'Definitely. Sadly, as it's not a Tiffany creation, and as I can't identify the maker's mark, I suspect you'll need to take your search elsewhere, perhaps to one of our . . . competitors.' He said this as if there was something bad in his mouth.

Holly looked at the charm, trying to figure out where it might have come from — Cartier, Harry Winston maybe . . . She thought about the multitude of luxury jewellery stores in the city — or on Fifth Avenue alone. Surely they'd keep records of such an expensive purchase?

'You're sure you don't recognise the maker's mark?' she asked Samuel.

'I'm afraid not. It could well be a bespoke piece, and very distinctive — which, on the plus side, should make tracing the owner that bit easier.'

'Thank you again,' Holly said, her mind awhirl with this new information. 'You've helped a lot, in any case. At least now I know to be more careful when carrying this thing around. Who knows how much the whole lot is worth?'

Samuel seemed to be wrestling with something and eventually he spoke again.

'Actually, I do know of someone who might be able to help you — help trace the origin of the egg charm, in any case.'

Holly smiled broadly. 'That would be fantastic!'

'Ever heard of Margot Mead?'

She shook her head. The name meant absolutely nothing to her.

'Well, she's pretty well known in society circles around Manhattan, and one of our regular customers, if you know what I mean,' he added delicately, and Holly figured this meant that Margot was rolling in the moolah.

'OK . . . ?'

'She's a collector. Adores jewellery. If there's one woman who could help you identify a charm that distinctive, or indeed someone who has the means to come by it, it's her. She has a lot of friends and, believe me, they buy a lot of expensive stuff.'

Holly looked at the egg again. It really was a marvellous charm; she was surprised that she hadn't noticed how much more expensive it looked compared to some of the simpler pieces on the bracelet. She wondered if it had been bought to commemorate a particularly special occasion — a significant birthday, maybe?

She noticed Danny edging towards her and looking fidgety, and figured that was her cue to take her leave. 'Well, Samuel, I really appreciate your help. I'll see if I can track down this Margot.'

'You're welcome. Best of luck to you,' Samuel said. 'It's a lovely bracelet and I'm sure the owner will appreciate your efforts.'

Holly was about to slip the bracelet back into her pocket, but then remembering how expensive it was, she instead carefully tucked it into the inside pocket of her handbag.

Margot Mead . . .

She sounded like one of those out-and-out New York society queens. How on earth was a lowly shop assistant like Holly going to inveigle an audience with someone like that?

9

At his parents' house on Park Avenue, Greg paused at the threshold of their bedroom, a lump in his throat.

It was the place he had run to in the middle of the night as a child when he had a nightmare, or didn't feel well. Not to mention all the times he would sit on the big four-poster bed and watch his parents getting ready to go out to some fancy event or other.

The morning light began to illuminate the room. He looked around; every item and every fabric had his mother's imprint on it. She loved bright colours, yellow especially, often saying that there had been little colour in Alphabet City, where she had been raised.

On the dressing table, among the various perfume bottles and lotions, he spied a framed photograph and picked it up. It was one of Jeff and Cristina, taken before they married. His mother looked like a film star, Audrey Hepburn-like with a pretty print dress and gloves and hat.

'Love you, Mom,' he whispered, carefully slipping the photo back on the dresser among her things.

Then Greg swallowed hard and went back into the living room where his father waited.

'Everything OK, son?' Jeff Matthews asked, watching him carefully.

'Sure,' Greg nodded and, going to the drinks cabinet, poured his father two shots of his favourite thirty-year-old Scotch.

Taking in the surroundings in which he'd grown up, he realised that the place was a bit like the Scotch: richly familiar, and little had changed in the last few decades. As always, there were fresh sunflowers on the living-room table. He didn't know where Jeff had got them, this time of year especially, but his father had bought his mother sunflowers every week of their marriage for the past forty years.

'Here you go, Dad, just what the doctor ordered.'

He passed the lead-crystal rocks glass to his father, and took a seat across from him on the settee that his mother had picked out when they first bought this classic pre-war apartment.

Jeff took a sip of the amber liquid and gave a small grimace as the liquid burned its way down his throat.

'Actually, this is probably the last thing that the doctor ordered, son. But really, who wants to listen to that old bastard? If it were up to him, I'd be on an all-greens diet with a water IV. No fun in that,' he chuckled. 'If I'm going to go out, I'm going to go out the good way: pickled in good Scotch and eating a cow.'

'Dad, come on: don't joke about your health. And besides, you are as strong as a horse,' Greg scolded, uncomfortable with such discussion. The past few months had been hard on everyone, and Greg still worried about his father rattling around in this huge apartment.

'So,' Jeff said, taking another sip of his drink and changing the subject. 'You quit your job.' He wore a serious expression that suggested: OK, let's talk business.

Greg sucked in his breath, but his dad started to laugh, slapping his knee jovially, which finally elicited a smile. 'Well, damn, good for you! In my opinion you should have quit that sweatshop years ago. So what's the plan now?'

Greg rubbed his hands together and reached for his own drink (a glass of red wine; he had never been much of a hard liquor drinker), took a sip and smiled. 'I'm going to make a go of it on my own, with my photography. You know it's always been a dream of mine, and since that photo of the Flatiron sold, I have been playing with the idea. Of course, there is a risk . . . '

'Life is a risk. Don't let that scare you — you can't live your life always afraid of putting yourself out there. You should do what you love, because in this economy,' he joked, 'you're gonna be doing it for a long time. And you're good at it, I know that. Taking pictures, your mom reckons you were like one of those Hudson River painters, except with a camera.'

Greg smiled, uncommonly proud at hearing this.

Jeff spread his hands around in the air, gesturing at the apartment. 'All this didn't happen overnight, and this is not why I went into trading. I did it because I loved it, standing in the pit, the excitement, the panic, the joy on my customers' faces when I made a good deal . . . ' He glanced over at the flowers. 'The rest just happened to be a perk, and — well, back when I was on Wall Street — your mom always said she didn't care what I did or what we had, as long as I could provide — for you of course!' He playfully pointed a finger at Greg. 'That's what love does, you know,' he added softly. 'Everything is more bearable with two. And speaking of which, what does Karen think of it all?'

Greg grimaced a little. 'Well, let's just say that she is still getting used to the idea.'

'Oh?' Jeff queried. 'She's upset with you for leaving?'

'I guess you might say that,' Greg replied, trying to choose the right words. 'But it's my own fault, really. In hindsight, I know I should have given her more of a heads-up, whereas instead I kind of just sprung it on her. I honestly thought she would be happy, but she seems worried.'

Jeff eyed his son, the wheels in his head obviously turning. 'Worried about what?'

'Well, I suppose that she is just a little intimidated by me going off on my own and her being the only one with the dependable, pensionable job. I told her I have a plan; I wouldn't have done this if I didn't, but, you know, she is my partner in all of this, in life. I'm probably the bad guy for not telling her before I pulled the plug.'

Jeff laughed. 'Well, most women can be uptight when they worry about the bills.' He paused. 'You aren't, are you? Worried about the bills?'

Greg smiled and shook his head. Just like his

father to still think he was an eighteen-year-old who needed to be bailed out. 'No, Dad. Trust me, I've been responsible. I'm not coming to you for a cheque.'

'Ha! You thought I was offering! You know, that time I quit my job before going out on our own, your mom was scared too, at first. We had just bought this place and the mortgage was hanging over our heads. But she eventually came round. And when I opened up my own firm, that risk paid off. I'm sure the same thing will be true for Karen.'

Greg nodded, and hoped his father was right. But while he thought about it, he decided he might as well get his input on one other matter that had been playing on his mind.

'So, I was thinking . . . '

'Yeah? Well, that makes a change,' his father joked. It was hard to find Jeff in a bad mood; he was always jovial.

Well, almost always.

'Dad, I'm serious,' Greg chided.

'OK, OK, so what is it?'

'Well, I'm thinking of asking Karen to marry me. I think it will help us get past this place . . . this problem, and refocus our relationship. And I suppose I wanted your blessing.'

Jeff looked at his son thoughtfully, all joking now set aside. 'My blessing? Shouldn't you be asking for *her* father's blessing?'

'Her father passed away a couple of years ago, remember?' Greg stated quietly. 'And she's not really that close with her mother. I just felt that I needed to talk to someone about it.'

Jeff nodded. 'I see. Do you feel it's right?' he asked point blank.

Greg thought for a second and nodded his head in the affirmative. 'Yes, I do. I love her more than I have ever loved any woman. And I want to spend the rest of my life with her. I want a marriage like yours and Mom's — the romance, the sparkle, the love. Everything that happened during the good times. I want that, with Karen.'

His father paused and looked away, out of the windows that let in a spectacular view of Central Park. The snowflakes hit and melted against the windows.

'You even willing to deal with the stuff that happens in the bad times?' he asked bluntly, causing Greg to shift in his seat.

'It's a part of marriage, isn't it?' he replied gently.

Jeff swallowed hard. 'Yep. As they say, for better or worse. Marriage is like life; no one ever said it was easy. And it's just . . . if this is what you want, then I say go for it. Karen's a smart girl; she's driven, talented, beautiful. The whole package, right?'

Greg laughed at the confirmation of his own perception. 'Yes, she really is the whole package.'

Jeff smacked the armrest of the chair he sat in. 'Well, I hope you have something special planned. Have you been thinking about how you are going to pop the question?'

Greg let out his breath and ran his fingers through his hair. 'Yes, so, I want to do something special, something really memorable.'

'Something that'll blow her socks off?'

Greg smiled, unable to remember the last time Karen had worn socks, if ever. She seemed surgically attached to her skyscraper heels.

At that moment, the doorbell rang, signalling Karen's arrival for dinner.

'Hold that thought. Don't want to let anything slip in front of her.'

'I know. Dad, I have one other question . . . '

'Hit me, but hurry,' he chided as he rose from his chair. 'Maria will let her in,' he said, referring to the hired help who ghosted in and out of rooms in the penthouse.

'Well, remember how Mom put Nonna's ring aside for me? I was going to ask her with that.'

'Wonderful. There are a lot of happy times associated with that ring, a lot of history, and of course your mother would be happy to see it live another great life. I'll need to search for it, though — she must have put it away somewhere . . . but I'll get it for you soon, OK?'

Greg beamed and stepped forward to give his father a hug.

'That would be great. Thank you.'

Just as he was about to head down the hall to the front entryway to meet Karen, Jeff called out to him, 'Greg?'

'Yes?' Greg turned round with raised eyebrows.

'Just a thought. When I met your mom, I knew within two minutes that she was the one for me. We had a great life before . . . ' He shook his head sadly. 'I hope it's the same for you and Karen.'

So do I, Greg thought, heartened. Karen was

the one for him, no question about that.

What his dad had said about his grandmother's ring — that it would be good to see it live another great life — was exactly what he felt, what he *hoped*, for him and Karen. He just hoped she felt the same way.

★ ★ ★

It was late evening, and Holly and Danny were back at the apartment and trying to keep warm in spite of the plunging temperatures. Upon leaving Tiffany earlier, they'd gone into the park for a walk and, on impulse, rather than going to the movie theatre, Holly bought two tickets to the zoo. As they passed through the turnstile, she remembered back to when the kids' zoo in Central Park cost only ten cents. Wow, things had changed in such a short time.

She watched Danny as he examined the mice and stood in the mouth of the blue whale, and then laughed as he tried in vain to feed the chickens, which refused to come out of their shed due to the snow.

'Hmm,' she said to him. 'We probably could have just seen mice at home, huh? How about some cotton candy?'

'You feeling all right, Mom?' Danny joked. She tried her best to keep him away from processed sugar and all the crazy things that passed for children's 'food' these days.

'I'm just fine,' she replied. 'Then let's go and see the penguins.'

At the penguin exhibit, the penguins were out,

themselves marvelling at the snow, and Holly realised the exhibition hadn't changed in the past twenty-odd years.

Danny tugged at her arm as she paused, lost in thought and memories. 'Seriously, Mom, are you OK?'

'Yeah, I'm fine. I'm just remembering when I use to come here with your grandpa. I really wish you could have known him.'

Danny shrugged. 'I know, you've said that before.'

Holly took note; maybe she was dwelling too much. She thought about who they did know. Maybe this year she should have Christmas dinner at her house, maybe invite Kate and be less dependent on her mother.

'You're right,' she said, hugging Danny, who this time didn't resist. 'Maybe we should concentrate on the living. How about we have Christmas at our house this year?'

Danny stared at her. 'Really? With a tree and everything? I mean a big tree,' he clarified quickly. They always had a tree but a tiny table-top one; certainly no competition to Eileen's full-size live tree.

'I guess so.' Why not go the whole hog? Holly thought, deciding to throw caution to the wind.

'Yay, Mom! I can't wait!'

Afterwards they made their way back home, Danny chatting excitably about Christmas all the way.

In the meantime, he'd also taken a keen interest in the mystery bracelet, having learned all about it following their trip to Tiffany that morning.

'So a flower, a handbag, a feather . . . ' He reached for the bracelet she'd once again been examining. 'It really is just like yours, except the charms are different.'

'That's a quill, Danny,' she corrected him.

'Really? It looks exactly like a feather to me.'

'Well, yes, this is a feather, but the kind they used to slice the end off, so they could dip it in ink and write.'

'Cool! I want to do that.'

Holly laughed.

'Well, if that feather thing is used for writing, maybe she's a writer?' he offered.

Holly shrugged. 'Could be.' A highly successful one if she was carrying around charms made of gold and diamonds, she thought wryly.

'And what's that?' Danny asked, pointing to a crescent-shaped object that looked a little bit like a tadpole.

Holly had been wondering about that one herself from the outset. She'd thought at first that it could be a chilli, but there was a definite wave to the design that suggested otherwise. 'Your guess is as good as mine, honey.'

'Well, what about these wedding bells — you think that maybe the owner of the bracelet is married?'

Holly nodded; she had already considered that, but unfortunately it didn't open any other doors for her. After all, people got married every day, and nothing on that particular charm gave a when or a where.

'I thought about that, but it doesn't lead me to anything — not that I can think of, at least.'

Danny inspected further. 'How about this one?'

Holly leaned closer to see what he was looking at. It was a horseshoe.

'What about it?'

'See on the back there's some kind of stamp?'

'Yes.' She had taken note of that too: a series of letters and numbers. She had no idea what they meant, and just assumed it was a jeweller's mark. 'I saw that, but I didn't know what to make of it.'

'Did you run it through Google?'

'What?' She looked at him, feeling stupid. 'No. Actually, the thought didn't even occur to me.' Leave it to her technologically savvy son to inspire a new avenue for the search.

Danny rolled his eyes in feigned disbelief. 'I can't believe you didn't do that first thing . . . Here, let me get the computer.' He scurried off to get Holly's laptop and then sat down on the edge of her bed. 'Can you read off what it says?'

Holly looked closer at the charm and deciphered the letters and numbers. Danny's fingers, entirely adept to a computer keyboard, quickly typed in the information and waited for the search to populate. Holly moved beside him and peered over his shoulder in curiosity as she watched her son do his magic.

'What are you getting?'

'Not sure, might be nothing. There's a bunch of hits for books, library call numbers and some other stuff . . . '

Holly looked at the search listings and,

143

admittedly, it seemed like a lot of gobbledegook. A thought occurred to her. 'Maybe it's a date or an address? And since we know this bracelet's home is most likely in New York, why don't you add New York to the search terms? This might be a zip code or . . . something.' She didn't know *what* it could be, but she thought her suggestion was reasonable.

Apparently, so did her son, who turned round with his eyebrows raised. 'Who are you and what did you do with my mom?'

Holly tapped him on the back of his head. 'Enough with the wisecracks, kid.'

She watched as he turned back to the computer and typed in her suggestion.

'Huh,' he said, after a beat. 'Mom, you might be on to something.'

'Why? What do you see?' Holly looked closer and found that the search had returned a list of websites related to an artist named Gennaro del Vecchio. He happened to be based here in Manhattan, and he owned an art gallery on West Twenty-Fifth Street.

'Do you think this means something, Mom?'

'I don't know, but I'd certainly say it's a shot in the right direction,' said Holly, feeling positive once again. 'Does the address of his gallery happen to be six-eighteen?' she asked, referring to the numbers on the inscription. Danny checked and shook his head.

But maybe the horseshoe charm had some kind of connection to the gallery anyway. 'Are you going to go there?' her son enquired. 'To the gallery?'

'I'd say that's my next port of call, wouldn't you? Maybe this Gennaro fellow can tell me something.'

'And maybe I should keep searching on the computer,' Danny offered with raised eyebrows, wondering if his mother's excitement over this new development might put off bed just a little while longer.

Holly was so busy examining the horseshoe charm that she barely took note of Danny's last suggestion. She nodded her head in agreement, albeit absently. 'Yes, that's a good idea, that's probably what you should . . . Hey, wait a minute,' she exclaimed, suddenly coming out of her daze. 'Nice try, mister, but not so fast. School tomorrow, so it's bed for you. Now.' She smiled, amused by her son's artful dodging.

'Awww, Mom — '

'Don't 'Awww, Mom' me. Bed. It's only a few more days till winter break and then you can be the Watson to my Sherlock as much as you want.'

Danny smiled. 'Or you can be the Watson to my Sherlock. Don't forget who took the search to Google.'

He jogged off, laughing merrily as his mother nodded in agreement. Indeed, because of Danny, they once again had a warm lead.

10

On Monday morning, Greg strode into the lobby of the *New York Times* building with his portfolio under his arm. He felt amazing. As he rode up in the elevator to Billy the photo editor's office, he realised he had no plan, no prepared speech, nor had he done a Q and A with himself in the bathroom mirror; he was just going to go in and show what he had and what he could do.

Billy's floor was pretty much the same set-up as Rob's, except that as a senior editor he was not only given a space on the common-room floor, but also a private office. As Greg was ushered in by Billy himself, he stopped to stare at all the photos on the wall. Every inch was covered. There was one of almost every New York mayor from the 1970s onwards, a few presidents and every angle of the city you could imagine.

Suddenly Greg felt like grabbing his portfolio and running back out through the door. But, before he could, Billy motioned him to sit. He did, his knuckles white over the edge of the leather case.

While the walls were covered with prints, the desk was clear except for a phone. It was a long, wide glass desk, with a light under it that would illuminate the whole thing to look at negatives and prints. Greg gripped his portfolio tighter.

'So what do you have?' Billy asked, getting

straight down to business. He held his hands out to Greg for the portfolio. When Greg paused, the editor scratched his ear and laughed a little. 'C'mon, they can't be that bad. You're here, aren't you?'

Greg slowly handed the portfolio over and held his breath as Billy untied the ends and dumped the whole thing out on his desk.

He sat and slowly went through every single photo, sometimes turning them over to read the date and description, sometimes putting them aside in a separate pile to go back over. After what seemed like an eternity, Greg cleared his throat.

Billy was behind a large print — one of the shots Greg had taken while out with the cops in Queens. 'Can I get you some water?'

'Uh, no, I'm good,' Greg managed. 'It's just, ah . . . you're not asking me anything.'

'Shouldn't have to.' Billy put the photo he was looking at down on the desk. 'Your work should be able to tell me anything I need to know. I'm looking for photographers, not writers.'

Greg nodded. 'True.'

'And these are quite good, really quite good.'

Greg felt relief wash over him like a hug from his mother.

Billy closed the portfolio and sat back in his chair. 'OK, now here comes the questions . . . Ever been punched in the face?'

Greg looked at him, startled, but could see from Billy's expression that he was not joking.

'Uh, I may have been in a bar fight in college once . . .'

'Good. Ever had someone try to run you over with their car?'

Greg shook his head, baffled.

'Ever been in the middle of a shoot-out?'

Greg shook his head again; this was an interview for photography and not the Marines, yes?

'I only ask — ' Billy got up and perched on the edge of his desk — 'because if I call you and say, 'There's a riot downtown and the cops are using tear gas,' you gotta go, right?'

'Sure.' Greg nodded, gulping a little.

'I mean, you can't be afraid to jump in there, and you may get hurt. You would get a press badge, of course, but when things get rough, no one's going to be looking at it, you know?'

Greg nodded again. 'I understand,' he said out loud. 'I can do it. I'm not scared.'

'Good, because I can reimburse you for broken equipment, but you'd be contract, so if you break your teeth, you're on your own.'

Greg felt his shoulders relax and smiled a little. 'Fine by me.'

Billy stuck his hand out. 'OK, great, consider yourself officially on trial.'

'Seriously?' Greg grabbed Billy's hand and shook it hard. 'That's it?'

'Oh no, that's not it; there's lots of legal now . . . papers for you to fill out and all that stuff. Mostly 'bout how you won't sue us if you break your teeth — ' he tapped on Greg's portfolio as he handed it back to him — 'and how any shots you take on assignment belong to the *NYT*.' He flashed Greg a big smile. 'Legal and HR will call

148

you to come in and fill that crap out. Now, let me think about what I want to do with you.' He leaned against the desk and squeezed his eyes shut. 'There's Christmas coming up and one of my regular guys has been bitching about vacation, so you can take the assignment.' Billy's eyes remained closed and Greg wondered if he had everything in a file in his head. 'Colour, of course — shots of all the traditional New York places New Yorkers go during the holiday season, so Rockefeller Center, Bryant Park . . . You figure it out, OK? The writer's name is Suzanne Lee. She's in our directory, which you need.'

At this he whipped open a drawer in his desk and pulled out a thick sheaf of papers stapled together. 'Copy it, I want it back. Call, introduce yourself as *her* photographer — it always goes better that way — and ask her what she wants. But you get that list.'

Greg nodded, suddenly overwhelmed.

Billy put his hand on his back and steered him to the door. 'At least no chance of broken teeth on this assignment, huh? Although, knowing Suzanne . . . '

Next thing Greg knew, he was standing outside a senior editor's door with an assignment and a *New York Times* staff directory in his hands. OK, so it was just a trial assignment, but . . .

He grinned, suddenly understanding how those football players felt when they dumped Gatorade on each other; it all made sense now.

This was what getting your dream felt like.

11

Holly gazed absently out of the window at work, still thinking about everything she had learned (or not) about the charm bracelet over the weekend. She was so deep in thought that it took her a moment to register a woman on the other side motioning like a mime.

Oh no ... After lunch she had been so distracted she'd forgotten to switch the sign on the door to 'Open'. Thank goodness Carole was away with her family for Hanukkah today; she'd kill her ...

Holly raced to the door and let the woman in. 'I am so sorry ... '

'It's OK,' the customer laughed. ''Tis the season to make you insane!'

She was dressed beautifully and her long brown hair streaked with blonde was perfectly cut and framed her face well.

Holly felt her hand self-consciously creeping up to the nape of her own neck. She had cut her own hair much shorter earlier this year because she could not afford the upkeep of it. No problem guessing which one of us works here and who shops here, she thought wryly.

'Can I help you with anything?' She gave the woman a huge smile and got straight into salesgirl mode.

'Yes, my mother adores Gucci. I was wondering if you had anything in good condition

150

— a bag or something? I want to really blow her away on Christmas morning.' She gave Holly a knowing look. 'My turn to be the favourite daughter, you know?'

Holly nodded as if she did know, which of course she didn't. She tried not to feel envious as she went about pulling bags off the shelves and giving a little back-story to each. She could count her relatives on one hand (and she included Kate in this, who was like a sister). That was the hardest part about the holidays really. The people she had in her life were special, of course, but she had always yearned to go to one of those big family dinners, where everyone sat around the table, joking and laughing over big piles of food. What was it like? she wondered wistfully, looking at her customer as she inspected a gorgeous Gucci satchel from the 1980s.

'What's what like?' the woman asked, peering at Holly, who realised to her horror that she must have spoken out loud.

'Well, this bag is like the one that Mia Farrow took to her in-laws for Christmas one time . . . ' she blurted, winging it.

'Mia Farrow has in-laws?' The woman looked at her with disbelief.

'She did — but way before she met Woody and adopted all those children, of course.'

'OK . . . '

'She was still working for MGM at the time and had just married Frank,' Holly continued, warming to her theme. 'He took her to Hoboken to meet his mother — his dad was long dead. I mean, how old was Frank when he married her?

151

Like fifty or something . . . So she ran out and bought a full Jersey ensemble: you know, Jackie O glasses, Gucci bag, pink Chanel suit . . . She thought it would make a good impression on Mamma-in-Law. And do you know what happened?'

The woman was staring, her green eyes shining and her mouth agape with interest. 'No.'

'Mamma Sinatra started yelling at Frank in Italian to get that transvestite out of her house, he wasn't fooling her.'

'No . . . ' The woman's eyebrows had crawled to her hairline.

'Because she had just gotten that pixie cut? True story — or so I've heard.'

'Wow, that was great!' The woman picked up the bag with delight and asked Holly to wrap it up for her. 'I'm Alexandra by the way,' she told her. 'Alexandra Konecki.'

'Holly. Nice to meet you, Alexandra — and I hope your mother loves the bag.'

When the customer had left, Holly smiled, wondering how her mind managed to save all these stories she'd come across years ago and then have her pop them out at will just like that. She just had one of those brains, she supposed.

Shortly after her most recent customer had departed, the doorbell chimed once again and Mona Sachs appeared.

'So what the hell happened to my Halston?' the stylist asked without preamble, and to her horror Holly realised she'd never sent over the garment as per Mona's request from the other day. While her mind was great at storing useless

152

information, clearly her attention to detail wasn't up to the same level.

'Oh, Mona, I'm so sorry, things have been crazy! I have it ready out back and everything. It just completely slipped my mind . . . '

She waved an arm. 'It happens, don't worry about it. My society queen just had to make do with Versace. Poor dear,' she added sardonically.

Society queen . . .

Holly paused, thinking of something.

'I'll make it up to you, I promise. But, Mona,' she asked, 'have you ever heard of a woman called Margot Mead?'

She raised an eyebrow. 'Sweetie, that's like asking me if I ever heard of Rudy Giuliani. Of course: Margot Mead is royalty among the Upper East Side set.'

Holly's expression brightened. 'Do you happen to know her personally?'

'Are you kidding me? Nobody knows these women personally, not even their own damn husbands. I've come across her assistant a couple of times, though. Jessica, nice girl.'

Holly's eyes widened. An assistant . . . She cleared her throat, deciding she should share the information about the bracelet with Mona. She didn't know why she hadn't thought about it before. It might even belong to one of her clients, although this was doubtful given that the box it was found in had been delivered directly to the store. And, as it was, Mona typically bought from them, and had never used them to sell anything.

When she'd finished outlining the details, as

well as Samuel from Tiffany's suggestion that Margot Mead might be the one to help identify the egg charm, Mona nodded slowly.

'There's a very good chance she would know who something like that belongs to — hell, it might even belong to Margot herself.' The thought had crossed Holly's mind too, but because she had no way of getting in touch with Margot, she thought she needed to explore avenues related to the other charms first.

However, it seemed Mona might well be able to short-circuit the search. She scrolled through her trusty BlackBerry. 'Here you go,' she said, finding the details for Jessica, the assistant she'd mentioned before. 'Give her a call. I'm sure she'll be able to help.'

Holly couldn't believe her luck. 'That's fantastic, Mona, thank you. I so appreciate it.'

'Don't mention it. But if you still happen to have that Halston lying around, I have another use for it . . . '

'Oh, of course.' Holly duly retrieved the shirt and wrapped it up.

She was still buzzing with anticipation when, after Mona left, she quickly picked up the phone and dialled Jessica Edwards's number. That buzz was soon deflated when she got voicemail.

She left a garbled message about how she urgently needed to get in touch with Margot Mead, with a mention that Tiffany had suggested Margot might be able to help with a query — figuring that the mention of the store might pique the assistant's interest enough to return her call.

Then she looked at the clock. It was almost closing time.

Having waited a few more moments for any late evening stragglers, Holly eventually grabbed her coat and turned the sign to 'Closed'. She had a whole rack of clothes to take over to Thuma for dry-cleaning, and a box of donations to take over to Sacred Heart, as per Carole's instructions.

Having dropped off the dry-cleaning, she popped back to the shop to collect the donations and, lifting the heavy cardboard box to her chest, went back out and made her way slowly down the street.

Pausing in front of Encore, she noticed how quiet it was inside. When she walked in, Frank the owner was waving at her from the register.

'So slow over there that you've decided to come over and help me?' he teased.

He was a slender man, with thinning reddish hair and a large moustache. He, like Carole, had been downtown for years, holding on to his little thrift store with all his might, except his shop had not so much evolved like the Secret Closet had but had simply become more overcrowded. Frank's checkout counter was up on a platform as they were in the old days, so he could have full view of the store to see if there were any shoplifters. As a result, his customers would have to strain to reach the counter in order to check out. The effect was amusing.

Holly smiled at him. 'Nope.' She indicated the box she was holding. 'Just popping down to Father Mike with a couple of things, if you wanted to add to them. It's pretty cold out these

155

days, you know,' she added pointedly.

Frank waved his hands in feigned annoyance. 'Well, I don't have time now. I'm just about to close up.'

Holly smiled inwardly; she knew he would try and get out of it somehow. 'It's OK; I'll just go through the racks and pick out a few things myself. Unlike you, I'm a pro at this.'

Frank practically flew down from his perch behind the register. He sighed. 'OK. Just nothing with too good a label — that's all I ask.'

The two of them slowly made their way along the racks, and Frank started to get into it, checking coats for tears and stains and actually picking out the best ones (though the labels weren't fancy) to serve as donations.

'So you have a heart after all,' Holly teased.

He waved his hand dismissively. 'Nah, I already told you, Max took it when he left me.'

Frank's partner had left him over a year ago, having hot-tailed it to Florida with a much younger man. The only good thing, claimed Frank, was that he had left behind everything he owned, which he immediately put up for sale in his shop.

'You haven't found anyone since?' Holly asked.

'Oh, I have found plenty of anyones!' he laughed. 'Just not *the* one.'

Holly nodded and the two of them continued to work through the racks in silence. She shook her head to herself. Here they were in the biggest, busiest city in the world, where you would think you'd easily bump into the person of your dreams. They could be passing through, or visiting, working nearby or even taking in a Broadway show. But it seemed everyone Holly knew was single, lonely and searching. Of course, she herself was not searching; she had too much going on with Danny. But it would be nice to have someone special in her life sometime.

'What about you, Holly?' Frank asked, as if reading her mind. They had reached the end of the rack and the box was now full to bursting. 'Any dates recently?'

She laughed. 'I have a date every night, remember? His name is Danny.'

'Oh please! How old is he now? Give it a few short years and he'll be out on dates himself — then what will you do?'

Holly paused. She hadn't really given it that much thought, but Frank did have a point. The last ten years had flown by. It seemed only yesterday that she was rocking Danny as an infant, and now he had just turned ten. It seemed unfathomable.

Frank smiled at her thoughtful expression and added some more fuel to the fire. 'And of course men age so much more gracefully than women. Let's see . . . fifteen is the age of staying out in this city. So that's just five years from now — which would bring you to the ripe old age of . . . what, forty?'

'Frank — enough!' Holly exclaimed. 'If that's the case, all I'll need to do is to come and hang out with you on a Saturday night, seeing as you're telling me you don't go anywhere.'

But his words had struck a chord with her. Danny was growing up so fast, and already she could see him pulling away. What would she do when he did?

Holly closed up the box and thanked Frank again, who gave her a dry peck on the cheek as she left.

Carefully making her way down the already slippery path, she headed up to Sixth Street. Sacred Heart was one of the oldest churches in the city, and Holly loved dropping off donations there. There was something very peaceful about walking into a dusty, empty church. She wasn't a terribly religious person these days — the family used to attend Mass back in Queens when she was younger, but her dad always said that all you needed for a church was a few people hanging around talking about good things. Which she figured was as good a description as any.

Holly frowned as she walked up the steps. Had she failed spiritually with Danny? She was concentrating so hard on keeping it all together, with providing for him and making sure his life was steady, it was easy to overlook that side of things. He had asked about his grandfather a couple of times, and Holly had told him that Seamus was in heaven, which seemed to satisfy him.

She heaved open the door and her boots clicked as she walked down the centre aisle towards the altar. Holly wasn't sure about heaven herself, and she remembered being so angry when her father died — at least until the arrival of her beloved bracelet.

She stopped alongside the altar and peered through the dusty air to the office in the back. 'Hello, Father Mike?' she called out tentatively.

'Holly? Back here,' a chipper voice sounded from the enclave.

Holly often wondered how the priest was able to recognise her voice with all the people he must talk to all day long, though — she glanced over her shoulder at the empty pews — maybe it wasn't such a mystery after all. But he also had some involvement with St Patrick's Cathedral uptown, which she guessed would be a much busier post.

'Hey there, good to see you. What have you got for us this month?' Father Mike appeared in the doorway and gratefully relieved her of the box. He was a short man, built like a boxer, with greying hair and a weathered face, and his life was dedicated to helping all and any who came his way. He had plenty of destitute and needy in his congregation who might not necessarily show up for Mass, but definitely showed up on Wednesdays for soup, and for provisions, like clothes and blankets. He placed the box on his desk in the tiny room and began sorting through the contents. The church basement was hopping with activities most of the time, Holly knew. There were flyers all over the place. Single parenting meetings, AA meetings, grief counselling, marriage counselling, choir, soup kitchen . . . the list went on and on.

'Oh, would you look at that?' He pulled out an oversize leather handbag that was a blatant Gucci knockoff. 'That has Stella written all over

159

it . . . ' He winked at Holly, who smiled in agreement. Stella was a local 'girl' — a transvestite who suffered from depression and was occasionally in need of help. Holly had only figured out who she was after watching her march by the store one day in some worn Versace boots Holly had dropped off a few days before.

'Nice, Holly, very nice . . . ' He sorted through the rest of the items — warm coats, more bags, things the few older women in his tiny congregation could use. 'It's a pity you don't get more men's clothing . . . that's what I really need, suits. Something to give them some dignity and some confidence.'

Holly shook her head. 'Sorry, I wish we did too. I got as much as I could from Frank, but you know what he's like . . . '

Father Mike smiled and closed up the box. 'I sure do. That man could find my grandmother's tea cosy and sell it as the Shroud of Turin.'

Holly laughed. It was true; Frank felt obligated to try and sell absolutely everything that came his way, which was one of the main reasons Encore was so crowded and disorganised.

'Thanks for this, and pass on my appreciation to Carole too, won't you?'

'Of course.'

There was noise in the front of the church and a few people started filing in in the dark, laughing.

'Ah, they're here to set up downstairs,' said Father Mike. 'We're having an alcohol-free mixer tonight — want to join us?'

Holly smiled and shook her head. 'I'm too bushed tonight, Mike, and I need to get back to Danny, but thanks for the invite.'

Father Mike patted her on the shoulder. 'Ah well. Now go home and . . . meditate or do yoga or whatever it is you heathens get up to these days.'

Holly gave him a hug and promised to try and weasel some additional menswear out of Frank next time.

When she reached home about half an hour later, the glow of the TV was on and Danny and Kate were on the couch watching a movie.

'Hey, guys.' Holly gave Danny a kiss and he looked up at her sleepily. 'You're late.'

'Yeah, I know, I just had to pop over to Sacred Heart. Did you eat?'

Kate nodded. 'Yep, we had hot dogs, just like you suggested.'

'Yummy . . . ' Danny added appreciatively.

Holly slipped off her coat and hung it on the hook by the door. 'Well, I hope you left some for your poor old mom.'

Kate stretched and got up off the couch, readying herself to leave. 'Course we did.'

Holly gave her a quick hug as she left, promising to talk again tomorrow. She put some ketchup and mustard on her hot dog, and sat next to Danny on the couch. 'What are you watching?'

'Oh, I think it's something about a falcon,' Danny said disinterestedly. 'It's kind of boring, though.'

Kate had become addicted to old movies,

probably from her days with Justin, but as a result she had got Holly addicted to them as well. On the TV screen, Humphrey Bogart looked passionately at the portrait of the woman he was searching for. Holly ate her hot dog, wondering if times were simpler back then.

'That's some apartment . . . ' she murmured.

'Yeah, in Hollywood,' Danny murmured back.

Holly watched as Bogart searched frantically for the love of his life, and wondered if anyone would ever do that for her. Relationships seemed so dispassionate nowadays . . . No one seemed willing to try hard, to fall in love so deeply you felt as though you'd got hit on the head with a shovel. Did love like that even exist any more? Did it ever?

Holly sat back on the couch, reminding herself that, in truth, she'd felt a little bit like that when she first met Nick . . .

*   *   *

Chelsea, Lower Manhattan, 1999

Holly couldn't help but feel that the stars were finally aligning for her and things were going her way. She felt like skipping she was so happy! But, considering just how loaded down her arms were at that particular moment, with grocery bags, her handbag, as well as the coat that she realised was too heavy to wear as spring started to make its debut, skipping probably would be hard to manage.

She took a deep breath as she considered all

that had been going on. She smiled as she thought of the meeting that she had just finished, with the owner of Village Consignment, a lovely little vintage store based nearby. She'd got the job, her first real job! She had wanted it so badly, ever since she'd walked into the store for the first time, and her imagination had gone wild as she'd perused the expansive selection of vintage evening gowns and flouncy skirts with billowing petticoats that had probably been worn at sock hops and school dances in 1956.

Holly couldn't help but wonder about all the sure-to-be fantastic stories associated with the beautiful clothes, and was quick to point out and explain to her prospective boss the history behind many of the classic cuts and hemlines — knowledge she had acquired during her college days, which had successfully ended last summer.

Since graduating, she had been sending out countless job applications and barely making ends meet with a string of waitressing and bartending jobs in Manhattan. Ideally, she'd love to own and run such a store of her own someday, but for now, this was a start.

She had to admit she was happy that she would have a regular salary; she didn't feel so guilty about splurging a little bit with the groceries she'd just bought. After all, a night like tonight called for a nice steak and a bottle of wine. OK, it would just be New York strip and not a fillet, but still . . .

She pulled a Motorola phone out of her pocket and flicked it open. Despite Holly's protests, Eileen had insisted she have this cell phone, especially since she lived in a walk-up apartment that was slightly lax on the security in an area that was borderline problematic. For once, she'd decided to humour her mother. Eileen paid the bill for the phone, because it was a luxury that Holly couldn't quite manage on her own at this point, as well as a habit she didn't particularly like.

She hated passing people on the street who were engaged in loud conversations with their pieces of plastic — a sight that was becoming more and more common these days. And while she had originally vowed that she would only use it for emergencies, now she really, really wanted to spread the news about her new job.

Holly quickly dialled a few numbers, first calling her mother, then her college roommate Laura, who had since moved back to her home state of Maine, and her old schoolfriend Sally back in Queens. She was quick about her calls — she didn't want to run up a big bill — and of course everyone was thrilled for her.

Holly hiked up the bag of groceries a little bit further on her hip and briefly considered calling Dylan, a guy she'd met a few weeks previously and whom she'd been seeing somewhat casually. She wasn't sure if there were any sparks between them, and Holly was a firm believer in the idea that if fireworks didn't go off immediately, then it probably wouldn't ever happen.

She had really tried to like him, and he was a nice guy, good looking and charming; but there was just something missing.

164

Being with him, and talking to him, it felt, well, forced, and the couple of times that he had been clearly interested in taking their dalliance to the next step, Holly couldn't get past the kissing.

Dylan also didn't understand why someone with a college degree would want to work in retail, of all things. Holly had explained that her background was in fashion merchandising, and that you had to start somewhere. When she went on the initial interview at Village Consignment, Dylan had rolled his eyes and compared it to working at the Salvation Army.

She knew that she would probably just have to cut him loose soon. After all, why waste time with someone who wasn't the one? Why sell herself short with someone who clearly had a lack of imagination?

Holly placed the phone back in her pocket, glancing down briefly. In that split second, she collided with what felt like a brick wall.

Caught off her guard, she was thrown off balance and landed in a heap on the path with all her bags and belongings.

'Oh, man, sorry. Are you OK?'

Holly looked up and was met with the deepest, most liquid blue eyes she had ever seen in her life. The man had dark hair, and a square jaw with stubble that said, 'I haven't shaved today, but I still look good.' She stared at him with her mouth open and felt her heart jump in her chest.

'I'm fine.'

'Can I help you up?' He smiled and a dimple appeared on his cheek. His eyes were heavily lashed and she suddenly thought about her current Hollywood crush, Leonardo di Caprio. This guy had those eyes.

But then she realised he was still waiting for an answer. Holly shook her head, as if she needed to clear the fog away. 'Oh yes . . . sorry, I . . . Right.' She smiled meekly, at a loss for words.

'Are you sure you're OK?' he asked, pulling her up from the ground.

'I think so . . . ' She looked at the bags strewn about her. 'Oh crap. But my wine isn't.' The bottle of wine that she had bought had not survived the collision.

'Oh no, that's my fault, I'm so sorry. Shit, I'm a klutz. I was walking with my head down. Messing with this stupid phone.' He held up a Motorola like Holly's.

'It's fine. It was just a cheap bottle, no big loss. It probably would have given me a headache anyway.' Then she considered her words. What if he thought she was some sort of lush? That she drank bottles of wine alone? 'I mean, not that I would have drunk the whole thing. I was just going to cook dinner — a steak. And, you know, red wine and red meat and all . . . '

Shut up, Holly! she thought to herself. She bit her lip. 'Anyway . . . '

A smile played about his lips. 'It's OK, I know what you mean. I like a nice glass of wine with a steak too. Can I make it up to you?' His grin was broad and open and Holly felt flutters in her stomach.

'Really, you don't have to do that,' she protested, but her heart wasn't in it.

'Please, I want to. It's the least I can do for running you over. I'm Nick. Nick Mestas.' He held out his hand again. 'Nice to meet you . . . erm, I didn't catch your name?'

'Holly. Holly O'Neill.'

'O'Neill? As in the bar chain?' he queried and she winced. The drinking connection again.

'Can't say. I've never been in one actually,' she told him.

'But you are Irish, yes? That hair, those eyes?'

Holly blushed furiously. 'Second generation,' she confirmed, not willing to get into the specifics.

'Me too. Second generation, I mean, although Greek in my case.' He laughed. 'My parents really thought about that one. Bet you never heard of a Greek named Nick, huh?' She giggled, and he flashed a smile that made her heart almost stop. 'So what do you say, Holly O'Neill? Dinner to make it up to you? We could go to an Irish bar if you'd like.'

Holly swallowed hard. She had planned to stay in, cook a steak, drink some wine from the now broken bottle that stained the path, and then probably take a bubble bath, but really she had just collided with one of the best-looking men she had ever laid eyes on, a man who was now asking her to dinner. Maybe her stars really were aligned today.

'So, what do you think? I swear I don't bite, and I will never knock you over again. If you like red wine, I know this little bistro down in Greenwich serving a cabernet that will literally make your mouth water.'

'Greenwich . . . I just came from there,' Holly said absently, feeling as if she couldn't control the words that were coming out of her mouth. 'I just got a new job in a store in the Village and — '

'Well, then you have to say yes. We have to celebrate.' He smiled again and Holly had to restrain herself from throwing herself at him right then and there. If there was such a thing as love at first sight — well, maybe lust at first sight — Holly had a bad case of it.

'OK, then, it's a date,' she smiled.

*　*　*

It was after dark when the cab pulled up to the kerb in front of Holly's walk-up. Nick jumped out of the car and ran round to Holly's side to open the door for her. She stepped gracefully out as she held Nick's hand and a shiver ran along the length of her spine as she wondered if he would try to kiss her.

'Mind if I walk you to your door?' he asked softly.

'Sure,' she replied, feeling suddenly shy.

Nick turned to the driver. 'Can you wait for me? Keep the meter running. I'll be back in a moment.'

Holly smiled at his chivalry and silently added another point to Nick's score, which had been accumulating all evening since she'd first laid eyes on him.

And what an evening it had been. From the moment he had helped her up from the

168

sidewalk, he'd been nothing but a complete and utter gentleman. Opening doors, pulling out her chair, asking questions. So unlike many of the guys she had encountered in Manhattan, who just wanted to talk about themselves, or sit at some bar drinking beer and watching whatever sport happened to be on TV. No, Nick was quite the opposite.

He was twenty-six, a couple of years older than her, and had been living in New York since he graduated from UCLA and left the West Coast in hopes of cashing in on the growing Internet boom that was sweeping the globe.

He had a background in the emerging field of computer science, and said that he was big into gadgets, especially his cell phone.

What's more, Nick seemed to completely get Holly's love for the city, as well as how excited she was to start work at Village Consignment. He was a rapt audience, and they had spent the better part of the last four and a half hours talking about so many things.

Holly walked to her door with Nick at her elbow and she felt nervous anticipation settle in her stomach. She *really* wanted to kiss him.

'So, I had a great time tonight, Nick. I'm glad we ran into each other. Literally,' she added, smiling.

'I am too. I'm hoping that you will say yes if I ask to see you again.' He took a step closer and glanced at her lips. He was going to kiss her . . . She knew it.

She gulped and nodded. 'Yes, I'd really like that.'

169

'How's breakfast tomorrow? Too soon?' He smiled and her heart beat faster.

'No, not too soon.' Her head moved closer to his and then suddenly he pulled her close, enveloping her in an embrace and covering her mouth with his. 'Holly . . . ' Nick whispered. She opened her eyes and wondered if he was going to ask to come in. Much as she wanted him to, she also hoped he wouldn't. She never slept with a guy on a first date. Although this time she was tempted to break that rule.

'Yes?'

'You are amazing. And I would love to stand here all night kissing you. I had a wonderful time tonight. But let's save some of this for breakfast in the morning.' He kissed her again and she was sure that her heart would beat out of her chest with happiness.

'I can't wait.' She took a step back and almost had to physically restrain herself from jumping back into his arms.

'Oh, there's something in front of your door,' Nick pointed out. He knelt down and picked up a small, box-shaped package. He looked worried as he glanced around at the apartment hallway. 'Can people just walk in and drop things off? That's not very safe.'

Holly focused in on the package and smiled, recognising the by now familiar shape. It had been a while . . .

'No, it's OK,' she told him. 'I have a . . . secret admirer, so to speak.'

Nick crinkled his brow. 'A secret admirer? I don't like the sound of that. I'll fight the guy off if I have to,' he joked, and Holly burst out laughing.

'No, not like that. I already know what this is. These boxes arrive from time to time, when I have stuff going on in my life.' Quickly she told him the story, of her charm bracelet, and showed him the individual charms that graced her wrist.

'And you don't know who sends them?'

She blushed. 'Well, I have my ideas, of course, but I feel a bit like Cinderella, like I have a fairy godmother.' She didn't want to get too deep into her theory about exactly who might be looking out for her from afar; it was information Nick didn't need to know just yet. Notwithstanding that, it was a deep topic for a first date.

'Aren't you going to open it?' he asked, studying the package. 'You have me intrigued. That's if you don't mind me seeing it,' he added quickly.

'Not at all.' Holly grinned and ripped open the package. Inside was the same lilac box from before. She untied the ribbon and popped open the lid.

'What is it?' Nick asked, moving closer.

Holly put a hand to her mouth. She grinned happily. 'It's a little dress, made out of silver — look!'

'Wow, your fairy godmother must know you got a job today, a job in fashion,' Nick said, leaning closer once again to kiss Holly full on the lips. At that moment, all thoughts of charms, fairy godmothers and everything else left her head immediately.

He was right, though. Her mysterious

benefactor must definitely have known about the job and how today had been a very big day for her, a memorable day. But whoever it was, they definitely didn't know about this, about Nick. Because if they did, they would have forgone the dress charm and instead almost certainly sent a trinket in the shape of a heart engraved with the word 'love'.

12

Light crept into Greg's apartment like a thief and, for once, when it hit his sheets and slowly made its way up to his pillow and rested on his face, he didn't leap out of bed as if his hair was on fire. Instead he stretched lazily and stared out through the window. With no five a.m. wake-up, he could now sleep in when he worked late the night before. What a novelty, and how civilised, he thought. He glanced at his clock: eight a.m. Sounded about right. He pushed the sheets off and walked over to the window, realising he really had never seen his own neighbourhood during the day.

However, Karen was still on the corporate schedule, and as she entered the bedroom, stilettos clacking on the wooden floors, it was obvious she was not impressed with his time-clock.

'I hope you aren't planning on sitting around in your pyjamas all day,' she commented.

Greg looked at her. Things around the house had been slightly tense over the last while, and he was sure the remainder of the tension would subside once he popped the question.

'Oh, babe, of course I'm not going to sit in my PJs. Just because I work at home doesn't mean I'm some sort of bum.'

'I know that,' she said tersely. 'Anyway, it would be great if you could pick up my dry-cleaning sometime today. There's a suit I need for my presentation tomorrow.'

Greg's face fell. Not that he minded doing errands and helping out, but it seemed as though Karen had been issuing a lot of these kind of requests since he'd started working from home, as if he had nothing else going on.

And that wasn't the case. He had been extremely busy. Not only had he been out and about taking shots for his *NYT* portfolio, but he had also gone about getting listed on several freelance websites, and had been in touch with a web designer to get going on a company website. He had touched base with a lawyer friend to get the paperwork organised for his newspaper gig, and had sent out numerous emails and made countless phone calls to let everyone in his circle of interest know what he was doing.

But he wasn't sure if Karen realised any of that.

He guessed she was still just getting used to this transition, and finding it hard to adapt. Every couple went through some tough times, but it was the serious ones who persevered. Take his mom and dad for example.

Greg knew that he had a tendency to put his parents up on a pedestal, but part of it was because he admired their relationship so much. Being an only child, he had grown up as an integral part of their love for each other, and was often a direct witness to their happy marriage and their way of coping with both the good and the bad. There was no denying that his parents had been soulmates. He wanted a love like that for Karen and him, and he had to admit that he felt somewhat troubled by the question that his father had posed to him days earlier, about how he had known that he wanted to spend his entire life with Cristina within minutes of meeting her.

That hadn't quite been the case for him, had it? If anything Karen had been the one who'd pursued him, shortly after they were introduced at a charity benefit at the Guggenheim a couple of years back. He remembered being silently impressed by her confidence, not to mention her beauty, but he was so busy with work (which basically ate up every daylight hour), he hadn't been looking for a relationship.

But as they had talked about careers and children and school and apartments for years now, the only thing left was to tie the knot. What were they waiting for? Until there was enough money? There never would be enough money, and Greg knew from experience that no matter how hard you planned, nothing in life was ever meant to go perfectly.

Pondering that thought, he then decided that his parents' courtship had taken place in a different time, a different era, even. Life today seemed so much more complicated than in years past.

It was then that he realised that he hadn't yet answered Karen's question about the dry-cleaning.

'Of course, honey. It's no problem. Listen, would you like to meet up for dinner later? I could meet you after work . . . '

Karen was already shaking her head. 'No, I

don't think so. I can't be out late, not when I have an early tomorrow.'

Greg raised a surprised eyebrow. 'You never used to mind going out on work nights. We did it plenty when I was at the firm.'

'Yes, but you are no longer at the firm, are you? And I can't risk messing anything up in case I'm out of a job too.'

Greg's smile fell as he watched Karen ready herself to leave for work. She shuffled through file folders and arranged them meticulously in her briefcase. He turned round and went to the closet, intent on getting dressed as soon as possible.

'It's not like I'm doing nothing around here, and I didn't *lose* my job,' he replied quietly.

Karen put her briefcase down and walked over to him. She put her arms around his waist.

'I'm sorry,' she whispered. 'I shouldn't be like that. I've just been a bit stressed recently. Really, I apologise. These last few weeks, there's been so much going on, what with this and then everything at work, and the holidays . . . '

He turned in her arms. 'I'm the one who should be saying sorry. I'm the one who sprung this on you, after all.'

She chuckled. 'I'll give you that much . . . '

He bent to kiss her, and breathed a sigh of relief, seeing the smile that graced her beautiful face. 'I promise you, Karen, that I will never, ever *not* tell you about something I am planning. *Ever* again. And I promise I am dedicated to making a go of this photography business. I promise you are not in this alone.'

Karen gave a small nod and Greg hoped against hope that she believed him.

'We're partners, you and me. You know that, don't you?'

'Yes, I know.' She leaned close to him, before eventually pulling back. 'You have a good day, and I'll see you later, all right?'

'No problem.'

Having got dressed and made coffee, Greg switched on his laptop and began editing some photos he had taken the day before. He had gone through five rolls of film in three hours. When he was out and about with his camera, the time just seemed to fly by. Whereas when he was trading, he had turned into a clock-watcher, and it had seemed as if getting to noon took the whole day.

He sat back for a moment and admired his work; all pictures of gleaming New York skyscrapers, but shot from slightly off-kilter angles, as was his signature. He had to admit, he thought they were pretty OK — very much along the lines of his Flatiron shot. No use for the *NYT*, but maybe he could shop these around to a couple of galleries and see if there were any bites.

Gradually, his thoughts began to drift again to how he could really wow Karen when he asked her to marry him. He didn't want this proposal to be anything ordinary or humdrum like a ring hidden in an oyster or a champagne glass; he wanted to stage a crazy romantic gesture that she would remember her whole life. Nothing obvious either, more something that could integrate seamlessly into her day. Karen was very intuitive and he didn't want to do anything that would make her suspicious. Nor did he want to do anything corny, as he remembered her saying how she hated public restaurant proposals, or aeroplanes writing the request in the sky. She called such things tacky and clichéd.

So it had to be romantic and private, but also something so special and original that she would never forget it. Something they would tell their kids about, Greg thought with a smile.

The proposal to end all other proposals.

But what?

★　★　★

Later, at the office, Karen shuffled through some print ads from the previous year's spring marketing blitz. The theme had been 'Magic', and the department had hoped to tie it into an event with Disney, but they had pulled out at the last minute, though unfortunately after the flyers promoting the theme had already been mass-printed.

The whole thing had left her and her colleagues looking foolish, and as a result they had already started on next year's campaign in the hope of redeeming themselves.

Amy, one of the copywriters, stopped by her desk.

'Trying not to repeat that mess?' She motioned to the old print ad. 'Why is it out?'

'A reminder,' Karen answered, 'to never let it happen again.' She sighed and pulled her makeup bag out of her desk. As she touched up her face, Amy picked up Greg's photo, which was situated beside her PC screen.

'So how's handsome and rich doing?' she asked with a grin.

'Still handsome, at least,' Karen said ruefully, putting her makeup bag back in the drawer and slamming it a little too hard.

'Oh?' Amy crossed her arms. 'What gives?'

Karen began neatening the pile of paper on her desk. 'He quit Wall Street. Now he's going to be a full-time photographer.' She looked hard at the papers she was straightening, avoiding her colleague's gaze.

'Oh my . . . Well, that's a big change. But I think you mentioned before that he was pretty good at it. Didn't he have some kind of exhibition a while back?'

'Yes, he is very good at it . . . ' Karen trailed off, and picked up the crossword she was working on over coffee that morning but hadn't finished. She was sorry now she'd made Greg's so-called 'exhibition' out to be something more than it was at the time. It was, after all, one photograph. Just one.

'So what's the problem?' Amy persevered.

'No problem.' Karen picked up a pencil and began filling in the remaining clues.

'Why do you do these anyway?'

'Because it keeps my brain active . . . ' she replied flippantly, but the truth was she had always felt somewhat inferior to the people in her and Greg's — well, mostly his parents' — circle. The society types with their rich and privileged silver-spoon backgrounds. Karen had always felt a burning desire to be part of that world, to be known as smart as well as beautiful, and perfectly put-together at all times, no matter what. And she'd been succeeding too.

But now Greg's out-of-the-blue career change was moving the goalposts. Everything she'd been working towards seemed to have taken a big step backwards since he'd told her.

Now, she thought irritably, she would have to introduce him as an out-of-work artist type rather than the successful broker he once was — a second-generation Upper East Side moneymaker. Having finished the crossword, she slipped it into her bag and checked the time. 'So are we ready for this presentation or what?'

'OK, OK, I'm going!' Amy grinned and gave Karen a sideways glance. 'And correct me if I'm wrong, but I thought it was the artist who was supposed to be temperamental, not the girl-friend?'

13

Holly made the short walk from Danny's school towards the store, passing the Christmas shoppers and people lugging fir trees through the streets. Fairy lights were everywhere and people were rushing about trying to get Christmas preparations done. It made her think about her own family festivities when she was a child, when her dad would finally close the hardware store the night before Christmas.

She had always complained that he should close early like the other shops did on the street, but he would remind her that a hardware store was sometimes the saving grace for someone's Christmas. Last-minute gifts for a husband or father, light bulbs, fuses, electrical tape: these were the things that held Christmas together, and who was he to deny the public that?

And he had been right, of course; there were always the late stragglers arriving in a panic because their fairy lights wouldn't work or they had forgotten to buy a tree stand, or because Uncle Charlie was coming to visit and he'd always talked about wanting a cordless drill.

Finally, around six p.m. on Christmas Eve, Seamus would shut the lights off at the hardware store and walk the few blocks home, where Holly and Eileen would be waiting eagerly for him. The turkey would be resting on top of the stove, flipped-over plates covering all the side dishes to keep them warm. Her mother would have a Bing Crosby or Johnny Mathis record on the turntable. All the lights would be dimmed or off, so that their own Christmas tree with its multicoloured lights would cast a warm glow around the small room. They had no fireplace in their house; that had been walled up years ago, like most of the fireplaces in the brownstones on their street. So they would compensate with a trio of candles on a make-do mantelpiece in the dining room. After her dad had gone upstairs to get changed, he would come down in a fresh shirt and tie to carve the turkey. And, even though it was only the three of them, they still all dressed up, and her mother polished the silver and unearthed the best china. After dinner, Holly would be sent to bed, under the threat that Santa might not come if she was up too late. She would hang her stocking with a thumbtack on the only bookshelf in the living room and go up to bed, stopping on each step to plead with her parents to stay up just a bit longer — but the pleading glances never worked.

Then Holly's mom and dad would sit on the tiny sofa, open a bottle of wine and turn Johnny Mathis up a little louder. Holly could hear them from her bedroom, talking and laughing, her father's low, rumbling voice giving Eileen a rundown of his day.

Finally Holly would drift off to sleep — then, as soon as the first slice of sunlight hit her bedroom, she would bound downstairs to see what Santa had put in her stocking. There would always be candy and foil-wrapped chocolate, usually a sample bottle of perfume, fancy socks with lace around the ankles, and — at the bottom of the stocking — a big fat orange. At this point, her mom and dad would be sitting on the couch, bleary-eyed, holding cups of coffee, and Bing would be back on the turntable. Finally her mother would let them all eat a hard-boiled egg to tide them through Mass and the three of them would make their way on the snowy, empty streets to the local church, where they would sit through a Christmas Day Mass that was twice as long as a regular Mass, and Holly's stomach would groan and gurgle at the thought of chocolate and candy back home. Sometimes her father would slip her a peppermint, putting a finger to his lips not to tell Eileen, and Holly would gratefully pop it in her mouth and quietly suck it through the sermon.

After Seamus died, they had stopped going to church altogether. Holly had come downstairs one Sunday morning, dressed and ready to go, only to find her mother still in her dressing gown at the kitchen table, sipping a cup of coffee.

'I just don't feel like going today, do you?' she had simply said.

At the time Holly had seen it as just another memory of her father that her mother was destroying, another source of comfort her mother had removed. Christmas in the O'Neill household had been different after that.

And Christmas this year would be completely different again. Because, for the first time ever, Holly and Danny would not be going to Eileen's house in Queens.

Instead her mother was coming to them.

She still wasn't entirely sure why she'd suggested to Danny they have Christmas dinner at their teeny apartment. But when Kate had mentioned that she wouldn't be going home to Minnesota this year, and was complaining of being at a loose end, Holly had decided for sure that she was going to host a big, old-style Christmas at her house, the kind she'd always wanted. It obviously had something to do with what she'd been feeling lately, about wanting to give Danny something other than just the basics. She wanted to create traditions and memories like her father had done for her.

Eileen had been surprised at first when Holly made the suggestion over the phone the night before.

'Are you sure? You know I'm always happy to have you and Danny.'

'I know, but this year I thought that maybe we could do something different. Danny would love it, and Kate would be here too.'

There was a brief silence on the phone. 'Anyone else?'

'What do you mean?'

'Well, I suppose I was just wondering if you'd met anyone, anyone interesting?'

Holly groaned. 'Mom, you of all people should know that's the last thing on my mind.'

'Still . . .'

'Still nothing.'

'OK, well, in any case, thank you. I'd love to come. Only problem is, because I thought we were having it at mine, I invited someone. A friend.'

Holly stopped breathing. No, her mother wasn't seriously . . . She couldn't comprehend Eileen seeing another man.

'I know what you're thinking and don't even go there!' her mother trilled. 'It's a girlfriend. She doesn't have any family left so — '

'Well then, bring her along,' Holly said before she could stop herself. 'The more the merrier.'

'Seriously?'

'Yes, why not?' Although how the hell five of them were going to fit in the tiny living space was a mystery. Especially alongside the Christmas tree that Danny had been asking for. He was so excited by the prospect that she couldn't turn him down.

As Holly pondered over the complexities of fitting guests into her apartment, let alone those related to preparing Christmas dinner, her cell phone rang inside her pocket.

'Hello?'

'Ms O'Neill?'

'Yes.'

'This is Jessica Edwards calling on behalf of Margot Mead. I'm returning your call from yesterday. You said in your message you're from Tiffany?'

Holly straightened. For some reason Jessica's tone made her feel as though she should be standing to attention. 'Not quite, but a lovely man from there pointed me in Ms Mead's direction.'

'And this is concerning a piece of jewellery?'

'Yes.' Holly went on to explain about the bracelet she'd found, and Samuel's belief that

Margot Mead might be able to help track down the origin of the jewel-encrusted egg charm.

'Really, I'm just hoping she could give me some more information about the egg charm and where it might have been purchased. The bracelet may even belong to Ms Mead herself, who knows?' This was a long shot, but Holly was trying to get the assistant on side.

'You do realise that Ms Mead is not a directory service?' the assistant said snippily, and Holly reflected that navigating the world of the Manhattan elite was truly like living on another planet. After all, at the end of the day, people are just people, and she was pretty sure that Margot Mead put her pants on one leg at a time just like everyone else.

But all at once, Holly felt sure that — whatever her love for jewellery — Margot Mead wasn't the owner of the bracelet. Even without meeting her, Holly understood that Margot had to be the type of woman who allowed assistants and stylists to dictate the shape and style of her life. A charm bracelet like the one Holly carried in her handbag was too full of whimsy, and too unpredictable, to belong to someone who had a third party do her bidding. She just knew it.

'Of course I understand that. But I just wondered if she could possibly take a look at the bracelet to see if she recognised it. The egg charm, I mean,' she added. 'I believe Ms Mead is quite the jewellery connoisseur.'

'Well, she certainly buys a lot of jewellery, Ms O'Neill.'

'Please, call me Holly,' she insisted pleasantly, noting that the invitation to familiarity was not returned.

'You said that this was found in a jacket where you work?'

'Yes, I work at a vintage store in the Village. I found it in a Chanel jacket, a lovely one, and really, I just want to return it to its rightful owner. You see, I have one myself and — ' she automatically jingled her own bracelet at no one in particular — 'I just figured if I could follow the breadcrumbs, so to speak, it might lead me back to the person who is missing this.' She chuckled self-consciously. 'I'm sure you're thinking I just read too many fairy tales.'

'No, it's a nice thing to do.' Jessica's voice softened a little. 'I'm sorry I was rude earlier. I apologise.'

'It's no problem, it's the holidays — everyone is busy. But listen,' Holly continued, hoping to make the most of the slight chink in Jessica's armour. 'Do you think Ms Mead might be able to take a look at it for me?'

'Well, it's like this,' Jessica replied, her brusqueness returning. 'Margot Mead serves on the board of about thirty different charities in the city. She has something going on almost every night, and barely has time to take a look at her own husband, never mind a . . . ' She trailed off and sighed. 'Wait a minute, did you say it was a jewel-encrusted egg charm?'

'Yes.'

'Well, it's the strangest thing, I think I might have come across something like that a while back — at one of our benefits. Like I said, Ms Mead is involved in a lot of charities, benefits, auctions, that sort of thing. And those prizes are often jewellery.'

Holly's heartbeat quickened. 'So you're saying the charm might have been picked up at one of those auctions or given out as a prize?'

Nice prize . . .

'Perhaps. Obviously we keep records of such things for tax purposes. Could you possibly email me over a picture of the charm in question and I can see if it rings any bells?'

'That would be fantastic. Are you sure you don't want to see it in person, though . . . ?'

'Believe me, I'll be lucky if I see the light of day for the next couple of weeks. There's so much to organise over the holidays this year, a soiree at the Plaza, a cocktail evening at the Four Seasons, not to mention the library benefit . . . '

'OK, I understand. Let me know your details and I'll send a photo to you as soon as I can.' Or, more likely, she'd get Danny to do it. But seeing as Jessica seemed to be so swamped with Christmas-related social arrangements, Holly didn't expect to hear back from her anytime soon.

'I can't make any promises of course, but if it was given out as one of our prizes, then there is a possibility that we'll have some more information about it. We rarely keep track of the winners, though . . . '

'Honestly, any help you could give me at all would be amazing. Thank you.'

'No problem. Where was it that you said you worked?'

'The Secret Closet, just off Bleecker Street.'

'Yes, I know the place.'

'Oh.' Holly was surprised. 'Well, perhaps Ms Mead has sent stock our way on occasion. I'd imagine she has an amazing wardrobe — especially with all those charities and the events.'

'I doubt it. Ms Mead certainly doesn't need the commission on anything like that, and she takes great pride in her wardrobe.'

'I'm sure she does.' With the amount of money she obviously spent on her wardrobe, she wondered if Margot Mead realised the irony of spending money on designers, instead of simply donating that money to the many charities over which she presided. Then again, she sounded like a woman who could probably do both and still put groceries on the table.

'You have to look good when you are raising funds for the children in Africa, or clean water in Southeast Asia, or breast cancer or what-have-you . . .'

Holly's ears pricked up. 'Breast cancer, you said?'

'Yes, among many others.'

She thought again about the pink ribbon charm. Coincidence?

'Does Ms Mead work on behalf of breast-cancer charities regularly?' she enquired. 'It's just that there is another charm on the bracelet . . .'

'Oh, I see,' Jessica said, when Holly explained her line of thinking. 'That might narrow the search down a little. I can cross-reference to see if there were breast-cancer events or auctions at which that egg charm might have been used as a

189

prize. Leave it with me.'

'Honestly, I really can't thank you enough.'

Holly ended the call, new hope in her heart. Margot Mead's assistant had not only promised to look into the egg charm, but might also be able to give her a lead associated with one of the others.

This, taken with the information Danny had gleaned from the horseshoe, meant that she was getting somewhere. She planned to head down to the gallery at lunchtime to see if she could find out anything more on that end.

Holly smiled. With luck she'd be able to reunite the bracelet with its (possibly by now frantic) owner very soon.

14

At his apartment, Greg was on hold with Suzanne Lee, his contact from the *NYT*. Billy was right: to say that this particular writer was highly strung was a huge understatement.

He picked up the tennis ball he had been rolling across the living-room floor to the opposite wall and sent it rolling again.

Finally Suzanne's clipped, businesslike voice came through. 'So do you get it? Do you get what I want? I don't want it to look like a Macy's ad, OK? None of that happy-clappy stuff, you got it? I want classic, old-style New York, so you're going to do Rockefeller, Wollman Rink, the Plaza,' She paused. 'Are you writing this down?'

Greg looked at the scribbles he had made since the beginning of the conversation. 'Yep.'

'Good, and I need a shot of Tiffany on Fifth and I want a bakery, one of those traditional kinds — '

'I know a good one.' Greg cut her off without thinking.

There was silence on the other end of the phone.

'Glaser's on the Upper East Side, German, been there for over a hundred years . . . ' He trailed off, uncertain.

'OK, great!'

Suzanne Lee hung up the phone and Greg was

left to wonder about deadlines and how to get her the prints. He leafed through the directory and saw there was an email next to the number. He'd start right away; Suzanne sounded like the kind of person who wanted things 'yesterday'. Obviously the woman was under a lot of stress, or maybe that's the way she was all the time.

Greg looked at his notes. He'd like to do the Rockefeller Center and the Plaza at night; they'd look especially festive and pretty all lit up. He would clean his equipment tonight, and tidy the darkroom, check fluids and that kind of thing. The bakery and Wollman Rink he could do tomorrow morning before heading over to his folks' place for a while. Then maybe the night shots the following evening.

He decided to do it in chunks and send digital photos through as he went: that way Suzanne could tell him if he was on the right track or not, which he suspected would be no trouble for her.

But for now, he planned to take a trip downtown to work on the second phase of his new career plan, something that he hoped would boost Karen's faith in him even more.

★   ★   ★

Holly walked with determination as she navigated the slush on Twenty-Fifth Street while taking special care not to ruin her black riding boots. She had to admit that she had possibly made a mistake in her wardrobe choice that morning and paid silent tribute to the Scotchguard she had applied when she first

192

bought the boots in a Century 21 sale during the summer.

She peered down the street and took a moment to check the address again. The street was awash with galleries, and she wanted to make sure that she had found the right one.

'It should be just here.' Holly looked up at the nondescript building in front of her and felt sure that she had found the correct one. Nothing said 'art gallery of the highest standing' like a brown brick building with no signs.

She pulled her mink-coloured shearling coat tighter around her, taking a few steps forward to tug at the heavy and ornate oak door.

A moment later she was welcomed by a blast of heat that was surprising considering the high ceilings in the space, and she welcomed the warmth.

Dark wood floors complemented the red paint on the walls and reflected bursts of light from the track and recessed lighting fixtures above. The space could have easily been considered for a wing at MoMA, it was so elegant, and Holly's gaze immediately wandered to the walls, which were covered in resplendent pop-art canvas paintings and photographs. Some were renditions of places here in New York, others of exotic locales around the world that Holly could only dream of.

Fascinated, she started to wander along the perimeter of the room, almost forgetting why she had come in in the first place, until someone approached her silently from behind.

'Welcome to the del Vecchio Gallery. Is there

something I can help you with?'

Holly turned round quickly to be faced with a dark-haired man who had the same sculpted jawline and arresting features as another man she had met in Manhattan many moons ago. The man in front of her spoke with an ever-so-soft Italian accent, an inflection that clearly indicated he had been in the US for some time, but had not yet given up his roots. His eyes were heavily lashed, but instead of blue like Nick's, they were warm amber. A smile graced his lips, one that suggested he was a rogue and knew it, and Holly steeled herself, almost out of habit, not to fall prey to yet another charming man.

However, as was Holly's nature, she also had a hard time being rude to a stranger and a smile found its way to her lips.

'Yes, maybe you can help me. I'm looking to speak to Gennaro del Vecchio.'

The smile grew wider. 'Well, then you are in luck, because I am he.'

'Oh,' Holly stuttered, somewhat disarmed.

The mere fact that she had asked for him directly seemed to make his body language suddenly click into overdrive, as if he was intrigued that he now had the audience of an attractive female.

'And you are?' he enquired.

'Oh, sorry, I'm Holly O'Neill.'

'Well, Holly O'Neill, what brings you here today? Are you looking for a new piece of artwork?'

Right, she thought to herself with a smile. Everything on the walls here probably costs more than I pay in a year's rent.

'The artwork is beautiful, but actually it's about something else. And it's sort of a long story. I wouldn't want to interrupt you if you are busy?'

She knew that she was the only person on the gallery floor just then, but she didn't know if there was some sort of backstage business that the owner engaged in when there was no foot traffic.

'Does it look like I am crushed with Christmas shoppers?' he teased. 'I run a business that is — how do you say it? — not the top priority when stuffing a stocking.'

Holly let out a laugh at his somewhat broken English. She had to admit that she loved a man with an accent, and he was definitely handsome. Unfortunately he reminded her too much of someone she tried not to think about regularly.

'And besides,' he added pointedly, 'I always have plenty of time for a beautiful woman.'

I bet you do, thought Holly, as she mentally channelled some imaginary armour to shield herself from his charms. 'Thank you.'

'So tell me your story, Holly O'Neill. What is it I can help you with?'

Holly extracted the bracelet from her handbag and once again recapped her mission: how she was trying to track the owner by way of the charms, as well as her path to Gennaro's front door. When she'd finished, she paused for breath and waited for the gallery owner to speak.

'May I see this bracelet of yours?'

She handed it over willingly, and he searched

through it. She thought he was looking for the horseshoe with the letters that had led her here, but instead he flipped directly to the tadpole-like charm that Holly couldn't identify.

'This *corno*, it is wonderful. The craftsmanship is spectacular,' he pointed out, displaying the charm in his palm.

She followed his gaze. 'Oh, what did you call it — a *corno*?' she asked, fascinated. 'What is that?'

'It's an Italian horn. A traditional talisman used to ward off evil.'

Interesting, Holly thought, her mind racing. Could the owner of the bracelet possibly be Italian, then?

'Yes, it's quite beautiful,' she replied, unwilling to admit that she hadn't known what it was.

'Surely, it is. I grew up around them,' Gennaro said, chuckling. 'And I may well have grown up around this very one.'

Holly's eyes grew wide. 'Excuse me?'

'This charm, I believe it came from a shop in my home town, in Florence. My father's shop, Corna Fiorentine.'

'Seriously?' Holly couldn't believe her luck.

'I take it this is the charm that led you here to me?'

'No, actually, but what a happy coincidence,' Holly replied, heartened that she was on the right track. 'Maybe your father could help me find who bought this?'

Gennaro's smile dimmed ever so slightly. 'Ah, I am afraid that is not possible. You see, my father, Giovanni, now rests with the angels.'

'Oh, I see,' said Holly, crestfallen once again.

'I'm terribly sorry to hear that.'

'Don't worry, it was many years ago. But even if he was still alive, please understand that he sold many of these through the years. I doubt if he would have been able to identify this one trinket.' He held the bracelet out to Holly, and she took it.

'Probably,' she agreed, trying to consider the angles. 'But it's so strange — that isn't the charm that led me here. It's this one.' She indicated the horseshoe. 'Isn't it odd that the bracelet has two very different charms that lead directly to you?'

Gennaro shook his head and his brow creased. 'Yes, it is odd, and very strange. But I cannot figure out the connection, as I've never seen this bracelet before. None of my own work, or the work I buy from freelancers, has anything to do with *corna* or horseshoes.'

Holly was thinking out loud. 'Well, you said the horn symbolises protection, as do horseshoes. What about the numbers: do they mean anything to you?'

Gennaro looked again at the inscription, 618. 'Nothing to me personally. Maybe it is a date?'

'Yes, maybe.' Then remembering her recent conversation with Jessica, a thought suddenly occurred to her. 'Would you happen to hold events here? Like a charity benefit or something? And have you ever heard of a woman called Margot Mead?'

Gennaro shrugged. 'I'm afraid I do not know this lady. And we do hold events here sometimes — not as you describe, but exhibits, where our artists sell their work, sometimes in aid of charity.'

Holly was thinking hard. 'Wait a minute, didn't you say you buy the work of freelancers?' When he nodded in agreement, she continued. 'And you showcase this work, at gallery events?'

'Yes, we do,' Gennaro confirmed. 'Ah, I see where you are going with this. Maybe this charm means 'good luck', because someone had their work showcased here on such a date, perhaps June eighteenth, yes?'

Holly smiled: that was exactly where she'd been going. 'Yes, so how long have you been open? Or actually, how many eighteenth of Junes have you been open?'

Gennaro put a thoughtful hand to his chin and started counting, what Holly assumed was years, on his fingers.

'That would be eight. I have owned this gallery for eight years.'

Holly felt like jumping up and down. She felt that they were close to discovering another piece of the puzzle. She was sure of it.

'And how many times have you had gallery events on June eighteenth?'

With that Gennaro threw up his arms. 'Well, that, I would have to check. My assistant keeps those records, but I can ask her to look. You are looking specifically for work exhibited by freelancers, yes?'

'And who might have an Italian connection of some sort — although that's not a given,' she added quickly, so as not to make the search too restrictive.

Gennaro smiled. 'You are quite the detective, Holly O'Neill.'

'My son calls me Sherlock.' She smiled,

thinking of her and Danny's recent sleuthing, and was surprised to see Gennaro's face change at the mention of a son. His eyes darted to her left hand, evidently in search of a ring. Holly had to purse her lips together to hold back a smile.

'Your son? How long have you been married?'

Holly shook her head and looked down at her hand. 'I'm not. And I'm no longer with Danny's father.'

Gennaro's face brightened. 'Ah, I see, and your son, how old is he? And does he like your current boyfriend?'

Talk about subtle . . .

'He's ten. And there is no current boyfriend.'

Gennaro looked Holly up and down. 'There is no way you are old enough to have a ten-year-old son. Not possible. I mean, you can't be a day over twenty-five, how beautiful you are. And to be single, that is a tragedy.'

Holly laughed out loud at this. 'Oh, Gennaro, what a smooth talker *you* are! Try adding ten to that.'

He feigned shock at her true age and put a hand over his heart. 'You must have fantastic genes. Do not tell me, you are Italian, yes? We Italians have good genes; Italian women are beautiful for ever.'

'Do I look Italian to you?' Holly pointed to her hair, and glanced at her watch. As much as she was enjoying Gennaro's flirting, she needed to get back to work.

'So is your assistant here? Do you think she could get this information for me?' She hoped her suggestion could get the flirtatious gallery owner back on track, but unfortunately he shook his head.

'No, Sofia is not here right now.' Holly hid a smile; *of course* his assistant was a Sofia. There was no way a man like Gennaro would have a Sally or a Jane as an assistant. 'But I can have her call you. If you leave me your number?' He smiled devilishly, and Holly was quite certain that if she left her number, Sofia wouldn't be the only person calling her. Nevertheless, she handed him her business card.

'My cell is on there, so is my email, in case Sofia finds anything.' She stressed the assistant's name, hoping Gennaro would take a hint.

He didn't.

'Fantastic, Holly O'Neill, and once we have some information for you, maybe I can take you to dinner? To talk about our ... er ... findings with this mystery bracelet.' As much as she hated the next words that came out of her mouth, she knew it was necessary in order to get Gennaro to ask his assistant to pull the event records, and not throw her card in the trash as soon as she walked out of the gallery.

'Sure, that would be lovely. As soon as Sofia calls me, we can figure something out.' She smiled coyly, hoping she wasn't overdoing it.

Flirting with Italian Stallions like Gennaro was not a speciality of hers, and frankly, since Nick, she felt long out of practice in the art of flirting. After all, she and Nick had stopped flirting a *long* time ago.

'Ah, *bella! Fantastico.* I know just the place too, you will see.'

'Sure, just don't forget to talk to Sofia about that, OK?' She pointed to her card. 'It's very important that I get this bracelet back to its owner. Remember, New York artists you might have exhibited work from, OK? Female New York artists.'

'You have my promise, Holly O'Neill.' He reached forward and took her hand, then bowed low to place a kiss on it. The door chimed behind them and Holly reclaimed her hand, placing the bracelet back in her handbag, making sure it was safe and secure. 'Until we meet again, *bella donna*. Ah! Now, you will excuse me: I have some business to attend to. Gregorio!' Gennaro cheered, looking over Holly's shoulder at whomever had just walked in the door of the gallery.

Holly turned abruptly and ran face first into the man she assumed was 'Gregorio'.

'God, sorry,' she said, rubbing her nose, which had connected squarely with the man's very hard shoulder.

'Oh, excuse me, sorry about that. Are you OK?' said Gregorio in a very non-Italian-sounding New York accent. His dark gaze met hers and he smiled kindly, brushing away a lock of hair that had fallen across his forehead.

Holly smiled absently. 'Yes, I'm sure my nose will recover,' she joked. 'Anyway, excuse me, I was just leaving.' She turned to Gennaro. 'Thanks again, Gennaro. I look forward to hearing from Sofia. You too.'

'*Ciao*, Holly,' Gennaro called over her shoulder. 'Until we meet again.'

Holly exited onto the street, just as her cell phone rang.

'Hello, is that Holly?' a crisp voice said on the other end of the line.

'Yes, it is.'

'It's Jessica, Margot Mead's assistant. I have some information for you regarding the jewelled egg charm. Is this a good time?'

Yes, Holly thought happily, right now is a great time.

15

'Gregorio! What's up, my man!' laughed Gennaro as he welcomed his friend to his gallery.

Greg smiled fondly at the nickname that Gennaro had given him, and continued to use, since they first met a year or so ago.

'Hanging in there, man. I hope I didn't interrupt anything,' he asked, looking back at the door through which the young woman had just exited. 'She ran off pretty quick.'

Gennaro waved a hand. 'Not a problem. It wasn't that big of a deal.' He took another glance at the business card he was holding and threw it on the reception desk. 'Pretty little thing, though.'

Greg shook his head; it was so like Gennaro to mix work and pleasure. He was the epitome of a ladies' man.

'Interested buyer?' Greg asked.

'No, no, nothing like that. Some great duck hunt that she was on, like a scavenger in my opinion. Looking to return a lost bracelet to some artist. She thinks the artist is a woman I might have done some business with.'

Greg laughed at Gennaro's use of English colloquialisms. 'It's a wild goose chase, not a great duck hunt.'

'Pardon?'

'Never mind.'

'Sadly, she wasn't interested in a thing on these walls. Can you believe that? Only interested in finding the owner of this bracelet that she had. I might have to give her a call to help her on her quest, you know? Maybe, just maybe, I can get her to dinner, and then maybe she will be interested in something else, yes?' Gennaro wiggled his eyebrows, leaving little wonder about what the 'something else' could be. 'Speaking of women, how is the beautiful Karen?'

'Actually, that's what I wanted to talk to you about.'

'Your lovely girlfriend? *Fantastico*, I'm all ears. I would be happy to take her off your hands.'

'No, not like that,' Greg laughed. 'I just popped by to let you know that I quit my job at the firm. I'm going full time with the photography. I'm hoping to sell some more of my work because I'm planning on proposing to Karen soon, and well, I feel I need to provide her with something that boosts her confidence in my decision, especially if she is going to say yes.'

Gennaro shook his head, seemingly not following how the two factors tied together.

'I don't understand. How does your proposal coincide with you selling your work?'

Greg quickly explained that he had sprung his decision to quit the firm and start up his own photography business on Karen. And that things had been a little tense around the old *casa* as of late.

'I am planning on proposing very soon, but I just want to prove to her that I'm already making a go of things with my new career.'

Gennaro frowned again. 'You know, my father, when he opened his store, he did so with very little money. He took a chance, but my mother always stood by him. To the very end she did.' Gennaro seemed to cringe when he saw Greg's face fall, and immediately realised his bad choice of words. 'Ah, buddy, I'm so sorry. I heard about your mother . . . I'm so sorry.'

Greg smiled sadly. 'Thanks. I won't deny it's been hard, but . . . I guess you just need to come up with coping mechanisms.'

'You Americans with your coping mechanisms,' Gennaro smiled. 'No, what I meant just then was that your parents had a wonderful love story. My parents had a wonderful love story. I hope that your love story with Karen isn't just based on some photographs.'

'I'm sure everything will be fine,' Greg replied, feeling a little uncomfortable. 'Anyway, I just wanted to find out if you were in the market for anything new?' He indicated the walls of the gallery.

Gennaro shrugged despondently. 'Ah, Gregorio, my friend, I'm not buying anything right now. In this economy, it's been slow, especially for the holidays. I have stockpiles of work in the backroom that I have yet to display.'

Greg sighed and looked around at the art that graced almost every surface of the gallery. 'Of course I understand. But, hey, thanks for hearing me out — and if you do need anything along those lines, keep me in mind, won't you?'

Gennaro seemed to be thinking. 'Well, I can't

promise anything, but why don't you email me some files and maybe we can do something together for the next gallery event in the New Year. Speaking of which, are you going to the benefit this year?'

He was referring to the annual New Year's Eve ball held in aid of St Jude's Children's Hospital, a big society event that Greg and his family usually supported with their attendance.

Greg sighed. He hadn't really thought about it. 'I'm not sure . . . Maybe. We've had the tickets for ages of course, so . . . I think it might feel odd going now, with everything. Will you be there?'

Gennaro nodded in confirmation. 'Yes, although I need to get a date for the night.'

Greg laughed. 'That's not like you. Less than a couple of weeks before an event and no date? You're slacking, man.'

'Please, you know me better than that,' Gennaro replied with a wink. 'I have a waiting list.' He looked towards the door. 'Although perhaps I will overlook the list and aim for someone new, like my pretty friend who just left.'

Greg sighed indulgently at his friend's antics, and felt grateful that he was no longer in the dating game. He knew Gennaro was telling the truth; the man regularly had several women hanging around, vying for his attention.

'Well, good luck with it anyway. And thanks again for agreeing to check out my work. But now I'd better get going; I'm doing a few bits and pieces for the *NYT* and I have to follow through. I hope you have a merry Christmas,

Gennaro.' He offered his hand and Gennaro took it, pulling him forward into a bear hug.

'You too, Gregorio. And good luck with Karen. She's a beautiful woman. And I'll bet she has been hinting about a ring for quite some time, eh?'

Greg shook his head. Actually Karen wasn't in the least bit pressurising in that regard. While she adored jewellery, she didn't get sappy about engagement rings, and he'd never once heard her use the words 'princess cut'.

'Really? Then she clearly isn't Italian,' Gennaro chuckled. 'Italian women like to know your intentions on date number one. No messing around wasting time, you know? That's why I adore Italian women, but I do not date them.' He smiled wickedly. 'At least, not after the first night.' He clapped Greg on the back. 'You are a lucky man to have such a level-headed woman.'

Greg smiled and said goodbye to his friend, but Gennaro's words had struck a chord.

It was true; Karen really wasn't the type of woman to buy pre-emptive bridal magazines or squeal over the news of a friend's engagement.

He thought about his mother, and how Cristina always rejoiced over weddings, baby showers and occasions like that. Sure, he understood that all women weren't the same, and he certainly wasn't trying to compare Karen to his mom, but he was struggling to remember if he had ever seen Karen show excitement over the life events of her friends. There was no denying his girlfriend had passion, of course, but the things she got excited about were often

207

holidays they were taking, or a deal she had just closed at work, or even her ability to score some in-demand purse at Louis Vuitton.

In any case, Greg hoped she'd be suitably passionate about how he was planning to propose. The idea had struck him out of the blue that morning, and the more he thought about it, the more he realised it was absolutely perfect for Karen.

Getting back on his bike, he made his way uptown to put the early stages of his plan in place.

A few minutes later, as he walked to the elevator in the *New York Times* building, he made eye contact with every single person and smiled. He'd have to start memorising faces and names soon.

When he got to Rob's office, his friend high-fived him before saying anything else.

'Way to go, man. Billy told me the good news. Lunch — and maybe with a celebratory beer?'

'Sounds good.'

'Have you got an assignment already?'

Greg nodded.

'Who's the writer?'

'Suzanne Lee.'

Rob made a face. 'OK, you'll need definitely a beer. She's a little . . . demanding.'

Greg laughed. 'Tell me about it.'

The two men strolled out of the office and out onto the street.

'Wanna go where all the *NYT* people go?' Rob asked.

'That would be cool,' he replied enthusiastically.

'Then go back inside and order out,' he joked, before leading Greg down the street to a diner where half the menu was in Russian.

Their elderly waitress took a long time to take their orders, but Rob and Greg didn't care; they were marvelling over the fact that after knowing each other for so long they would now be working for the same company.

'I can request you, you know,' Rob told him. 'So if things get light, let me know.'

Greg nodded, digging into a beet soup. It was stone cold and made absolutely no sense on such a frigid day. He had only ordered it because the old lady had barked, 'Beet soup?' at him and he had nodded, afraid to contradict her. He was hungry, but food was far from his mind.

The men ate in an enjoyable silence for a while, until Greg finally broke it when the beers arrived. 'I feel bad asking, seeing as you've already done so much, but do you think you could check something out for me?'

Rob nodded uncertainly and listened as Greg outlined his request.

When he'd finished, his friend looked at him as if he was crazy. 'You're sure about this?'

Greg stiffened. 'What — the proposal or the favour?'

'Well . . . the favour of course. I've got to tell you, Christmas morning could be a little tricky, but I'll certainly ask. Will's a buddy — he might OK it.'

'Thanks, man. I owe you a lot.'

'You sure do.' Rob took a swig of his beer. 'So you really think Karen's the one?'

'I know it.'

'How is she feeling about the big lifestyle change?' he asked carefully. 'Shit-hot broker to lowly shutterbug?'

Greg let out a breath. 'It's been hard on her, I know that. But we'll get through it. There are worse things,' he added, thinking of what his poor dad had been dealing with.

Definitely worse things.

16

Outside the gallery, Holly fumbled with her phone for a moment as she juggled her handbag. She pulled her coat tighter around her as a brisk arctic blast of air hit her in the face.

'I'm sorry, Jessica, I'm here. Sorry, struggling a bit. This weather is pretty rough today.' Holly smiled into the phone, just as another torrent of wind flung a strand of hair in her mouth. 'Eek, OK, out of the wind now.' She moved into a doorway that provided some level of shelter.

'No problem,' Margot Mead's assistant said. 'I've been in the penthouse since six a.m. Most times I can barely remember what sunlight is.'

Holly bit her lip, thinking that working for a woman like that was probably no easy task. She was already picturing Jessica as one of those twenty-two-year-olds who wore black from head to toe, invested in spray tans and had bleached-blonde hair.

She probably bought expensive Christian Louboutin heels with her below-average pay-cheque, and chose to eat ramen noodles in her tiny apartment. All just so she could keep up with appearances. But then again, that was the life of a young, trendy New Yorker who was probably desperate to break into the upper echelons of the city.

'Well, I hope you get out soon. The winter weather is rather lovely, so long as the wind doesn't blow you over. Days like today remind me of a snow globe. From the outside everything looks fine, then you shake it and it all gets jumbled up.'

There was silence on the other end of the line, as if Jessica was thinking about the analogy. When she finally answered, she said, 'Huh, I guess I'm more of a beach girl.'

Of course she is, Holly thought with a smile. Quickly, she changed the subject.

'So you were calling about the egg charm. What can you tell me?'

'Well, there's good news and bad news. The good news is when you sent over the photograph, I immediately recognised the charm as something that was earmarked as a prize for one of our bigger benefits. We kept records of the purchase, but unfortunately the bad news is, we don't keep records as to who might have won it.'

'Oh, right,' Holly said glumly, her mind racing to consider other options. 'So, there is no record at all of the winner?'

'Nothing,' answered Jessica, reconfirming her own statement.

A thought occurred to her. 'You said it was used at a benefit?'

'Yes, as I said, Ms Mead is involved with many charities.'

'Great. So what was the purpose of this particular benefit — I mean, what charity was it in aid of?' She was wondering again about the pink ribbon charm.

'I'm not sure about that — we're involved with lots of big events. It was bought in autumn last year, so it could have been one of many. There was a breast cancer event that would have been in October . . . ' Holly heard a shuffle of paper and a pause. 'Then there was the environmental 'thing' in November, and then the children's benefit in December.'

Holly thought quickly and some type of recognition of *something* played around the edges of her brain. She extracted the bracelet from her handbag and shuffled quickly through the charms, wondering if there was something that could be related to the environment — the one that looked like a flower, perhaps? The pink ribbon charm could also hypothetically connect the owner to the breast cancer benefit in October.

'Could you by chance get me a list of the people who were at those events?' Holly asked, thinking that if the gallery owner sent her the freelancer information in the meantime, she might be able to cross-reference this with the names of the people attending Margot Mead's benefits.

Once again she heard Jessica sigh. Clearly this sort of task was outside her pay grade.

'I don't know. I mean, I have a *ton* to do and with Christmas in a few days, I just don't know if I can pull this sort of information. I have to finish up all Ms Mead's shopping, and I'm still arranging for couriers for some of these other gifts for her friends, and then I am trying to get New Year's Eve finalised. I don't know when I am going to do my *own* Christmas shopping, and I have my parents coming to town tomorrow for the holidays. As it is, I'll be lucky if I get to spend five minutes with them, let alone have any time off. Ms Mead already said how she was going to need me to deliver something on Christmas Eve, and I just know that this is going to carry over on to Christmas itself and, well, . . . ' Jessica stopped talking and Holly could practically feel the stress coming from the other end of the line. She couldn't help but feel sorry for her; Holly was sure it was hard to do other people's bidding all day, especially when it left you no time to do your own.

An idea popped into Holly's head, and she prayed that this level of bribery would work.

'Jessica, you don't know how much this would mean to me if you could pull those lists for me. I know it is just a few days before Christmas, and I know just how hard you must work. If there is any way that you can get the names of the people who attended the benefits, and possibly email them to me, I would truly appreciate it. And just to show my gratitude, if you wanted to swing by the store I work at sometime, maybe when you are out running some errands, I would be happy to let you use my staff discount on anything you might like. We have some really fantastic party dresses in stock right now, and you sound like the type of girl who probably has big plans for New Year's Eve.'

There was a pause, and Holly held her breath.

'I have to work New Year's Eve,' Jessica said tartly. 'Like I said, there's a benefit. I mean, I love my job, but I'm still *working*.'

Holly couldn't help but think that while it

might be glamorous to be an attendee at some of these benefits, it was probably a different story when you were handling guest lists and juggling the desires of your employer.

'I see,' Holly said, trying to figure out how she could spin this. 'Well, I bet you still need a new dress for it, though? I'd imagine dealing with wardrobe changes for all of Ms Mead's events can get expensive. I bet it also gets tiresome when you have to wear the same dress over and over . . . '

Holly heard Jessica take a sharp breath on the other end of the line and knew she had struck a nerve. No would-be Manhattan fashionista would deign to be seen in the same ensemble multiple times, even if it was for an event associated with work.

'So maybe you could come into the store, pick something out and oh, I don't know, wow your employer and her friends at this benefit? We have some divine flapper dresses, or some really great gowns from the fifties. That era is so hot at the moment. In fact, we have something very similar to what Reese Witherspoon wore at the *In Style* awards last week.'

'Really?' Jessica squeaked. 'I love Reese. Anyway, OK, fine. I'll try and pull those lists for you. And I will stop by, maybe tomorrow or the next day. Will you be at the store?'

'Of course.'

'Fantastic. Maybe I owe myself a reward. Fat chance of getting one from her,' she added, referring to her errant boss. 'I'll try to pull up the lists and bring them with me. Is that cool?'

Holly grinned. 'Jessica, that is the coolest thing I have heard all day.'

★　★　★

Later that evening, she filled Danny in on the progress that she had made that day. She toyed with her own bracelet, finally taking it off and laying it next to the mystery one. She had far fewer charms than the other, which led her to suspect that perhaps the bracelet belonged to an older woman.

So many charms from so many different stages of life — the flower, horseshoe, handbag, Tiffany key, *corno*, the wedding bells, Eiffel Tower, baby carriage, a carousel . . . all milestones, important moments in someone's life.

Looking at the two bracelets side by side, Holly was struck by how much more living she had to do.

'So the guy from the gallery says the horn charm is from Italy?' Danny was saying. 'So now you know that this person was in Italy. On vacation or something.'

'I would think so.' Holly pulled her son close. 'I bet it's a magical place, don't you?' she said dreamily. 'I've always wanted to go to Italy, Florence especially. It seems awfully romantic. Think of all that history, all that art. It gives me goose bumps to think about the people through the ages who must have walked those streets.'

He looked at her. 'Why haven't you ever gone?'

Holly smiled, considered the innocence of

216

childhood, of being Danny's age. He still existed in a world where responsibilities, work and commitments were a far-off thing, and while Holly was a firm believer in whimsy, she also knew that exotic vacations became less important (or indeed realistic) when you had bills to pay, children to take care of and a job to attend to. But she still knew it was important to keep such mystique open to him.

'Oh, I don't know, Danny. I guess I need to win the lottery. Or put you out to work.' She smiled cheerily, but tilted her head in question when a frown appeared on his face. 'What's that look for?'

'Mom, maybe if you had someone else around, like my dad or something, then maybe you could travel, because it wouldn't be just you.'

Holly felt a familiar trepidation at this line of conversation.

'Now, Danny, even families who have two parents around can't always afford to take extravagant vacations. You shouldn't think that way.'

He shook his head and Holly could see that they were rounding to the familiar discussion of how a dad around here might make things easier. Her mind raced, trying to think of a way to avoid it.

'Anyway, who needs a vacation when we've got so much going on these days? Our first Christmas dinner at home: that's a big deal. Maybe tomorrow after school, we can go out and pick up a Christmas tree?' she suggested.

'Yeah, that would be cool!'

Holly exhaled, relieved. Problem temporarily averted. She held up the bracelet and jangled it. 'And of course, in the meantime, we still have this great big mystery to solve.'

17

An oak door loomed in front of me, and it was with excitement and trepidation that I looked to my husband as he placed a hand on my lower back to guide me forward.

'Are you ready?'

I nodded my head, feeling slightly dazed. Were we really considering this?

'Yes, I think so.'

He smiled happily and propelled me through the open door. I must be honest — the moment that I stepped over the threshold, I felt as if I was walking on air.

'Oh my God, look at this place!' I exclaimed, and he shot me a look that said, 'Remember what I said? Don't get overly excited or we will lose our ability to negotiate.' But I couldn't help it. This place was . . . amazing. It was a Classic Six penthouse, one of the six-room pre-war apartments that are much sought-after in Manhattan — and already I could feel the history from each of those rooms.

I put my hand on the wall, stroking the crown moulding that ran down the middle of the hallway, then entered the living room — or maybe this might be called a 'sitting room', a place where society types ended up greeting and receiving guests. I had to stifle a giggle. Right now I 'received guests' in a cramped living room that was the size of the foyer in this place.

My daydream was interrupted as the real-estate agent, Theodore, turned round to face us. I wondered if he ever went by the name Ted.

Probably not in this part of town, I decided.

'And this is the sitting room,' he confirmed. 'This room was actually just redone by the previous owner. The interior is attributed to Donghia Associates, under the direction of the extraordinary Angelo Donghia.'

I nodded knowingly, even though I had no idea who he was talking about.

'That's fantastic,' I said somewhat vaguely, looking around at the ornate woodwork. Obviously, Ted saw through my bluff, because he felt the need to clarify just who Angelo Donghia was.

'Mr Donghia is a visionary. He designed the Opera Club at the Metropolitan Opera House at Lincoln Center, which met with superb acclaim.'

I had never been to either, but I smiled just the same. I knew he wanted me to feel like some sort of hick, but to be honest, I didn't know anything about opera, and I certainly wasn't going to pretend that I did. However, I was far too used to New York snobbery to be upset by this guy. It took a lot more to shake me up.

I might want this apartment with every bone in my body, but only because it was beautiful and the house of my dreams. Social climber, I was not.

'Can we see more?' I asked, wanting to get past the sitting room and on to the rest of the place.

'Of course,' he said. I knew he was holding

back a sneer. I'm not sure if he was put off by our age, still being relatively young, or if he was just upset that he pegged me as someone who might not be as cultured as his other clients.

Whatever it was, it was water off a duck's back.

Ted led us on and I had to do my best not to start skipping. Every room we entered was even more beautiful than the one before, and in my mind, I'd already started decorating.

I could envision that green velvet settee that I spied at an antique shop in the West Side right over in that corner, next to the fireplace. And I had this great idea about a brass headboard that I saw just last week at Bloomingdale's for the spare guestroom. I knew it would be a perfect fit.

And then there was the fact that there was also this other room, a space that looked out onto Central Park, where lofty clouds seemed to float by and the sunshine gleamed into the room happily. Currently painted in a neutral ivory colour, it would be a perfect room for a baby's nursery.

I found myself separated from the others and walked across the hardwood floors, the heels of my slouched boots clicking merrily and echoing across the empty rooms.

I closed my eyes for a moment and allowed myself to feel the air move around me. This was a very old and classic building, and had probably seen many tenants in its lifetime.

It had been a home several times over, and had a history, had probably known its share of happy times, as well as sad.

The people who had lived within these walls had loved and lost, laughed and cried, been born and possibly also died. And right now, all of them were talking to me.

They were telling me this is where I would live my life, where my marriage would bloom and blossom, where our children would be born, where we would experience joy as well as sorrow. They told me that all of those things, those experiences, would colour my life.

At that moment, I knew. We had come home.

I heard footsteps behind me and turned round quickly. There stood my husband with a small smile on his face. I opened my mouth to speak and he put a finger over my lips.

'You don't have to say a word, your face says it all. This is it, isn't it?' he whispered.

I nodded my head.

Pulling me close, he kissed me and I closed my eyes. At that moment, I saw the years stretching out before us. I imagined what our life would be like here. I dreamed about the memories we would make and I honestly felt like crying with happiness. This was all too good to be true. Someone needed to pinch me, because I had to be dreaming.

And well . . . Ted did that for me. Not pinched me exactly, but he 'ahemmed' loudly enough to indicate that he had walked into the room and was slightly uncomfortable with our public display of affection. I quickly opened my eyes and grinned.

'You're absolutely sure?'

I nodded again. 'Outside of marrying you, I have never been so sure about anything in my entire life.'

'OK, then'. He stepped away from me and clapped his hands together once, his indicator that now it was time to do business.

Moments later I was left alone as the two men went to make use of the kitchen counters to discuss offers. When I was finally by myself, I did a quick little jig and tapped my heels in a makeshift sort of dance on the wood floors. I opened the patio doors and walked out onto a private terrace that was attached to the space. Oh my God! We were going to have a private terrace.

Resting my arms on the thick decorative stonework that lined the terrace and protected me from falling, I let the wind whip my hair around my face as I thought about everything that had led us to this point in our lives.

We were so lucky, to even be able to consider living in a place like this. But then again, I have to admit that my husband was also a talented and forward-thinking businessman. I'd always known he was going places, and apparently so did his boss, seeing that he was promoted to a management position after only two years with the firm.

There was no denying that I was wildly proud of him. I couldn't believe that he had already accomplished so much. How many couples at this stage in their lives could afford to live in a Classic Six? I certainly didn't know of many.

Of course, I was nervous too. We were making

a big investment. But it was a good investment too. The kind that you lived your life in, a permanent sort of thing, not like buying clothes or shoes or other frivolous things that didn't mean much, not in the scheme of things.

Yes, I loved buying clothes and shoes as much as the next girl, but this was real estate and, truth be told, I knew it was the type of investment that would shape our lives. Hopefully for the better.

I had never known a pair of shoes, or a jacket or piece of jewellery, to ever shape my life.

Although that wasn't strictly true, I realised, as my charm bracelet twinkled in the sunlight. Confining one's life to a small number of events is always difficult, but as with the bracelet, there was always room to add more. And this journey was far from over.

★ ★ ★

'So it's official, the Classic Six is ours!' my beloved husband informed me a few days later.

'Are you serious? They accepted our offer? Oh my God, oh my God! When can we move in? Goodness, there's so much to do and plan . . .'

We were going to be homeowners. Spectacular homeowners!

'Shh, soon, soon. The closing will be handled by the lawyers. I'm sure that we can be in by the end of the month.'

I started to do calculations. That was three and a half weeks' time. Suddenly, my cramped living room threatened to close in on me and I pictured the space that we would be able to grow into, instead of continually tripping over ourselves trying to manage living life in a veritable shoebox. I had a longing to move tomorrow.

'OK,' I said, thinking hard. 'Well, I wish we could move sooner, but I suppose there's a lot to do in three weeks.' I gave him another kiss and extricated myself from his embrace, looking for a pen and paper. 'I need to start making lists. And, you know, I think that this occasion serves for it, so I am going to order these divine change of address cards that I saw in a stationery store over on Lexington to send out to our friends and whatnot. I also think we will have to throw a housewarming party. Now that we are going to have the space, I think it will be so fun to be able to entertain and . . .

' . . . What?' I asked, looking up at my husband, who stood there smiling.

'Do you know you're beautiful when you are all wound up?'

I swatted at him with the pad of paper I had found on the end table. 'Oh hush. I'm a planner, you know that.'

'Yes, you are. But I think you are forgetting one important element. Something that needs to be attended to before anything else.'

I thought briefly. Organise movers, start thinking about furniture, change of address cards, housewarming party — what was I missing?

Seeing the puzzled expression on my face, he put his hand in his pocket. When he pulled his hand out, I saw he had something in his palm.

'You are forgetting about this,' he said, displaying a small charm. 'Isn't it how we always mark an occasion?'

I squealed with delight as I took in the small piece of jewellery. It was a skyscraper. No, actually it was a high-rise building. Looking closer, I realised that in fact it was *the* high-rise building, the one that housed our new Classic Six apartment.

'Oh my God, look at this. Is this really our building? A model of the building we are moving into? How in the world . . . ?'

'I had it made. After we made the offer, I knew that you would need a charm to mark this step in our lives. And I thought about how to represent it. I didn't want to buy a house charm, because, well, our place isn't a traditional house. And I found all these other skyscraper-like charms, but they weren't right either. So I decided to take a picture of our building to a jeweller on Seventh and have a charm made. That way, it would be extra-special. Do you like it?'

I looked at the intricate design on the charm and my heart swelled. This was just so special, and of course he was right, our place wasn't a normal house, and how do you really represent an apartment, even if it is a Classic Six? The picture he'd taken to the jeweller must have been a good one, because this was the work of a true artist.

'Like it? I love it. It's perfect.'

I clasped the charm tightly in my closed palm and wrapped my arms around my husband, getting up on my tiptoes to kiss his lips. I thought of the weeks ahead of me, and all that I knew I would have to do before moving, but at the top of my to-do list would be to get this charm added to my bracelet.

This made it official. We were moving in our new home. The charm in my hand served to acknowledge this landmark occasion that would take us into the next chapter of our lives. Who knew what the future held? All I knew was that right then, the present was perfect.

18

The following evening, as promised, Holly and Danny went on the hunt for their first proper Christmas tree.

After work, she picked him up from school and they scanned the nearby streets for Christmas-tree vendors close to home.

'There's one,' Danny called out, pulling Holly in the direction of one of the bodegas renting out their sidewalk space to a tree vendor.

'They look like they have plenty, honey — slow down.'

Holly released his hand and let him spin away from her. She smiled as he raced ahead.

He was literally jumping up and down in front of a huge spruce tree when she finally made it up the block after him.

'This is it, Mom. This is the one!' he said excitedly, pointing at it.

She shook her head. 'Danny, it must be seven feet tall. How big do you think the apartment is, let alone how wide . . . ?'

Suddenly, a young man appeared from the depth of the trees. He was bundled up from head to toe in warm clothes so that only his frosted-up glasses showed.

'Do you want me to pull it out for you, ma'am?' he asked.

'Yes!' said Danny. 'Yes, yes, yes!'

Before Holly could protest, the man had

228

pulled the tree off the wooden bar it was leaning on and was shaking it out for them to inspect.

'Perfect,' Danny proclaimed.

'Too tall,' she insisted.

'I can cut her down a bit for you and trim the top?' the man asked hopefully.

Danny turned to her with pleading eyes. Holly looked from the tree to her son then back to the tree again.

'Fine,' she sighed, unable to resist that look. 'Can you whittle it down at least a foot?' she asked the vendor. He nodded and disappeared with the tree; they heard the saw start as he went to work.

Danny was so excited he was fit to burst. 'Ornaments, Mom, what about ornaments?' he asked.

Holly hadn't even thought of that; they really didn't have any. Well, they had a few, to hang on a garland, ones that Danny made at school.

'I guess we could stop in on Frank and see if he has any?' she suggested. Encore really was more of a thrift store than a clothing store anyway, despite the spin Frank tried to put on it.

Danny nodded enthusiastically and Holly waited for the young man to reappear with the shortened-down tree. When he did so, the spruce did indeed look much more manageable and Holly was relieved. She paid for it and he agreed to hold it while they went round the corner to find ornaments.

She and Danny made the short walk over to Encore. Frank was rearranging some clothing racks and glaring at a pair of teenage girls who seemed more interested in trying on old clothes and laughing at each other than actually buying them.

'Paying customers, I hope?' he announced pointedly as Holly and Danny approached him. The girls ignored him and continued to pull things off the rack.

Holly realised she would have to rescue him. She went up to one of the girls and studied the leather jacket she was trying on.

'Excuse me. Are you going to buy that?' The girl looked at Holly and shrugged noncommittally. 'Because I would really like to see it.'

'Sure,' the girl said, and shrugged the jacket off.

Holly made a big show of going over it in every way, turning it inside out and examining the label up close. She even pretended to examine the buttons on the sleeves. Then she turned her back to Frank and said to the girls in a loud whisper, 'Can he see me?'

The girls shook their head, as Frank was engrossed in conversation with Danny. Still, their interest in what she was doing was piqued.

'Can you believe he only wants twenty-five dollars for this? Man, oh, man . . . '

'What do you mean?' the girl Holly had taken the jacket from asked a little defensively.

'Well, you do know Joan Jett . . . ? Oh, never mind,' she said quickly and began walking away with the jacket as if about to buy it.

'Wait a minute, I was trying that on . . . ' The girl held out her hand, demanding the jacket back.

Holly held on to it for a moment, as if unsure of what to do.

The other girl chimed in, 'Lady, my friend was trying that jacket on, do you mind?' She looked as if she were trying to get eye contact with Frank, who really was ignoring them now.

Holly begrudgingly handed the jacket over. 'Well, I just hope you know what you have there.'

The girl snatched it from her. 'I certainly do!' she announced, marching up to the counter to buy it.

Holly watched the two girls waltz out of the store and turned to Frank, who was smiling behind the cash register.

'I really wish you would come and work for me, Holly . . . '

She smiled guiltily. 'Where'd Danny go?'

'Back section, something about Christmas-tree decorations? I think there are a few in the boxes back there.'

At the rear of the store, Holly found Danny standing amid boxes Frank apparently never bothered to unpack, but had simply arranged on long buffet tables, rummage-sale style.

'Oh, brother . . . '

'Plus everything smells like mothballs,' Danny said dejectedly.

'No worries, we'll search through it for a few minutes and if we don't find anything, we'll just go to Rite Aid and stock up on cheesy plastic stuff, OK?'

Danny nodded and the two of them dived in, searching through the boxes for anything that might work on their newly bought tree.

After a few minutes Holly called out, 'Bingo.'

'What? What did you find!' Danny crossed to her side of the table excitedly.

She'd salvaged two faded boxes with twelve ornaments in each, the old-fashioned kind made with mercury glass. The colours were faded, but they were charming, in various shapes of Santa, angels and silver bells.

'Perfect,' Danny grinned.

Danny sought out an old tree stand but when they brought everything to the front towards the register, Frank waved them right out of the door. 'Go ahead, you got me a sale. Merry Christmas and whatnot . . . '

Bidding him a grateful goodbye, they made their way back to the almost frozen tree vendor, who handed over their tree.

'How the heck are we supposed to get this thing home?' Holly asked, daunted by the shortened but still disarmingly large spruce. She handed the boxes of ornaments to Danny. 'OK, you take these and I'll drag it,' she said, tossing the tree to the ground so she could get a grip on its trunk.

Danny watched her anxiously, as if she were about to pick up a human body.

She managed to get her hands around the trunk, and to her relief it was not that heavy, regardless of the look of it. She started to drag it down the street, with Danny giving directions.

Reaching the walk-up, she handed the keys to Danny to get them into the lobby, and hauled the tree through the slender double doors, miraculously not breaking any branches. Finally

232

making it to the apartment, she shoved the tree into the living room, relieved.

They decided to set it up across from the couch, next to the little TV.

The two of them shoved the trunk into the old metal stand, and Holly held the branches straight as Danny screwed the anchors in. When he was finished, they stepped back to take a look at it.

'It's big,' Holly said.

'Now, we have to water it, to make sure it doesn't dry out.' Danny bounded off to the kitchen to fill a cup with water.

'How do you know so much?' she asked.

'Well, my friends have Christmas trees and everything,' he answered, getting on his knees to water the tree.

'Oh, of course,' Holly replied, watching him carefully. Did he take everything in like that? Every detail when he went over to a friend's house? She hadn't really thought about it before, that he was getting to the age where he might very well notice domestic issues. Like if someone's apartment was clean or dirty, if they watered their Christmas tree — if there was a father in the home.

Holly bit her lip; she was not going to obsess over this. She wasn't the only single mom among Danny's peers, but she knew she was certainly in the minority. Joey, his best friend, came from a traditional home and a large family, and lived in a huge apartment with a live-in housekeeper. His mom, Rita, was always very kind to Holly, often pressing her to come over and have a cup of coffee, a cup of tea, a glass of wine or something.

But Holly was always too busy. She had to work, and when she wasn't working, she wanted to have that free time with Danny. Maybe she would take Rita up on that cup of coffee sometime.

Holly wondered what else he saw at his friends' houses and it broke her heart. A dad, a big apartment, vacations, Xboxes and iPads . . . Holly sighed. They would just have to make their own memories this year, so what if they were a bit different from the mainstream? So they got their ornaments out of an abandoned box in the back of a thrift store . . . It would build character and tolerance and a real appreciation for what they could afford.

Danny had finished watering the tree and sat back next to his mother on the couch.

'We need lights,' he said matter-of-factly.

Damn, Holly had forgotten about that. Where was she going to get fairy lights at this hour? Then she had a brainwave.

'Tell you what — we'll take them off the fire escape.' They had a whole string of fairy lights they hung on the fire escape every year to make it festive. She would simply crawl out there and get them.

'But when, Mom?' her son asked, and she knew he was trying his best not to sound impatient.

She grinned, getting up from the couch and crossing the small room to her bedroom area. She pulled the window open and the cold air came rushing in.

'I'll make you some tea!' Danny cried, and ran into the kitchen, as if she were about to embark on a major expedition.

Holly crouched on the fire escape, unwinding the lights carefully with freezing fingers. 'Oh, the things we do for Christmas . . . ' she grumbled good-naturedly.

Once the fairy lights were unwound, she hopped back inside. Danny met her with hot tea. She handed him the lights and took the warm mug, basking in the steam.

Holly nodded. 'Go ahead, you do it — you don't need me for this bit.'

His eyes brightened as he immediately began to navigate the tree with the string of lights, trying to figure out how they would look best. When he was finished, he shut off the main light, and he and Holly sat on the couch and stared transfixed at their newly decorated tree.

'Why haven't we ever had a tree before?' Danny asked, his youthful face illuminated by the lights.

Holly took a sip of her tea and thought about it. The truth was, it had always seemed like a man's job. Her father had done it at home. When she left Nick, she hadn't much felt like celebrating Christmas anyway. Then after Danny was born, her mom had swooped in and they were always invited to Queens for holidays.

'I don't know,' she answered. 'That's a good question.'

'Can we do this every year?' he asked hopefully. 'Whether we go to Nana's or not?'

'Yes,' said Holly firmly, 'we can. Absolutely. I

think it's your best idea yet.'

Danny snuggled close to her on the couch, and the two of them sat there, happy in the glow of the lights, and each other's company.

'Next step, a puppy,' he grinned, and Holly nudged him playfully with her elbow.

19

The following morning began with Holly and Danny walking briskly to his school. Well, Holly was walking briskly; Danny was lagging behind her. She guessed that most kids got that way around this time of year: they knew time off was on the horizon and simply couldn't bring themselves to bear another day of school.

'Come on, Danny, you'll be late and I am not writing you an excuse note.' She ploughed ahead without turning round; she was running late — again — so he would just have to keep up. She heard him grumbling a bit behind her, but when they approached the entrance to the school, he suddenly let out a whoop.

'Dad?'

Holly felt all the blood rush to her face. There was Nick, bundled up in a puffy coat from North Face, sitting on the steps of a building next to the school, a cigarette dangling from his lips.

Her heart pounding, she let Danny run ahead of her to give his dad a hug. Nick looked sheepishly at her over Danny's head, which was now buried in the puffy coat.

'Really, Nick, smoking? In front of an elementary school?' Holly was not going to waste her time with formal hellos.

'Oh sorry, I forgot.' He stubbed out the cigarette and gave her the 'are you happy now?' look that she hated. It always made her feel like a nagging harpie.

'So, what brings you here?' she asked, her tone even.

'Came to see my son, of course. Hey, buddy!' Nick punched Danny in the shoulder, who beamed widely. He was trying not to, but couldn't help it. Holly sighed. Of course he was happy to see his dad; he always was. Problem was, of course he'd be angry with his dad later when Nick let him down again.

'Well, he's got to go in now — the bell rang, he'll be late.' Holly pointed at the lines of children filing into the school building.

'Aw, does he have to go today? I have a day off . . . ' Nick watched her face darken and added quickly, 'I know, I know, I should have called, I should have, but it was kind of a last-minute thing.'

Danny looked hopefully at his mother.

'No way, absolutely not. He has tests this week, he can't make them up, he's got to go.' She softened as she looked down at Danny. 'Sorry, honey, but you know you've got to go.'

Nick scratched his head. 'OK, how about after? Can I pick him up after class?' His voice was getting a little tense.

'Fine,' she capitulated, and Danny jumped up and down, grinning.

'Thanks, Mom!' He gave her a kiss, and punched his dad on the arm. 'See you later. Three o'clock OK?'

Nick nodded and Danny sped down the street, just making it to the door as it started to close.

Holly studied Nick, trying to figure out where

this newfound interest in Danny had come from all of a sudden.

'What's going on, Nick?'

'Nothing, just wanted to see Danny — you know, with the holidays and all.'

'You know, to a ten-year-old, a birthday is considered a holiday,' she replied icily.

'Right, you're still mad about that, huh?'

'I'm not mad for me; I'm *sad* for Danny.' Holly started to walk away from him but then changed her mind. 'And I'm sad for you too, Nick. You have no idea how you are going to be paying for this later, when he gets older and starts putting it all together.'

'What? That I'm a shitty father?'

Holly pursed her lips and said nothing.

'OK, I admit it, I'm not the best dad in the world, but I'm gonna try a little harder from now on. Is that OK with you?'

'Why? Why now, I mean?' Holly knew him well enough to guess she was not getting the whole story.

'Diana's pregnant.'

She almost felt like laughing at the absurdity of it all. That he was acting as if she actually knew who Diana was, or that he showed up unannounced — not to mention the fact that he was having another kid, which would be bound to have a negative effect on Danny.

Nick rubbed his eyes and Holly could tell he was itching for a cigarette. Against her better judgement she felt a little sorry for him. He had at least admitted he was not a good father.

'Do you want to walk with me to work and we

can talk on the way? I'm going to be late otherwise.'

'Sure, yeah.' Nick immediately pulled out a cigarette, as she had known he would, and they started walking back up the avenue together. She was about half an inch taller than him in her heels and felt very much like the together, confident woman she had strived so hard to become after leaving him. But instead of feeling powerful over him, now she just found herself feeling sorry for him.

'So Diana . . . that's your girlfriend I take it?'

He grimaced. 'I didn't tell you about her?'

'No, Nick, you didn't, and you probably didn't tell Danny either,' she chided.

'Right, I should do that.' He puffed nervously on his cigarette. 'Anyway, she's pregnant, and she says unless I can prove to her that I can be a better father to Danny, she wants nothing to do with me.'

Holly felt nauseous. So now Danny was being used so Nick could hang on to his latest girlfriend?

'Right, well, being a better father should probably be done for Danny's sake before anyone else.'

'Yeah, that's what our counsellor said too.'

Holly stopped in the middle of the sidewalk. 'You're seeing a counsellor?'

'Yeah, can you believe it? She's really got me, this girl.' He shook his head. 'Says there's a lot of work to be done . . . ' He trailed off and stared at Holly. 'What?'

She started walking again. 'Nothing, Nick, nothing at all.'

'So, I thought maybe I could try and be more regular in Danny's life, like a real dad would.'

Holly didn't look at him, but let all the thoughts

240

and emotions crowd her brain and her heart. It was great that Nick was in counselling, and kudos to this Diana person for getting him there. But telling Danny he was going to have a little brother or sister? Letting Nick into his life again after he'd screwed up so many times? She didn't realise it but she was instinctively shaking her head.

'Oh, come on, Holly, don't be that way, please? I know the odds aren't good with me, but things are different now . . . ' he trailed. 'I swear I'll do better by Danny from now on. I mean it. Come on, take a chance, roll the dice.'

Holly took a deep breath. They were nearing the store by now. 'OK, but I'll still have Kate pick up Danny today. You can take him for pizza or whatever, but she'll be there too, OK?'

'Fine, whatever.' Nick nodded at her and walked away.

She could tell by his tone that he was annoyed that he was going to be chaperoned later, but what did he expect? He shows up out of the blue and thinks he's going to take over? What if he forgot to pick Danny up? God forbid . . . Holly shook her head. Lord only knew what can of worms this was going to open. She pulled out her phone before going in the store to text Kate and let her know that Nick would be there later.

Roll the dice, he'd said.

Holly sighed, looking down at the pair of silver dice on her charm bracelet. She'd heard that one before . . .

★ ★ ★

Nick raised the taster of sangiovese to his lips and took a small sip. He swirled it in his mouth for a moment and then looked to the sommelier and nodded.

'It's pretty good.'

The sommelier turned to Holly, poured her a glass before filling Nick's, then placed the bottle on the table and took his leave.

'So what do you think, babe? Isn't this spectacular or what?'

Holly smiled nervously. This whole experience was indeed spectacular, but she couldn't help but feel slightly out of her element. This was her first time in Vegas and she had to admit everything truly was larger than life. They were here on a 'work retreat' or, at least, that's what Nick and his partners were calling it. In truth, little or no work was being done, and Holly knew that the term was only being loosely batted about so they could write the entire trip off. Nick said that jaunts like this were needed so as to keep morale up, keep the motivation going, but Holly couldn't help but view it as excess.

Especially the amount of money that Nick was spending.

Yes, the Internet start-up he was working for was absolutely booming, and like Nick said, he deserved to not only work hard, but play hard too. And Holly agreed, to a point. However, she couldn't get over her discomfort at some of the lavishness of it all.

Then again, maybe she should just go with the

flow and have some fun.

She smiled and looked across the table at the man she'd now been seeing for just over a year. Ever since their first date, they had really clicked. There was no denying he treated her well, and he had told her openly that he was head over heels in love with her.

'It is spectacular, Nick, all of it. I'm very happy for you.'

He reached across the table and took Holly's hand in his. 'Happy for *us*, babe, happy for us. This is about you and me. And it's going to impact our future. For ever. Don't forget that.'

Holly had never known a man who talked about 'the future' as much as Nick did. Or rather, talked about a future with Holly, specifically. She had to admit that she still got goose bumps every time he alluded to the idea that they were in it together, for the long haul.

'I know, Nick, it's all a lot to get used to. I have to be honest, I've never drunk wine from a bottle that costs over two hundred dollars before,' she said, and then bit her lip, raising a hand to tug at the top of the strapless Versace that Nick had insisted on buying earlier. Holly had planned on wearing the pretty 1920s flapper dress she had packed, but he'd insisted she was deserving of something new, rather than something that had already been worn by 'someone else'.

Actually, Holly thought the vintage dress to be quite lovely, but she went along with the Versace even though the price tag made her feel slightly nauseous; now she was just terrified of spilling something on it.

'Babe, don't fidget, you look beautiful,' Nick reassured her, before taking another drink and refilling his glass.

Holly put her hands in her lap and sat up a little straighter.

'I'm sorry, Nick, I didn't mean to fidget. This all is really wonderful. I suppose maybe I'm just a little nervous.'

'Well, let me be the first to tell you that you look ravishing when you're nervous. So, what do you think of the hotel?'

They were staying at the Mandalay Bay, one of the hottest hotels on the Strip, and Holly was still marvelling over the size of their suite. 'It's beautiful of course. And our suite . . . well, I've never been in a hotel room so big,' Holly joked. 'I think I could probably fit my apartment in it several times. So what's planned for tonight after dinner? There are several shows that look really great,' she continued, as their appetisers arrived. She looked at Nick's choice of escargots and cringed. She didn't consider herself a picky eater, but at the end of the day, these were snails.

Nick shrugged and used the tiny seafood fork to pop a snail into his mouth. 'I just figured that we would see how the night goes. Pete and Mack were talking about hitting up the craps table, and maybe checking out this club that just opened up — I think it was at MGM.'

Holly nodded and fought back a grimace. She loved to dance as much as the next girl, but that's exactly what they had done last night. Plus, though she liked the others, she honestly thought that maybe she and Nick could have a night alone, without Pete and Mack and their respective girlfriends.

'Not sure I'm up for that tonight. Maybe you and I could do something alone?'

Nick's face fell. 'So you just want to go back to the room after dinner?'

Holly shook her head. 'No, no, nothing like that. I'm not a stick-in-the-mud. I just thought that maybe tonight could be about us, you and me. Maybe we can find a nice cocktail lounge, listen to some music, drink some champagne and then take advantage of that Jacuzzi in our suite.'

Nick's face lit up and he rose ever so briefly from his chair and leaned across the table to kiss her. 'You know what? That sounds ideal. I'll tell the guys that we pass.' He quickly pulled out his cell phone and began dialling. Holly sat back in her chair and looked around nervously. Personally, she hated it when people talked on their phones, especially in fancy restaurants.

'Nick,' she called out under her breath, 'not in the restaurant.' He held up a finger to her; he was already talking to Pete.

She felt her cheeks flush red as a woman at the next table looked in their direction and shook her head, whispering something pointed to her dinner companion.

Holly sighed. She knew Nick's heart was in the right place, but really she didn't understand why he couldn't have got up and left the restaurant to make the call. Certainly it wasn't the first time it had happened, and he knew it got on her nerves, but insisted that technology didn't wait and instant information was the way of the future. But Holly didn't see why 'instant information' couldn't get some manners.

'So where were we?' Nick said, and Holly turned to meet his eyes. Except they weren't on her. They were focused on a long, red velvet box that had suddenly appeared on the table.

'What's this?' she asked, surprised.

'Why don't you open it and find out?'

Holly reached for the box with shaking hands. She knew it wasn't a ring box, so this wasn't a proposal, but it was definitely jewellery. And she knew enough about that shade of red to know this particular box had come from Cartier.

Holding her breath, she opened the lid. Inside was one of the most spectacular diamond bracelets that she had ever seen. Her breath caught in her throat.

'Oh my goodness . . . Nick, oh, you shouldn't have.'

Nick smiled happily as he reached for the box and removed the bracelet from within. He then left his seat and came round the table to place it on her wrist.

'Here, put it on. A beautiful dress like that deserves beautiful jewellery. Take off that other bracelet.'

Holly froze when she realised what he was talking about. 'My charm bracelet?'

'Yeah, come on, it doesn't go with the dress. This does. I figured you needed something fancier than that thing.'

That *thing* was the bracelet that Holly had worn every single day since her father's funeral when she was sixteen years old. She'd barely taken it off since and couldn't comprehend doing so now.

She paused, a worried expression on her face.

'Holly, really, this bracelet was made for that dress. It's in a totally different league to that one.'

She swallowed hard, feeling as if her heart might break, even though she knew that she would only have to remove her charm bracelet for a couple of hours while she wore the Cartier substitute. She paused, deciding she was being silly.

'Well . . . ' Reluctantly, she undid the clasp and placed her beloved charm bracelet in her evening bag, double-checking to make sure the clasp was securely closed and it wouldn't open and the bracelet couldn't fall out.

The moment her hands were free, Nick put on the new one and, as he did, Holly felt a sudden surge of irrational panic.

'There, look at that, it's beautiful,' he said in admiration, as he took his seat across from her again. 'What do you think?'

Holly glanced down at the bracelet. She had to admit it was truly a stunning piece of jewellery. She had never owned anything like this, yet the sheer heft of the piece made her arm feel heavy and weighed down. The complete opposite to the reassuring jingle of her charm bracelet.

'It's really lovely, Nick,' she managed absently. 'Thank you.'

Nick studied her face. 'You don't look very happy, babe. I hope you're not disappointed.'

Holly's head sprang up and she looked at

247

Nick, confused. 'Disappointed? Why would I be disappointed?'

He shrugged and placed his napkin back in his lap. 'Well, you know, guy brings out a jewellery box . . . Some women get upset if it's not a *ring* box.'

'Oh no, that's not it at all.' Truthfully, Holly wasn't feeling upset about that; she was feeling all out of kilter because she wasn't wearing her bracelet, her talisman.

'Anyway, I just thought that maybe you might like something to remember this trip by,' Nick said, shrugging, evidently put out at her reaction to his extravagance.

Holly smiled, but it didn't reach her eyes, and Nick seemed to take this as another sign that she was truly disappointed that he hadn't given her a ring.

'Babe, you know I love you, but there is just so much happening right now. And, well, don't you think that we have other stuff to do before deciding to get married? Really, we are watching this company take off, all this stuff happening, and that needs pretty much all of my focus and attention. Besides,' he added, his expression lightening, 'don't you think that maybe . . . ' He cleared his throat. 'Maybe we should live together first?'

Holly's eyes widened. They had never before talked about anything like this.

'Are you serious?'

Nick threw his arms wide. 'Would I have mentioned it if I wasn't? Yeah, I think that maybe the time is right; we should take the chance. We could get a bigger place — my lease is up soon, and I know you just signed a new one on the walk-up, but maybe we could sublet yours. How does that sound?' The smile that was already on Nick's face got turned up a notch and Holly got an idea of how he wooed his clients.

She couldn't help but laugh.

'You're really serious, aren't you?'

'Of course, honey, when have I ever played with you? It's you and me, OK? You and me. So let's do it. Let's move in together.'

She took a deep breath, her head spinning at this sudden shift in the direction of their relationship. 'It's a big move, Nick. I've never lived with anyone, I mean, a guy, before.'

'And I've never lived with a girl either. Come on, Holly, take a chance. As they say in Vegas, roll the dice.'

Holly took a deep breath and then vigorously nodded her head. His enthusiasm (and possibly the fact that they were in a city known the world over for gambling) was infectious. 'OK then, yes, let's do it,' she grinned.

'That's my girl. This calls for champagne. Come on, let's go celebrate!'

Minutes later, Holly and Nick were rushing hand-in-hand through the expanse of the casino, laughing like children. Holly wasn't sure if her giddiness was due to the wine, the recent development in their relationship or if it was a combination of both.

As they passed a gift shop, she came to a stop. 'Hey, Nick, hold on for just a second, OK? I'm going to run in here.'

He was slightly ahead of her. 'No problem.

The cocktail lounge is just up here. I'll go in and order the champagne.'

'Great.' Holly walked into the gift shop, well aware that her Versace dress and Cartier bracelet looked sorely out of place among the 'Vegas Vacation' souvenirs and knick-knacks. She found her way to a jewellery case that contained myriad trinkets and baubles of every shape and size. Briefly looking inside, she found exactly the thing to commemorate such an occasion.

Peering down into the glass case at a selection of silver Vegas-themed charms, she asked the clerk to remove one in particular. A set of dice.

She paid for her purchase, slipping the small charm into her evening bag alongside her bracelet, reflecting that Nick could have saved a lot of money if he had just thought of a charm as a souvenir of their time here as opposed to the Cartier bracelet.

And as Holly headed to the lounge where Nick waited for her with a bottle of champagne, a new thought occurred to her, a much more troubling one, and the hairs on the back of her neck stood up.

Roll the dice . . . he had said.

Could it be that Nick was reducing their relationship to a simple game of chance? And what's more, Holly thought regretfully, hadn't she just agreed with him?

20

Greg packed up his camera and some film and loaded himself and his kit bag onto his bike. Billy from the *NYT* had very kindly thrown him another bone — this one with the New York Historical Society, of which his wife was curator.

The society was one of the oldest museums in New York and located on the Upper West Side. His parents donated money to them, and he and Karen had gone to a few charity events there.

'She wants to know if you would be interested in doing an instalment of a show they're working on, called 'Right and Riots' or something, about people protesting down through the ages.'

Greg didn't need to be asked twice. It was exactly along the lines of his 'People of the City' portfolio and he couldn't wait to get started.

When he got to the building, Billy's wife was waiting in the huge marble lobby. She was short and energetic and zipped over to him with her hand stuck out.

'Greg. Hi, I'm Ingrid.' Before he could even say hello, she had pinned a visitor's badge on him and was shepherding him into one of the galleries.

'I'm sorry; it's always crazy when we plan a new show. We never have enough staff, or money . . .'

She paused and blushed a little. 'Speaking of which, did Billy tell you anything about money?' she asked meekly.

'Only that I probably wouldn't be getting much of it . . . '

Ingrid squeezed her eyes shut, like a child trying to ignore a bad deed it had done.

'How about . . . none?' She opened one eye and peered at him hopefully.

Greg stood in the middle of the gallery, with its beautiful high ceiling, marble floor and heavy oak doors. He was standing in the oldest museum in New York City and they couldn't afford to pay him. Yet, in truth, he wouldn't want to be anywhere else.

'OK, so what do I get?' he chuckled. 'A Hudson River Valley painting? Free membership for life?'

She laughed with him, relieved. 'No, but I think we can put your name in lights. In here at least.'

Greg stuck his hand out this time. 'Sounds great to me. I'm in.'

'Phew!' Ingrid shook his hand again and brought him through the empty gallery, pointing out where things were going to go, and showing him how she wanted the photos to be blown up and hung. When they got to the end of the gallery, she led him through another pair of huge wooden doors to the other end of the main hall.

'Let's go up to my office, we can go over paperwork, and you can meet a few people.'

She pushed a big brass button for the elevator; when the doors opened, Greg found himself entering the largest elevator he had ever seen.

'I know,' said Ingrid as they stepped inside, 'it's pretty amazing, isn't it?'

They went up to the third floor and he

followed Ingrid into her office. He sat and filled out paperwork, amazed at himself for making financial and copyright decisions without a lawyer, but feeling pretty confident anyway.

Ingrid beamed as she gathered up everything. 'Wonderful, now you meet our resident photographer.'

They took the elevator back to the basement where he was led into a huge workroom. There a little man sat at a stool going over prints with an eye piece. 'Greg Matthews, this is Ed Rushton, out staff photographer — he's in charge of the exhibition.'

Ed looked as if he were in his seventies, with short grey hair and rimless glasses. He had a slight build and was wearing a pale peach woollen sweater, which seemed to help him blend in to the cold white walls around them.

They shook hands and Ed motioned for him to sit. 'I've already seen some of your stuff via Billy — it's great.'

The three of them spent a little while going over the preparations for the upcoming exhibition and what was required. By the time they were finished, Greg felt more confident that things would work out brilliantly. Imagine, his work being part of a major exhibition in the Historical Society. It didn't get much better.

Eventually, Ingrid excused herself and Ed and Greg were left alone.

'Coffee?' Ed offered. Greg nodded, shivering; it sure was cold down in the basement.

Ed laughed. 'Teeth chattering yet?'

'Almost. How do you stand it?'

'Have to: no money for oil in this joint.'

Greg warmed his hands around the coffee mug and let the steam warm his face.

'So, just breaking into the business, huh?' Ed continued.

'Yep. Bit of a baptism of fire, I suppose.'

'These sneakers aren't just a fashion statement, you know.' He stretched out his feet to admire his own footwear. 'I often have to run up and down the hall to warm up.'

Greg laughed.

'I'm serious,' Ed insisted.

'No money in the arts, is that what you're trying to tell me?' he said woefully, thinking about Karen's likely reaction to his newest work colleague. 'I think I'm beginning to figure that out.'

After leaving the gallery, Greg headed to First Avenue and Eighty-Seventh Street in the hope of racking up work that, while not quite lucrative, was at least paid.

Glaser's bakery was right where it had been when he'd first visited with his mother so many years ago. He crossed the street to take some photos from the outside. When he thought he'd shot it from almost every angle possible, he went inside.

In almost thirty years, nothing had changed. The bakery string was still unwound from a spool that hung from the ceiling, the floor was still intricate marble mosaic, and the display cases the same wooden and glass. There was a huge cracked mirror on one wall and another slanted mirror on the other. The old cash register was just the same, big and bronze and old-looking. He felt six years old again, hanging on to his mother's hands as she picked out bear claws and scones.

'Why is there a slanted mirror?' he had asked her.

'So they can see behind them,' she had replied. 'They're looking for thieves.'

And Greg had felt sad. If you were hungry enough to steal from a baker, maybe you really needed it.

Greg snapped back to the present as a young woman, dressed in traditional baking clothes and apron, asked him if he needed help. She looked to have come straight out of another era, save for the pierced eyebrow and arms covered with tattoos.

He took out the release forms the *NYT* had faxed him over earlier that morning and explained about the Christmas piece, asking for the owner.

The owner was young — a fourth-generation baker — and he willingly signed the forms and let Greg take as many pictures as he wanted. As Greg wandered around the premises and snapped away, he wished his mom was here to see this; she'd have loved it.

When he'd finished, he thanked the girl behind the counter and shook hands with the owner, who pushed a bag of fresh-out-of-the-oven doughnuts into his hands.

Greg took them willingly and strapped them to the back of his bike — but not before taking one out to sample. Tasting the doughnut was like stepping back in time, and he felt nostalgic as he pedalled over towards Central Park and his next stop.

He had just taken photos of the bakery he and his mom used to visit when he was a child, and now he was going to take pictures of the ice-skating rink he used to frequent as a teenager. His throat constricted.

Wollman Rink was a popular meeting spot. In the past Greg and his friends would meet here for hot dogs and hot chocolate, and then speed off on the ice looking to bump into pretty girls.

Reaching Fifth-Ninth Street at the edge of the park, he got off his bike to walk the rest of the way. A thin string of fairy lights was looped round the edges of the rink and, as it came into view, Greg could see a few skaters making lazy figure eights on the ice. He chained his bike up and made his way down to the entrance.

He spoke briefly to the girl at the ticket kiosk, outlining his intentions, and waited while she took the time to clear it with the top brass.

He decided to get some hot chocolate as she did so. Sitting on the bench overlooking the rink, he gazed at the skaters and wondered what each of them did for a living.

A few teenagers skated by with their girlfriends — obviously ditching school. They kept trying to bump each other on purpose to impress their ladies. Next came by a more reserved older couple — making the most of a day off from work, perhaps? Or tourists even — the woman had a look about her that could have been European. Then an older woman with grey hair pulled into a ponytail passed by. She had on a purple cashmere sweater and a black skating skirt with black leggings. Greg raised his eyebrows; there was a story behind that one, for sure.

After about half an hour or so, the girl from the kiosk finally reappeared, giving him the signed release forms and allowing him to shoot.

Greg duly took a few shots on the ice and then from the benches. As he did, the old lady in the purple sweater walked on her skates over to him. 'You a student?' she asked.

He laughed. 'No, I work for the *NYT*.' He felt the words roll off his tongue as if he had been saying them his whole life.

She raised her eyebrows. 'Really?' Greg could detect a slight Russian accent. 'Well, sorry to bother you. You were so tall and lean, I thought maybe you were a new skating student . . . '

'Why — are you a teacher?'

She snorted slightly. 'Yes, you could say that. I am Madame Vera Treynovitch, ex-ballerina of the Paris Opera Ballet Company and full-time skating instructor. My specialty is *pas de deux*.' She placed hands on her hips and Greg studied her; she looked at least ninety.

'Can I take a picture of you?' he asked.

'Yes.' She said it in a no-nonsense tone (no coyness where she was concerned) and immediately struck a pose, her skates crossed and her hands lifted into a graceful position, her head tilted to something beyond his shoulder. As he raised his camera, Greg had the sense that she had suddenly gone back in time a few decades.

When he'd finished, he asked her if she gave lessons to couples.

'Of course,' she said, her eyes sparkling.

She gave him a card with her full name, Madame Vera Treynovitch, written in purple script, and Greg thanked her, thinking that it could be an additional Christmas gift for Karen. Naturally her main present would be the big surprise proposal and Nonna's vintage ring, but this might be a nice idea for a romantic outing over the holiday season.

His mother had adored skating and he recalled countless Christmas outings with her and Jeff here and at Bryant Park and over at Rockefeller. But sadly those days were over.

He noticed the older woman smile at him, a strange expression on her face, almost as if she'd been reading his mind.

'This woman, she is very special to you, yes?' Madame Vera asked, and Greg wasn't quite sure if he was referring to his mother or Karen.

His response worked either way.

'Very much so.'

'Well then, come back soon and let me teach you and your lady how to move together as one. Skating, it is a bit like true love — both parties must move fluidly in tandem together in order to achieve true perfection.'

Greg gulped a little at her words. Ever since he'd packed in the job, it felt as though he and Karen were the very opposite of 'in tandem'. Still, he reassured himself, the proposal would sort that, and soon he and Karen would be on course for 'true perfection' yet again.

21

Later that day, Holly stood behind the checkout tallying store totals. Briefly, she checked her watch. Still two hours to go until close.

Glancing out through the front windows of the store, she saw that it was snowing again.

'How are things?' Carole asked, approaching Holly from behind. Somewhat startled, she jumped.

'Oh, I didn't hear you! I should put bells on you to stop you from sneaking up on me.'

Carole laughed. 'You look a million miles away.'

She shook her head and shrugged, going back to reviewing the store totals. 'Oh, I suppose it's this bracelet. I have to admit, I've been somewhat consumed by it.'

Carole bent down to pick up a stray piece of the tissue paper that they used to wrap customer purchases. It had drifted to the floor like some sort of deflated ghost, tired of haunting.

'Well, you've certainly been doing your due diligence in finding the owner, I'll say that much. And from what you have told me, you seem to be making progress.'

Holly shrugged again, somewhat half-heartedly. She pressed 'Print' and waited for an inventory list to be ejected from the printer. 'I've been trying.'

'I salute your detective skills. Danny's too.'

Holly smiled, thinking of her son's brilliant insight into the horseshoe charm. 'I probably wouldn't have found the art gallery without him,' she said, then gave a rueful smile. 'He doesn't get his technological savvy from me, that's for sure.'

Carole pursed her lips. 'Well, at least Nick contributed that much. Being a techie in today's day and age isn't a bad thing.'

Holly nodded her head in agreement. 'There's no denying Danny is his father's child.' She'd already told Carole about Nick's sudden appearance that morning. Ranted, more like.

Carole held up a hand before Holly had the opportunity to take a walk down melancholy lane. 'And he is also most definitely his mother's son. He wouldn't be the person he is today — ' she paused, and put a finger under Holly's chin, raising her gaze to her own — 'he wouldn't have the opportunity to become the man that he will surely be, if it weren't for you. Never forget that.'

Holly smiled and looked at her boss, mentor and friend. 'Thanks, Carole.'

Carole moved to the other side of the counter, straightening a shirt on a hanger. 'Anyway, changing the subject, do you have plans for New Year's yet?'

This time it was Holly who snorted and rolled her eyes. 'Carole, you know my opinion on all that. New Year's Eve is pyjama time.'

'Don't let your life pass you by, Holly. You're only young once.'

Holly was about to counter Carole's advice when the front door of the store opened and along with a blast of cold in came a young woman. She was expertly coiffed with bright blonde hair and high black patent Christian Louboutins, and dressed head to toe in black. Before she said a word, Holly knew exactly who she was.

'Jessica?'

Holly had indeed pegged Margot Mead's assistant to a tee from their telephone conversations.

'Are you Holly? I brought the lists.'

'Fantastic.' She turned to Carole to give her a rundown on Jessica's involvement in the search so far.

'Sounds promising,' her boss commented.

'I hope so. But — ' she turned to Jessica — 'first things first — didn't we also talk about finding you something to wear for that New Year's Eve work thing?'

Jessica smiled gratefully as Holly rushed forward to help her out of her coat, hanging it up on a store coat rack as gently as if it had been the Queen's ermine cape. She flitted around the store, showing Jessica dress after dress, and giving her a keen account of who had owned what, what the garment had most likely experienced during its 'other life' and just how divine each piece would look when put on.

Her heart broke just a little when Jessica emerged from the dressing room in Anna Bowery's amazing Givenchy. It was absolutely perfect on her. And as much as Holly loved the dress herself, at least Jessica would have somewhere to wear it.

'It looks really good on you,' chimed Carole as Jessica twirled the voluminous skirts and

261

admired her reflection in the mirror.

She smiled and flipped her hair. 'I suppose you have to splurge every now and then, and you know, you're right, there's something about this dress — a sense of magic or something,' she said to Holly, who had wasted no time in giving her a rundown of the dress's likely history. 'You know, this store is just awesome. I can't believe some of the great stuff you have.'

'Thank you, and be sure you tell your boss that if she ever feels like getting rid of any of her clothes, we would be happy to take them and provide her a nice commission,' Carole put in.

Jessica rolled her eyes. 'Like she needs the money. I mean, she's great, and smart, and she does a ton for charity, but really, I've never seen her wear the same thing twice.'

'Must be nice,' laughed Holly. 'So which dress do you think you are going to get? The Givenchy or the red silk curve-hugger that makes you look like Marilyn?' she asked, indicating a very sexy and tight cocktail dress that most definitely channelled the late Ms Monroe.

Jessica shrugged. 'I don't know. I'm really torn. I mean, this dress is gorgeous, the tulle and the crystals and everything. But the other one is super sexy, and just a bit more modern. I'm trying to figure out which one I would get more wear out of. Admittedly, both would be great for the benefit . . . The Givenchy, well, I could wear this for ever too; it will never go out of style. Whereas the red one, well, you can't wear stuff like that after you turn thirty.'

Holly couldn't help but laugh. Jessica couldn't

be more than twenty-two, twenty-three tops. Thirty probably seemed like a long time away. Holly wondered if she could convince her that turning thirty didn't mean you had to start wearing burlap sacks.

'Well, while you decide, I'll take a look at those lists you brought me — see if anything jumps out.'

'Oh, of course. Here you go.' Jessica dug into her handbag and brought out a scarily thick sheaf of papers.

Holly gulped, looking down at the lists of names from the charity events. Right off the bat she had realised that there were several duplicates, meaning that some of the people on these lists had attended all three events. Where was she supposed to start? There were literally hundreds of people to sort through.

'So you just found the bracelet in the pocket of a jacket? Wow, I'm guessing the owner must be frantic. You do know that egg charm cost over four thousand dollars?' Jessica said airily.

Holly's mouth went dry and she reached under the counter for her handbag, in order to take another look at the bracelet. 'Four thousand, seriously?'

She laid the bracelet on the countertop, and Jessica moved closer for a better look. 'Yep, I definitely remember coming across this one,' she said, pointing out the egg. 'Or something very similar in any case.' She began studying the others.

'I so hope we can find something in this list,' Holly said. 'At least something that ties in with what we know so far.'

'Which is . . . ?'

'Well,' Holly began, 'besides having attended one of your boss's charity benefits, there's a strong possibility she's an artist and maybe a writer too. And perhaps has been affected somehow by breast cancer. She's married, with children, possibly has a penchant for handbags, and has most likely spent time in Florence and Paris . . . '

Carole shook her head. 'Goodness, Holly, it's a bit like searching for a needle in a haystack, isn't it?'

Jessica frowned. 'Not necessarily. Trust me, I do this every day. Ms Mead will approach me with some request like 'Can you call that person who I saw at that restaurant in October?' and I have to figure it out. It isn't impossible. You already have quite a few clues; now you just have to try and put them together.'

The blonde-haired girl leaned closer to the counter and again started inspecting the charms individually, pausing when she came to the one in the shape of a skyscraper. Holly had noticed it before without any sort of recognition.

'Hmm.'

'The skyscraper? I was thinking that was maybe where she worked, or maybe she could even be an architect, or — '

Jessica was already shaking her head. 'No, no, it's not that. It's not a skyscraper.'

Holly's brow furrowed and she exchanged a glance with Carole, who gave her a confused shrug.

'But it looks like a skyscraper . . . sort of art deco, like the Chrysler Building, although I

264

don't recognise it . . . '

'But it's not. It's an apartment building,' Jessica said with conviction.

'What? How do you know?'

'Because there are four of them, exactly like this, in a row on Park Avenue. I walk by them every day.'

Holly's mouth dropped open. 'Are you sure?'

'Yes, I'm sure. This is what my job entails, noticing things. I would bet you a million dollars that the owner of this bracelet lives in one of those four buildings. Or used to.'

'Oh my goodness . . . ' Holly felt like hugging the girl in front of her.

'Yeah, but those buildings are sure to contain hundreds of tenants,' Carole pointed out. 'What are you going to do? Go door to door?'

Jessica was already shaking her head. 'No, it's much simpler than that. If the person does still live in that building, all we have to do is compare those lists that I brought against those addresses. From there, the list may well be narrowed down even further.'

Holly felt like cheering. 'Oh my God, Jessica, you're brilliant!'

Jessica smiled and waved a hand. 'No sweat, that's why they pay me the big bucks,' she added sardonically. At that second, her phone buzzed and, looking down at the screen, she grimaced. 'Speak of the devil . . . ' She turned away and headed towards the dressing room, walking fast and speaking even faster. 'Of course, Ms Mead. Absolutely, right away. Yes, the caterer has already confirmed for New Year's Eve and he understands the constraints. Yes, he understands that too, as does the florist. Yes, they know it's an annual thing — same time, same place.'

Same Time, Same Place . . .

Just then something clicked in Holly's brain, but her train of thought was quickly interrupted when at that moment her own phone buzzed from her inside pocket. She looked at the display. It was Kate.

Holly turned away and pressed the green button on her BlackBerry, connecting the call. Seconds later, all colour drained from her face. 'Oh my God, is he OK? Hold on, I'll be right there.'

'Holly, what's going on?' Carole asked, concerned. 'Are you OK?'

She was already grabbing her coat. 'Yes, but Danny's not. He's at Lennox Hill Hospital. He had an accident at the Rockefeller Ice Rink. I have to go.'

But what the hell was he doing there in the first place? Stupid, stupid Nick . . . she knew she should never have . . .

'Is he hurt?' Carole pressed.

'He needs stitches. Kate couldn't stay on the phone for long, and well, I just have to . . . Oh God, I still have so much to do here,' she cried, tears welling up in her eyes.

'Holly, just go, I'll take care of all of it. Go take care of your son.'

Her mind whirling, Holly grabbed her things. 'Oh God . . . Jessica, thank you for everything, and thank you too, Carole. I'll be in touch . . . ' With that she rushed from the store, hailing a cab before she was barely out of the door.

22

A few minutes later, she threw open the doors to the Lennox Hill Emergency Room and hustled to reception. Breathless, she dinged the small silver bell on the counter. 'Excuse me!' she said frantically, unable to make eye contact with the nurse behind the counter.

The young redheaded woman at reception snapped her gum and turned bored-looking eyes in Holly's direction.

'Um, excuse me,' Holly continued, feeling the blood pound through her veins and tension sweep across her chest. 'I'm looking for my son, Danny Mestas. He was checked in just a little while ago by Kate — '

'Holly, over here!' called a voice to her left. It was Kate.

Thank God.

'Kate, oh my God,' Holly cried as her friend rushed towards her and enveloped her in her arms. 'What happened? Where's Danny? Is he OK? What happened?' she repeated, thirsty for answers.

Before Kate began, she turned to the bored-looking nurse. 'It's OK, she's Danny's mother, the boy I checked in.'

'Sure,' the nurse said, shrugging.

'Tell me, Kate, is he all right?'

'Shh, shh, the doctor's with him now. Sit down and I'll tell you everything.'

Holly took a deep breath as she tried to relax herself. It wouldn't do Danny any good to see his mother in a state. She took two more deep, stabilising breaths and wiped her sweaty palms on her jacket. She couldn't help it, though: worrying about Danny was something that she did as naturally as breathing. After all, it was just the two of them. Or it should be.

'Was it Nick? Did he do this? I can't believe I let him — '

'Calm down,' Kate insisted. 'It wasn't Nick's fault.'

'Well, I think I'm as calm as I can be when I'm told my child is in the ER.'

Kate took Holly by the elbow. As they walked to where Danny was being inspected by the doctor, she filled her in. 'So we were at the ice rink, Danny and Nick were skating, and then, well, Danny got involved in a bit of horseplay with some of the other boys out there. From what he told me afterwards, they were simulating a Rangers/Islanders hockey game . . . '

'Oh Lord . . . '

'Anyway, so one thing led to another, and things got a bit too rough, and well . . . ' Kate pulled aside a curtain that separated a small portion of the triage area from the rest of the ER. 'He doesn't look that pretty, but the doctor says he will be fine.'

Holly's breath caught in her throat as her son was revealed. Lying on an examination table, as a doctor gingerly inspected an arm, Danny looked as if he had been the victim of a dozen two-hundred-pound NHL defenders. The right side of his face was swollen, with black and blue bruises settling in, his lower lip glossed over with what seemed to be an antibiotic cream, and his eye puffy as if he had been punched in the face. The worst thing, though, was his arm, which was now being carefully cleaned and set in a cast.

'Holy shit!' she exclaimed as she laid eyes on her boy before throwing a hand over her mouth at her outburst. 'I mean, holy cow.'

Danny opened the eye that was not swollen and regarded his mother. 'It's OK, Mom, you can say that; I know what I look like,' he smiled weakly.

'How did this happen? Who did this?'

'We were just playing.'

'Just playing? This is not just playing! This is assault!'

Danny put a meek hand up. 'It's no big deal, Mom. I'll heal.'

Holly was about to launch into a protective tirade over how this could happen when the doctor spoke up.

'Ms O'Neill?'

'What? Yes, I'm sorry. I mean, yes, I'm Holly O'Neill, his mother.'

'I'm Dr Chapman,' the man said, smiling kindly. 'And in Danny's defence, it looks a lot worse than it is, but — '

'There's a but?' Holly said, feeling exhausted.

'He does have a concussion. Just a mild one.'

'A concussion.' She looked down at Danny and ran a hand across his forehead lovingly. 'I can't believe this.'

'I'm OK, Mom.'

269

Holly sighed. 'Danny, there's a reason hockey players wear helmets and protective gear. It's because of stuff like this, and those guys still end up getting hurt!' She rubbed her temples. 'So what's the prognosis, Doctor. What should I do?'

Dr Chapman was finishing with the cast. 'Well, we would like to keep him overnight for observation. The bruises on his face and the broken arm, which is only a hairline fracture, those will heal on their own, but we want to make sure his head is OK. We will move him to a room upstairs, and of course, you can stay.' The handsome doctor smiled kindly.

She nodded. 'OK, thank you.' She breathed a sigh of relief and delicately planted a kiss on her son's hand. 'Danny, you scared the life out of me, do you know that?'

Kate put an arm around her. 'I'm sorry about this, I really am. I should have told him to stop.'

'Never mind that, where was Nick in all of this?'

Danny's eyes were downcast. 'It wasn't Dad's fault.'

Kate moved her aside. She spoke quietly. 'It was and it wasn't. It was Nick's idea to go skating, but then he got a call — some emergency with his girlfriend and the baby — and had to leave. He wasn't there when Danny ran into trouble. He doesn't even know that it happened.'

Holly was in two minds whether to be annoyed at Nick for leaving early or relieved that she didn't have another battle to face. Still, if there was an issue with the baby, she could

270

hardly blame him and she hoped everything was OK. She shook her head at Kate. 'I suppose it could be worse. I only have to worry about one boy. As the saying goes, if I had a girl, I would have to worry about *all* the world's boys. I'll take concussion over that,' she said wearily, giving her friend a hug.

She knelt back down by Danny's bed. 'And you, mister, don't scare me like this ever again. Don't you know my heart couldn't handle it if anything bad happened to you?'

Danny grimaced. 'I'm sorry, Mom. I'll think it through next time.'

Hours later, Holly and Danny were settled in a room in another wing of the hospital and Danny was sleeping peacefully, under the doctor's watch because of the concussion, and due to his own exhaustion and some strong pain medication.

Holly, however, was struggling to get comfortable on the hospital-issued cot next to his bed, and she was having a hard time feeling calm. Too many scary thoughts were going through her mind, and the idea of anything serious happening to Danny terrified her. With a bubble of panic in her chest, she closed her eyes and fitfully tried to sleep, only to toss and turn, remembering all the other situations where she had been worried about the welfare of her child.

'Anyone who ever said having a child was easy was clearly crazy, or a liar,' she muttered under her breath, remembering what her mother had said when Holly first told her that she was going to have a baby.

'You never stop worrying, ever,' Eileen told

her. 'From when they are just a tiny baby to the time they become a teenager and then an adult. It never stops. You'll see.'

Holly swallowed hard and fought back her tears, remembering several moments where this particular sentiment rang true, but then she remembered something else and modified the thought.

Her mother was only half right. It wasn't just when they were babies that you started worrying. It was long before that.

* * *

Manhattan, February 2001

Holly placed the small white plastic stick on the marble counter of the sink and sat down on the edge of the claw-foot tub that Nick had insisted on having installed just two months before. The behemoth, usually so comforting when filled with warm water and bubbles, now chilled her as she sat on its side. She felt hesitant to touch it, as if it was pulling all of the cold from outside where a New York February was in full swing.

She swallowed hard and stared at the pregnancy test on the counter. It was the first time that she had ever taken one. And this was the first pregnancy scare that she had ever had.

She was five days late. She was *never* five days late.

Holly knew that while she might be punctuality-challenged in her day-to-day life, her period did not subscribe to that particular personality trait.

272

That was one area of her life where she was like clockwork. Until this month.

The idea of possibly being pregnant was so remarkably new to her, she still couldn't get her head around the idea.

What was more, she didn't know exactly what she would do if it happened to be positive.

Another thing that she and Nick hadn't spoken about.

Sure, their relationship was good. And she enjoyed living with him. Their new apartment was practically palatial compared to her place, which she was subletting now. If they wanted a baby, there would be room.

She always knew that she would want children *someday*. So why on earth, two years into their relationship, had they never talked about this?

Holly didn't consider herself a shrinking violet, not by any means. And she certainly was in love with Nick. Maybe it was just because the opportunity for that talk never seemed to be there.

Just as their marriage conversation had more or less started and stopped that night in Vegas, expectations over where they were going, together, were never directly addressed, or more often than not revolved around what they (Nick) were going to buy, or where they (Nick) were going to live.

Putting her head in her hands, Holly sighed deeply and fought back the tears that were threatening to spill, based on sheer frustration and fear.

'When did we stop communicating? Did we ever?' she moaned.

Allowing a few tears to make trails down her

cheeks, she looked up at the sink.

Nevertheless, things would change, starting today. No matter what the result, there would have to be more talking about big life events, and not just work.

Holly took a deep breath and stood up. She took two quick steps towards the sink and put both hands on the counter, as if steeling herself for what would come next. She closed her eyes ever so briefly and thought of how her life could change in the next couple of seconds.

Holly shifted her hands ever so slightly, and her charm bracelet dinged on the marble surface. She opened her eyes and looked down at the test.

It was positive.

* * *

Hours later, as she lay curled up on the bed she shared with Nick, she heard the front door open. Looking at the clock, she realised that she had been lying there thinking for hours. And in that time, she had come to a decision. But first, she had to tell Nick.

'Babe?' he called out. Immediately she could hear something in his voice. There was a jubilant edge to it. Few days passed without some new development or triumph at work. Nick was rarely in a bad mood; never did he come home angry at a boss, or frustrated with some new piece of corporate legislation. He loved what he did. But that might just be the problem. It was a one-track mindset, and it didn't allow for any other life developments to take place. Nick's job was the third person in the relationship.

So he might have news today, but this time, she did too.

'Holly? Are you home? The front door was unlocked and . . . ' Nick entered their bedroom and turned on a light. 'Hey . . . what are you doing in the dark?' A touch of concern entered his voice. 'Are you OK?'

Holly turned to look at him, and it was as though she was seeing him for the first time. She noted his dark hair, and his eyes — two deep oceans of blue that still made her heart thump. His broad shoulders and muscular arms that were so good at holding her. His kind smile. All the things that had attracted her in the first place.

And now, he was the father of her child.

'Holly? Hey, are you there?' he said with a smile on his face. He waved a hand as if trying to get her attention.

'Sorry, just spaced out for a moment. Listen, Nick . . . I need to talk to you . . . '

Nick smiled and crossed the room in four quick steps. He sat on the bed next to her and held her hands. 'Great, because I have something to say to you too. Today was a huge day, Holly, just huge — '

'Really, can we just wait a second. I need to talk to you . . . '

It was as if he hadn't heard her.

'You will never believe what happened. I can barely still believe it myself. It's going to change everything. It's going to change our lives . . . '

'Well, I have something to say and I'm pretty sure it's going to change our lives too . . . '

It was as if Holly was invisible, or mute.

'I mean, we thought there was a possibility of this happening, but never did we think in a million years it would happen so fast. I mean, a year and a half! A year and a half in business and now this . . . '

Holly sighed heavily and clenched Nick's hands with more force, practically digging her nails into his palm. He didn't notice.

'Nick,' she said sharply.

'We were bought by Yahoo!'

'I'm pregnant.'

'Yahoo! Can you believe . . . Wait, *what* did you say?' he said, his smile fading. He dropped her hands and placed his palm down on his legs, as if trying to wipe off whatever she had just exposed him to.

Holly felt her chest tighten as Nick's eyes grew wider.

More quietly this time she repeated, 'I'm pregnant.'

Nick sat there for a moment, shaking his head, as if it couldn't be possible. As if the sheer *biology* wasn't possible. The silence went on long enough until Holly grasped eagerly for Nick's hands, shaking them.

'Say something, please.'

'I . . . I don't know what to say. I hadn't exactly planned on this . . . '

'Well, that makes two of us,' Holly countered. 'I'm just as shocked as you are. But . . . I know what I want to do.'

Suddenly, his eyes bore into hers intently. 'What?' he asked hesitantly.

'I want to keep it,' she said with a small smile. 'I want to have the baby.'

Nick was silent, and he pulled his hands away again. Gently this time, as if he thought she wouldn't notice him recoil. He stood up and walked to the wall where a sliding glass door opened up onto a patio. He put his hands on the glass and placed his forehead against the cool pane. Holly waited for him to speak, all the while feeling as if her heart would pound out of her chest in anticipation.

Finally, she broke the silence. 'Well?' she asked, her voice barely above a whisper. 'What do you think?'

More silence still.

'Nick, please, I understand. I was freaked out too. I didn't expect this, didn't plan on it. But I think we should talk about it.'

Holly hated sounding as if she was pleading. After all, this wasn't just about her; this was about the both of them. The *three* of them actually.

Nick turned slowly round to face her.

'What do you want me to say?' he asked bluntly, with a new edge to his voice.

Holly crossed her legs, Indian-style, on the bed and put her hands in her lap. She had never felt smaller in her life. 'I guess I want you to say that you love me, and that we'll figure this out together.'

Nick pursed his lips together. 'Holly, I don't want it.'

Holly felt as if she had been slapped, and her breath rushed from her lungs. 'What did you say?'

This time, Nick's response was quick. 'I said I don't want this.'

Eyes welling up with tears, Holly held out her hands. 'How can you say that? This is you and me — it's ours. Our baby. I know it's scary, and it's a lot to take in. And I know we've never talked about it. But maybe it'll be a good thing . . . ' Holly reached for him, hoping that he would pull her into his arms, tell her he was wrong, that he was just joking, that he wanted their baby.

But he didn't. If anything, he backed further away from her.

'We never talked about it because it's irrelevant. I don't want kids.'

Tears fell from her eyes. 'But you always talked about the future, and being together, and — '

'Holly,' he said matter-of-factly. 'Yes, together, with you. Not together with a baby.'

'But I want the baby,' Holly pleaded, crying. 'How can you be so cruel?'

Nick sighed and walked to where she sat. 'Babe, I'm not trying to be cruel. This just doesn't fit in with what I want in my life. In my future.' Holly froze; she was keenly aware of the switch from 'our' future to 'my' future. 'And like I was telling you, Yahoo bought the company today.'

Holly threw up her hands. 'So what does that mean, that now you have more money?' she said sharply. 'Does it mean that you don't have to

278

work as much? If that's true, why can't we have the baby?'

Nick looked her straight in the eye and replied, 'Because I am moving, to Silicon Valley. I'm included in the buyout. I was offered a permanent position. And I'm taking it.'

'Silicon Valley? But I thought you loved New York? You always said that this is where you wanted to be. And what's with *you* moving? What about me?'

He shrugged and regarded her with cool eyes. It was as if a switch had been flipped and nothing was the same. As if their relationship had been irrevocably altered in five minutes. Then again, Holly supposed that it had.

'When I walked in that door just a few minutes ago, I wanted to ask if you would come with me.'

Holly nodded, the gravity of the situation setting in, and the reality of who Nick was unfolding before her eyes. She realised at that moment what was most important to him — it was his work, his money, his career, and it would never be her. Nor would it ever be their baby.

She felt numb.

'And now?' she asked, already knowing the answer.

Nick took a deep breath. 'Look, I already said it. Don't make me say it again. I don't want a baby.'

'And if I do?' she enquired. 'Does that mean that my invitation to move with you to Silicon Valley has been rescinded?'

There was barely a pause. 'I'm sorry,' he replied.

Holly moved out of Nick's apartment the next day after spending the night in the guest bedroom. She didn't feel sorry to leave, and it didn't appear that Nick felt sorry to see her go. What few things she had that she hadn't put into storage when she sublet her apartment, she took with her to her mother's, who invited her to stay with her until her apartment had been vacated and she could move back in.

Even though it was all a shock to her system, she stood by her decision. Holly knew that she had never wanted anything in her life the way she wanted this baby. She wondered if it was possible to already love it, that little ball of cells, the way she already felt that she did, wholeheartedly and with every fibre of her being. She knew without a doubt that she had made the right decision.

She patted her tummy, evicting Nick from her mind and thinking about the road ahead. It would just be the two of them and she smiled in spite of herself. While she never imagined herself as a single mother, she didn't feel scared, but rather emancipated. And as she continued walking down the street in her old neighbour-hood in Queens, she passed a jewellery store on her right.

Holly felt like laughing out loud when she walked into the tiny store and her eyes immediately travelled to the only baby-themed charm in the display case. A little stork, carrying a bundle. She put down her Visa without a second thought, knowing for sure that this was a milestone that deserved to be commemorated.

My little bundle, she thought with a heart full of love as she inspected the newest addition to her charm bracelet. Walking bravely on and thinking about the future, Holly jingled her bracelet happily.

23

Karen Bennet's iPhone buzzed in her lap just as the cab pulled up in front of the 21 Club on West Fifty-Second Street. Swallowing hard as she looked at the display, she took a deep breath.

'Hey, Greg, how are you?' she said airily as she connected the call. The cab driver turned round in his seat and opened his mouth to speak, but Karen threw up a hand, silencing him. The last thing she needed was him making some sort of announcement that identified where she was or what she might be doing.

'Hi, babe. I got your message about being late tonight. That's no problem. You said you were having dinner with a contact?'

'Potential contact actually. Bradley asked me to play a part,' she said, referring to her boss.

'Well, good luck with that. No worries on my end. I think I'm just going to order a pizza and get some work done.'

Karen felt like rolling her eyes but caught herself. She knew it was unkind, but she had to admit that she was tired of the whole 'order a pizza' spiel, which seemed to be occurring with more regularity around their house.

'Well, sounds great,' she replied. 'So, I'll see you later, OK?'

'Um, one more thing.' Greg cleared his throat on the other end. 'Are you still OK for dinner tomorrow night at Cipriani? I know Dad is really looking forward to it. He hasn't been out much since . . . '

Karen thought about it. While she wasn't exactly in the mood for playing happy families, her heart hurt for Greg's father, Jeff. She had always liked him and knew that he was really struggling over Cristina.

'Oh, right, sure, of course.'

'Great.' She could hear Greg smile down the phone. 'Well, have a nice night, and good luck. If anyone can land a new contact, it's you.'

* * *

Back home, having hung up on Karen, Greg made another phone call and smiled while waiting for his dad to answer.

He felt giddy with excitement. On Christmas morning, when Karen opened the *New York Times*, she would be in for the surprise of her life.

The first stage of his plan was arranged; now all Greg needed to do was to make sure that the second and possibly most important part was in hand.

Moments later, Jeff answered, and after a brief catch-up on how things were, Greg got round to the other purpose of his call.

'So, I'm hoping that you can bring the ring with you to Cipriani tomorrow and give it to me on the sly?'

While it was cutting things close, it was the perfect opportunity for Greg to ensure he had his grandmother's ring in time for Christmas morning.

'I'm sorry . . . I know you asked me for it before, but it completely slipped my mind . . .' Jeff said with a hint of tension in his voice, and Greg immediately felt terrible that his request was so self-serving, given everything that his dad was going through. And here he was making all this fuss about proposing.

'Dad, I'm so sorry. Of course I know you have better things to be doing. I apologise. I was only thinking of myself.'

Jeff chuckled into the phone. 'Nah, you're OK, and like I said, things are OK, I'm OK. But let's not talk about that now. Anyway, I know how it is when you are planning to propose; it's kind of all-consuming. I'm guessing you figured out exactly how you're going to do it?'

'Absolutely. I contacted my buddy at the *Times* and we worked out a plan.' Relieved that his father's tone sounded brighter, Greg explained how he'd arranged for the proposal to be worked into the newspaper on Christmas morning.

'Well now . . .' Jeff laughed, but Greg felt it was somewhat forced. 'That's quite a grand gesture.'

He smiled. 'I suppose Karen's kind of a grand gesture sort of girl.'

'I suppose.'

Greg's forehead creased with concern. 'Do you think it's too much, Dad? You sound worried.'

Jeff took a deep breath on the other end. 'Well, no, I'm not worried. I just have to give you credit. You're a brave man for being so public.'

'I'm not being public,' Greg commented a little defensively, thinking his plan through again. 'Nobody but Karen will understand what it means.' He paused for a moment, worried about his father's subdued reaction. 'What is it, Dad? Do you think she might say no? I wouldn't have thought all this out or planned things if I thought she wouldn't accept.'

'No, no, Greg. I don't think she's going to say no. That's not what I meant. I suppose . . . Well, I don't know what I mean. Maybe I was just thinking about your mom and when I proposed. I'm sorry, I shouldn't compare. I think the idea is great. It's unique.'

Greg thought back to how Jeff had asked Cristina to marry him. He had opted for the simple idea of getting down on one knee in Central Park, no bells and whistles. His parents' relationship had been very much a great love story, and the simplicity of the act seemed to complement them and who they were. Instead of detracting from the power of their feelings for each other, the privacy of the moment was just right.

Greg suddenly worried that he was doing the wrong thing.

He swallowed hard. 'You promise you don't think it's too much?'

'No, Greg, no. I'm sure it will be perfect. Don't worry about that,' Jeff said. 'It will be like something out of the movies.'

Greg felt himself relax ever so slightly. 'I guess I'm just nervous.'

'You wouldn't be human if you weren't nervous about asking a woman to marry you. And where is Karen tonight? I'm assuming she's not home at the moment if you're talking freely about rings and proposals.'

Greg pushed his worry aside and embarked on a new line of conversation. 'I just got off the phone with her actually. She has a meeting.'

'Quite the spitfire, isn't she? Working two days before Christmas, when everyone else in New York is knee-deep in festivities. She has quite the work ethic.'

Greg heard the smile in his dad's voice. 'She does,' he confirmed. 'I'm proud of her. She is doing so well. She deserves her success.'

'As do you, Greg. Don't forget about what you're doing either. It's important, and remember that I'm proud of you too.'

Greg felt his hands shake ever so slightly. He certainly felt appreciative of his father's praise, but knew that he would feel better when he actually sold something and made Karen feel confident about his choice.

'Thanks, Dad, I appreciate it. And I'll see you tomorrow, OK? Just don't forget about the ring.'

'I won't. Looking forward to seeing you, and Karen too.'

Greg ended the call and couldn't help but feel sad for his father. For too long now, his dad had tried putting on a brave face, but he knew that the holidays must be hitting home for him. Greg missed the way things used to be, his mother's bright smile when he walked through the door, her laugh as she described something funny. He could only imagine how it must feel for Jeff, who had to face the situation day after day, and try and find the strength to get through it. Greg felt a lump in his throat. His father was a hell of a lot braver than he was.

24

The following morning — the day before
Christmas Eve — dawned clear and bright in
Manhattan. Jeff Matthews lay in the large
king-sized bed with his eyes closed, enjoying the
last few moments of that state that was
somewhere in between the dream world of sleep
and wakefulness.

He was still in a place where dreams were
reality and the harshness of daylight was nothing
but a small blur on an otherwise clear horizon.
He automatically reached to the other side of the
bed, intent on pulling his lovely wife close to him
for a kiss and a snuggle. But as he stretched his
arm out, he was only greeted with empty space
and cold sheets. It was then that he remembered
that his wife was no longer beside him.

He thought that he had been dealing well with
everything up until now, but the last couple of
weeks had been hard. The mere fact that the
holiday season was in full swing wasn't making it
any easier, and many of the feelings that he
thought were starting to normalise in his soul
were once again amplified, and throbbing, like a
healing wound that had just been freshly split
open.

Jeff sat up in bed once he felt ready to face
the day ahead, and looked out of his bedroom
window to where Central Park lay under a sheet
of white. He loved the way the park looked in

winter and he remembered how Cristina always said that around Christmas time it was an island in a sea of wonder.

'OK, enough of this. It's time to stop feeling sorry for yourself and start your day,' he told himself in a committed and commanding voice. He smiled as he remembered another of his wife's favourite sayings — this one about life: 'You bring your own weather to the picnic.' It was a good philosophy, as were most of Cristina's views on life.

He gave a small laugh and pushed himself out of bed. The world wasn't going to wait and he did have plenty to do today.

'I have to get that ring for Greg — that's important job number one — and then I have to get these presents wrapped,' he said thoughtfully. While the ring was easily found, Jeff had to admit the idea of wrapping presents for his son and soon-to-be future daughter-in-law was daunting in and of itself. Cristina had usually done all the wrapping of the presents and they had always looked lovely. Like something right out of a department-store display. Whereas he knew anything wrapped by him was sure to look like a first grader's attempt at arts and crafts time.

And that was probably insulting to first graders. Jeff laughed. He thought for a second and remembered that Maria was coming in this morning — he would ask her. Getting dressed and then pulling the presents that he had bought out of the closet, he stacked the gifts on the kitchen island in two piles, one for Greg and one for Karen. Then he started writing some cheques for everyone else and stuffing them in cards. There was one for Maria, one for the concierge downstairs, one for the building's doorman, elevator attendant, mailman and superintendent. All the people who kept day-to-day life on track. He'd be sure to distribute all of them that afternoon in order to ensure that Christmas cheer was efficiently delivered.

As he was finishing up, he heard the key turn in the front door lock and he knew that Maria had arrived. Putting her gift envelope to the side, and then thinking again and putting it in his pocket, he turned round with a smile on his face just as she walked into the room.

'Ah, Maria my dear. Merry Christmas, or should I say, *Feliz Navidad?*'

Maria laughed and rolled her eyes. 'Nice Spanish accent, Mister Jeff,' she said, in a voice that indicated that she had been born and raised in Brooklyn.

'I just thought I would honour your heritage.'

'You know I'm Puerto Rican and not Mexican, right?'

'Same language,' Jeff said.

'Yeah, and you speak about as much Spanish as I do,' she laughed, swatting him aside to put her purse down. 'In Brooklyn, we just say, 'Merry Christmas.''

'All right, all right, point taken.' Jeff reached into his pocket. 'And this, my dear, is for you.' He presented Maria with the envelope.

She smiled. 'Aw, thanks, Mister Jeff. Is this a bribe?'

'Of course not. It's your Christmas gift!' he said with his hands up, and then he gave somewhat of a guilty grin. 'OK, but I also need your help.'

Maria shook her head playfully. 'I knew there was a 'but'. OK then, spill it.'

Jeff flicked his eyes to the pile of presents on the kitchen island. 'Um, well, I was wondering if you might . . . '

Maria followed his gaze. 'Wrap the presents? I have been wrapping presents for my kids until my fingers bleed just so I wouldn't have to do it at the last minute, and where does that get me? Wrapping presents for you at the eleventh hour, jeez!'

Jeff smiled. As much as Maria pretended to be inconvenienced, he knew she didn't mind really. She was witty and amusing, and her ability to 'call it like she saw it' was something that had always tickled Jeff.

'Please, Maria? I'll be absolutely lost without your help.' Jeff presented his hands as if in prayer and got down on one knee.

Maria laughed. 'You ever hear of gift bags?' Then she sighed. 'All right, get up off your knee, old man, before you break a hip. That's the last thing I need today is another trip to the ER. Had to go yesterday, and if there is anywhere crazier than Fifth Avenue at Christmas, it's the ER. Nothing says 'Happy Holidays' better than wounded kids and sick people.'

'You were at the ER?' he said, concerned. 'I hope everything is OK?'

Maria threw up a hand. 'Oh, it was Pete the

maniac,' she said, referring to her oldest son. 'Needed a couple stitches after getting into some horseplay on the ice rink at Rockefeller. Part of it was Pete's fault, but thank God the other kid's mother was cool. I told Pete he was lucky that he didn't get charged with assault.'

Jeff patted Maria on the shoulder. 'It was an accident. Pete is a good boy, you know that. Boys will be boys,' Jeff said. 'We had plenty of those scares ourselves when Greg was growing up, being both ends of plenty of trouble.'

Maria laughed and shook her head. 'It's a stressful thing, raising kids.'

'You can say that again.'

★   ★   ★

The doors of Cristina's closet loomed in front of Jeff, and it was with a tentative hand that he reached out and opened the French doors protecting his wife's worldly possessions.

He swallowed hard, hearing a small squeak as he pulled the doors towards him.

'Going to have to get some WD-40 for that,' he muttered under his breath. Cristina always complained about that squeaky door but he had never done anything about it. He felt bad about that now.

Jeff slowly walked into the closet that served both as a dressing room and a home to all her clothes, jewellery, handbags and other treasures. As beautiful as Cristina's things were, nothing compared to the luminescence that she gave off when she walked into a room.

Feeling weak, Jeff sat down on a velvet-covered stool where his wife used to put on her jewellery while taking in her reflection in the mirror atop the small vanity. Jeff turned round and opened a bottle of her perfume, still where it was since she'd last touched it, and breathed in its scent. A small, almost invisible breeze ruffled the silk robe near to where he sat and he closed his eyes.

He felt a tear leak from his right eye.

He turned his back to the vanity. 'It's hard, you know, sweetheart, so hard. Especially now. With the holidays, with Greg ... It's just not fair, and I know, I know you would say, 'Life's not always fair.' But it can be so hard sometimes ...'

Jeff withdrew a handkerchief from his pocket and blew his nose.

'You know, I had a dream last night about that Christmas we spent in Paris. Do you remember?' Jeff smiled to himself through watery eyes. 'That was the Christmas that you gave me the best gift ever. You told me at the Eiffel Tower on Christmas Eve that you were pregnant, that we were going to have Greg. Oh, we were so lucky. Our whole lives in front of us.' He took a deep breath. 'I'm pretty sure you would tell me to stop feeling sorry for myself now.' He looked up to the ceiling and closed his eyes.

'Greg asked for your mother's ring, but I suppose you know that already. I'm so proud of him, so nervous for him, but I think that he and Karen will do well by each other. He's going to propose soon, some grand gesture in the *New York Times* of all places.' Jeff paused, as if waiting for a response, and then he shook his head. 'I know that wouldn't be your style, but I bet Karen will like it.' There was another silence before Jeff continued. 'Now, I also know that you've always had your concerns about Karen, but I hope that you will wish him well. Every marriage needs good wishes, after all.'

Jeff reached out a hand and touched the silk of the robe. 'Help your son out, OK? Sprinkle a little bit of fairy dust on him. I think he's been having a rough go of it lately.'

Jeff paused again and considered his next words. 'I would be lying if I said I wasn't worried for him. I know you were always a bit more protective of him than I was, but there is something, oh, I don't . . . off . . . about what is happening, I guess. I give him my blessing of course. I only ever want him to have what you and I did.'

Jeff looked around the space once more before blowing his nose again and standing up. He turned round to where his wife's jewellery box sat on her vanity and gently opened the lid of the wood box. She had always had quite an array of jewellery and, as their income had grown, some of the pieces had become more ornate and elaborate. Nevertheless, and no matter what type of wealth they might have acquired, Cristina had always stayed true to her roots. She might have associated with society types in her life, but never once had she asked for an upgrade on her engagement ring, and she had loyally worn her heart, so to speak, round her wrist for as long as she could.

Jeff easily found her ring and picked it up, along with a velvet box to give it to his son in. Then something about the appearance of the jewellery box struck him as funny, and he began to paw through the rest of the items.

He found the diamond necklace he gave her three Christmases ago, as well as the sapphire pendant that she had loved to wear on their annual outing on New Year's Eve, but something was missing.

'Now where did you put it?' he said in frustration, wishing she would answer.

Jeff thought back quickly. When did he last see her wear it?

Getting to his feet, Jeff frowned, perplexed. 'Sweetheart, where on earth is your charm bracelet?'

25

I could barely handle how excited I was. I just hoped that the sheer pride that I felt was written all over my face. I couldn't believe it; my son had sold one of his photographs. To an art collector!

I didn't care that it was only one picture; I felt as if I had been responsible for raising an artist of the likes of Steve McCurry. I also knew that this would be the first of many. As his mother, of course, I felt as if he had talent. Real talent. In fact, I knew he had talent, but I felt buoyant that others had recognised this spark in him too.

It made me hopeful for his future. He was too good, too imaginative and full of wonder to be stuck in some cramped office. He was of a different breed, not some stiff corporate type, and this was simply another recognition of this fact.

'Darling, ask the driver to stop here. I want to walk the rest of the way. I like to look in all the windows on Gallery Row,' I said, tapping my husband on the shoulder.

He turned to me with a concerned expression. 'Are you sure you are up to it? You feel OK?'

I waved a hand at him. 'Oh, I'm fine. Some walking will do me good.'

Understandably, I knew why he was concerned about me; after all, I had started chemo just recently, and admittedly, it was wearing on me just a bit.

But I knew that it was nothing that I couldn't

get through. After all, I still held to the belief that I had a lot of living to do. A lot of dreams that I still had to accomplish and things I wanted to experience.

'OK, if you insist.' He turned to the cab driver. 'Excuse me, could you pull over here? You don't have to pull down Twenty-Fifth; we will walk the rest of the way.'

The cab slowed and then stopped. We handed the driver a twenty and told him to keep the change. It was a warm summer night, and you could tell that Manhattan was just turning its attention to summer. There seemed to be an influx of tourists and the locals hadn't yet abandoned the city for the sea breeze and cooler air of the Hamptons. Right now the bars and the restaurants lining the streets had thrown open their doors and windows, as happy diners and drinkers pulled out their summer wear and indulged in the warm nights and the joviality that went with them.

I was happy to feel among them. Recent months had been stressful and I was in dire need of a night out. And the mere fact that our son's work was being exhibited at a gallery was exciting enough in itself.

We walked slowly, hand in hand, down Twenty-Fifth Street, and I was content taking in the sights and smells. Smells of garlic and pizza and other things cooking at the host of restaurants around me drifted through the air and I took a deep breath. I knew, though, that my husband was keeping a careful and watchful eye on me.

'You OK, sweetheart?'

I smiled and playfully rolled my eyes. 'Yes, Doctor, I'm fine.'

'Hey, don't fault me for worrying about you. I happen to love you and all that jazz.'

He pulled me close and placed a kiss on my lips. As he pulled away I put a finger to the side of his mouth and wiped away the lipstick.

'That colour looks good on you . . . '

He laughed and put an arm around my shoulders. 'You know, I was thinking . . . you and I, we could take a trip to the Mayo Clinic. And get another opinion on what we should do.'

I stopped on the sidewalk and turned to face him. 'Sweetheart, we have already gotten three opinions, here in the city, by some of the top oncologists on the planet. I trust what they are telling me.'

'I just don't want to do anything too hasty, or flippant . . . '

I shook my head. 'I would do neither, with my life, yours or any other. I promise. But I think that right now we should be taking heed of what my doctors are saying. And if they think that chemo is the right course of action, then I will do that.'

'But it's making you so tired, and sick. I'll never understand a form of medicine that doubles as poison. Future generations are sure to think we were insane.'

I shrugged, agreeing. After all, people of our age look back two hundred years and think that the idea of bloodletting is absolutely barbaric. 'Well, with each generation comes new development, and we can only trust in what we have right now.' I put a hand to his face. 'I'm not so vain that I am worried about losing my hair, and I have faith in the idea that the doctors know what they are doing. So let's just try to let this work, all right?'

We started walking again in silence, but his grip tightened, as if he was afraid that I might disappear in front of him.

I knew that all of this had been tough on him. It had been tough on both of us. After all, no one ever liked the idea of being faced with their own mortality. Each of us walks around with the understanding that we are not permanent fixtures on this earth, but at the same time, being stared in the face by possible doom isn't an easy thing to handle.

However, I had to stay strong. It would do no good to anyone if I fell to pieces. Even in my most private moments, when I did have to admit that I was scared, frightened even, of the future, I tried to focus on the good as well. In many ways, we were so fortunate, more fortunate that many people who faced this. I had access to great doctors and some of the most skilled surgeons in all of New York. And we had the funds to pay for what was very expensive treatment. Many times, I thought that this disease was also a blessing, as it had opened my eyes and made me realise that my own experience could assist in increasing awareness about the condition and its challenges. I was happy to get involved in many different charities around the city, and taking part in these events allowed me to hear the stories of others — the success, sometimes the heartbreak. It helped me keep a healthy perspective that I was not, nor would I ever be, alone in my battle. I glanced down at my bracelet and instinctively picked up the pink ribbon.

But for tonight at least, I wanted to put some of those things out of my mind, and enjoy my son's success.

'I think this is it.' He stopped as he looked at the gallery's address.

'Fantastic.'

'I wonder if they're here yet.'

I sighed a little. 'Wouldn't it be nice if it was just us tonight — just our family, I mean?'

He looked sideways at me. 'Now, now, behave.'

'Oh, you know me.'

He followed me inside. 'Yes, I do. That's what I'm worried about.'

Moments later, we entered the gallery. It was a beautiful space, all rich, dark wood and vivid red walls. The high ceilings exposed the original brick of the building and, even though there wasn't an Italian corno in sight, there was something about this place that sent me back almost forty years to a memory I had held fondly in my heart all throughout the course of my marriage.

'Doesn't this space remind you of that store in Florence where we got my corno? What was that man's name?' I searched my memory banks looking for the answer, but Jeff spoke first.

'Giovanni.'

'And his little boy.' I smiled, remembering the

young child. 'Wow, he must be in his forties now. At least.'

'Probably closer to fifty actually.' He put his hand around my waist and ushered me further into the gallery. 'Time flies.'

'It sure does,' I said wistfully.

Suddenly we spotted the rest of our party. 'Look, there they are.'

Making our way through the considerable crowd that was forming in the gallery, I realised that my handsome son was camped out in front of the photograph that the gallery's owner had bought from him. It was a beautiful shot of the Flatiron.

I greeted my son and pulled him close for a hug. 'Hey, darling. Congratulations, it looks amazing. All this is amazing! I am just so proud of you.'

He kissed my cheek and returned my embrace. 'Thanks, Mom. Dad. Thanks for coming. I'm just so incredibly excited.'

'As you should be. It's quite an accomplishment for an amateur.'

His girlfriend, who had stayed silent up until this point, finally said hello. 'Jeff, Cristina . . . how are you?'

I greeted her with a small hug and a kiss to the cheek, but if I was being honest, I had to admit that Karen and I weren't terribly close. As much as I wished the opposite were the case, we had never truly warmed to each other.

In the beginning, much effort had been made, at least on my part, but privately (and only to Jeff), I had taken to calling her 'the ice queen'.

She seemed to make Greg happy, but there's something about her cool, calm and calculated exterior that I can't get around. It's not that she is emotionless, but something in the way she always seems to be thinking of her next move, or sizing a situation up and trying to determine how it could be used to her advantage.

There was a lack of loving spontaneity about her, and maybe that's what I didn't understand. Greg, Jeff and I had always been a close-knit family, but it's not that I was one of those mothers who was against adding another to our group; it was that Karen's inclusion to our family felt forced. Like oil and water, they simply didn't mix.

At the same time, Karen and Greg had been together for a couple of years. So clearly there was something about the relationship that worked, and maybe I should butt out.

Regardless, I just want my son to be happy. He's such a loving, thoughtful and creative man, and I know that his father and I raised him well. He's a definite catch and I suppose I'd always hoped that he would have a woman in his life who would not only appreciate him, but also complement him, in thought, desires and imagination.

'Karen, you look lovely tonight,' I said with a smile, taking in her chic black cocktail dress, her flawless complexion, perfect red lips and expertly coiffed blonde hair.

Indeed, she was beautiful, stunning even. She was the type of woman who men and women alike would stop to stare at. She was always so well put together, never a hair out of place, and maybe that was part of it too. She wore her beauty like a shield, like a piece of armour. There was nothing vulnerable about her, nothing ever amiss. A woman like her would never break a heel while walking down Fifth Avenue. She would never trip over a kerb while daydreaming, absentmindedly crash into a stranger or slip on a patch of ice. In the winter, there would never be a salt stain on an expensive pair of boots, and she would never have to deal with windblown hair. That was just the type of person Karen was, and I had to admit, I had a hard time relating to her.

After all, I was a woman who regularly ran into things, who tripped and who sometimes felt frazzled. I found that some of the best things in life happened when you accidentally bumped into them.

'How are you feeling?' she asked evenly. I smiled, feeling as if she was appraising me under that cool stare.

'Well, my hair hasn't fallen out yet, but I'm sure it's just a matter of time,' I said, chuckling. 'I'm going to have to invest in scarves, I suppose.'

'Mom, don't joke about such stuff,' Greg said.

'Oh, honey, if I can't laugh at myself, then who can I laugh at?' I offered, patting his arm.

Karen continued to look at me. 'I have to admit that you are taking it all very well.'

I shrugged. 'It's a part of life. You never know what you are going to get; you just have to be strong enough to deal with it. Keep a positive attitude and have a little faith. I was listening to Springsteen earlier today and I think 'Thunder Road' could be my theme song. The bit where he sings about showing faith, how there's magic in the night? And I might not be a beauty, but hey, I'm all right.' I smiled. 'I like that idea.'

Jeff pulled me close. 'You'll always be a beauty. Hair or not.'

'Well, faith might be fine,' Karen said, 'but you certainly can't trust magic to offer you a cure.'

'Karen . . . ' Greg looked horrified.

I simply nodded. 'I disagree actually. I have read that those people who are surrounded by love, compassion and the positive attitude of others — while also believing in their own ability to heal, or having a type of dedication to a greater energy, be it karma, God, magic, whatever — have a surprising survival rate. Hence, I choose to make sure my interests in this area are equally balanced.'

Karen said nothing and Jeff quickly moved to change the subject. 'Greg, your mother and I were just commenting that this gallery reminded us an awful lot of a place we visited in Florence. What was the name of the store?'

'Corna Fiorentine,' I exclaimed, suddenly remembering out of the blue.

Greg smiled. 'Well, the owner is from Florence. Maybe he knows it. Hold on, let me introduce you.'

Greg signalled to a man standing across the room in conversation with some of the other guests. He was rather handsome, and he knew it.

He sauntered over to us, and I could imagine him quite at home in Florence, wearing tight black jeans or maybe even leather pants.

'Gennaro, meet my parents, Jeff and Cristina Matthews. And you already know Karen. Mom, Dad, this is Gennaro del Vecchio, the owner of the gallery.'

Gennaro took my hand and placed a kiss upon it. 'Ah, surely you cannot be Greg's mother, you look too young . . . Surely his sister? I will never believe that you birthed this friend of mine.'

Leave it to an Italian Romeo to talk about 'birthing' within mere seconds of meeting a woman. I waved a hand and blushed. 'Stop, I'm old enough to be your mother.'

'We actually were just talking, about a store that my parents visited in Florence. What was the name of it again, Mom?'

'Corna Fiorentine,' I said, confirming the name once again. At that Gennaro's face lit up.

'Well, indeed it is a small world! And of course I know the name well. It is my family's store!'

I put a hand over my heart. 'You've got to be kidding! We met your father back in the nineteen seventies — seventy-two to be exact. Giovanni.'

Gennaro crossed himself. 'Sadly, my father is with the angels now. My older brother runs the store.'

'Lupo!' I exclaimed. 'We met him when we were there. He was this big.' I placed a hand up to my hip, indicating that the Lupo I had known had been just a child.

Gennaro laughed. 'Indeed, this is a wonderful coincidence. Just goes to show you how fate works in strange ways. What are the chances that I buy a piece of work from a man whose parents met my father forty years ago? I say it all the time, all of us, we are all connected to each other. I believe there is a saying about this. What is it now? 'Seven degrees of separation'?'

'Six,' I said, and then, remembering something, I started to pull back my sleeve to show him my charm bracelet, and the Italian corno his father had crafted, but at that moment a young woman walked up and pulled on Gennaro's elbow.

'Excuse me, Gennaro, you are needed.'

He held up a finger to her. 'One moment, Sofia.' He turned back to us with a smile. 'I'm sorry, you will have to excuse me. How do you say? 'Hold that thought', I shall return.' And he quickly walked off.

I dropped my arm back to my side. 'I'll show him later.' I looked at Jeff and smiled. 'It's amazing how things work, isn't it?'

'Speaking of charms, Mom,' Greg said quietly. 'I have something for you.' He pulled a small pouch out of his pocket and handed it to me. 'Something to mark this evening.'

I took the little cloth bag from his hand and opened it, looking inside. 'Oh goodness. Look at this!' I dropped the contents into my extended palm and admired the gift. It was a tiny horseshoe. I picked it up and examined it closely, noticing a small engraving on the rear.

Greg smiled. 'I had today's date, six eighteen,

engraved on it, and the rest relates to this address. As for the horseshoe . . . well, I guess that if it weren't for luck, I might not be here tonight.'

I smiled, my heart filling with love and pride for my beloved son. 'Yes, part may be down to luck, but there is true talent there too.' I smiled fondly at what would become the newest addition to my bracelet. 'But, Greg, this is your night, not mine.'

'Perhaps, but I know I wouldn't have had this night if you hadn't encouraged me, if you hadn't believed in me. If you hadn't insisted that I follow my dreams, I don't know if I would have ever discovered how much I enjoy being behind the camera. Besides, so much of my life is already outlined on that bracelet.'

At that comment I saw Karen subtly look away, sipping her champagne and glancing elsewhere, as if she paid no heed to the exchange. I knew her opinion on Greg's photography, though.

I reached forward and hugged my son, touched by the gesture. 'I will always believe in you, Greg. Always. No matter what. Give your full heart to whatever you do. It will ensure that you stay rich in happiness. If you have that, then you will always be exactly where you are supposed to be in life.'

26

First thing the following morning, when she was sure Danny was still asleep, Holly slipped out of the room and dialled Eileen's number. Her mother picked up on the first ring.

'What's the matter, pet?' she asked without saying hello.

'How did you . . . ?'

Then, shaking her head, she outlined what had happened to Danny. Once she'd reassured Eileen that her grandson was OK and should be home soon, she got to the real purpose of her call, the sudden reappearance of his father.

At the end of her tale there was a brief silence.

'OK, so, Nick's back,' Eileen said eventually. 'That has to be good for Danny, doesn't it?'

Holly took a deep breath. 'I don't know, it's just more — '

'More of what?' Eileen interrupted softly. 'More of life? Yes, it's hard, and I know it's been tough for you, but some things you just have to let go of. For your own good, and for Danny's. He needs his dad, irrespective of what you think about him. If Nick wants to see him, let him.'

Holly stared at the receiver. She thought her mom hated Nick, but now it sounded like she'd forgotten all he'd put them through.

'Oh, Holly, I was the happiest woman in the world when you left him, but I can't pretend he's not Danny's father, and neither can Danny

. . . Just try and let it go.'

'Let it go?'

'Yes, honey, let it go. Your whole life is ahead of you, so why wallow?'

She realised her mom wasn't being flippant or dismissive, but was instead being realistic. How could she keep Nick out of Danny's life? She couldn't of course — it wasn't her decision to make.

'You're right,' Holly said softly into the phone.

'So you're sure he's OK?' Eileen asked, referring to Danny. 'What about Christmas? Do you want to just come here instead?'

Holly groaned inwardly. She'd forgotten all about hosting Christmas dinner in two days' time. But she knew that it would break Danny's heart if she changed their plans now (or worse, that he was the cause of it), so she might as well see it through. 'No, I think they're letting him out today so it should be fine.'

'Still OK to bring Vera too?'

Holly grimaced. She really wasn't in the mood for entertaining strangers, but what could she say so close to the day?

'No problem.'

'Great. I can't wait to see my grandson — you too. And don't worry, everything will be OK.'

Holly nodded, trying to shake any negative thoughts about Nick out of her head. At least Danny would be happy, and maybe it would be good for him.

OK, so Nick might not have been there, back when she needed him the most, but people changed, didn't they?

Saying goodbye to her mother she instinctively reached down for the bracelet on her wrist, and sought out another charm that had arrived mysteriously, not long after Nick had told her he was leaving for California.

It was a tiny mustard seed enclosed in a glass ball. At first, Holly had no idea what it was, let alone what it was supposed to represent. All the other charms had been so self-explanatory but this one was a real mystery. Until one day she happened across a quote from her old Bible.

'*For truly I tell you, if you have faith the size of a mustard seed you will say to this mountain, 'Move from here to there,' and it will move; and nothing will be impossible for you.*'

The mustard seed signified inner strength.

Holly figured she might be needing a lot of that in the weeks to come.

★　★　★

'Karen, you look lovely!' smiled Jeff as he reached out to take Karen's hand and kiss her cheek.

'Thank you, Jeff. Merry Christmas to you.'

'And to you, my dear. Son,' Jeff said, turning to Greg, 'Merry Christmas.'

Greg embraced his father. 'Merry Christmas, Dad.'

The three took their seats at a cosy table located in the back of the chic and famous restaurant, and Karen looked to the waiter who had shown up to greet them.

'Is it possible to get a black napkin?' Karen

asked, indicating the fact that the white cloth napkin provided would leave lint on her dark pencil skirt.

'Of course, madam,' the waiter smiled.

Jeff cleared his throat. 'I took the liberty of ordering a bottle of Veuve Clicquot. I don't think it would be Christmas Eve without a little bubbly.' Jeff turned to Greg. 'We all know how much your mother loved celebrating with champagne at Christmas.'

'How are you holding up, Dad? Are you OK?' Greg said with concern in his voice as he patted his father on the arm.

Jeff smiled somewhat weakly. 'I'm OK, kid. Making it through. It's what your mom would want me to do.'

At that moment, the waiter arrived with the champagne and Karen excused herself to go to the ladies' room.

Greg watched Karen get up and move gracefully across the dining room; when she disappeared from sight, he turned quickly to his father.

'Did you bring the ring?' he asked urgently.

Jeff's hand disappeared into his jacket pocket and he extracted a velvet box. 'Yes, here you go. I found it in your mom's jewellery box this morning. Open it up. You might have to have it sized after, of course.'

Greg flipped open the box and smiled. 'I know.' He shook his head. 'Man, it really is a beautiful ring,' he said, admiring the diamond cluster in an antique gold setting. 'Thank you, Dad. I appreciate you doing this.'

'I'm glad to. It's what your mother always wanted. Now put it away before Karen comes back.'

Greg did as he was told, putting the box in an inner pocket in his coat. Looking back to his father, he asked, 'Always wanted what? Me proposing to Karen, or using the ring?'

Jeff's brow crinkled. 'What do you mean? Both of course.'

Greg shrugged. 'I'm not sure. Maybe I'm imagining things, but I get the impression that she and Mom have never seen eye to eye.'

'Why would you say that?' Jeff questioned carefully.

'Oh, I don't know, I suppose that they're both so different, Mom and Karen. We both know how sentimental Mom's always been and Karen . . . well, she's all business, a straight shooter. I'm sure you know what I mean.'

Jeff did indeed know what Greg was talking about, but didn't see the need to expand on it. Not that it mattered now in any case. 'So is everything all set for the big day?' he asked, quickly changing the subject.

Greg smiled proudly. 'Yep. I was able to get everything confirmed this afternoon. Karen wasn't feeling well earlier, and while she was holed up in the bedroom, I was able to call Rob and make sure all was in hand. I can't wait to see her face on Christmas morning when she realises . . . ' His eyes sparkled with excitement.

His father smiled. 'That's great. Now, better hush, here she comes.'

Seconds later, Karen resumed her seat at the

table and placed her napkin on her lap. She smiled easily at her dinner partners.

'OK, what'd I miss?'

Greg cleared his throat. 'Oh nothing much, just catching up on everything.'

Jeff nodded. 'I understand you weren't feeling well earlier, my dear. I hope you're feeling better now?' He picked up his flute of champagne.

Karen picked up her own glass, somewhat gingerly Greg noted. 'Yes, I'm fine now, just a bit of a headache. I didn't sleep well last night.'

'Ah yes, I hear you had a client dinner. How did everything go?'

'Oh, just business. Same old same old,' she said airily. 'So what are we toasting?'

'Let me offer a toast,' Jeff said. He raised his glass. 'We all know that this year has been tough,' he said, and Greg noticed his father's eyes shimmering a little. He put a hand on his arm and Jeff gave him a grateful smile. 'But we all know that if Cristina were here with us now, she'd want us to rejoice in the past, be happy in the present and look forward to the future.' On this last sentiment, he fixed his gaze squarely on Karen and she provided him with a nervous smile. 'To Cristina!' he said, holding his glass up for a toast.

Greg and Karen chimed in, 'To Cristina . . . '

Setting his glass down, Jeff turned to Greg. 'Oh, and speaking of your mom, there was something I wanted to ask you. This morning, when I was going through . . . er . . . some of your mother's things — ' he looked at Greg pointedly, who got the reference — 'I noticed something was missing and I wanted to know if you knew what had happened to it.'

'What is it, Dad?' Greg asked, leaning forward in concern.

'Your mother's charm bracelet. It wasn't in her jewellery box, and I can't remember the last time I saw her wearing it.'

Greg frowned and looked away, thinking hard. 'She, ah, . . . didn't have it on before, um . . . ?' He stuttered nervously and Jeff shook his head.

'No, I thought of that too, and then I realised that I hadn't seen her wear it for a while. Do you remember when she last had it?'

Greg thought back. He had countless memories of his mother wearing that bracelet, and the charms provided so many lovely reminders of the past. Hell, much of his family's life was on that bracelet.

'Well, she definitely had it on at the Met benefit,' Karen put in quickly. 'Remember when she won that prize? That beautiful jewelled egg.' She shook her head enviously. 'Leave it to Margot Mead to spend thousands of dollars on a charm that was just given away.'

Greg nodded. 'Yes, you're right there. I took the bracelet to Seventh Avenue afterwards myself to have it added for her. But I can't remember her wearing it after that, can you, Dad?'

Jeff bit his lip thoughtfully. 'I have to be honest, I can't either. Everything was so consuming over the last few months . . . I'm afraid I wasn't paying attention to much, other than the way she was feeling or her doctors' appointments, or well, the fear of losing her.' His eyes went glassy again. 'I wasn't paying attention to those kinds of details. Although I'm sure that she'd have told me if she'd lost it. You and I both know she guarded that bracelet with her life.'

Feeling worried, Greg thought harder. 'I know. I remember the last charm I bought for her, that time at the gallery,' he said sadly. 'I wish now that I'd given her more of them.'

Jeff reached across the table and patted his son's arm. 'Hey, kid. Really, don't beat yourself up. I didn't buy her anything for it recently either. I guess I didn't think there was much to commemorate in anything that was happening. Even that breast cancer charm, I could never understand why she'd want to carry that around on her wrist. Of course, your mother would say that that was me being foolish and that the sickness was simply part of her life, same as everything else.' He smiled at the thought. 'The last charm I bought for her was that 'Date to Remember' disc. She promised me she'd be around to honour that this year, but . . . ' Jeff's voice thickened and he started to choke up. He looked away as if it would prevent the others from seeing his display of tears. He dabbed his eyes quickly. 'Sorry about that.'

Karen reached out to pat his back and Greg smiled at the gesture, his heart filling with happiness at the thought of spending his life with her. 'It's OK, Jeff. We know how you are feeling.'

'I guess I thought if I had that sentiment engraved on the charm, it might make it real, give it a better chance of happening. But maybe things don't quite work that way.' Jeff pulled out a handkerchief and blew his nose. He returned his gaze to his son and Karen and provided a watery smile.

Greg smiled but felt broken-hearted, both over his father's sadness and the fact that this important bracelet, which was a part of his mother for as long as he could remember (and long before the time he was born) was now missing. Since she'd been pretty much bedbound for the last six months, save for occasional trips out onto the terrace of the penthouse when she was feeling better, he was sure the bracelet had to be *somewhere* at home.

'I'm sure it will turn up, Dad. We will just have to look for it, that's all.'

'I'm sure you're right, Greg.' Jeff gave him a half-hearted smile. 'It can't have just disappeared. Bracelets don't get up and walk away on their own, do they?'

27

'And look at how cool this app is, Mom. You can actually access any comic book that's been made, ever!' Danny laughed as he shoved his brand-new iPad under Holly's nose, a Christmas gift from his father.

She chuckled fondly as Danny grabbed a cinnamon roll with his bad arm (his hand still worked fine) and ran off into the living room with the iPad to discover more new 'cool apps and stuff'. Even with a broken arm and a banged-up face, Christmas morning at their house had not been compromised in the least.

Holly had been able to check Danny out of the hospital the previous afternoon, as he had made it through the night without any difficulties. Kate had come over to spend Christmas Eve and to help Holly keep an eye on him, as well as give her a hand with the preparations for Christmas dinner.

'Ah yes, the much-needed comic book app,' Holly said sardonically. 'Just what would life be like if we couldn't access every comic book known to man?'

'Oh stop, you never know, your son might be the next Steve Jobs.' Kate swatted her with the newspaper, before getting up and going to the coffee-maker.

'Do you want a refill?' she asked, holding up the fresh pot.

'Please,' Holly replied a little too eagerly. The stress of the last few days had left her dog-tired. 'And maybe put a little Bailey's in it while you're at it. That sort of thing is allowed on Christmas morning, isn't it?'

Kate giggled. 'I won't tell if you won't tell,' she whispered as she poured some liqueur into the mug. 'I'm sure Santa does the same thing once he gets back to the North Pole.'

Feeling content and toasty on the sofa while a fire raged in the hearth and festive noises on the TV sounded from the corner, the two women sat in companionable silence as each read their own section of that morning's *New York Times*.

After a time, Kate averted her eyes from the paper and looked at her friend. 'So, are you feeling OK now? About Danny, I mean. You were a bit . . . unglued when we were at the hospital.'

Holly put down the entertainment section of the paper and smiled easily. 'Well, I could only feel better once I knew he was resting comfortably. It's just such a terrifying thing to get a call at work saying your son is in the ER. All kinds of dreadful scenarios were running through my head.'

'I can imagine, and sorry again to have been the bearer of bad news.' Kate peered across the room and watched Danny alternate his attention between the TV and his new Christmas gift. 'He looks fine now. In a technological wonderland.'

Holly laughed. 'Yep, there's no denying he is Nick's son,' she said with affection, for Danny, if not for his father.

Although to be fair, while they were still at the

317

hospital, Nick had phoned being apologetic about having to leave the ice rink, and had also been suitably horrified to hear about Danny's accident.

'I can't believe it,' he told Holly. 'We were having such a blast — in fact I took some shots on the phone . . . ' And much to her surprise (and delight) he sent through a picture he'd taken of Danny on the ice that day, her son grinning with his thumbs up, looking happier than she'd seen him in a very long time.

Her heart had melted when she saw it, and then late the night before, he'd turned up at her door with the iPad, gift-wrapped and everything. Maybe he really was trying to turn over a new leaf.

Holly ran a hand through her hair and her charm bracelet jingled, reminding her of something.

'Oh, I forgot to tell you. I was asked out the other day. By a very handsome gallery owner. He's Italian,' she added, chuckling.

Kate's eyebrows rose. 'Well, I hope you said yes!'

Holly laughed. 'Just because you're all loved up at the moment,' she said and Kate smiled coyly. She and Dr Chapman, the handsome physician who'd tended to Danny at Lennox Hill, had hit it off, and a big date was planned for the following week. Holly so hoped it worked out for her friend; the doctor seemed like a lovely man and her friend deserved someone special.

'As it happens, I didn't say yes or no,' she continued. 'I am waiting on some information

318

from him, and really, this guy was such a Romeo, I'm sure he's already forgotten all about me.'

Kate shook her head. 'Not possible. Any guy would be insane to forget about you. And what 'information' exactly are you waiting on from him? Sounds very covert.'

Holly went on to update her about the information she'd gleaned so far from the charms on the bracelet, and how she hoped Gennaro would be able to help her get even closer to finding the owner.

''Course, I don't know if I will be able to find the time to keep searching for her much longer. After all, with Danny in the condition he's in now, I can't exactly be traipsing all over Manhattan.'

Hearing his name, Danny approached them on the sofa. 'What about my condition?' he asked.

Holly smiled and put her arms around him, pulling him close. 'I said that I needed to be paying more attention to you, playing nursemaid and getting you back to health.'

He rolled his eyes. 'Mom, I'm fine, you don't need to worry about me.'

'Even so, I can't very well continue this wild goose chase, not with my only son injured.'

'But you already have so many clues!' Danny insisted. 'So I cracked my skull open a little bit . . . no big deal. I'm OK.'

'Well, we'll see . . . '

Holly idly turned her attention back to the newspaper and opened it to the crossword. She picked up a stray pencil nearby and started reading through the clues.

'I agree with Danny — you certainly can't give up now,' Kate persisted. 'Think about it. Someone is out there, frantic about losing their precious bracelet, and searching high and low for it. You are the person who is going to make that happen. You know, if you think about it, there's a reason this ended up in your hands, Holly. It's karma or something. You are the perfect person — the vessel even — to deliver the treasured memories associated with that bracelet back into the hands of its rightful owner.'

Holly's eyes widened. 'Seriously, Kate, you should run for office with a speech like that.' She laughed. 'And of course I'm going to try my best to get it back to the owner but, right now, I'm going to try my best to finish this crossword.'

Kate got up for another refill, and Danny once again turned his attentions to his iPad.

Holly sat back on the sofa and immersed herself in following yet another line of clues — this time from the crossword. It seemed far simpler to uncover those mystery words than finding a proverbial needle in a haystack in New York City.

But as she started to decipher the crossword, her inbuilt radar for intrigue and mystery began to go off as, bit by bit, she uncovered the clues. As she gazed at the page, something was becoming clear, but she wasn't sure what.

Five across: Singer of 'Two Lives'. Five letters. *KAREN* (Carpenter)

Seventeen down: Mr Darcy's maiden. Six letters. *BENNET* (Elizabeth)

Two down: Editor of *NYT* crossword. Four letters. *WILL* (Shortz)

Sixty-four across: Not I, me, him, or her. Three letters. *YOU*

Fifty-two down: '—— the Night' by Gaga. Five letters. *MARRY*

Fifteen across: Not I, him, her, or you. Two letters. *ME*

Ten down: Barry's Westdale high-school student. Four letters. *GREG* (Brady)

When Holly finally finished encoding the message plain for all to see in the crossword, her eyes widened. 'Oh my goodness . . . ' she swooned, putting a hand to her mouth. 'Kate, you have to see this. How romantic . . . What an absolutely amazing thing to do.'

Kate came and peered over Holly's shoulder. 'What is it?'

She held up the newspaper. 'Look, someone's being proposed to via the *NYT* crossword. On Christmas morning, can you believe it?'

Kate read the message aloud. ''Karen Bennet, will you marry me?' Oh wow, that's so amazing!' Ever the softie, tears appeared in her eyes. 'That's possibly the most romantic thing I've ever seen — or read even. What a way to pop the question! I hope she sees it, this Karen Bennet.'

'I'm sure she has — or will. She must be a crossword addict, otherwise why would — ' she looked back down at the message — 'Greg do it this way?'

Kate was staring dreamily into the distance. 'Oh, I really hope she says yes!' she exclaimed, getting carried away by the drama of it all.

Holly read the message again. 'Well, of course she will. Clearly this guy went to a lot of trouble putting this together, just for her.' She looked at her friend, for once sharing in Kate's mushy sentimentality. 'What woman would say no to a proposal like that?'

28

Greg was up on Christmas morning just as the sun was starting to emerge above the horizon. He had barely slept the night before, so nervous was he in anticipation of what would unfold on this day. Still, he felt wide awake and completely alert. Not to mention excited.

He gingerly got out of bed, slipped on a robe and padded silently across the bedroom, stealing a glance at Karen's sleeping form. He didn't want to wake her until he was absolutely sure everything was ready to go downstairs.

Quietly opening the closet door, he sought out the jacket he'd been wearing a couple of nights before at Cipriani. Reaching into the inside pocket, he found the ring box and slipped it into the pocket of his robe. He momentarily considered changing out of his pyjama pants and getting ready for the day, but that wasn't how they typically did Christmas. morning here and he didn't want Karen to suspect anything amiss.

Smiling, he patted his robe pocket and left the bedroom, shutting the door quietly behind him.

He systematically went around the house turning on their Christmas-tree lights and the ones on the mantel wreath — setting the tone for a warm, festive atmosphere. He couldn't deny it, he hadn't felt this excited on Christmas morning since he was a child.

Reaching down to rearrange the presents

under the tree, Greg guessed that there would be more when his father came over to join them later.

He disarmed their security system and walked to the front door, crossing his fingers on the way out that their paper delivery guy hadn't decided to sleep in or skip his route that morning. That would certainly put a spanner in the works, and Greg didn't fancy having to slip out to a newsstand to find a backup paper.

Outside, the air seemed to sparkle, as if he could see individual molecules floating around him. He admired the crisp new covering of the snow and the icy brightness of the sun as it reflected off the smooth surfaces outside.

Hoping against hope that the *New York Times* would be lying on the doorstep as usual waiting for him, he gave a sigh of relief when he saw that the blessed paper was exactly where it should be. At his feet, in its protective plastic wrapper, just waiting to be picked up. He would have to remember to give the delivery guy a good tip next time he saw him.

Greg picked up the paper and shook off the snow that had settled on the outer covering overnight. Now that he thought about it, maybe he should run out for another one — might be nice to have an unused 'souvenir' copy of that particular edition. Something to show the kids someday.

Greg glanced up at the clouds and he thought of his mother. Oh, how he wished she could be here to see this!

Easing back inside the foyer and shutting the

door, Greg took a deep, cleansing breath and thought back to last Christmas. Their last Christmas together as a family.

Even though Cristina had been very ill at that time, due to the robust chemotherapy she'd been getting, she had been feeling more positive.

Two days before Christmas last year, her doctor had told her that it seemed the cancer was responding to treatment. By this time, she had lost her hair, and his normally curvaceous mother had been reduced to a shell of her former self, but she was there, smiling, and as always staying positive about the future. No matter what it might hold.

Greg smiled as he recalled her words. 'If you live every day like it's your last, then you have no regrets, because each new dawn is a blessing in itself — a gift you didn't know you were being given.'

Her smile never even faltered when, a few months later, even after the encouragement from the doctor, a fresh piece of news was conveyed. Yes, while the breast cancer seemed to be controlled, a new mass had been found on a recent chest X-ray. They would have to operate immediately and another round of chemotherapy was ordered, with radiotherapy to follow.

At the time, Greg and Jeff had taken the news badly, but Cristina had simply said, 'We just have to roll with the punches. It's just another challenge and we'll get through it.'

Greg sometimes wondered where his mother found her reserves of strength. A lesser human being would have easily crumbled under the stress and strain, let alone the fear, of dealing with such a disease, a disease seemingly dedicated to morphing and changing into a new type of monster every day. But still Cristina marched on, head held high.

Thinking of her words, Greg smiled as he edged back in the door and shut it behind him. Automatically his thoughts segued to their conversation in Cipriani about her missing bracelet.

After he got through today, it was next on his list of priorities. He *had* to find his mother's bracelet. It was a family heirloom.

★   ★   ★

Karen awoke and stretched out her arms. A full night's sleep for what seemed like the first time in ages had done her the world of good and she felt like a new woman today.

Glancing to her left, she discovered that Greg was no longer in bed, and felt briefly thankful — she wasn't in the mood for any Christmas-morning nookie.

Karen swallowed hard as she thought about all that had happened recently and she tried to make sense of it.

There was no doubt she had been struggling with the idea of Greg becoming some sort of freelancer and, quite frankly, she would be lying if she tried to say that she was OK with it. There was no point in sugar-coating it any more.

She thought back to the countless times when Greg had said that they were partners, equal in everything. But he took that away from her when he decided to quit his job without even getting her opinion on it. It made her responsible for everything — the finances, the mortgage, everything. And that was not what she'd signed up for.

She had always imagined herself with a certain type of man. A man who was interested in the finer things in life, in being a member of a certain level of society and having possessions that were reflective of his status, not one who was necessarily interested in sitting in Central Park all day long selling photographs to tourists. She thought that she had found the former in Greg, and it frightened her that she might have actually found the latter.

It was fine to frequent galleries if you were there to rub shoulders with people who mattered, and buy conversation pieces that meant you had money, if not taste. But not if you were there hoping to sell your wares so you could pay this month's rent.

Her iPhone beeped at the very same time the bedroom door opened. Karen jumped. She looked up to see Greg standing in the doorway, a huge smile on his face.

'You're up? I was just coming to wake you.' He crossed the room and, sitting down on the edge of the bed, pulled her towards him in a huge hug. 'Merry Christmas, sweetheart. I think it's going to be a great day.'

'Merry Christmas,' she said, a little taken aback. He seemed weird . . . almost as if he was ready to jump out. of his own skin. It worried her a little.

Breaking apart from him, she swung her legs out of the bed and found her footing on the floor. 'I'll be right down. Just give me a moment to get myself together.'

'Take your time.' Greg smiled and left the room, allowing Karen to put on her robe and retrieve her phone. Her gaze quickly scanned the message and she smiled, placing it carefully in her pocket.

She brushed her hair and washed her face, taking a moment to rub some Creme de la Mer onto her skin, which was certainly showing the effects of dehydration from her exploits a few nights before.

Karen winced, thinking about it.

Having approved her appearance, she got ready to join Greg.

Based on the way he was acting, you'd think Santa himself was downstairs. Yes, Christmas was fun, and yes, she liked to get presents (preferably expensive ones in either blue or red boxes), but there would likely be none of that this year. After all, these days they had to think about their *finances*. Which meant that such goodies (not to mention all-round fun) would be limited.

Karen sighed deeply. *OK, let's get this over with*.

Her suspicions were confirmed when she spotted the dearth of elegant gift boxes and bags in her pile beneath the tree. Instead there were a couple of very obviously store-wrapped packages and a simple white envelope.

Reaching for the envelope first, her jaw

dropped when she read the card inside. 'Skating lessons?' she said, looking up at Greg in bewilderment.

He laughed. 'I know it's not usually our thing but I met this great lady in Central Park and I thought it would be different — a fun thing for us to do together.'

She smiled, trying not to betray her disappointment. *A lady in Central Park suggested this? Jeez, next he'll be looking to raise pigeons . . .*

Once they'd finished opening the rest of their rather modest gifts to each other — some perfume and a skincare set for Karen, and tickets to a Yankees game for Greg — they sat in their living room, drinking mimosas, as was their usual Christmas-morning custom.

Greg went to get a garbage bag for the discarded wrapping paper, and when he came back, he placed the newspaper in Karen's lap.

'Here's your paper, honey. I know that even Christmas morning doesn't separate you from your crossword.'

Karen smiled and took a sip of her drink. 'I must admit I particularly enjoy the holiday ones.'

Skating lessons aside, she had to confess she was feeling pretty good today. Maybe Greg's giddy mood was rubbing off on her a bit. Or maybe it was just the champagne. Nevertheless, she was going to sit back and enjoy the day.

'My lady,' he said, handing her a pencil. 'Do your worst.'

Karen placed her drink on a side table and curled her legs beneath her. She went right to the entertainment section and flipped through the pages, finally finding what she was looking for. Folding the section into quarters, she studied the crossword and set out about solving the initial clues.

Greg watched her with nervous trepidation, knowing that it would only be a few minutes until she found the hidden message. His stomach suddenly sick with anxiety, he decided he needed to do something to pass the time. He unfurled the trash bag and began picking up wrapping paper, all the while keeping a surreptitious eye on Karen.

He couldn't help but grin to himself as she filled in each clue, a studious expression on her face as she worked towards the completion of the puzzle.

Greg bent under the tree taking his time.

When he heard her issue a startled gasp, he knew it was time.

'Oh my God . . . '

He turned back to face Karen, expecting to be met with a huge smile, a delighted bowled-over, you've-blown-my-socks-off smile.

His stomach lurched when he met her eyes and instead saw utter confusion, a look of sheer disbelief.

Was it really that unexpected?

Before he could utter a word, Karen held up the section of newspaper. 'Greg, what is this?'

'And here I was thinking you were good at these things,' he teased. 'Need some help with that?'

He moved forward. Then, reaching into his

pocket, he extracted the ring box and got down on one knee.

Karen's mouth dropped open.

'Greg . . . ' she said breathlessly.

'I wanted to do something special for you, to show you just how dedicated I am to us, and how committed I am to our relationship. I know that there have been some big changes recently, but we have been through so much together already — this year especially — and I know we can weather anything. Karen, if that crossword didn't spell out the message clearly enough, let me. Will you please do me the honour of becoming my wife and making me the happiest man on the planet?'

'Greg,' she said softly, shaking her head, 'I'm sorry but no, I can't marry you.'

'Wh-wh-what?' he stuttered, his face falling.

Karen reached out for his hands, helping him to his feet.

'Greg, please sit down. We need to talk.'

29

Holly was readying the table for Christmas dinner. It was set with all her mismatched china and mismatched glasses and, she thought ruefully, there was no denying it looked more like a rummage sale than the height of elegance. She lit the candles in the middle of the centrepiece: a small holly wreath with a few red berries on it. She felt Danny sidle up next to her. 'Wow, it looks great, Mom!'

She hugged him. 'You really think so?'

'Yeah, it looks cool, like a real Christmas table!'

Holly squeezed him tightly; her little man, he saw the joy in everything.

'Thanks, honey.'

There was a knock at the door and he rushed to answer it.

'Mom!' he called out from the living room. 'Nana's here! And some strange lady.'

'OK ... here we go,' Holly mumbled to herself, going to the door to meet her Christmas guests.

Eileen had Danny enveloped in a bear hug, and then she quickly pushed her friend into the apartment. 'This is Madame Vera Treynovitch,' she said proudly. 'Vera, meet my lovely family.'

'Nice to meet you,' Holly said, her eyebrows rising.

She graciously extended her hand to a very

old, grey-haired lady wearing glasses with huge lenses that made them look more like goggles. She wore a short black skirt over leggings and a purple wrap stole beneath a short fur coat, which looked barely enough to keep her warm. Her hands were shrouded in long leather gloves as she took Holly's hand.

'Thank you so much for inviting me.'

Holly looked quizzically over the woman's head at her beaming mother. 'No problem. Can I take your coat?'

Vera happily gave up her coat and peeled off her gloves. As she did, her bare hands briefly touched Holly's. 'Thank you again . . . Oh!'

'What is it?' Holly asked anxiously. 'Are you OK?'

'Yes — it's just . . . ' She looked at Eileen. 'I am clairvoyant, and when I feel the naked flesh . . . ' She clutched her chest dramatically.

Eileen hid a smile as Danny led his grandmother away to show her his new iPad.

Perturbed, Holly gently tried to slip her hand away, but Vera clung on.

'You are going to meet someone tall . . . dark — '

'And handsome, I'll bet?' Kate interrupted from where she sat on the sofa, trying not to laugh.

Vera suddenly gripped Holly's hand tighter. 'Yes,' she gasped. 'Yes, handsome, but . . . I know him . . . I *know* him and he believes he is bound for another, but . . . '

Holly looked helplessly at Kate, who shrugged and made the universal sign for crazy behind Vera's head.

'With another . . . but there is a puzzle . . . '

'I'm sorry. I really have no idea,' Holly said politely.

'Yes, a puzzle — literally!' Vera enthused. 'A crossword puzzle.' Still grasping Holly's hand, she then spotted the charm bracelet and stroked it with her fingers. 'Is this yours?'

'That's right,' Holly said, feeling slightly unsettled at the mention of the crossword puzzle, especially in view of the one she'd been working on earlier that morning.

'I'm sorry . . . the vision is lost. Or perhaps I'm just confused, and tired . . . '

Finally Vera released Holly's arm and dramatically raised her own to her head. 'Do you have any wine?' she asked.

'Yes, of course. Kate, would you, please . . . ?' Holly pleaded, desperation in her eyes, and Kate duly led Vera to the couch, promising to fetch her a glass of red, while the older woman continued to stare at Holly as if she made no sense.

'So, Mom, how did you two meet?' she asked her mother brightly.

'Well, not only is Vera a dancer but she's also an usher at the Lincoln Center. We've known each other for years, isn't that right, Vera?'

Vera took a big gulp of wine. 'Yes, years. We first met when your mother tried to sneak from standing room to a free seat during a Wagner opera. I let her, of course. I mean, it was Wagner . . . it goes on for ever . . . no one should have to stand through that.'

'So, anything we can do to help?' Eileen asked Holly.

'Maybe you could start lighting the candles.' Holly gestured to the expanded kitchen table and the old-style candelabra she'd also picked up from Frank's.

'No problem. Oh, and I almost forgot . . . ' her mother said, thrusting a medium-sized box into Holly's hands.

'What's this?' she asked, surprised. Lifting the lid of the box, her breath caught, as the scent evoked a million and one memories. Tears came to her eyes. 'You made Irish Christmas pudding?' It was perfect. Just the perfect addition to Holly's first Christmas dinner here and tasting it would no doubt evoke memories of the wonderful Christmases of her childhood back when Seamus was still alive.

Eileen smiled bashfully. 'It's been so long, I was worried I'd forget the recipe.'

Her mother duly began the task of lighting the candelabra, ably assisted by Danny, and feeling much calmer now, Holly went back into the narrow kitchen to check on everything. 'Cranberry sauce . . . ham . . . cloves . . . ' She held a wooden spoon to her head and tapped it as she went down the list. Kate followed her into the tiny kitchen.

'Well, *that* was a little weird,' her friend commented.

'Who — Madame Vera? Tell me about it. Anyway, she seems quite old, and obviously doesn't have any family around.'

Kate looked at her. 'You've got family on the brain lately, haven't you?'

'At the moment, I've got Christmas-dinner

nerves on the brain . . . '

'Can I help with anything?'

'Yeah, pour more wine — for me.' Holly gestured to the bottles on the counter.

'No problem.' Kate uncorked a merlot and passed a glass to her. 'Do you know, maybe you should show the bracelet to Vera, seeing as she's a clairvoyant and all?' she teased.

Holly said nothing, but kept the idea in the back of her mind, unwilling to dismiss the idea out of hand. Oddly, the strange old woman had been right about the crossword puzzle, so maybe she could pick up on something random about the bracelet that might help? But as far as tall, dark and handsome went . . . well, that just sounded like the usual guff those types pulled out to make a buck.

Soon afterwards, Holly announced that dinner was ready, and they all crowded around her table, which had been extended with the help of a card table — another donation of Frank's.

Kate brought out the ham and vegetables, and Holly followed with the turkey, stuffing and berries to applause. When the table was full and they were all seated, everyone hesitated, as if unsure what to do next.

As it was her first time hosting Christmas dinner, Holly wasn't sure what to do either.

'A prayer?' Eileen suggested, smiling encouragingly at her daughter.

'Yes.' Glancing around briefly, Holly scrunched up her eyes and took a deep breath. 'Let us . . . let us always be happy . . . ' she stumbled. 'Let us always . . . ' she started again' . . . be

336

grateful for the wonderful things in life — family, friendship and good health.' Feeling stupid, she opened her eyes, but everyone was smiling. No, actually — Danny was beaming.

'Amen!' he cheered along with the others before digging in and eating.

Kate slipped away from the table to put on some festive music, and before Holly knew it, the whole table was laughing and talking and devouring everything faster than she could put it in front of them.

She glanced again at her son and felt happy tears spring to her eyes. He had a mouthful of ham and was laughing at something that Vera had said. His nana was on his other side spooning roast potatoes onto his plate, while Kate was trying to balance a paper hat on his head. This was it, Holly thought, realising that this was what she'd always wanted for him. Danny was surrounded by people who loved him, wanted to protect him . . . everything he deserved. She hoped against hope that Nick understood that too, and would go on to give him the same thing.

When dinner was over (and Eileen's Christmas pudding devoured), Holly cleared the table while Kate made coffees. Everyone else collapsed in the living room to watch TCM.

'Ah yes,' she heard her mother exclaim, 'An Affair to Remember . . . Cary Grant.'

'Nineteen fifty-seven,' Danny said factually.

'Deborah Kerr is so — '

'Beautiful!' Kate called out.

'Annoying,' Vera said sourly at the same time.

Holly and Kate glanced at each other and smiled as they cleaned up.

Her friend poured her a cup of coffee. 'Get out there and spend time with your family. I'll finish up here.'

'Are you sure?' Holly took the cup gratefully.

'Of course. You've done enough.'

She walked out into the living room and looked at the small crowd gathered around the TV.

'Come on, Mom,' Danny ordered. 'Sit.'

'Yeah, Holly,' said Eileen. 'Hurry up, they're about to meet at the Empire State Building.'

As there was no more room on the couch, Holly sat on the floor in front of the glowing screen, and watched as Cary Grant waited patiently for Deborah Kerr at the top of the Empire State Building. As she watched, something tickled in the back of her brain — but what she didn't know.

Frustrated, she got up and went back into the kitchen.

'What's up?' Kate asked.

'I dunno . . . it's weird, but remember the bracelet — that charm . . . ?'

'Which one?'

'The 'Date to Remember' charm, the one with the New Year's Eve inscription: *Same Time, Same Place.* What if . . . ?' She trailed off, shaking her head as if the idea was too absurd for words, yet . . .

'You think it might be referring to a meeting place — like in the movie?'

Holly grimaced. 'It sounds stupid, I know.'

'But if it is, then the owner of the bracelet should show up at the meeting place, just like Cary Grant and Deborah Kerr — or Tom Hanks and Meg Ryan! Oooh exciting. Do you think it's the Empire State Building?'

'Kate, I'm not even sure if it's anything like that, but the charm does suggest . . . '

'And even better, this is supposed to happen on New Year's Eve, only a week from now!' Kate had dropped her tea towel and was getting seriously carried away by the drama of it all. 'Oh, Holly, you're right — that has to be it. The charm must be referring to a romantic meeting spot for the bracelet owner, and the love of her life, here in Manhattan!'

Holly bit her lip, wondering if her imagination was running a little too far ahead of her this time. 'Like I said, it's just a thought . . . '

'So all you have to do is figure out the meeting place, then go there on that night too and find the owner.' Kate was shaking her head with wonder. 'But where could it be? I wonder. In Manhattan alone there must be hundreds of — '

'Actually,' Holly admitted hesitantly, thinking back to the conversation she'd overheard Jessica having with Margot Mead, a few days before, 'I think I already have an idea.'

30

Lying on the couch, still in his pyjamas at five o'clock on Christmas evening, Greg had his arm over his eyes, as if nursing an almighty hangover.

He couldn't believe how the day had turned out and was completely flabbergasted by what had happened with Karen.

After pulling him up from his prone position on bended knee, Karen had, in a very businesslike manner, outlined all of the reasons why she couldn't marry him. Greg had listened with an open mouth, aghast at her level-headedness, and at how flawlessly she had been able to provide her reasons. He had pleaded with her, and told her that he would wait for her to get accustomed to the idea. And then he had foolishly suggested couple's counselling, to which Karen had simply shaken her head no, explaining that counselling of any sort was for weak-minded people, individuals who had no control over their lives.

That was a slap in the face itself — had she really called him weak? Or even alluded to the fact that he had no control over his life?

No, Greg reassured himself, he was none of those things, but he felt that if you wanted something to work, that if you were dedicated to making something work, you took the necessary steps. But Karen had replied that there was no longer anything to make work, before adding something that cut him to the quick.

'Greg, it wouldn't be worth it. To either one of us. It would be like putting a Band-Aid on a broken arm.' Then she frowned. 'That's weird, I have no idea where I got that saying from.'

But Greg knew. It was one of his mother's expressions. And, just like that, it had all come full circle. It was a sign. He and Karen were finished.

Which was reinforced tenfold when she simply stood up and said that she thought it best if she went to a hotel, in order to 'create some distance'.

As she went back to the bedroom, Greg had stared numbly after her, looking around the room like a shell-shocked war survivor. That is, until something buzzed on the couch. Karen's iPhone had fallen out of her robe pocket. He picked it up, meaning to call after her, but then he read the text message displayed on the screen.

Think you can get away for a while today? I'm at the Plaza and I have nothing to do but think about you.

From someone named Jack — who was at the Plaza. Probably the same hotel Karen was headed to now for her 'distance'.

He had simply laid the phone on the coffee table, and when Karen re-entered the room, resplendent in skinny Versace jeans and a pair of Manolo Blahniks, he motioned towards it, stating, 'Jack says he's at the Plaza.' Karen's cheeks pinkened a little until she regained composure. She didn't even attempt to explain; she simply picked up the phone, offered a quick 'thank you' and left.

She was so calm and cool and collected about it all. But really, was it any surprise? Karen would only get upset if she wasn't prepared for something. It wasn't in her nature to have emotional outbursts.

Which was so unlike him. And his family. They laughed, they cried, they argued, they talked about their dreams and hopes, they disagreed, they loved, they *lived*.

Greg wanted to be mad, and he was sure that there was a part of him that would fume and be angry later, but right then, after all that had happened, he simply couldn't. He was exhausted.

'Here you go, kid. I thought you might need something stronger than the wine.' Jeff handed him a crystal glass filled with Scotch, which he had brought over for what he had believed would be celebratory drinks.

Greg uncovered his eyes. 'Thanks, Dad.' He took the glass and threw the majority of the liquor back in one gulp.

Jeff grimaced. He had to admit that, when he arrived, he hadn't been altogether shocked that Karen had said no. What had struck him more deeply was the realisation that he was happy she had done so.

Not that he wanted to see his son hurt; no, not by any stretch, but rather, he realised now that clearly Greg and Karen just weren't right for each other. There should be no second-guessing when it came to a marriage proposal and, if anything, he admired Karen's honesty in the matter. Her bluntness would probably save his son from a world of hurt later.

Plus, if the tart was cheating, which it appeared that she was, then so long, farewell and don't let the door hit your skinny ass on the way out.

Jeff turned his attention to Greg as he struggled to sit up on the couch. He was sure that he had a nice little buzz on, if he wasn't completely drunk. But no matter, a break-up was a break-up and the guy was entitled to a couple of drinks.

Greg groaned. 'I'm such an idiot. That stupid proposal. How could I have thought that was a good idea? I'm a laughing stock.'

'No, you aren't, and besides, save for you, me, Karen and your buddy at the *Times*, no one knows that it was from you. There are probably a hundred, if not a thousand Karen Bennets in this city. At least you didn't work your full name into the puzzle.'

Greg shook his head. 'At least.' He paused. 'I just don't know how I could have been so blind. Why couldn't I see that there were cracks?'

'Because you are your mother's son. As savvy as your mom could be, she was always a sucker for romance. You get that from her. Plus, well . . . you like to see the best in people.'

'But Mom always had reservations about Karen . . . ' he ventured questioningly.

Jeff exhaled. 'Perhaps. But she also resolved to accept something — or rather someone — who apparently made you happy.'

Greg put his head in his hands and ran his fingers through his hair. 'She said that if we stayed together, it would be like putting a Band-Aid on a broken arm. I swear to God, when she said that, I was convinced Mom was in the room, standing right behind me.'

'To all things there is a purpose,' Jeff said. 'More Cristina words of wisdom. And indeed, and maybe you don't know it right now, but maybe that purpose will reveal itself to you soon, Greg. Your mother always had a canny knack of knowing what's best for you and me both. Even before we knew it for ourselves. I always teased her of having a secret crystal ball, the way she could always work out what the future held.'

Greg chuckled. 'OK then. Maybe part of that purpose was making sure we didn't have to eat any of Karen's cooking today.' His laugh grew. 'You know, she really was completely terrible in the kitchen, and completely beyond cooking anything remotely edible.'

Jeff laughed heartily. 'Amen to that. So then, what do you say for Christmas dinner? Chinese or pizza?'

★ ★ ★

The following day, Holly listened to Carole outline down the phone all the reasons she should stay home with Danny and not worry about coming back to work for a few more days.

Even though she was still a little concerned about him, she felt guilty for rushing out on her boss a few days before, leaving her short-staffed for the Christmas rush.

'Honestly, don't worry your pretty little head

about it — it's already all taken care of,' Carole assured her. 'I'm going to have my niece come in and help me. She's looking to earn a little extra pocket money over the school break. You stay home and look after your budding hockey player, OK?'

'So what you are telling me is that I am easily replaced by a seventeen-year-old, is that it?'

'Not quite. I certainly won't be letting Tasha loose on the deliveries or we'd be seeing lots of *haute couture* on Father Mike's crew,' Carole laughed jovially. 'But she's competent enough to man the cash register, answer the phone and clean up the dressing rooms, which is more than enough for the moment. It will be fine, Holly, and besides, you need to be with Danny. If you're here, you'll just be worried about him. Anyway, I suspect you don't have a whole lot of options for a sitter over the holidays. Unless you and Nick are really back on good terms.'

'Not that good,' Holly told her, although Nick had phoned on Christmas night and talked to Danny, much to her son's delight. Maybe her ex really was dedicated to being a better father from now on. She hoped that this time he truly meant it, unlike after 9/11, when he'd come back from California full of promises and great intentions to be there for Holly and the baby. That day had given him a huge shock — had brought him to senses and reminded him of what truly mattered, he'd said.

And for a while Nick had been true to his word, until eventually life got in the way of good intentions . . .

Nonetheless, she was a long way from calling on him to take care of Danny while she went to work.

'Well, I'd certainly appreciate it while he's still off school, but I promise I'll be back before the end of the week, OK? You are bound to be busy with last-minute crowds coming in for stuff for New Year's Eve. Speaking of which, did Jessica end up buying any of the dresses?' she asked, referring to Margot Mead's assistant, who'd been in the store when Holly had had to rush off to the hospital.

'Yes, she ended up buying a couple actually.'

'Great. The red one *and* the Givenchy?' Holly felt a little sad, knowing that she would never see Anna Bowery's stunning dress again. It had been so wonderful to admire and daydream about it in the short time it had been at the store. 'Good for her. It looked amazing on her, and she'll have lots of occasion to wear it. I think I might miss it, though,' she chuckled.

'Speaking of Jessica, any more progress on the bracelet?' Carole asked.

'Well . . . ' She wasn't sure whether or not to mention to Carole her theory about the 'Date to Remember' charm and a supposed meeting place on New Year's Eve. It was just that — a theory and a bit of a long shot when she thought about it.

'I'm going to start cross-referencing those lists she gave me,' she told Carole. 'See if there's anything that jumps out from there. And I might give that gallery owner a call too, see if he's found anything out in the meantime.'

She reached for her bag and pulled out the masses of paper she had thrown in there a few days before. The lists were by now in complete disarray, and she picked out Danny's hospital discharge and treatment papers, which she had shoved in there as well. She tried to organise the lists as she spoke to Carole, realising everything was by now hopelessly out of order.

'I think I've made a mess of it already, though. I don't even know which list is which. Damn . . . ' Holly said, shuffling through the paper before casting the lot aside. 'It's like every time I turn around there is more information to consider, not less. Given what I've already discovered, I would have thought that the possibilities would have started to narrow themselves down now.'

'Well, good luck with it anyway. I'm sure you'll work something out,' Carole said. 'On the plus side, it'll give you something to do while you're playing nursemaid,' she teased.

Holly thanked her again and the two women said their goodbyes.

When she hung up, Holly checked on Danny, who was happily engrossed in his trusty iPad, before turning her attention to the bracelet once again.

Part of the paperwork Jessica had given her was a list of attendees at a charity benefit that took place yearly on 31 December.

Following her revelation during the movie on Christmas Day, Holly wondered if it were as simple as that — that the owner of the lost bracelet was somewhere on the list and might turn up at the same event on New Year's Eve this year.

Same Time, Same Place?

And, even if this was the case, what was she supposed to do — turn up at the benefit on New Year's Eve and just stand outside asking people on the way in if they'd lost a bracelet? She'd probably be chased away by security.

No, Holly thought, deflated, in truth it was highly unlikely she'd be able to figure everything out by New Year's Eve — which was now only days away.

31

I lay my head back against the mass of pillows that Maria has so expertly arranged on the bed. I feel restless, and that 'cool spot' that I so eagerly search for proves to be elusive. I decide to think of cold things — maybe it would help. The feel of the ocean in the Hamptons; some delicious ice-cream treat from Serendipity; snow. Like the snow that yearly flutters down onto Central Park just outside my window.

What I wouldn't give to go lie in the snow! The thought is so fleeting, it makes me wonder about the last time I voluntarily lay down to make a snow angel, or felt gentle snowflakes on my skin. I look longingly at the window across from my bed; it is my one companion in this room.

Just feet away, on the other side of the glass, is New York, and I imagine the wind that rushes down Fifth Avenue right at this moment, the smell of hot chocolate as it cascades out of a café, and the ice skaters at Rockefeller. I imagine myself in those places; at the very least I wish that I could press my cheek against the cold glass that presents all of the city to me. A city I have known so intimately my whole life.

I shake my head, thinking of times past, before everything happened. I wish I could take back all of the times I complained about being too hot, or too cold, or being bored, or too busy. I wish I could have all those times back, and just be happy to be in the moment. All of my little complaints seem so silly, so trite, especially now.

I sleep and wake again, not sure if it is the same day or another day.

I feel confused sometimes, and I'm not always sure if my pain is real or just imagined. Or how much of it is due to the battle raging in my body or the fear that seems to have settled upon my heart.

I don't want to think this way, about that. I really want to believe, just like any challenge of my life, that this, too, will be something that I will eventually conquer, overcome. That I have the opportunity to go on. Yes, I've had a good life — an amazing life — but when does one ever stop wanting more? Dreaming of what is yet to come? It just isn't fair.

But no one ever said life was fair.

I close my eyes and let out a sigh. I feel the tears stinging the backs of my eyes and I struggle to keep them at bay. Those tears seem to come all too easily these days, and it is even harder to keep trying to hide them.

I move my left hand and cover my right wrist. It's funny to think that such a little charm bracelet can offer such feelings of protection. But that's what I need these days, some level of hope that will ultimately assist me in enduring.

This little trinket never fails to remind me of the happy times; it is proof that I have lived.

So this is what it feels like to hold your life in your hands.

I gently caress each charm, briefly recounting the memories, the significance, the joy and the happiness associated with it. Who will remember my story when I am no longer here? Who will know what these little things mean?

I don't need to look at the individual charms any more; I have committed all of them to memory over the years. Each little addition is so special, so important to me. Every charm contains a host of memories, and all of them — if not completely happy — still make me who I am.

I remember when Jeff presented it to me. Right back at the beginning, the year before we married.

I feel the little pickle with a diamond chip on it: the first charm, a salute to the pickle barrel and his version of an engagement ring. Tears spring to my eyes unexpectedly and I catch my breath. It all went by so fast.

I ball my fists around the bracelet so I won't cry, feel the little Italian corno dig into my palm and start to breathe again.

We were on our honeymoon, and I was wearing . . . a red and white print dress cinched at the waist with a wide red belt. I just wanted to look like Jackie O back then. Jeff was in a suit with no tie, just a little blue neckscarf. Oh, we thought we were so European — we were so silly! My hand hurts so I release the bracelet a little bit, and with my fingers I find our wedding bells, white gold this time.

My fingers keep circling the bracelet. Next the quill; Jeff always used to tease me about being a compulsive list-maker. The handbag, an obvious one and a true homage to an unfortunate addiction. I have always had a particular

351

weakness for Chanel.

Then Greg's baby carriage, the happiest day of my life. Lost in the memory, I smile and stare at the ceiling — there is a pretty pattern of light playing on it. I feel like a baby staring at a mobile. Is this what it was like? Not for me as a baby, no crib mobiles back then, just the tin ceiling of my parents' deli to keep me entertained. Greg had a mobile themed Curious George; it was from a little toyshop on East Eighty-Sixth street.

When I was a girl, I wanted brothers and sisters so badly, it was awful. I ached for them. I had to help at the deli, so I was not allowed to stay and play with any of my schoolmates after school, or on the weekends. It was books on the deli counter and get cracking. My dad would have me make the egg salad, and later let me work the slicer. Think about it, letting a child work a meat slicer — we were so crazy back then. This brings a smile to my mouth as I think of buying Greg's first car-seat straps, unheard of in my day, when you just got tossed around in the back seat. Or how I cut up his meat until he was eleven. Eleven! I was so afraid he'd cut himself with a knife. Jeff used to scold me that I was babying him, but I wasn't. I was just being his mom, a good mom, because I could. I had no deli to run, no other obligations. I could devote all my time and attention to my beloved boy. I was unable to have any more children, and Greg himself was nothing short of a miracle. I could not get pregnant for the life of me after Jeff and I got married. I remember talking to Father Mike about it, who told me that God was good and that I shouldn't worry too much about it.

Jeff and I took his advice and simply decided not to obsess about it from then on; after all, as Doris Day sings, 'Que sera sera.' Do young people watch old movies any more? I must ask Greg. He used to park himself in front of the TV with me now and then to catch an old movie. Cary Grant was my favourite, of course. Jeff always reminded me of him a little bit. I must ask Greg when he comes again. Maybe we can watch one together . . . if I have time. I have to laugh. If I have time? I sound like I'm getting ready to catch a flight.

It's strange how I worry more for Jeff than I do for Greg. Parents are supposed to go before children, it's the natural order of things, and though I know Greg will grieve, he'll move on.

Jeff, he's the one I get so nervous about. I wonder if I should arrange a full-time girl to help him. Maybe Maria could use more work, to help him out full time — I should ask her, although she's already assumed that role.

I can't help it; I have visions of Jeff eating old yoghurt and getting botulism. He never thinks of those naturally life-preserving things like I did, like if something smells funny, don't eat it.

I hate the fact that my illness and all its accoutrements have prevented us from sleeping in the same bed any more — in the same room even. I miss my husband's strong arms around me at night, the time I am most scared and oddly most awake.

But I don't want to think about that just now.

It is too depressing.

Where was I? Oh yes, I had just traced the outline of a tiny snowflake, one of the first charms I received from my son. Christmas was always my favourite time of year and we used to take Greg to see the Rockefeller Center tree lighting every year, even through high school.

I smile at the thought of my tall, handsome son, still humouring his silly old parents as time and time again they bring him to see the tree.

The lights go on and he claps along with the crowd, just to make us happy.

We had since stopped taking him skating, though — that I couldn't subject him to. After the lighting, we would 'release him', and let him go off to find his friends and go sledding on garbage-can tops in the park. I wonder if Greg will bring his own children to the tree lighting some day. I sure hope so.

When I was told that there was nothing more they could do for me and hospice might be the best thing, I was angry. I was frustrated, too, and almost cleaned out our checking account donating money to breast cancer foundations.

It's why Dr Chang bought me the little cancer ribbon charm. She really is sweet, though young. She sits on the board of one of the foundations — they told her we were donating a large sum. She didn't get all emotional on me, thank God, even though I know it's what her own mother died of. She simply sent me something she knew I'd love. A little pink ribbon charm for my bracelet. A symbol of the now that was happening to me.

She was the one who agreed to let me come home to our apartment, and let Maria and Jeff do my checks. When she had me settled in the first week, I complained about the morphine, the way it made me always so sleepy and gave me strange dreams, and how it ruined my appetite. What I hate the most is being apart from my husband, though.

I move on to the next charm. It's . . . the carousel! One of my favourites. Jeff gave it to me after Greg turned three. We had just taken him to Coney Island and Jeff sat on a horse with him, the two of them leaning out as far as they could to try and catch the brass ring. Afterwards we walked on the boardwalk and ate Nathan's hot dogs . . . I am missing it acutely now, so I let go of the charm.

I feel in a dreamlike state all the time now. Jeff and Greg come in and out of the room and try to talk to me, but their voices are mostly a fog.

I am not afraid of dying. When I was first diagnosed, I was — it haunted me all the time. I wasn't ready, I was afraid for what was on the other side, but now I just don't think about it.

It's like sleep to me now. Someday soon, I will slip into unconscious sleep and I won't wake up, that's all. No big deal. Except I have to leave all earthly pleasures behind, and earthly people. That's the hard part. Is there anything more to say? Or do? How many times can I tell my family that I love them before they let me go? I feel Jeff holding on to me with every bit of force he can. I know he prays constantly for a miracle. But he's just keeping me here, not letting me go.

I think of my parents and how they died young. They had worked hard, seven days a week and holidays, at that deli. My father had been so proud of it when he had finally purchased it. They had seemed bewildered but pleased when I married Jeff. It had just been the three of us for so long. I knew there was always sadness at my leaving behind my mother's smiles. Jeff and I had offered to have them live with us but they had refused, instead opting to keep the small rooms above the deli as they had for years. They died soon after I left, Father of a heart attack and Mother of . . . they were never quite sure what — loneliness? I had tried to get her to sell the deli after Father died, and again she had refused. When it was all over, I didn't go back down there for a few years, not until after Greg was born. The change in the old neighbourhood was so shocking to me that I made a promise to myself that I would be faithful to the places in New York that I knew and loved. I wouldn't neglect them and I would go and visit them on a regular basis.

It became like a game when Greg got into photography, fun to look through the lens and try and catch the small, subtle changes. A building going up over a period of months, the signs on a movie marquee changing.

Oh, how I love this city, how I have always loved it. I wonder if this will be my last year here, or if I might be able to keep our yearly appointment, the promise we made.

32

Greg was on a mission. After waking up late that morning he'd got a text from Karen telling him that she'd be stopping by to pick up some of her things.

As a result, he'd decided to head over to Park Avenue; he didn't want to be there when she came back. He understood that he would have to face her eventually, and even have an adult conversation with her, considering they would have to figure out what to do with many of their shared possessions in the townhouse.

He replied saying that she should feel free to let herself in, and that he wouldn't be there.

Greg wondered briefly where Karen was going to live or where she was going to stay until she was able to figure out something more permanent. And then he realised that he didn't care. She could hole up at the Plaza with 'Jack' for the rest of her life. At this point, Karen and her affairs were no longer his business.

Still, he couldn't believe that his entire world had changed in barely forty-eight hours. Karen had been such a big part of his life and now she was gone — just like that. And all because of money, it seemed. Because she was afraid he wouldn't be able to support them in the way she had been accustomed to.

Greg tried to put himself in Karen's shoes and think of how he would feel if she had suddenly changed careers, suddenly announced she wanted to join the Peace Corps or something. Unlikely, he thought, smiling. Even so, he knew for sure he'd have supported her, had always supported her in anything she'd done.

Is this what he had to be on the look-out for now? he wondered. Women who were only interested in him for his money? Although, he reminded himself, there wasn't much of that any more.

Another fresh start, he thought ruefully, as he closed his front door behind him and took the bike out onto the street. Sometimes you needed to be careful what you wished for.

He arrived quickly, and said hello to the building's doorman, Conor, a veritable fixture of the building itself. Going up in the elevator, he let himself in to the penthouse and found his father in the kitchen with Maria.

'Good morning, guys.'

'Oh, Greg, I'm just so sorry to hear about . . . ' Maria said, approaching him and giving him a hug. He accepted the embrace, somewhat uncomfortably. Even though he knew her well, it was still slightly embarrassing having other people know that you had been dumped. Especially after such a dramatic and public proposal.

'It's OK, Maria, thanks. I'll be fine.'

She looked up at him, a mischievous smile on her face. 'If it makes you feel any better, I could arrange to have her taken care of? Us Puerto Ricans, we don't mess around, and I have a cousin who — '

Greg laughed for the first time since Christmas Day. 'Thanks for the offer, but I don't think that will be necessary.'

'Well, don't say I never offered to do anything for you.'

Greg turned his attention to his father. 'I thought I'd come over — Karen's coming round for some of her things later and I didn't want to be there.' He reached into his pocket. 'And I brought Nonna's ring back,' he said sadly. 'I guess I'll put it back in Mom's jewellery box.'

'For a while at least — until you need it again,' his father added kindly, but Greg figured it would be some time before he'd be looking to use the ring again, if ever.

'Has the charm bracelet turned up yet?' he asked, the mention of the jewellery box reminding him about it.

'No, we've searched high and low for it by now, haven't we, Maria?' Jeff replied.

'Well, I might as well take a look around myself while I'm in there.'

His mother's plush walk-in closet was one of those places that lived in the dreams of most women, but for his lucky mother, was a reality.

Reaching out to touch the delicate fabrics, Greg couldn't help but reflect on the memories associated with each piece of clothing.

The pretty floral dress she had worn at his college graduation, and the deep red silk two-piece she'd had on that night at Gennaro's gallery when his photograph of the Flatiron had been on display. Or the time she had sat reading a book out on the private terrace in this pale violet cardigan. Greg felt in its pocket and pulled out some crinkled-up Kleenex, seemingly nothing but a scrap of trash, but he knew that his mother had probably used it to dry her eyes after reading a particularly heart-wrenching passage in a novel. He held the crumpled tissue in his hand and felt a lump form in his throat.

Placing the cardigan back on the hanger, he threw the tissue away in a nearby wastepaper basket.

He sat down on the edge of the bed. 'I know you didn't lose it, Mom. I know you *wouldn't* lose it. This bracelet was your whole life — hell, it had your whole life on it. So what on earth did you do with it?'

He thought back to the last time he'd seen her wear it. Karen mentioned that it had been at the hospital benefit on New Year's Eve last year and that was true, but . . .

Then, looking again at her closet, he remembered something.

The red suit . . . Greg got up and crossed to the wardrobe, holding the delicate silk jacket up in front of him. His eyes moved to the sleeves. Yes, it had been June and warm outside when his mother had worn this at the gallery.

That was the last time he'd given her a charm, the horseshoe charm to commemorate the occasion. So she'd definitely been wearing the bracelet that night.

He reached into the pockets of the jacket, wondering if maybe she'd taken it off for some reason and left it in there.

And as he did, a sudden thought struck him

360

— a new and much more recent memory concerning Gennaro's gallery came to mind. It was last week, when he'd called in to the gallery and collided with that woman on her way out.

When Greg had enquired if the woman was an interested buyer, Gennaro had told him something about her trying to find out something about a bracelet, because one of the charms had led her to his gallery.

Greg felt his spirits lift. Somehow his mother must have lost the bracelet and this woman, whoever she was, had found it and was trying to give it back.

But then why didn't Gennaro recognise it as Cristina's — especially with the *corno* — made by his very own father — attached?

Then Greg thought back to that night, when his mother had attempted to show Gennaro the Italian *corno* she'd bought in Florence all those years ago, but he'd been interrupted by Sofia. So Gennaro wouldn't have recognised the bracelet, because Cristina never got the chance to show it to him.

Thinking back to that day at the gallery, and the woman with the striking auburn hair, pretty face and bright green eyes, Greg knew he was on to something. But if she did happen to be in possession of his mother's bracelet, how on earth was he supposed to track her down now?

He tried again to think back to what little his friend had said about her. Didn't Gennaro mention something about asking her out? In which case he must have a phone number for her.

Greg felt heartened. For once his friend's

Romeo tendencies would come in handy.

'Don't worry, Mom,' he said with conviction. 'I'll get it back . . . '

He put his mother's silk jacket back where he'd found it and went outside. Then he quickly grabbed his coat and put it on.

'Where's the fire?' Jeff asked in confusion.

Greg quickly explained his train of thought. 'I think that somehow Mom lost the bracelet a while back, and that someone has found it and is searching for us, just like we've been searching for the bracelet. And I think I met that very same person the other day. At Gennaro's gallery.'

Jeff's face lit up. 'Problem solved, fantastic.'

'It's not that simple unfortunately.' Greg shook his head. 'I don't know her name, but I am going to find out.'

'But, Greg, I don't understand. How would Cristina's charm bracelet end up with some random stranger? How would it even get outside the house?' Maria asked in confusion.

'That I don't know, Maria, but if I happened to bump into this woman at the gallery, I wonder how she came to end up there?'

'She must have tracked down the origin of the Italian *corno* and somehow traced it back to Gennaro via his father's place in Florence,' Jeff stated simply. 'What are the chances? I always said that bracelet was like the story of this family's life, laid out for all to see.'

Greg nodded. 'Well, Gennaro will know who this mystery woman is and he'll be able to tell me where to find her. And with luck we'll have Mom's bracelet back in no time.'

33

Holly was taking the decorations down off the Christmas tree. It was just too darned big to remain in their apartment (and for she and Danny to live comfortably alongside it) any longer.

She wrapped the various angels and bells in tissue paper while Danny half-heartedly unwound tinsel from the branches. In order for the tree to be picked up kerbside, it had to be completely bare, otherwise City Sanitation wouldn't take it.

'Mom, my arm hurts,' he complained, not nearly as interested in the tree as when they were dressing it before Christmas.

'Oh, poor baby . . . funny how it doesn't hurt so much when you're playing Nintendo,' Holly teased. 'Go on then,' she told him, ruffling his hair as he bounded off.

Dry needles became entangled in her clothes as she struggled to remove the now bare tree from its stand.

After some exertion, it finally came loose, and as it did something shot out from the branches and nearly hit Holly in the eye. She shrieked and stood back, thinking for a moment it was a mouse or some other creature that had taken up residence in the tree.

But very quickly she realised that it wasn't an animal but a package.

A tiny box wrapped in lilac paper with a little purple bow on it.

Picking it up, she studied the gift and found a little tag with her name written on it.

She sat cross-legged on the floor, wondering how long it had been there. Since Christmas Day obviously.

Smiling at the familiar lilac packaging, she carefully untied the bow and opened the box, an action that was by now almost ritualistic.

Inside was a silver charm in the shape of a fir tree with a tiny diamond chip in the middle of the star. She turned it over; on the back was inscribed, *Holly's 1st Christmas.*

She felt a tear slide down her cheek, warm and inviting.

Another little gift of love and hope.

Wiping her face, Holly unclasped her charm bracelet and attached the tree in the best available space — the hourglass, the first charm she'd received all those years ago, on one side, and on the other, a little charm in the shape of a dove.

Fitting really, Holly smiled, thinking back to the particular day she'd received that one.

★ ★ ★

New York, 11 September 2001

Holly opened her eyes and yawned widely. Stretching out her arms and legs, she turned and faced the window, where bright sunlight was already peeking through the slats of her blinds.

She looked at the clock and smiled: seven thirty a.m. Just enough time to get ready for

364

work and grab a green tea at Starbucks on the way to work.

It was then that Holly realised that someone else was awake too. A determined kick came from inside her evergrowing tummy. There was no denying it, her baby was definitely healthy, but she was worried that with each passing day she resembled an elephant more than a woman. She wondered how big she would be when she reached the full nine months.

'OK, little man, I know you're awake. Just hold on a minute and let your poor mother get her bearings.'

She put her feet on the ground and stood up, her protruding abdomen stretching out in front of her. She had to admit, pregnancy had been an experience. Not that anything bad had happened; it was more that she felt constantly in awe of what was taking place in her body, and she couldn't believe that soon she would have a son to call her own.

Some of her friends had been perplexed by her decision to find out the baby's gender beforehand, arguing that it took all the surprise out of the main event. But Holly insisted that, even though she knew that much, she would be surprised just the same. After all, how many times did you get to meet face-to-face a person that you had a hand in creating? The wonder and magic of that thought alone was enough to get Holly through until the day her child was born.

And she had to admit that she was happy she was having a boy, she thought, going into the bathroom to freshen up. She hadn't talked to

Nick in months; the last time had been when she had officially moved the rest of her things out of his place, and she had no intention of doing so anytime in the future. After all, what was the point? He'd made it clear he wanted no part of this baby. And that was fine by Holly. Her child would be hers alone, and she was dedicated to the idea of making him into a man who was strong, considerate and courageous — instead of a materialistic commitment-phobe who only thought of himself.

Holly smiled at the notion as she came out of the bathroom and lumbered to her closet to search for something to wear. It was still ridiculously hot in the city and while she appreciated summer stretching into September, she would be happy when she was able to breathe a bit easier when she was walking around on the hot concrete of Manhattan. She hated being covered in sweat by the time she got to work at nine a.m.

'So the sundress it is again,' Holly said as she stepped into a light summer outfit that had served her well this past season. While she had stocked up on maternity clothes as her bump grew ever bigger, the one indulgence she resisted was buying her beloved vintage. After all, no point in spending all that money on clothes that would definitely not be required for very long. She did have the financial future of a baby and herself to think about, so best to be wise in her decisions.

She stepped into a pair of sandals and wiggled her toes. Yes, much easier than heels.

Holly grabbed her handbag and put some

earrings on. Her charm bracelet jingled as she did up the clasp and deemed herself ready to go.

Moments later, she was on the streets of Manhattan.

Darting into a Starbucks on Church Street, she was happy to find that the line wasn't that long, allowing her to stay on schedule. She smiled contentedly and took her place at the back.

Seeing many regulars, several of whom greeted her and asked how she was feeling, she felt peaceful. Anyone who ever said New Yorkers were rude, loud or self-involved had obviously never lived here. Holly believed that many of her neighbours and the people she regularly saw out and about around the neighbourhood were some of the nicest and kindest in the world.

'Here's your green tea, ma'am,' the barista smiled. Throwing a dollar in the tip jar, Holly thanked her and waved goodbye.

She glanced at her watch as she started walking up Church Street and headed towards Greenwich Village. She was ahead of schedule, for once, and she felt quite proud of herself. So many women had told her that they seemed to become flaky and all over the place when they were pregnant. But not Holly — if anything, she had become more organised.

The baby gave her another sharp kick as she finished this thought and she patted her tummy and took a small sip of tea.

'Yikes!' It was red-hot, and Holly stopped for a moment and rubbed her lip. 'Damn, I should remember to ask them to put some ice cubes in next — '

But she didn't finish that thought.

Overhead a deafening roar reverberated off the buildings around her. Holly put a free hand to one of her ears as she looked up and saw a low-flying plane . . . no, not a plane, a *jet*, burning a path through the sky above her.

Mouth agape at how close to the ground it seemed to be flying, she followed its trail as it surged forwards overhead. Holly took a fleeting glance at others on the street who were looking upwards in sync with her, watching the plane as it flew towards Lower Manhattan.

It was then that her heart started to race. She dropped her tea on the ground and jumped as the hot water splashed her bare legs, but even then she couldn't take her eyes off what was unfolding in front of her, above her.

Holly walked a few paces in the opposite direction to where she was supposed to be headed, but she couldn't help it. There were throngs of people standing around, watching and engaging in speculation about what was going on. While she knew that standing here gawking was akin to chasing ambulances, she couldn't help it.

She put her hands over her abdomen as the baby gave what seemed to be a vicious kick and she doubled over.

The woman next to her took note of Holly, clearly distressed and very pregnant.

'Honey, are you OK? Can I call your husband, or a boyfriend? Can I do anything for you?'

Holly crumpled to her knees. At the lack of an answer, the woman looked around, seemingly trying to catch the attention of anyone, even though all eyes were turned to the skies.

'Somebody help! I think this woman is in labour!'

★ ★ ★

Holly hadn't been in labour. But her heart was broken.

As the day developed, she saw the world that she had known change drastically. Even after she had convinced the kindly woman on the street that she wasn't in labour, the woman had understood that she was still in danger, especially as she had stood frozen in place, unable to move.

It was only when another nameless New Yorker grabbed them both and propelled them away from the oncoming onslaught of dust and debris that Holly had willed her feet to move. They'd rushed to the Starbucks she had been in just minutes before, looking for a sanctuary from the hellish cloud that threatened to consume them.

And it was in that Starbucks that Holly sat on the floor, her back propped against a wall, studying the faces around her and the TV screen in the corner. It was all so surreal. A frightening realisation struck her as the news bulletins and terrifying headlines flooded in all around them. Her child would never know the safe and secure world that she had grown up in, the one that she had lived in up until this day. That world was in the rear-view mirror and Holly knew that she would never be the same.

Even when the grey ash on the street outside

settled, she felt hesitant to leave. But she also knew that she had to get home, and walking was the only way she was going to get there. Her phone had stopped working hours ago; so right then she was effectively invisible. She needed to call her boss and she needed to call Kate. Justin worked in Cantor Fitzgerald. Please, God, let him have got out before . . . Holly put a protective hand over her tummy and heard her charm bracelet jingle reassuringly. Moving into the street, she felt particles of dust, the remnants of destruction, falling onto her head and shoulders, and she put her head down to shield her vision. This was not her New York; this was a nightmare. Where had the beauty and wonder gone? And would it ever come back?

★   ★   ★

Wearily climbing the steps to her apartment, Holly felt as if she had lived four lifetimes since she'd woken up on what had been a cheery, sunshine-filled September morning. She put her key in the door and turned it hesitantly, for a moment wondering if she would find her home suddenly altered from the way she had left it as well.

But when she opened the door, she found her apartment exactly the same as it had been when she'd left it that morning — although by then it seemed like a lifetime ago. The blue baby clothes that she had been folding on her small coffee table the night before were still in their pile. The plate from her English muffin that morning was still in the sink. Her bed was still unmade.

She didn't know how long she had stayed there in her doorway, but finally she noticed the blinking messages on her answering machine.

Crossing the small living room, she pressed 'Play'.

There had been numerous calls. All from friends and loved ones who were worried about Holly and the baby. Even Nick had called, and Holly felt relieved to hear from him. Right now was not the time to hold grudges.

Her throat closed over, though, when she heard Kate's frantic and tearful tones. 'Holly, have you heard from Justin? Please say you have. I can't reach him and . . . I just don't know what to do!'

Holly immediately phoned her back but just got the answerphone. She hoped against hope that her friend hadn't tried to go down there — it was no place for anyone. Yet how could Kate not, when Justin could be caught up in it all? Crying silently for her friends, Holly sank onto the nearest chair.

Having tried Kate a number of times — still to no avail — she worked to return the other calls, and made promise after promise that she would stay safe. The only other person she couldn't reach was Eileen. Feeling worried, but by now emotionally exhausted, she dragged herself into the shower to try and remove the remains of the day from her skin and hair.

And she tossed the sundress that she had been wearing in the trash. She never wanted to see that dress again.

Emerging in a robe, Holly saw the sun setting outside her window. This horrible day was ending. She picked up the phone to again call Kate and then her mother.

No answer from either of them.

The following morning dawned in Holly's apartment and as she opened her eyes, she wondered if the previous day had been a dream, a horrible nightmare that just couldn't be real. When she looked out of her window and saw the dust still in the air, she realised it was not and her heart sank. She sat back on her bed and cradled her stomach, unsure what to do or think.

A knock at her door made her break from her reverie. When she peered through her peephole, she couldn't believe it. It was Eileen.

Flinging open the door, no words were said between the two women as they threw their arms around each other.

'How did you get here, Mom?' Holly cried, tears spilling from her eyes. 'The bridges . . . I thought the roads were closed?'

Eileen smiled. 'Oh, honey, I walked. I had to get to you. I didn't care that the subways weren't running. I didn't care that they weren't allowing traffic. I walked.'

Holly burst into tears again.

'Shh, pet, everything's OK. Are you all right?' she asked, looking down.

Holly sniffed and followed her gaze. 'We both are. But, Mom . . . what happened yesterday . . . everything is changed. Nothing will ever be the same. This poor baby, what sort of world will it be for him? He'll never know . . . he'll never know the world that I knew, the happiness and carefree sense that — '

'Holly, listen to me.' Eileen took her daughter's tear-stained face in her hands. 'That's not true. The world is still magical. There is still *hope*. Your baby, my grandchild, will still have every opportunity to wonder and explore the world, but he will only have that if the wonder and joy in your heart aren't lost. OK? The world you create for your son depends entirely on *you*.'

Holly felt more tears escape from her eyes and her vision blurred, but not before she noticed the small box in her mother's hands. It was a box she recognised all too well.

'Mom . . . what's that?' she asked, sniffing.

Eileen looked down at the box and handed it to her daughter with a small smile.

'I have had this for a bit, and I was planning to send it to you when the baby was born, but I thought that now might be a better time. I usually like to surprise you, as I'm sure you know . . . '

Holly looked at her, shocked. 'The other charms? Those were you too?' she questioned.

Eileen gave a small nod.

She reached for her bracelet and handled it delicately. 'But how? I mean, these can't be from you. I always thought that they were from . . . '

A knowing smile graced Eileen's face. 'I know who you thought they were from, and I know you enjoyed the fantasy, even though you never said it out loud.'

Holly blushed. 'Oh God, I'm sorry, I feel so stupid now.'

'Why feel like that? Of course there's something magical about the idea of someone, a fairy godmother, looking out for you. And I also know there's a lot of unknowns about your birth mom in your mind, and that's perfectly normal.'

Holly looked away, embarrassed at her mother's perception. Once the thought had entered her mind that time back in college — that it might be her real mother who was looking out for her — it had been difficult to shake. She was young and highly imaginative, and there was no denying that it was a comforting notion, especially when she was still missing her father and her relationship with Eileen was still suffering the after-effects of being told the truth.

Eileen took her hands. 'I know the truth about your birth was still all very fresh in your mind when your dad died and you'd been through a lot. I could see you start to slip away from me, when I knew you needed me more than ever. We needed each other. That's why I started sending the charms, and I continued to send them because I knew you enjoyed the intrigue and mystery.' She smiled. 'To be honest, I enjoyed picking them out and trying to second-guess your reaction.' Eileen squeezed her daughter's hand. 'I'm only coming to you with the truth now because . . . well, at a time like this, I wanted to make sure you know that there is someone who loves you very much, and who is always looking out for you. Someone who would walk for hours and miles to get to you. Me.'

Holly collapsed in a new round of sobbing and

found solace in her mother's arms. She buried her face into her neck and felt, once again, as if she was about five years old. Eileen stroked her head and soothed her crying daughter.

'You're like Santa,' Holly finally got out.

'I know. I thought you'd just decided not to try and find out where they were coming from, so that they wouldn't stop coming,' Eileen chuckled.

That had been the rule when she was a child: the moment you stopped believing in Santa, he stopped coming. Holly had held out until she was eleven, finally letting it slip that she had seen her dad eating the same kind of chocolates that appeared in her stocking.

'I'm sorry, it was so horrible for you to find out the truth the way you did. I was so angry at myself for blurting it out like that. Then, when your dad passed so soon after, it felt like you and I were growing further and further apart.'

'It was the heat of the moment,' Holly said. 'I know that.' Yet there was no doubt that the knowledge had created a huge chasm in her relationship with her mother and since then, and especially after Seamus's death, Holly had struggled to reconnect with her.

'No matter, it was all wrong. But in truth, there was a lot of stuff I didn't get right.' Eileen gave a watery smile. 'You'll find that too when you become a mother yourself.'

'I'm sorry I never put myself in your position, how it must have felt for you too — until now. I'm so sorry, Mom.'

'So in all that time you never looked for her?'

Eileen asked. 'Even when you thought she was sending the charms?'

Holly sniffed. 'No. Maybe there was a part of me that knew it couldn't be her, but like you said, I didn't want them to stop.'

'Oh, I'll always be sending you something, pet,' Eileen went on. 'You just keep on amazing me with your resilience and strength. Now dry your tears, and why don't you open that box?'

Holly sniffled and pulled away, a smile on her face. 'OK, Fairy Godmother.' With nimble fingers she unwrapped the small box, and when she saw what was inside gave a watery grin. 'Oh my, it's so pretty,' she whispered, lifting out the tiny silver dove.

'It's a symbol of hope, and I thought that today, of all days, you might need some. I bought it for the birth of the baby because, as a new mom — biological or not,' she added with a smile, 'it's easy to feel like the world is swallowing you whole, that you don't know how you will ever manage, and you very quickly realise what a big job you have in front of you. It's all too easy to feel overwhelmed. But I know you, sweetheart, and I know that you probably feel that way today, when the world seems to be falling apart. But it's not, and it never will, just so long as you have hope.'

34

Greg hustled across town on the bike, trying to make it through the heavy traffic that littered the Manhattan streets.

Doing his best to navigate the messy, slushy street without slipping and crashing off, he made it to the gallery about fifteen minutes later.

Only to realise that it was closed.

'Damn,' he spat, as he peered inside the gallery. It was dark, except for a small light coming from somewhere in the back.

Taking a chance, Greg got off the bike and knocked on the window, just in case Gennaro was inside.

Getting no response, he tried just a little bit harder and gave several more loud raps — still nothing. He pulled his phone out of his pocket and scrolled through the numbers, finally coming to Gennaro's. Pressing 'Call', he waited to be connected.

Only to be sent directly to voicemail.

Now what? he wondered to himself.

Then, to his surprise, the front door of the gallery swung open and he felt himself jump. Turning to his left, he expected to see his friend, but it wasn't Gennaro. It was a slight woman with long black hair and almond-shaped eyes. She was dressed in black from head to toe. Gennaro's assistant, Sofia. Greg recognised her immediately.

'Can I help you?' she asked with an impatient edge in her voice. 'The gallery is closed.'

'Sofia, isn't it? Hi. I'm Greg Matthews. Gennaro has exhibited some of my work in the past and — '

'Gennaro's not here,' she interjected quickly.

'Right, I gather that. I just tried his number and — '

'He flew to Barbados. On the twenty-fourth. With some *woman*.'

Clearly, Sofia was not impressed with this getaway. Greg briefly wondered if Barbados had been promised to her, only for Gennaro to change his mind and bring someone else. His friend's taste in women seemed to morph on a daily basis, and he wondered just how many different females he had in reserve at any given point in time.

'I spoke with him the other day and he didn't mention anything about that.'

Sofia snorted. 'Out of the blue he tells me he needs me to take care of the place for a few days. So here I am, while he is on the beach with some bimbo.'

Greg wondered just how involved Gennaro had been with Sofia. Clearly, she was miffed about much more than having to work.

'So,' he continued gently, trying to change the subject, 'I'm actually here because of something that Gennaro said the other day — '

Sofia cut him off quickly. 'He hasn't spoken to me about commissioning any new artwork, so I can't help you until he gets back.'

'Actually, it's about something different.' Greg

went on to explain the situation he was in, and the comment that Gennaro had made about the woman coming to the gallery to identify the owner of a lost bracelet. 'Did Gennaro happen to mention anything to you about it before he left? Anything about a bracelet?'

'He didn't say a word about any such thing. But apparently I am in the dark about a lot of matters these days, so no surprise there,' she said, huffily crossing her arms across her chest.

Greg sighed, wondering if this was the end of the road for him. At least until Gennaro got back from his break, and he could talk to his friend directly.

Then he considered another angle. Maybe Gennaro hadn't mentioned the bracelet, but maybe he had mentioned something else that could well be related. He'd got the impression that Gennaro had agreed to help the woman in some way and, knowing his friend, he was likely to have pawned off such a task.

'Is there anything else?' Sofia asked curtly, clearly anxious to go back inside and out of the cold.

'Just one more thing. Maybe Gennaro didn't mention the bracelet specifically. But would he have asked you to do anything out of the ordinary over the last few days?' Sofia looked at him and her eyes narrowed. Greg quickly clarified his request. He was sure Gennaro had many unusual requests outside of work (and most likely inside the bedroom). 'Anything that wasn't business-as-usual? Like additional admin-istration perhaps?'

Sofia was already shaking her head. 'Everything Gennaro does could be considered out of the ordinary.'

Greg winced, feeling sorry for his friend. Based on this woman's tone, Gennaro was certainly going to have some explaining to do in the very near future.

'OK, well, thanks anyway,' he said, guessing this conversation was going nowhere. 'Happy holidays.'

He started to turn away, when suddenly Sofia spoke again.

'I wasn't finished,' she continued, shaking her head as if to say, 'Typical man, refusing to listen.'

'Oh, I'm sorry. That was rude of me. Please go on.'

She sighed. 'I was about to say that for instance, the other day out of the blue, Gennaro asked me to pull all of the records for events on every June eighteenth that we had been open. How's that for random?'

Greg thought of the date, 18 June, and knew he'd hit pay dirt. 'Completely random. I agree.' And then he broke into a smile. It was the horseshoe charm he had given to his mother, not the *corno*, that had led the woman with the bracelet to the gallery. Or, more specifically, the numbers on the charm, 618 — 18 June.

'Do you mind if I come in to talk about it? It will just take a moment, I promise.'

Sofia nodded her agreement and held open the door for him as he fixed the bike to a nearby lamppost. 'He didn't tell me what I should do with the list when I compiled it,' she said, as

380

Greg followed her into the darkened gallery. 'He just gave me a name and a number to call.'

He immediately perked up at this. 'He gave you a name?'

She nodded as she entered the office of the gallery and rummaged around in a drawer, before taking out a sheet of paper. 'This is what I pulled,' she said, handing it to Greg. 'It's all names of artists who were featured at gallery events on that date for the past eight years.'

Greg looked at the list, and his brow crinkled in confusion when he didn't see his own name. 'Why are there only women listed on this?'

Sofia sighed. 'Because that is what Gennaro requested. I thought he was looking to expand his little black book, but if it is about what you say, then that makes sense.'

Greg shook his head, not getting it. 'How so?'

'Well, you say that there is someone who is trying to find the owner of a bracelet? Obviously, she is looking for a woman, not a man. After all, would *you* wear a charm bracelet?' Sofia rolled her eyes at having to explain the obvious again.

Greg nodded and couldn't help smiling at Sofia's exasperation. She probably put up with a lot of crap having Gennaro as a boss. But indeed it did make sense.

At the same time, if Sofia had provided a list of only women to the mystery woman, there was little chance of their paths crossing.

'You also said you had a name and a number? For the woman you sent this list to?'

'I have not yet sent it — I have not had the time to send it. I was going to, but . . . ' She sighed again. 'It's right here, written on the top of the page.'

Greg looked and to his relief saw a list of digits handwritten beside the name 'Holly'. It was a local number, here in Manhattan.

'No last name?' he asked.

This elicited a bitter laugh from Sofia. 'If she did leave one, I'm sure Gennaro is keeping it to himself, especially if she is attractive . . . '

She is, Greg recalled silently.

He also remembered Gennaro mentioning that he was going to call this Holly to ask her out. So if she did happen to leave a last name, it was probably currently in Gennaro's possession.

Nonetheless he didn't need it. Now that he had Holly's number, all he had to do was call and introduce himself, and explain how he came by it. He took a moment to program the number into his phone. 'Thanks, Sofia, you have been a big help — a really big help,' he said, buoyed by the new information. 'In fact,' he added mischievously, 'if I were Gennaro, I would tell you to take the rest of the day off.'

Sofia's eyes glittered. 'Can I tell Gennaro you said that?'

Greg laughed as he turned towards the front of the building. 'Sure. Blame it on me.'

Going back out onto the street, Greg didn't hesitate in immediately calling the number he had just been given, and was looking forward to speaking with this Holly and retrieving his mother's missing bracelet. It sounded as if she was a very kind person to have found it and then go to the trouble of trying to get it back to its rightful owner. And how clever of her to try and do so through the charms. Greg was pleased that it had been one of 'his' charms that had led her to Gennaro's and, thus, to him.

He listened as a phone rang on the other end of the line, somewhere in New York. Three rings, four rings, five rings, no answer. Then a voicemail message came on.

'Thank you for calling the Secret Closet. Unfortunately, we are unable to take your call at this moment as we are either on the other line or currently serving customers. Kindly leave a message and we will get back to you shortly. If you are calling to arrange a pick-up or a donation, please call back during the hours of four and six p.m. Thank you once again for calling the Secret Closet.'

'The Secret Closet?' Greg muttered to himself as the message ended. Clearly it was the number not for Holly directly, but the number of a store. But what was that on the message about leaving donations? Was she the owner of some kind of charity store? His mind quickly went through the possibilities.

Actually it made sense, Greg thought. His mother routinely donated to charity, and he guessed that would have extended to clothes too. More than once, he'd heard her talk to Maria about sending boxes down to the Sacred Heart. But he'd never heard anything about a place called the Secret Closet.

Greg quickly punched in another number and waited for his call to be answered on Park Avenue.

383

'Matthews residence,' said Maria easily into the phone. Greg launched into his line of questioning without delay.

'Maria, it's me. Did you happen to send out any of Mom's old clothes for donation recently? To charity, I mean.'

'Well, yes, I did actually,' she said, confirming Greg's suspicions. She sounded hesitant. 'Should I not have? I mean, I remember she put some things aside and asked me to box them up for Father Mike.'

'Father Mike, from the Sacred Heart?'

'Yes. And I did box them up, but then with everything . . . I kind of forgot about them for a while until I discovered them in the front closet recently and remembered her request.'

'How long ago was this?'

'Um . . . a couple of weeks ago, I think. Why?' Then her voice changed. 'Oh no . . . is that what happened to the bracelet? Did I do something wrong and it got in there by mistake? Oh no . . . '

'Maria, you didn't do anything wrong,' Greg insisted quickly. 'But does a charity store called the Secret Closet ring a bell to you? Is that the place you sent the boxes?'

'It doesn't sound familiar. But your mom donated to a lot of different places. Still, I'm pretty sure I sent that stuff to Father Mike. Do you want me to call . . . ?'

'No, it's fine, Maria, thanks. I'll call you back if I need to.'

Greg was beginning to get a better picture of what had happened. If this Holly person owned

384

or worked for a charity store, then she must have found the bracelet among one of Cristina's donations. He guessed that kind of thing happened all the time, which is why the store had gone out of its way to try and get the bracelet back.

But while everything was beginning to make sense, he still had no idea where to find Holly.

Frustrated, Greg called the number a second time, but again it went straight to messages. Damn, maybe they were closed for the holidays? If so, he'd have to wait until the New Year to reach them and get back Cristina's bracelet — and he really didn't want to wait. Who knows, by then the store could have given up on finding it and maybe put the bracelet out on sale. If that happened, and it sold in the meantime, there was no chance of finding it thereafter.

Bringing up Google on his phone, he did a search for the Secret Closet charity store. There were a couple of places listed, but they either weren't charity stores or were based outside of Manhattan. Whereas Greg knew from the number that this place was local. Darnit . . .

He looked at his watch, not sure what to do next. Karen would be at the townhouse round about now.

So seeing as he was at a loose end anyway, and Maria seemed pretty certain she'd sent his mother's things to Father Mike and not to that store, he might as well head down to the Sacred Heart and see what he could find out.

★ ★ ★

385

A few minutes later, Greg locked the bike and approached the front door of the church. He hesitantly pushed on it and to his surprise it swung open. If there was no service in session, most churches in New York were kept locked now as a safety measure.

'Hello?' he called out, feeling a little spooked. The place was cold and dark, and it felt as though someone was going to reach out and grab him. He heard voices coming from out back so he started making his way up the aisle alongside the pews.

Finding the door partially open, he knocked on it. A trim man who looked to be in his sixties turned round. 'Yes?'

'Father Mike? You might not remember me. I'm Greg Matthews, Cristina's son . . . ' He trailed off, not quite sure if the priest would recognise him. While he knew his mother and the priest had been friends for what seemed like for ever, Greg didn't know him particularly well, having had little involvement with him over the years.

Father Mike had thinning brown hair and the kind of leathery skin that betrayed years of smoking and being out in the elements without sunscreen or a hat.

'Yes — of course!' The man's face lit up. 'Cristina's boy. How are you?' he said, pumping Greg's hand. 'Please, have a seat.'

He pulled a rickety wooden chair close to his desk for Greg. The desk was littered with clothes and handbags.

The priest smiled. 'Don't mind the mess, just

going through some donations for the needy.' He swept everything back into a cardboard box and put it on the floor, before switching on a little electric heater nearby. Greg was grateful for it; it was freezing in the small, dark space.

'Actually, that's sort of what I wanted to — ' he began.

'So how's everything?' Father Mike interjected kindly. 'I spoke to your dad just the other day.'

Greg frowned. 'You did?' While his mother had always been a regular churchgoer, he didn't realise Jeff knew the priest that well too.

'Yes. He sounded good . . . well, as good as can be expected, I suppose.'

Greg nodded. 'Yes.'

'And how are you, Greg? What can I help you with? Did you have a good Christmas? Oh, forgive my manners.' He jumped up. 'Can I get you coffee or water?' he asked, and Greg shook his head.

'No, thank you, I'm fine. Those donations,' he continued, getting to the point. 'Maria told me she'd sent a couple of boxes down to you lately. Some of Mom's old stuff.'

Father Mike looked thoughtful. 'Well, our donations tend to be numerous at this time of year, and there are a lot of boxes coming in, but yes, I think you're right — I do remember something.' He smiled. 'Your mother's always been a great friend of the church, so generous. Your dad too, of course.'

Greg looked at the box of items that Father Mike had just cleared off the table. 'Do you go through all of the donations yourself? Check through them, I mean?'

'Mostly, but not always. I have a lovely volunteer who comes in on Tuesday mornings. She often helps with the sorting and the distribution. Why?' The priest looked at him quizzically. Then his eyes widened. 'Oh dear, was there something among the donation that your mother didn't mean for us to have? That happens a lot actually, more than you could imagine — items get mixed up, or the wrong things go into the donation pile.'

Greg quickly told him about the missing bracelet.

'I remember the bracelet. She never took it off, as I recall.' He looked thoughtful. 'I can see it in my mind's eye as we speak. Lots of lovely little trinkets that tinkled as she walked.'

Greg nodded. 'Yes, and we're thinking it somehow got mixed up in a donation. The thing is, even though Maria insists she sent the stuff here, the bracelet somehow ended up in a charity store. You mentioned someone helps you with distribution. Do you happen to distribute donations to charity stores?'

'Well, no — the opposite actually. They often pass on clothing that doesn't sell for whatever reason, usually because it's in such bad condition that only the truly desperate would want it.' He looked at Greg. 'You're saying the items your mother sent us ended up in a charity store? I can't see how — '

'Yes, a place called the Secret Closet. The reason I know is because — '

But Father Mike was shaking his head. 'My

dear boy, the Secret Closet isn't a charity store, it's a *vintage* store. Although I suppose that's a common enough mistake . . . '

Greg sat up straight. 'You mean you know the place?'

'Yes, of course. Carole Greene's spot. Just off Bleecker Street. I know them well. She and Holly often — '

'You know Holly too?' Now Greg was very excited.

'Why, yes, of course. Such a lovely girl. One of the loveliest you could meet actually.' He looked at Greg and smiled. 'Well, if Holly and Carole have somehow got hold of your mother's precious bracelet, then you needn't worry. They'll take good care of it for you.'

Greg stood up, feeling elated. 'The shop's on Bleecker Street, you said?' On the bike, Greg could be there within minutes.

'Just off it. Three blocks down on the left coming from this direction.'

'Are they open today, do you think?'

'Yes, I would think so. Hanukkah is over . . . Carole, the owner, is Jewish,' he added by way of explanation.

'Thank you, Father, you've been such a great help.' Greg stuck his hand out. 'I do remember seeing somewhere in the Village when I did a Google search, but for some reason I thought I was looking for a charity store.'

'Don't tell Carole that when you get there — she takes pride in stocking only the very finest!' the priest joked.

Greg smiled. 'Thanks again. I'm going to head

down there now.' He was about to turn and go when suddenly he thought of something. 'I meant to ask, how do you know my folks? Were they part of the congregation here one time or . . . ?'

Father Mike laughed. 'No, I was a butcher at the A&P down the street from your grand-parents' deli, so I feel like I've known Cristina for ever. After I got back from Korea, there were no jobs, so I signed up here.' He winked. 'Told everyone I had 'the calling', but the funny thing is, after I started here, I *got* the calling. Toughest job I've ever had.'

Greg decided he liked Father Mike. He was a kind man who probably had lots of interesting stories to tell. He took another glance around the little room, noting the pile of donated clothes in the box, the calendar on the wall with almost every square filled up with an activity or task, the side table covered with cans and dry goods — presumably for a food drive. Then his desk with the flashing phone messages and papers and cards piled high. 'Do you think I could come back here someday and photograph you and your office?'

'Sure.' The priest was neither surprised nor daunted. 'Anytime. Just stop in, I'm usually free. Unless, of course, I'm counselling someone.'

'Thank you, I will.'

'And I'm glad I could help you with your search.' Father Mike smiled as he walked him to the door. 'And rest assured that if Holly has your mother's bracelet, it really couldn't be in better hands.'

35

In Greenwich Village, Tasha Geller languished behind the counter of her aunt's store, twirling her hair, snapping gum and talking on the phone. This job was, like, so easy.

'So what did Dana say then?' Tasha said to her friend Gretchen. She paused for a moment, waiting for a response. 'Ugh, what a bitch. I saw she changed her Facebook status to 'in a relationship'. I mean, someone should tell her that just because you make out at a party doesn't mean that you are, like, in a relationship.'

She laughed at whatever her friend said, and then turned and jumped up to sit on the counter.

'Yeah, it's OK, a bit boring. It's my aunt's store. I really don't have to do anything and she is, like, paying me ten dollars an hour. Not too shabby.' A pause. 'Yeah, I don't know, some girl quit or something. I can't remember. Whatever, she's not working and my aunt needs some help, so I said I'd do it. I don't have anything else to do. Besides, like I said, it's not like I really have to *do* anything. It kinda smells a bit, though.'

Another pause.

'Just a clothing store,' she continued. 'A used clothing store. Beats me, I don't know why anyone would want to wear someone else's crap, you know?' She laughed. 'Right, like hand-me-downs? I know, gross.'

Suddenly, Tasha's attention was turned to the front door as the bell chimed, signalling that someone had just walked in. She rolled her eyes and jumped down from the counter, looking at the customer who had entered, glancing around expectantly. 'Ugh, Gretch, I have to go. I'll call you back. There's someone here and I have to go *wait* on them . . . Yeah, OK, call you back. Bye.'

Tasha placed the phone back on the receiver and looked at the customer.

'Like, hi. Can I, um, help you?' she said, smacking her gum.

She wished that the guy would just hurry up and figure what he wanted or needed and leave. She wanted to get back on the phone with Gretchen. They had lots to talk about. 'Is there, like, something you are looking for?'

Tasha still didn't know her way around the store really, but her aunt said that she didn't need to do much more than man the cash register and make sure people didn't make a mess of the rails. She figured that if someone came in looking for something in particular, they could find it on their own, and if they couldn't find what they needed, they could leave. Hopefully promptly and without annoying her too much.

'Actually, yes. I'm looking for Holly?' The man wore a hopeful expression.

'Um, she doesn't work here any more. She's gone.'

He frowned. 'What do you mean — gone?'

Jeez, how much plainer could she get? She meant that Holly didn't work here now. Adults could be so dumb sometimes.

'I mean, like, she doesn't work here. She used to, but now she's gone. Can I help you with something else?'

'Um, well . . . well, I was looking for Holly because she might be in possession of something that belongs to me, or rather, someone close to me. I'm looking for a piece of jewellery. A bracelet.'

Tasha snapped her gum. OK, she knew the answer to this. 'Well, we don't sell jewellery.'

The man held up his hands, looking annoyed. 'No, I'm not looking to buy anything. I'm actually looking for something that was lost, and I think Holly was trying to track down the owner of this bracelet that she might have found. The bracelet belongs to my family.'

Hearing the buzz of an incoming text, Tasha pulled out her cell phone and flipped it open.

'Well, I don't know,' she mumbled idly, as she read the message. 'I don't think we have a lost and found — '

'No, that's not what I am saying.' The man started to raise his voice a little. 'Are you Carole?'

'No, and she's not here either.' Tasha shrugged, and the man now looked as if he was about to explode. Jeez . . .

'Well, do you think that maybe you could give me another number where Holly can be reached and I'll get out of your hair? I only have the store's number.'

At this request, Tasha's eyes flew up to meet Greg's and narrowed.

She didn't like the way he seemed to be losing his cool and getting more animated. She might not be the brightest bulb in the box, but kids her age understood the meaning of 'stalker' well enough to remember the 'stranger danger' lessons taught in childhood.

'Sorry, I can't.' Tasha didn't know Holly from Adam, but she knew that she was doing her a favour. 'We don't give out personal information about employees, past or present,' she added with conviction, sure her aunt would be proud of her ability to confidently assert store policies.

Greg sighed. 'Well, is there anyone else I can talk to here, please . . . ? Carole, will she be back later?'

'No,' Tasha said sharply, looking to the phone. 'And if there's a problem, maybe I should just call the police.'

The guy backed off quickly. A bit too quickly, Tasha noted. 'No, that's not necessary.' He ran a hand through his hair and puffed out a breath. 'Look, maybe if you could just pass on my information? Here's my name and phone number. Maybe you could ask Carole to call me when she comes back. It's really important, so maybe you could be so kind as to pass this along. I really need to talk to Holly.'

Tasha took the card and glanced at it.

'Sure. Whatever.'

Greg Matthews, photographer. Stalker, more like.

When the guy finally backed off and left, she peered warily at the business card. 'Whatever, you're a freak.' Spitting out her gum, Tasha

394

wrapped it in the card and threw it in the trash.

Just as she reached for the phone, her aunt walked through the door. Quickly, she moved her hand away. She should at least look as if she was working. She stacked some papers on the counter.

'Hey, Aunt Carole,' Tasha said sweetly.

Carole smiled and came round the counter to where her niece stood. 'How's it going? Was it busy?'

Tasha rolled her eyes. 'Not really. A guy was just in. He didn't buy anything, though. It was a bit creepy actually. He was, like, looking for Holly or something, like a stalker guy. I told him to scram.'

Carole frowned. 'What do you mean, 'a stalker guy'?'

'Um, I don't know. This guy was looking for Holly. He wanted her phone number and stuff, but I told him she wasn't here.'

Carole was confused. Could it have been Nick? But Nick and Holly were in touch again so she couldn't see why he'd be asking for Holly's number. Her mouth set. She didn't like the idea of strange men in her store, looking for her friend, let alone looking for personal information.

'Did you tell him that that information is confidential?'

Tasha beamed. She knew she had done a good job. 'Yup, and I told him that I would call the police.'

Carole nodded, but something still felt off, something wasn't adding up. 'What else did the guy say? What did he look like?'

Tasha gazed up at the ceiling. 'Um, he had dark hair, and he was tall, kinda good-looking, I suppose,' and Carole thought she was mistaken; it must have been Nick. That is, until she heard the next words out of her niece's mouth. 'And he said something about some bracelet or something, I told him that we didn't, like, sell jewellery.'

Carole stopped short. 'He said he was looking for a bracelet . . . Are you sure?'

Tasha took a step back at her aunt's intensity. 'Um, like, yeah . . . '

Carole rushed towards the front door. 'Which way did he go?'

'Um, I wasn't really paying attention . . . '

'Think about it, Tasha,' Carole snapped, quickly losing her cool.

Startled, Tasha answered, 'Like, right, I think?' She watched her aunt rush from the store and head towards Bleecker Street. She rolled her eyes. 'No need to get snippy about it.'

She didn't understand what the big friggin' deal was. Why would Aunt Carole want to talk to some stalker guy? Adults were so weird.

Shrugging, she flipped open her phone and pulled up her Facebook account. Quickly typing a new status update, she smiled to herself at the wisdom of the words that she had just written.

'*Hey, idiots! When you yell at me, I feel less inclined to tell you what you want to know, OK?*'

She closed her phone and went back to leaning on the counter. Maybe Aunt Carole should learn that she shouldn't shout at her employees. Not if she wanted them to do their jobs properly.

Tasha smiled to herself and picked up the phone again, her attention now on continuing her conversation with her best friend. 'Hey, Gretch?' she said. 'Yeah, I'm good now. This place is dead again. It's so boring actually. I can't believe I have to be here for another three hours.'

When Carole got back to the shop, empty-handed and without finding the man who had been in the store, she found Tasha hard at work. On the phone.

'Yeah, and did you see what she was wearing? I know! Like, barf city.' Tasha's eyes at that moment locked with her aunt's. 'Um, I have to go. OK, bye.' She quickly put the phone away.

Carole raised her eyebrows and put her hands on her hips.

'It was a customer searching for something that we didn't have. I mean, there's, like, nothing in this store that could be called 'barf city',' Tasha said meekly.

'Really . . . '

'I swear — '

Carole held up a hand. 'Forget about that for a moment, Tasha. I need you to think. This is very important. Did the man say anything else? Did he mention his name?'

Tasha's mind went back to the trash can, but she knew she would be in trouble if her aunt knew that she'd just thrown the message away without giving it to her. And she already knew that she was walking on thin ice with Carole at the moment, by being caught on the phone.

'No, Aunt Carole,' Tasha said sweetly. 'I'm sorry, should I have asked? I just thought he was kind of a creep. He *scared* me,' Tasha said exaggeratedly, hoping that acting terrified would get her off the hook. 'I mean, this is my first day here. I don't know what to do in situations like that; you didn't tell me.'

Carole's expression changed and softened ever so slightly. 'I know, you're right. You wouldn't have known and you were just going with gut instinct when it comes to dealing with strangers. Just . . . excuse me for a second. I have to go call Holly. Just keep manning the fort up here, will you?'

Tasha agreed and, as Carole walked away, her niece called after her, 'Um, Aunt Carole?'

'Yes, Tasha?'

'Is Holly, like, going to be OK? She's not in trouble or anything, is she?'

'I don't think so, sweetheart. At least, I hope not.'

36

Holly's mouth dropped open when Carole called to tell her what had happened.

'I tried to chase him down, but it was too late, I lost him. Oh, Holly, I'm so sorry that I wasn't there at the time. If only I had been, this whole thing would have been sorted out by now and — '

'Carole, it's not your fault. It's mine! I should be at work today.' Damn, she thought, biting her lip. 'He didn't leave a name or anything?'

'No. Tasha practically called the cops on him; she thought he might have been a stalker, poor guy. You know what teenagers can be like.'

'And he definitely said he was looking for a bracelet. Anything else?'

'That's all I got out of Tasha.'

'So presumably the charm bracelet must belong to his wife, or a girlfriend or whatever . . . '

'I would think so. Tasha would have *definitely* told me if he'd looked like a cross-dresser,' Carole laughed.

A giggle escaped Holly's lips. 'It's just so ironic. Here I've been working to track down the owner, and now the owner — or her boyfriend or husband or whatever — is looking to track me down.'

'But how did he know you had the bracelet? Or your name and where you worked?'

Good question, Holly thought. She thought back over the search thus far. She'd started with Lila at the UPS store — who had her details but hadn't called her back. Next was Tiffany, but she definitely hadn't left her name or any contact information with Samuel, had she? Holly didn't think so, so the guy couldn't have traced her back from there. After that, she'd tried to get in touch with Margot Mead via Jessica. Then . . . Holly remembered where her next port of call had been, and had a brainwave. The gallery. She had left her card with the Italian gallery owner.

'Did Tasha say what this guy looked like?'

'All she said was that he was tall and had dark hair. I wondered if it might have been Nick at first, but then when she mentioned something about the bracelet . . . '

The gallery owner was tall and dark, but why would he call at the store if he had information to share with her? He had her card and could easily call her cell if he was looking for her.

'Did he actually say he was looking for a bracelet, or that he had information about one?' she asked Carole, wondering how reliable Tasha's memory was.

'I'm not sure. Hold on, I'll ask her.'

Holly waited, while Carole went to talk to her niece again. She guessed that she was right; it was probably just the gallery owner after all.

Carole came back on the line. 'No, Tasha says he was definitely *looking* for a bracelet, because she suggested something about a lost and found. What are you going to do now?'

Holly shrugged. It was unlikely to have been the gallery owner, then. 'I suppose I'm just going to have to call whoever had my number in relation to the search and find out if anyone's been looking for me,' Holly sighed. 'Still, I can't help but feel I am back to square one.'

'No, not square one. You've made progress. Because of your persistence, the bracelet's owner, or someone who knows the owner, knows you have it and are trying to give it back. Someone is looking for you, and you are looking for that same someone. Now it's just about putting you both in touch with each other. What is the phrase? Six degrees of separation?'

'Maybe you're right. Either way, I'd better go and make some phone calls.' She was about to say goodbye when she remembered something. 'Oh, and Carole?'

'Yes.'

'Do me a favour,' she said, a smile in her voice. 'Don't let your niece deal with any more of my customers.'

Carole laughed guiltily. 'Consider it done.'

★ ★ ★

Holly quickly confirmed with the girl at the UPS store that no one had come round looking for her. 'I'm sorry I didn't get back to you before, but I've been waiting for head office to come back with more information about the delivery tracking,' she said apologetically, once Holly reminded her who she was.

'Don't worry — I'm not sure the information

401

would have helped anyway,' she reassured her.

Next, she called Jessica and, once again getting her voice-mail, asked her to call back as soon as she could. Then she phoned the gallery and was told by an answering service that the place was closed for the holidays and would not reopen until the New Year.

Unsure what to do next, Holly put the phone down and joined her mother on the sofa. She had in the meantime told Eileen all about the missing bracelet, and her mother had proved just as intrigued by the search as she was. She'd come over earlier to spend time with her wounded (but thankfully improving) grandson.

'It's just so frustrating; I don't know what to do next,' Holly said, exasperated, after she'd outlined the latest developments.

'But it just goes to show how much progress you've made, if the owner now knows you have the bracelet, doesn't it?'

'Yes, but thanks to Carole's niece, he has no idea where to find me. Don't get me wrong, I'm glad she didn't give out my number or address to a complete stranger, but it's a pity she didn't think to ask *him* to leave a number.'

'I wonder how he did track you down, though?' Eileen mused.

'That's what I'm wondering too. I'm thinking it must have been Jessica — after all, from what we could tell from the charms, she — the owner of the bracelet, I mean — sounds pretty well off, what with the fancy egg, and the Park Avenue apartment, the very people who run in Margot Mead's circles.' She looked at her mother.

'Actually, now that I think about it, maybe the guy who called looking for me today isn't the owner's husband or boyfriend, but her go-to guy?'

The male equivalent of Jessica, perhaps?

Her mother shrugged. 'It's possible. Either way, you're obviously doing something right, otherwise this fellow would have never been able to find you.'

'Even so, I'm still no closer to getting it back.' Holly sighed, just as her phone buzzed. Speak of the devil . . . it was Jessica.

'Hi, Jessica. Thanks for calling me back.' She explained the reason for her call and her face fell when Margot Mead's assistant told her that no, she hadn't sent anyone connected to the bracelet her way.

'Damn, I have no idea who this guy is and how he knows I have it,' she said, frustrated.

'Sorry,' Jessica replied. 'Hey, sorry you had to rush out the other day. How's the little guy?'

'Danny's great, thanks,' Holly smiled. 'And I hear you did some shopping afterwards. Which dress are you going to wear to the benefit on New Year's Eve?'

'Oh, the Marilyn one, definitely,' Jessica confirmed. 'Not that I'll have a lot of time to worry about how I look on the night. The girl I had to help out has let me down so I'll be lucky if I get a chance to reapply my freakin' lipstick.'

As she said this, Holly was struck by something.

New Year's Eve. *Same Time, Same Place.*

Was there a chance that the guy who was

403

asking for her today — and who knew she had the bracelet — might be at that benefit? Clearly he'd tracked her down as a result of her own efforts, all related to the charms. She'd already established that the owner moved in higher circles and might possibly be a guest at the event that night. So maybe her assistant or boyfriend would be too?

It was worth a shot and, at this point, the only avenue related to the charms that she had left.

Same Time, Same Place . . .

Even if she was wrong and the New Year's Eve benefit wasn't the meeting place, perhaps finally being able to meet Margot Mead would point her in the right direction.

'Jessica,' she began, unsure how to word it exactly, 'seeing as you've been so great in helping me with all this, and you've just said someone has let you down, would you like a volunteer, an extra pair of hands that night?'

She wasn't entirely sure what Jessica's role was at these things, or even what the work entailed, but given that the girl always seemed so harried, Holly figured she'd be able to help out in some way. And while she was there, keep an eye out for anyone who might just happen to fit the profile she'd built up of the bracelet owner so far.

'Well, yeah — of course . . . but seriously? You'd do that?'

'Yes — if I can get a babysitter,' she added suddenly, but alongside her, Eileen was nodding and giving her a big thumbs-up.

'You're sure? That would be so great! I should warn you, it's a pretty fancy gig — strictly black

404

tie, so even though you're working, you'll still need to look the part. Oh, what am I talking about?' she laughed. 'Nobody better than you to find a great dress for the night.'

Holly gulped. The last time she'd gone black tie was . . . well, it must have been that time in Vegas with Nick. And that was, what . . . over a decade ago?

'Sure, I guess I can find a dress,' she said, thinking about the entirely functional contents of her closet. 'Just tell me what you need me to do, and more importantly, where to go.'

And when Jessica outlined the details, and told her where the New Year's Eve benefit was being held, Holly smiled.

'OK, great. See you on the night.'

Hanging up the phone, she took a deep breath, unable to believe what she'd just agreed to. 'I think, at this stage, it's my best shot of finding the owner of the bracelet,' Holly said, outlining her train of thought to her mother.

Eileen smiled fondly at her. 'It doesn't matter either way, honey. For once, you'll be doing something fun on New Year's Eve.'

37

A few days later, Holly resumed her post at the Secret Closet. 'Oh, are you a sight for sore eyes,' Carole said as Holly hung up her coat and bag.

'So I am apparently not that easily replaceable?'

Her boss laughed heartily. 'Not by a long stretch. And people wonder why I never had children.'

Holly had to admit that it was nice to get into a routine again. Danny's bruises were fading, and once his arm healed in a few weeks' time, he'd be as good as new.

'To be honest, Carole, I'm glad to be back. It's nice to get my mind off this thing tomorrow night. I'm not sure what I was thinking really . . . '

It had been a moment of madness, offering to help Jessica out at the party like that. Yes, there was a chance that Mystery Bracelet Guy (as she'd taken to calling him) might be there, but how did Holly seriously think she would be able to pick him out from among the crowd?

She couldn't very well wear a sign on her forehead, announcing that she was the Holly who'd found his girlfriend's/wife's/boss's bracelet. She groaned at her impulsiveness.

Carole laughed. 'I think it's a fantastic idea. Why are you having second thoughts about it?'

'Well, for one, I really don't remember the last

time I went out on New Year's Eve — never mind anywhere fancy, so I need to find something to wear. And for another, what if I do find the guy who's been searching for me and the bracelet?'

Carole raised her eyebrows. 'I'm not sure what you mean . . . '

'It's just all along, I was operating under the illusion that I was searching for a woman. Someone like me. I suppose I felt some kind of kinship with her. And now, with this third party — well, I suppose I'm just not sure what to expect.'

'Think positive, Holly,' Carole said, patting her friend on the back. 'I'm sure it will be fine. Either way, you'll probably have a great night. I know I'd give anything to be mixing with the rich and famous on New Year's Eve.'

'Ah . . . taking care of their coats is hardly mixing,' Holly said, although she had to admit she was kind of excited about that side of it. She'd never got within throwing distance of a Manhattan society event before. 'Well, with any luck, I can get there, help Jessica, find out who this bracelet belongs to and then be home before the ball drops.'

Carole looked at her, shocked. 'But why on earth would you want to do that?'

'I'm just going to see if I can finish a job,' Holly reminded her. 'Plus, I've never spent a New Year Eve's away from Danny . . . '

'Who is usually tucked up in bed long before midnight anyway,' Carole reminded her. 'I've told you before, Holly, you need to get out and have some fun. Who knows, you might even meet someone at this thing.'

'Yes, forget the society ladies, I'm sure all the stockbrokers and hedge-fund guys only have eyes for the cloakroom girl at these things,' she teased. She walked over to the nearest rack. 'But speaking of society ladies, I still need to find something to wear.'

Suddenly, Carole's eyes started to sparkle.

'You mean you haven't decided on a dress yet?' she asked innocently.

'I can't decide on a dress, because there isn't a single one in my closet — nothing that would work for an event like this, anyway.' She paused and flicked through the rails. 'Anything new in lately? Just something simple, and preferably cheap; I don't want to spend too much.'

Carole smiled mischievously. 'Wait right here.'

'What? Where else would I be going . . . ?' But she was talking to herself, as her boss headed out back to the stockroom. Seconds later, she emerged with a large white box with an elegant black ribbon tied round its middle.

'What on earth is that?' Holly asked.

'*That*, my dear, is a surprise for you. And with it, I need you to make me a promise.'

'What kind of promise?'

'I'll tell you in a minute. First, open it.'

'You're the boss,' Holly laughed, untying the ribbon. Then she lifted off the top of the gift box, tore back the tissue paper and immediately sucked in her breath.

'Oh, Carole . . . it's Anna Bowery's Givenchy! But I thought Jessica bought it . . . '

'I never said that, you did.'

Holly playfully swatted at Carole as she admired the dress. It was just so beautiful and, in truth, would be absolutely perfect for the benefit tomorrow night. When she thought about all the amazing events this dress had seen in its lifetime . . . Certainly, many more than she had, that was for sure.

'Try it on,' Carole urged, as she had when the dress first came in.

'Oh, I don't know — '

'Please, just humour me.'

'It doesn't matter, I can't afford it.'

'Try it on! Like you said, I'm the boss, and that's an order.'

'OK . . . ' Holly reluctantly picked up the dress and turned towards the small dressing room at the other end of the store.

A few moments later, she emerged to look in the mirror.

'Oh my . . . ' Holly gasped. 'This is exactly what Cinderella must have felt like.' She walked towards her reflection in the mirror, then twirled slowly, allowing the boundless tulle of the skirt to float around her, the crystals catching the overhead lighting and casting a disco-ball effect on the floor.

Carole approached her from behind and gazed at her reflection. She patted her shoulder. 'My goodness, Holly, it was really made for you. These nineteen fifties dresses can be so severe with their tailoring, especially on women's shapes today. You look like you've just stepped out of the fifties yourself. It hardly needs any alterations, just a little bit here . . . ' She took a pin out of her pocket and clipped it to the shoulder area, which was slightly loose. So delicate, and what's more you already have the accessories. Your charm bracelet is perfect with it.'

Holly duly held out her arm. The bracelet did indeed look great with the dress.

'You said it yourself,' Carole continued. 'This dress has seen so many things and has such a rich history — it should belong to you.' Holly was about to protest that there was just no way she could afford it, when Carole put her hand up. 'And it does now because I bought it for you. So please, promise me that you will wear this tomorrow night, and even if you don't find the owner of the bracelet, that you will have fun, that you will give that dress another great outing.'

Holly felt tears playing at the corners of her eyes and nodded. 'I would so love to wear it, but you have to let me pay you back for this. It's just too much.'

'No, Holly. It's just enough. Do Anna Bowery proud. Have a New Year's Eve to remember in that dress, OK?'

Holly held up the dress and had to admit to herself that she couldn't wait to put it on. Maybe it was a sign. Maybe, just maybe, she would find the owner of the bracelet while wearing this beautiful confection of an outfit.

Conspiratorially, the crystals on the skirt seemed to twinkle and wink at her, as if they understood that they were about to embark on another adventure with their new owner.

Holly turned to Carole and smiled. 'Well, then I suppose I'm all set. New Year's Ball, here I come.'

38

'Why is it I have never been able to get the hang of bow ties?' Jeff asked his reflection as he struggled with the black piece of silk round his neck.

Greg walked up behind his father and shook his head.

'Because Mom coddled you too much by always doing it for you? No surprise, you're hopeless.' He chuckled and tapped Jeff on the shoulder. 'Turn round . . . '

Moments later, Jeff's tie was perfect, compliments of his son. He admired the handiwork in the mirror. 'Not bad. Where did you learn to do that?'

'Where do you think?' Greg asked.

'Thank God you inherited more of her genes than you did mine.'

'Oh, I think I probably did pretty OK from both sides. How are you feeling, Dad? Are you absolutely sure about coming along to this thing tonight?' He knew today's date as well as the significance of the evening would be weighing on Jeff's mind — especially when this would be the first time they would be attending the annual New Year's Eve ball without Cristina.

His father raised a smile. 'Don't worry about me, kid. I'm fine. Anyway, your mother would kill me if I even thought about giving it a miss. The St Jude's benefit has always been one of her favourites.'

411

'I know.'

'You seem a bit distracted yourself,' Jeff commented as the two left the penthouse fully bedecked in classic tuxedos. Greg punched the elevator button, and father and son waited for the doors to open.

'I just wish that the woman who found Mom's bracelet would get in touch. It's been days now.'

Greg chewed ever so briefly on one of his nails. Despite leaving his number with that awful teenager, he'd heard nothing from Holly or the owner of the vintage store and it worried him. Didn't Father Mike say that they were decent, dependable women? Yet Holly no longer worked at the store and her boss had ignored his request to call him back. Greg was worried now that something had happened in the meantime, that he was too late, and maybe they had indeed sold the bracelet on to a customer. After all, who knew how long they'd been looking to give it back? With these places, there might be some rule that after a certain length of time trying to contact the owner, they just give up and put it out for sale. And who could blame them — if the bracelet had been among items his mother had requested be donated or sold on, then they were perfectly entitled to do so.

He tried to think back to his brief encounter with Holly on the way in to the gallery that time. How frustrating to think that their paths had already crossed. Neither one of them could have realised the importance of that brief meeting.

'I'm sure she'll get in touch. Don't forget it's still the holiday season and everything's a bit crazy. She sounds like a good person — going to all that trouble to try and get it back to us,' Jeff smiled.

The elevator pinged and both men got inside. Greg shrugged. 'I don't know — maybe she just has too much time on her hands.' But he was secretly impressed that this Holly seemed to have used the charms themselves to try and track the owner down. Cristina would be tickled pink by that, seeing as she always joked that the bracelet was a roadmap of her life.

★　★　★

'Your carriage awaits, my lady,' Eileen smiled, as she watched her daughter elegantly descend the steps outside the apartment building, Kate and Danny standing alongside her at the doorway.

Fully bedecked in the Anna Bowery Givenchy, Holly looked as though she had stepped out of another era. She had pulled her hair up into a loose chignon, which highlighted her elegant neck and showed off the bejewelled comb that expertly complemented the 1950s style. The dress sparkled and showcased Holly's attractive figure while the opera-length gloves that she had discovered in a drawer gave a nod to the past parties that this dress had surely seen.

Reaching the bottom of the steps, she blushed. 'I can't believe you hired a car to take me there, Mom. I could have just caught a cab.'

'That dress, and you, deserve better than any old yellow cab,' said an earnest Eileen.

Holly bit her lip. 'Well, thank you, I appreciate

413

it. So I guess I'm ready.'

'You look awesome, Mom,' Danny smiled.

'Why thank you, young man. Are you sure you don't mind me leaving you tonight?'

'Nope, Nana says we can watch Jay-Z. He's performing tonight on TV.'

More like Jay-Z was sipping champagne in a mansion in Beverly Hills, Holly thought knowingly. Danny didn't need to know that the majority of 'New Year's Eve Live Telecasts' were filmed months ago in studios.

'Don't worry about us; we'll have lots of fun,' Eileen said, putting an arm around her grandson's shoulder. 'And you, my dear, enjoy yourself. Don't even attempt to come home too early.'

Holly reflected on how times had changed . . . half her life ago, Eileen would have been telling her not to get home too late.

'We'll see. I might well be home in no time watching Jay-Z in my PJs with you guys.'

'You wouldn't dare,' Kate said ominously.

'Yeah, Mom, go out, have fun,' Danny encouraged.

Eileen patted her grandson's head. 'Yes, please have a good time. Just go and enjoy yourself. Regardless of whether or not you find the bracelet's owner.'

Holly looked down at the full tulle of her skirt and swished it, once again hypnotised by its crystals. Maybe she did deserve a little fun.

'Keep in mind, Holly, that no one probably ever had to tell Anna Bowery to have fun in that dress,' Kate called out. 'Time to do it justice.'

Giving the three of them a final hug goodbye, Holly got into the waiting black town car.

The trio on the steps waved after her as the town car pulled from the kerb and drove slowly up the street, before a moment later turning north in the direction of Fifth Avenue.

★　★　★

The Cadillac that Greg and Jeff were in pulled up to the kerb and Greg stared intently at the mass of people who were arriving for the hospital benefit, the majority of them being dropped off in sleek black cars much like the one that they were in right now.

Greg scanned faces in the crowd. Some he knew from his mother's work on various other charities, as well as their past attendance at this event. Others he didn't know personally, but recognised because of their penchant for appearing on Page Six of the *Times*. Still, most of the people he didn't recognise at all.

The car rolled forward in line and then stopped. Greg threw open the door of the car, not waiting for the kerbside valet to open it for him, and stepped out.

Jeff followed suit, straightening his jacket.

Father and son walked up the granite steps at the front of the building and Greg felt impressed, as he always did, by the grand façade. A regal lion statue sat to his right, a silent and noble sentry, seemingly unimpressed by all the glam and glitter of the people who strode around him. Corinthian columns soared overhead and

415

Greg thought back to what his mother had said last year as they walked up these same stairs together.

'It's comforting to know that people still have it in them to build temples to knowledge. These places will still be here long after we are gone.'

As Greg and Jeff neared the entryway of the building, both men reached into the breast pocket of their jackets and extracted their tickets to the event, ready to hand them to the striking blonde woman who was standing at the door, checking off names on a clipboard.

She wore a figure-hugging dress that looked as if it might have come out of Marilyn Monroe's closet, and Greg took note of her startlingly high gold platform shoes. She was practically as tall as him in them — he never could understand how women had the ability to totter around on six-inch heels. He would definitely fall on his face if faced with the challenge.

'Good evening,' the blonde woman said with crisp efficiency.

'Happy New Year,' Jeff replied. 'The name is Matthews, both of them.'

The young woman consulted her list and checked off the names. 'I have a total of four for your party. Will Cristina and Karen be following?'

Jeff shook his head. 'They couldn't make it,' he said by means of explanation.

The blonde girl nodded. 'Noted. Have a great evening.'

★ ★ ★

416

Holly swallowed hard as she took in the scene around her. Dozens of black town cars were pulling up to the kerb in front of the building and she felt a flutter of anticipation run through her stomach. She opened her small silver clutch and grabbed her lip gloss, touching up her lips. Placing the tube back in the tiny evening bag, she once again verified that the bracelet was inside. It was about the twentieth time that she had checked to ensure that she hadn't forgotten it.

Just in case.

She smoothed her skirt and glanced back out of the window. Men in tuxedos and women in stunningly beautiful evening gowns milled about outside. Some called out in greeting to one another, while others pointedly made for the entrance, eager to keep their feet on the red carpet and to get in out of the cold.

As Holly's car pulled forward once again, and then stopped, the driver turned round.

'Have a fantastic night, miss. Whenever you are ready to leave, just call this number — ' he handed her a card with his direct number on it — 'and I will come back and pick you up. Doesn't matter what time. I'm yours for the evening.'

Holly smiled and couldn't deny that she was tickled pink by the special treatment. 'Of course.' She looked at the name on the card. 'Thank you, Douglas,' she smiled again.

'Just call me Doug. I like it better,' the man replied. 'I keep Douglas on there just for the stiffs.' He nodded to the people who were outside the car, the people he was clearly used to driving around. 'Doug sounds like a guy you meet at the bowling alley, you know?'

She grinned knowingly. 'Well, I don't know about you, Doug, but I happen to like bowling.'

'You and me both, sister,' he replied in his thick Brooklyn accent. 'Now you go and have a great time.'

'Well, I'm sort of working, but thank you.'

At that moment, the kerbside valet opened the door for Holly, and she extended a graceful leg.

'Oh, and miss?'

Holly turned back to Doug, giving him her full attention. 'Please . . . it's just Holly.'

Doug smiled and nodded. 'Nice dress, Holly.'

Tentatively, she made her way towards the stairs, following the lead of those around her. She'd arranged to meet Jessica at the door, but right at that moment, and wearing that dress, she didn't feel like Holly the Help; she felt just the same as any of these glamorous people.

She glanced around, taking in the faces, wondering if any of them happened to be the bracelet owner, and at the same time recognising several of the people around her.

Wow, Mayor Bloomberg . . . and was that Gwyneth Paltrow? She gulped, trying her utmost not to be star-struck, otherwise she'd be useless to Jessica once she got inside.

Holly looked down at her dress and whispered to it as if it were a living thing, 'You probably feel right at home here, don't you?'

Then, as she ascended the steps towards the door, she reached down for her charm bracelet, seeking out a particular charm, the tiny book she'd received way back in college.

'Nothing exciting ever happens in a library, huh?' she said, echoing her old roommate's words from all those years ago.

With that, Holly took a deep breath and followed the crowds inside the New York Public Library.

39

She met Jessica in the foyer as arranged. 'Oh, you look gorgeous! I told you the Marilyn suited you.'

'Thanks. I've been getting compliments all evening actually.' Jessica grinned and put down her clipboard. 'I'm so excited you're here. Thank you for offering to help me — I really appreciate it. And wow, I know I said you needed to look the part, but . . . '

Holly flushed and looked at the dress, embarrassed. 'What — it's too much?'

'Are you kidding me? It's amazing — so amazing that I feel bad for setting you to work. You should be in there partying with the rest of them.'

'Seriously, it's wonderful but not quite my thing.' She loosened her throw. 'So where do you want me?'

'Well, to start . . . ' Jessica nodded to the rail of coats nearby. 'There's a room just down the hall set aside for all that. If you could just move the rails as they fill up, that would be great. Just take care not to mess up the numbering system.'

Relieved, Holly nodded. This, she was used to. Taking note of Jessica's directions for the makeshift cloakroom, she wheeled away the first rail of coats, noting that the majority were heavy wool for the men, and predominately fur for the women.

Not in the least controversial for a children's hospital benefit, but she guessed things might be different if this was in aid of an animal charity. Or would it? Again, the rich never seemed to recognise the irony in such things.

⋆ ⋆ ⋆

Greg and Jeff were making their way through the crowd. Several times they were stopped by friends and business acquaintances, people looking to say hello or express condolences over Cristina. Thankfully no one asked Greg where Karen was. He wasn't sure if it was because news had already spread about the break-up, or because people were aware of his very public proposal and didn't want to embarrass him about the gesture that turned out to be less than romantic.

That is, until he bumped into Margot Mead.

'Greg! How are you? Wonderful to see you again,' Margot gushed, reaching forward to air-kiss him. 'Is Karen here?' she continued, looking over his shoulder, as if expecting to see his ex bringing up the rear.

He reluctantly returned her embrace. 'Nice to see you again too. No, I'm afraid she's not. We aren't actually together any more.' He exhaled, preparing himself to go through more small talk before he could take his leave.

'Oh, I'm so sorry to hear that. Of course, I guessed something was off,' she said conspiratorially. 'I saw her, I believe the day after Christmas, at the Plaza. She was with some man, and well, you know, there needs to be a level of discretion, but still I was surprised . . . '

Discretion my ass, Greg thought, struggling to keep a smile on his face. Margot knew well that something was up. He knew that women like her lived for gossip, and he wasn't going to be an active participant in spreading the goods about himself.

'Well, it's no surprise to me actually. But you will have to excuse me: I see someone I must say hello to.' Greg motioned vaguely in the direction behind Margot. He didn't see anyone, but just didn't want to get stuck any longer with her.

'Oh, of course. I must go and say hello to your father. So sad about Cristina, you know — we all miss her terribly,' Margot said with some sincerity and feeling in her tone. 'How's everything at home? I can't believe that just a year ago we were all here together.'

'Thank you, yes, it's been a long year,' Greg said evenly. 'Now, if you'll excuse me. Happy New Year.' Greg figured he might as well get the greetings over with, as he wasn't planning on staying within an ass's roar of Margot Mead or any of her dreadful society friends for the rest of the night.

Going through the crowds, he headed for the bar that had been set up and ordered a beer. Sipping his drink, he continued to scan the crowd.

Just then, there was a tap on his shoulder.

'Gregorio, good to see you!'

Greg smiled, immediately recognising the distinctive Italian accent, and turned round to be met with Gennaro's smiling face. The tan he was sporting was definitely not Manhattan in origin.

'Hey, have a good time in Barbados?'

The other man looked taken aback. 'Yes, fantastic. But how did you know?'

'I swung by the gallery the other day and met with the wrath of Sofia. She was less than impressed about that, you know.'

'Yes.' Gennaro's expression was sheepish. 'Which is why I am making it up to her.' He nodded across the room towards a dark-haired woman in a silver evening gown whom Greg immediately identified as the gallery manager. 'I didn't have a date for tonight, so she is happy. For the moment at least.'

Greg shook his head indulgently. 'You're such a dog.'

'Don't I know it, buddy? Best-of-breed too.' He grinned proudly. 'What were you doing at the gallery anyway?'

Greg filled him in on what had happened since he last saw him, and that the woman at the gallery was likely in possession of his mother's bracelet. When he finished, Gennaro's mouth was shaped in the form of an 'O'.

'Holly O'Neill? It was your mother's bracelet that she showed me? I wish I could have known.'

'O'Neill?' Greg repeated. So now he had her full name. Whether or not he could do anything with the information was another matter.

Gennaro nodded. 'Yes, thinking back, and remembering what she told me, she was trying very hard to get the bracelet back to you. She found me through a horseshoe, and when I showed her my father's *corno*, she said it added a little more to the picture she was painting about the owner. Smart and sexy, eh?'

Greg listened intently to his friend, taking in every word.

So Holly really was trying to trace his mother back through the individual charms. That took a lot of dedication. The notion made him feel heartened: if she was putting so much time and energy into the search, it was unlikely she'd just give up and let the bracelet be sold on to some-body else. Hopefully she identified the importance of the bracelet to Cristina in sentimental terms.

Gennaro scrunched up his face, as if trying to recall what else Holly had told him about her quest. 'And do you know,' he added, 'she also mentioned that she had information about a charm related to a benefit? I think it was an egg?'

Greg nearly choked on his beer. 'The egg my mom won as a prize at the Met Gallery?'

'I don't know about that, but I do recall her asking me if I knew a Margot . . . what was her name now?'

Greg's pulse quickened. 'Mead, Margot Mead. Did she definitely mention her? She's the organiser of this event.'

'Yes, I believe so.'

Greg couldn't believe that Holly had made another connection. She really must have been doing everything in her power to get the bracelet back. He bit his lip.

'Keep an eye on that beer for me, will you?' he told his friend. 'I have to go and find the woman

I just tried to avoid.'

Thankfully, Margot Mead was easy to find, and was holding court in pretty much the same place as Greg had left her. However, getting through the mass of people who were surrounding her, vying for her attention, was not so easy.

Not wanting to be rude and push his way through, he looked for a way to get closer. Spotting his father, who was not more than an arm's length away, he gently made his way to Jeff's side.

'Dad,' Greg said, tapping his father's shoulder, 'can you get Margot's attention? I don't want to butt in.'

Jeff nodded. 'Margot? Excuse me? Margot? Could I talk to you just a moment?'

Margot turned her attention to Jeff quizzically. She looked to the woman who had been talking to her and held up a finger.

'Can't get enough of me, Jeff?' she laughed.

'Actually, I think my son needs you.'

She turned her attention to Greg but, before she could get a word out, he launched into what he had just learned from Gennaro.

'Margot, I need to know something. Did someone, a woman actually, recently come to you about a bracelet? Someone named Holly?'

Confusion flashed across her features. 'I don't think so. When you say 'come to me about a bracelet', do you mean as a gift?'

'No, not like that. It's just somehow . . . probably among all the upheaval . . . my mother's bracelet went missing, and I think that whoever found it may have found a connection to you

425

through one of the charms — the egg one, I think.'

'Really?' Jeff stepped forward, interested, and Greg nodded encouragingly at him.

Margot was frowning. 'The diamond one? Of course I remember Cristina winning that at the Met benefit, wasn't it? But really, I don't recall anybody asking about anything like that, not personally anyway. I could check with my assistant, though. She'd certainly remember something like that — never forgets a thing.'

'Would you? We'd be most grateful.'

Obviously recognising the urgency in Greg's voice, Margot continued, 'Of course. I could do it now, if you like. Jessica, my assistant, is here.'

'That would be wonderful, thank you.'

She pulled her iPhone out of her evening bag and quickly typed a text message.

Greg smiled at his father, hope and adrenalin surging through him.

This was good; this was really good.

★   ★   ★

Having safely moved all the coat rails to the designated cloakroom, Holly moved to the edge of the crowd in the Catalogue Room. Jessica had told her to go and take a breather until she needed her again, so Holly did as she was bid, anxious to see if she might be able to identify anyone who — from the picture she'd built up of her — might be the owner of the bracelet.

She'd been approached a few times by people thinking they knew her, and by a few men

426

obviously looking to hit on her. Small talk was made, but the moment Holly began talking about the bracelet and if they knew anybody who might be missing one, she'd been rewarded with strange looks and protestations that they'd seen someone they needed to say hello to.

With the way things were going, she'd be lucky if security didn't cart off the crazy woman propositioning people with mad stories about bracelets. She smiled. Oh well, she supposed there were worse ways to get on Page Six.

Looking at her watch, she took note of the time. Almost eleven o'clock, just over an hour until the ball dropped. She took in the happy couples and partygoers around her enjoying themselves, and suddenly wished she had someone to talk to. As much as she remembered her promise to Carole and the others to have a good time, and do the dress proud, she couldn't deny that she felt a little lost, not to mention hopelessly out of place.

She strolled slowly through the crowd, and as she did was awarded with appraising glances from several dashing-looking gentlemen, as well as a few dirty looks from the women who were obviously said gentlemen's dates.

She really didn't belong here.

Holly moved towards the bar area, thinking a glass of water might soothe her dry mouth and calm her nerves. As she approached the bar itself, she again attracted the attention of an appreciative man. But this was one she recognised.

Holly smiled as she looked at Gennaro, the

attractive Italian gallery owner. And he clearly recognised her.

'Holly? I have your name right, yes?'

She nodded and smiled, happy to run into a familiar face, even if it was this shameless flirt. Although, at the moment, Holly realised he was looking at her rather strangely. She coloured, somewhat embarrassed. Did she look *that* out of place here?

'Hello again — Gennaro, isn't it?' she replied. 'Happy New Year.'

'I can't believe you're here.' He didn't return her greeting, just continued to stare at her as if she'd just landed from outer space.

She blushed self-consciously. 'Well, I'm not here as a guest actually. I'm helping out a friend. Well — '

'Do you still have that bracelet?' he asked, cutting her off. She looked at him, surprised at the intensity in his voice.

'Well, yes . . . Why do you ask?'

'You do? Oh, this is just wonderful . . . '

So it *had* been Gennaro who had come looking for her at Carole's the other day, Holly realised. A surge of anticipation rushed through her veins. 'Why? Did you find out who it belongs to? Was it one of your artists after all?'

But then Holly recalled what Tasha had said about the man saying the bracelet was important to his family, and confusion bloomed yet again.

'Yes, and he is here tonight,' Gennaro said theatrically.

'He . . . ' Holly stammered, again perplexed.

'Yes, you are looking for him and he is looking

428

for you — wonderful! Come,' he said, reaching for her hand. 'We must find him, my friend. He will be so happy to see you.'

She looked at Gennaro expectantly, hardly able to believe it. She was right. Her hunch about the *Same Time, Same Place* charm was right. She had followed the breadcrumbs correctly and they had led her here to this place, on this night.

The owner of the bracelet — or at least someone who knew her — was here. Now all Holly had to do was get it back to her.

40

Greg turned round to see the Marilyn Monroe look-alike in the six-inch heels from the door approaching. She was carrying a clipboard, the guest list.

'Ms Mead?' Jessica said, nearing her employer. 'You were looking for me?'

'Yes.' Margot placed a hand on her employee's arm. 'Jessica, may I introduce to you Greg Matthews and his father, Jeff.' Jessica nodded and smiled politely, as if fully expecting to have to do their bidding as well as Margot's.

Impatiently, he smiled a greeting in return, wishing they could quickly get through the formalities and get on with it.

'Jessica, I believe that you might be able to help us. Do you recall anyone enquiring about a charm bracelet recently?' her boss continued. 'Or perhaps an enquiry related to an individual charm, more specifically one of the jewelled eggs we used as a prize at the Met benefit last year?'

Was it Greg's imagination or did the assistant's eyes grow twice the size?

'You mean Holly?' she gasped, and he breathed an internal sigh of relief.

'Yes, my mother's charm bracelet went missing recently and it seems that this woman, Holly, might have happened across it.'

'Yes, she did,' Jessica confirmed excitedly, abandoning her earlier decorum. 'And she's been

430

searching high and low for you these last few weeks.'

'Would you happen to have a contact number for her?' Greg asked, hoping that she might have something other than the store number, as this had already proved to be a dead end.

Jessica looked as though she was stifling a smile. 'I can do one better than that, Mr Matthews,' she said, grinning. 'She's here.'

Greg looked at Jeff in disbelief. 'Here tonight?'

'Yes, she offered to help out in return for my helping her with the charm. I can take you to her right now if you'd like.'

'That would be fantastic.' Greg couldn't believe his luck. He stole a delighted glance at his father, who was looking at his watch. Greg did the same as he followed Jessica through the crowds out towards the corridor. It was eleven fifteen — forty-five minutes until the clock struck twelve.

As they walked, Jessica told him all about Holly and her repeated attempts to track his mother down.

'She was very determined. Worked me even harder than Ms Mead trying to put the pieces together,' Jessica told him. 'Hey, you guys don't happen to live on Park Avenue, do you?'

'My parents do,' Greg confirmed. Then he thought of something. 'The building, she identified the building from the charm?'

'I did actually,' Jessica said proudly. 'But I think Holly was about ready to stand outside every building on the park hoping to find the right one.'

'I can't believe she was so committed. I'm very

431

grateful.' He was also really looking forward to meeting Holly properly. She did sound like a good person.

'I went to the store in Greenwich. Apparently she doesn't work there.'

'No, that's not it. She's just been out for a couple days. Her son had an accident just before Christmas and she was at home with him.'

Greg nodded. A son. And probably a husband too.

As if Jessica could read his mind, she quickly provided, 'She's single — really great. You'll like her, I think.'

Greg wasn't entirely sure why she'd felt the need to offer this piece of information, but from what he could remember of Holly from the gallery, he was surprised that she wasn't attached. She was very attractive.

'So it's true then, she definitely has the bracelet — you've seen it?'

'Yup. Seen it, inspected it and hypothesised over it too. Don't worry, Holly has it.

'Excuse me, excuse me, please,' Jessica said, trying to stay as professional as possible as they moved through the crowd, when at that point all Greg wanted to do was start tossing people out of their way.

'Come on, she's just down here,' Jessica said, leading him to a small room down the hallway that looked as though it might be a conference room but was now being used as a cloakroom. It was empty.

'She was just here . . . ' Jessica said under her breath.

Greg shook his head ruefully. It was as if somebody somewhere was trying to stop him from getting the bracelet back.

★   ★   ★

Holly felt faintly excited as she allowed herself to be led through the crowds.

She couldn't believe that after all the searching she would finally be able to reunite this precious bracelet with its rightful owner.

They wandered around for quite a while, until eventually she had to tell Gennaro to slow up, her feet were hurting.

'There are so many people,' he complained, looking frustrated. 'I don't think it is possible to find him in this way.' He took out his mobile phone and scrolled through it. 'With luck he will have his phone.' Holly watched expectantly as he put the phone to his ear and waited. After a few moments, he shook his head.

'It doesn't seem like he has his phone. Or,' he said as if a thought had struck him, 'maybe he just cannot hear it. Come, let us go through to the ballroom.'

'There's a ballroom in the New York Public Library?' Holly repeated in confusion.

Gennaro winked. 'There is on New Year's Eve.'

Then suddenly Holly was being led towards the famed Reading Room, which truly looked like something out of a fairy tale. The books that usually lined the large open space had been covered with light satin gauze and the flowers that bedecked the room uplit by soft candlelight.

'Wow,' she gasped, unable to believe what she was seeing.

Just then her own phone began to ring and she guessed it was Jessica.

'Oh darnit. Sorry, Gennaro, I don't think I can do this now. I'm needed. Like I said, I'm actually here working and — '

Gennaro, who was looking into the distance, shook his head. 'Wait just one moment. I see him,' he said, and before Holly had the chance to say any more, he took her hand and led her to the other side of the room.

Feeling guilty, she fumbled in her bag with one hand, trying to get the phone out. She'd promised Jessica she'd help out at this thing, not wander around the building with a handsome Italian.

But Gennaro was on a mission and, as she followed his course through the path of people up ahead, she saw a red dress and a mane of blonde hair. Jessica.

She looked seriously on the warpath, and Holly hoped she wasn't about to get a major dressing-down.

But when they got closer, Gennaro began to slow his pace; as the crowds parted, another person she recognised came into view. Standing beside Jessica was the man she'd collided with that day on the way out of Gennaro's gallery. Holly was sure of it.

He happened to see her at the very same time and his eyes brightened the moment their gazes connected. Instant recognition bloomed on both of their faces.

Gennaro dropped her hand and stopped about a foot in front of Jessica and the guy from the gallery.

'There you are!' Jessica exclaimed.

'Sorry, I know you've been looking for me, but — '

'Not me, him.' She nodded with a smile towards Greg.

'Seems you have both been looking for each other,' Gennaro commented mischievously. Jessica whispered to Holly that she would catch up with her later, and Gennaro followed her, an intent gaze on Jessica's backside as she walked away.

The man and Holly looked at each other.

'It's you . . . Gregorio,' she said, remembering how Gennaro had addressed him at the gallery.

He took a step forward and offered his hand. 'Actually, it's just Greg.'

'I'm — '

'I know who you are, Holly.' The look he gave her sent a warm flush to her cheeks. 'And I understand that you have been looking for me.'

As she took in Greg's fine features, his broad shoulders, warm chocolate eyes and dark hair that was practically pleading for fingers to be run through it, Holly thought, Remember, Holly, he's not looking for you — he's looking for the bracelet. She nodded. 'Well, I didn't know it was you, but yes, I have.'

Reluctantly she dropped her gaze to the clutch, and opening the bag, she put her hand inside it, feeling for the bracelet. Pulling it out in one swoop, she smiled and handed it to Greg. 'I think this belongs to you,' she laughed, 'or rather, your girlfriend or wife or . . . ' Her eyes danced around quickly, looking for any sign of the woman who not only owned the beautiful bracelet, but was also lucky enough to have laid claim to this gorgeous man's heart.

'Actually, it's my mother's,' he clarified and she felt her heart lift a little. 'Holly, thank you so much.' He picked up the bracelet and studied it, running his fingers along the individual charms. His eyes seemed to glisten as he did so, and she guessed she wasn't quite getting the whole story. 'You don't know how much this means. Really. This is so important to our family. Thank you from the bottom of my heart. My dad's here and I know he'll want to thank you too.'

She smiled kindly. 'It was my pleasure.'

For a moment the two of them stood there, unsure of what to say.

'Well . . . I probably should be going.'

'Actually, would you like to go get a drink?' Greg asked quickly. 'I feel I owe you that much at least, especially since I know you've gone to a lot of trouble to get this back to us.'

'You don't know the half of it . . . ' Holly smiled and self-consciously put a hand up to push a stray hair out of her face. 'But it was no trouble really.'

'Hey, you've got one too.' Greg noticed the bracelet on Holly's wrist and he put a gentle hand under her arm. A surge of electricity shot through her and her mind whirled. What was going on? Who was this man? 'It's beautiful. If it's anything like my mom's, I'm assuming all of these charms, they mean something too?'

She nodded, trying her utmost not to betray how she was feeling. 'You assume right.'

'So that's why you tried so hard to get it back,' Greg said. 'I was wondering about that.'

'This bracelet — it's the story of my life really.'

Greg smiled. 'Well then, it gives you an unfair advantage.'

'How so?' she asked, curious about his meaning.

'Well, you already know a lot of the stories behind the charms on my mother's bracelet ... so I'm thinking you should let me buy you that drink, right now, and tell me your stories so we have a level playing field.'

He looked expectantly at her but Holly had already fallen under his spell. She knew she wasn't supposed to be here sharing drinks and stories with handsome men; she was supposed to be working. But she couldn't resist the idea that something — and not just the bracelet — had drawn her here, to Greg. Almost as if to reiterate this, right then, the music changed, and recognising the song, she gave a little laugh.

'What's so funny?' Greg asked.

'That song — it's my favourite song in the whole world, and I'm just thinking about what my son said about it the last time I heard it.'

'What did he say?'

'He said it was a song about pizza,' she smiled, as the sound of Dean Martin's 'Amore' filled the room.

'Well, I suppose he's right in a way,' Greg said, chuckling. 'He sounds like a sensible guy.'

'Sensible, Danny?' Holly scoffed at the thought.

'Well, OK then, if you won't let me buy you a drink, then let me have this dance. Seeing as it's your favourite song . . . '

Holly looked around at these people, the beautifully dressed women and rich, handsome men. Never in a million years did she think she'd be among people like these in a place like this. Wearing a dress like this. With a gorgeous man who wanted to dance with her.

'Just say yes,' Greg said, closing the space between them and reaching for her hand. This wasn't her world and would never be her world, but maybe like Carole said, the dress deserved another great memory.

And as a matter of fact, so did she.

Feeling impulsive (and unable to resist Greg's smile), Holly held out her hand. 'OK.'

And as she danced around the Reading Room in the New York Public Library to that wonderful song, with a gorgeous man she'd only just met, she guessed Anna Bowery would approve.

As Greg held her hand up while they moved, Holly's bracelet dropped down along her arm and into her field of vision. She smiled, realising that she certainly wouldn't need a charm to remember tonight — this particular memory would be with her for the rest of her life. And in the end, wasn't it also the links — the people, the love and the memories — and not just the charms, that made the bracelet complete?

The song was just about to come to an end when another man tapped Greg on the shoulder.

'Son, I'm going now. I'll see you later. Happy New Year.'

'Oh, Dad, I didn't realise the time,' Greg said, turning but not letting go of Holly. 'I was hoping to talk to you before you go. This is Holly,' he said to the man whom he quickly introduced as his father, Jeff.

The man's eyes twinkled with humour and warmth. Rather like Greg's, she thought as he shook her hand. 'Holly, so good to meet you.' He looked at Greg. 'This is the lovely lady who was keeping Mom's bracelet safe for us?'

'Yes, I have it here actually.' Greg reached into his pocket and handed it to Jeff.

'This is just wonderful. On behalf of my wife — Holly, how can I ever thank you?'

'It's no problem, really. And I think your son is doing a pretty good job of that,' she smiled, meeting Greg's warm gaze.

When Jeff had taken his leave and they continued dancing slowly across the floor, Holly looked at Greg, confused.

'Where's your dad going?' she asked. 'By my watch it's another twenty minutes till count-down.'

'Exactly,' Greg said with a knowing smile. 'But Dad has a standing appointment every December thirty-first, and there's somewhere he needs to be.'

41

Jeff Matthews walked out of the library and made his way further up Fifth Avenue, his wife's bracelet safely in his pocket.

It was fitting, he thought, that they'd got it back.

Just in time.

Checking his watch once more, he quickened his pace and made his way along the street, past the stores and office buildings, his footsteps echoing on the footpath as he walked.

Reaching St Patrick's Cathedral, he noticed the car parked outside and tears came to his eyes.

She had made it. Despite her pain, despite the medication, and frail as she was, his beloved wife still hadn't let him down.

As she never had throughout their entire wonderful life together.

Their standing appointment at St Patrick's Cathedral at midnight every 31 December had begun the night of their wedding all those years ago. Jeff and Cristina had been married at midday in St Patrick's Cathedral. Following the wedding celebrations they had returned that very night to give thanks for their happiness and ring in a brand new year and the start of the rest of their lives, not knowing that it would be a tradition that would last for over forty years.

Jeff had been reluctant that Cristina should try to keep to the appointment this year, what with the second bout of illness.

But his brave (and obstinate) wife wasn't hearing any of it.

'An hour or so out of that stupid bed won't kill me,' she had insisted, when Jeff tried to convince her not to leave the apartment and forget about the tradition — just this once.

She was such a trooper really. Nothing fazed her, not the illness, the chemotherapy and now the radiotherapy she had been having these last few months, which had kept her holed up in the bedroom of their Park Avenue apartment.

The morphine was making her sleep so much that she was in and out of consciousness most days. Jeff was worried, but the doctors proclaimed that the therapy seemed to be working well, and the cancer slowly abating. It had been a hugely stressful and worrying year, but given time, his wonderful wife might well be on the road to recovery.

Going up the steps, Jeff knocked lightly on the door, and waited as it opened a fraction.

Father Mike was shaking his head. 'I don't know how I let you two keep talking me into this,' the priest said. 'Every single year . . . '

'Is she here?' Jeff asked.

'Yes, sitting in the last pew. Maria's with her.'

'Thanks, Mike, you know how much this means to us — especially now.'

'Yes. I know.' Father Mike shook his head indulgently. 'And actually I think it's wonderful.'

Going inside, Jeff approached his wife and took her hand. 'Ready, sweetheart?' he said. 'It's almost midnight.'

Cristina turned round and, despite her frailty, gave him a radiant smile that reminded him of how she'd looked on their honeymoon in Florence all those years ago. Like a movie star.

'Of course.'

Taking her hand, Jeff — aided by Maria — led his beloved wife to the back of the church, towards the area where the candles stood.

And as the midnight bells began to toll, signalling the end of one year and welcoming another, as always Jeff and Cristina Matthews lit a candle to celebrate all the things for which they were thankful that year, and the good things they hoped would come in the next.

'Oh, I almost forgot,' Jeff said, when they'd finished the yearly ritual. He reached into his pocket. 'I have something for you . . . '

Cristina's eyes lit up as she set eyes on her treasured bracelet. She looked at her husband. 'But how . . . ?'

He shook his head. 'Seems you lost it somehow. How we got it back is a complete mystery.'

Cristina smiled knowingly. 'Oh, I think you'd be surprised . . . '

★   ★   ★

A bell jingled happily behind me as I entered the charming little vintage store in Greenwich Village. I never knew this place was here, and I wish I'd discovered it before. I looked around at the beautiful displays and the gorgeous clothes.

It was then I realised I wasn't alone.

'Hi! Welcome to the Secret Closet,' a cheery

442

voice sang out. I turned my attention towards the register and saw a striking young woman with sparkling green eyes smiling brightly at me. 'Can I help you find anything?'

I shook my head. The last thing I needed, especially now, was more clothes, but still I smiled back.

'Oh, I'm just looking. There are some beautiful things here. Your store is very nice,' I said as I browsed.

'Well, thank you. It's not my store, per se, but I feel like it is sometimes.'

I walked in her direction, looking around at the clothes as much as I was looking at her. 'You know, a lot of these clothes, they remind me of another time. My youth.'

The young woman became wistful. 'I know, isn't it amazing? Clothes are like magic. Every time we get a new shipment in and someone asks us to sell some of their wardrobe, I wonder about what those garments might have experienced, what they have been through, what they have seen.'

I looked at the spark in the young woman's eye and understood exactly what she was talking about.

'I agree with you. I never understood people who would just go in for the latest trend or fad. These clothes,' I said, motioning around me and thinking of Karen, with her penchant for the latest and greatest, 'these clothes have lived. They're like works of art.'

She was nodding her head vigorously now. 'Yes, they're old souls. That's what I always say.'

I regarded her quietly as I circled round the store; I had a feeling that this young woman might be an old soul too.

'Have you worked here long?' I enquired.

'Yes, four years now. I know it's a while to work in one place, but really, I love it. And I figure you should do what you love, shouldn't you? Life's too short to settle for a job you don't enjoy.'

I paused, considering her words, and what I just learned from my doctor, what I had not shared with anyone, not yet. 'Yes, life is too short.' I neared the counter where she stood. 'I might actually have some clothes that I would be willing to donate. How does that work?'

She smiled and reached under the counter for a business card. 'Well, anything you have you can ship directly here, or if you call, we can send someone to pick it up. We pay a commission on anything that we sell and — '

I waved a hand. 'I don't need a commission.'

'OK, in that case, that's fine too — we automatically donate the commission to charity. Again, you can ship to us or we can pick up.'

I regarded the young woman for a minute more. She had to be around Greg's age. I liked her; she was sparkling, vibrant, so full of life. Why, oh why, couldn't he meet a girl like this?

A girl who laughed and understood the wonder in life and who made people feel warm just by being around her. But what were the chances of his path crossing with hers? Slim to none at best, especially in this city of millions.

'I'm Cristina Matthews,' I said. 'It's nice to meet you . . . '

She held out her hand. 'Holly, Holly O'Neill. Lovely to meet you too.'

It was then that I noticed her bracelet. It was a charm bracelet, just like mine.

'I really like your bracelet. I have one very like it. I've been collecting charms my whole life. I usually have it on, but it's having a new charm fitted at the moment.' I smile, thinking of Jeff's hopeful 'Date to Remember' charm. We'll see . . .

She smiled and shook my hand. The charms jingled around her wrist. 'It's fun, isn't it? Many of these were given to me over the years, but I collected some myself too. And I find that anytime I feel lonely, or feel sad, all I have to do is look down and I realise I am carrying all kinds of memories with me, most of them filled with joy and meaning. I suppose that when you think about life like that, it's hard to be sad, isn't it?'

I felt my eyes temporarily well up. 'Do your charms only highlight the happy times, though?' I asked.

She thought for a moment and then looked down. She played with a charm or two and then settled on a pair of dice, twirling it around her fingers. Then she returned her gaze to me. 'No, they're not all happy, but even the bad stuff in life can teach you something, shape you. After all, every story has both good and bad in it, and life can be like that too. I guess it's what we take away from it that counts. You wouldn't be able to appreciate the happy times if you didn't sometimes experience sad times as well. At least, that's what I think,' she added, blushing a little

445

self-consciously. 'What about you?'

'I couldn't agree more.'

'Are all of the charms on your bracelet happy?'

I shook my head and thought about one of my most recent additions, the breast cancer ribbon. It wasn't a happy reminder, but it was a lesson. 'No, they aren't all happy,' I admitted. 'But they've made me the person I am today.'

She smiled at me. 'Me too. My son always jokes that the story of my life is laid out on this bracelet. He's almost ten.'

'A son? How lovely. I have a son too. Yours sounds wonderful.'

'He is.' She paused a little and said the next words almost under her breath. 'I just wish his father realised it.'

'You're no longer with his father?'

She looked up, as if forgetting herself. 'No, not since before he was born. It's hard sometimes, but I do the best I can. At least, I hope it's the best.'

'I can't imagine you doing anything other than your best.'

She grinned. 'You should hear my boss: she thinks I'm a bit crazy. Especially when I try to tell her the stories I imagine behind all these clothes.'

I smiled, realising how much I liked this girl and how much she reminded me of myself when I was younger. Happy and optimistic, and so open and enthusiastic about her joy for life. I try my best to be that way still, but it can be hard sometimes. Yet I have to believe that I'll get better. I refuse to not believe it. It's the only way

I'm managing to get through this.

'It's funny how things turn out sometimes, isn't it?' I said.

The girl, Holly, had a quizzical expression on her face but smiled, probably wondering if she was dealing with a crazy woman, but yet I had a point I was trying to make.

'What do you mean?' she asked.

'How something as simple as, for instance, walking into a store like this instead of just passing by affects things? Like, if I hadn't decided to walk in here today, I wouldn't have met you and I wouldn't have known just how wise you are. Such a small thing.'

Holly smiled. 'It is. And it might be a small thing, but I've always believed that every little moment leads us to where we are going — where we are supposed to be. It's a big old world, but we are all just waiting to bump into one another, stumble across our next great adventure. Sometimes, we just get a push in the right direction.'

Her words struck a chord with me. Especially the bit about a push in the right direction.

She picked up a shirt and started to fold it and, as I watched her, an idea began to form in my mind.

'Well, it was so nice to meet you, Holly,' I said, turning to leave, the idea burning strongly in my brain. Yes, it was a long shot and beset with risks, but that never stopped me before. And just like Holly, I've always been a big believer that life has a way of working things out. 'I'll certainly be sure to send some clothes.'

'That's great! I'll look out for them. I'm sure you have some wonderful things and I can't wait to see what you send. And don't worry, I'll try not to guess too hard about the stories behind them. Although, now that I've met you, I know they're sure to be lovely ones.' She gave a little wave. 'It was great meeting you, Cristina. Have a lovely day.'

'You too. And please, let your imagination go wild, I don't mind. But do look out for them, and make sure you look closely at each and every piece.' I smiled as I reached for the handle. 'You just never know what you might find.'

We do hope that you have enjoyed reading this large print book.

Did you know that all of our titles are available for purchase?

We publish a wide range of high quality large print books including:
Romances, Mysteries, Classics
General Fiction
Non Fiction and Westerns

Special interest titles available in large print are:
The Little Oxford Dictionary
Music Book
Song Book
Hymn Book
Service Book

Also available from us courtesy of Oxford University Press:
Young Readers' Dictionary
(large print edition)
Young Readers' Thesaurus
(large print edition)

For further information or a free brochure, please contact us at:
Ulverscroft Large Print Books Ltd.,
The Green, Bradgate Road, Anstey,
Leicester, LE7 7FU, England.
Tel: (00 44) 0116 236 4325
Fax: (00 44) 0116 234 0205

Other titles published by
The House of Ulverscroft:

SOMETHING FROM TIFFANY'S

Melissa Hill

On 5th Avenue in New York City, two very different men are gift shopping for the women they love. Gary is buying his girlfriend, Rachel, a charm bracelet — partly as a 'thank you' for their holiday in New York — but mainly because he's left his shopping too late. Whereas Ethan seeks an engagement ring for the first woman to have made him happy since losing the love of his life. But in a confusion of shopping bags, Rachel ends up with Ethan's ring, and both couples' lives become intertwined. Ethan's efforts to reunite the ring with the woman it was intended for become unexpectedly tricky. Does fate have other ideas for the couples? Or is there a bit of Tiffany's magic in the air?

BEFORE I FORGET

Melissa Hill

Abby's memories are her most precious thing. Even though they're sometimes painful, she can't stop herself looking back, reliving the love of her life. Until a freak accident means that she could lose it all: every memory and experience she has ever had. Abby can't believe it's true. She feels fine. She is fine. How could she possibly forget all those moments that make her who she is? She's determined to fight it. With the help of her friends and family, Abby makes a list of things she's always wanted to do. She's going to save her memory by having the most unforgettable year of her life . . .

BETTER TOGETHER

Sheila O'Flanagan

Journalist Sheridan Gray believes she's going places, but loses her job, her boyfriend and her flat, and ends up working for a small-town newspaper — writing horoscopes and reporting on dog shows. Home-loving Nina Fallon's life is shattered when her actor husband's exploits become national news. Trying to avoid friends, she runs Ardbawn's guesthouse alone. When Sheridan moves into the guesthouse, she realises that Nina is key to the story that would make her name as a reporter again. But Sheridan's desire to uncover the past puts her on a collision course with the present, and with the man she's come to love. Sheridan could lose more than she dreamed possible. Is she better off going it alone? Or is love the greatest prize of all?

IOU

Helen Warner

Amy's charming life, spent shopping and lunching whilst the nanny cares for her children, is thrown into disarray when husband Ben's business collapses overnight. Their house and savings lost, Amy must now be the breadwinner — but can their marriage survive the upheaval? Meanwhile, her sister Kate always struggles: juggling her job with two children and husband Miles. But then, by chance, she meets enigmatic Jack. Increasingly estranged from Miles, Kate wonders if Jack can offer her a fresh start. But there's something about Jack that Kate doesn't know . . . And their mother Jennifer, recently recovering from her husband's death, contacts old flame Hugh — unlocking a dangerous Pandora's box. She's desperate to find the answer to a question that has long tormented her, but will she be able to cope with the truth?

THE SATURDAY SUPPER CLUB

Amy Bratley

Eve had her world torn apart three years ago when the love of her life, Ethan, disappeared and she never found out why. But now her life is rosy. With a lovely new boyfriend, Joe, and the prospect of a cafe-opening, things finally seem to be falling into place . . . until she agrees to take part in a supper-club competition for a local newspaper. Eve is cooking the first dinner, and who should turn up on her doorstep expecting a three-course meal, but her long lost love?